THE
UTOPIA

CHRISTIAN JERRY MARCHIONI

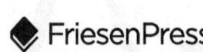 FriesenPress

One Printers Way
Altona, MB R0G 0B0
Canada

www.friesenpress.com

Copyright © 2024 by Christian Jerry Marchioni
First Edition — 2024

All rights reserved.

No part of this publication may be reproduced in any form, or by any means, electronic or mechanical, including photocopying, recording, or any information browsing, storage, or retrieval system, without permission in writing from FriesenPress.

ISBN
978-1-03-831732-2 (Hardcover)
978-1-03-831731-5 (Paperback)
978-1-03-831733-9 (eBook)

1. FICTION, DYSTOPIAN

Distributed to the trade by The Ingram Book Company

THE UTOPIA

PROLOGUE

Gather round, kids, as I tell you this story. Those were the words floating in his head, words that he initially found a bit bizarre for a moment like this. He hadn't heard them in that particular order since he was a little kid, back when Teacher Lee used to read to their group. But that was many moons ago, and Teacher Lee wasn't here. No one was here but for one other person. And neither of them had a book. He hadn't read one in years.

The human mind was certainly a strange place. In his twenty-three years of life, he had come to discover that. It seemed to work at random a lot of the time, filling his head with thoughts that often seemed out of place.

But the more he thought about it, the more it seemed like perhaps this wasn't one of those times after all. Teacher Lee's story time—that was one of his favourite childhood memories, something he looked back on fondly with a radiating smile. And the more he thought about it, the more he realized it was almost like he was in one of those stories right now, finding happiness in what the Utopia had blessed him with, the same way many of the characters in those stories had. He could now even imagine what the first words of this particular tale would be.

Once upon a time, in a land not so far away, a man and a woman were enjoying the serenity of a crisp summer night. Staring off into the abyss, the couple of lovebirds didn't exchange words, didn't exchange any overt affections. They simply sat peacefully, reflecting on the beauty of the world that surrounded them.

They saw no princesses or castles, no dwarfs or wolves, no witches or ogres or beanstalks or glass slippers. Truth be told, a few of these concepts they had never even heard of.

And it didn't matter a lick. All the same, there was magic in the air. They smelled it in the cool breeze that floated ever so elegantly around them, felt it in the soft sand beneath their legs, heard it in the ocean waves breaking gracefully at their feet, saw it in the little balls of fire floating mysteriously in the sky. They feasted on the elements, and the taste was decadent.

For the man especially, it was quiet nights like these that were his favourite: simple nights where he could put everything else aside, where his normally restless mind could focus on the here and now, where it was finally put at ease. It didn't happen often, but on nights like this, it was possible—when the moon was bright, when the temperature was just right, when the stars in the sky almost spoke to him as friends. On a night like tonight, he could probably get there on his own.

But mostly, it was thanks to her.

When he looked at her, all those other externalities became afterthoughts. Of no greater importance than the words that represented them. On many days, she was his moon. She was his perfect temperature. She was the star that made the universe come together. She had been for as long as he could remember.

He smiled at her, but she paid him no notice, her mind distracted by the wonders abound, the magnificence of the great big world and all that was out there. One day she would see it. She had told him that since they were young.

They sat hand in hand on this clear summer night at Wexin District Beach, abandoned at this hour by all inhabitants except themselves, both staring up at the stars. They were beautiful this evening, the brightest either of them could remember seeing in some time, a reflection of the warmth each felt within their core, a symbol of the heat they felt for each other, occupying their place in time and space in much the same way—heaven and earth combined into one.

It was a sad moment when he remembered that in real life, love stories didn't come with a fairy tale ending.

CHAPTER 1

The beginning was the hardest, or so he had thought. Hearing the words, feeling the bracelets tighten around his wrists—it was all such a shock. And none of it made sense.

It had started out as such a normal Tuesday—such a normal day in general, really: wake up at one in the afternoon or therearound, grab a beer from the perpetually understocked fridge, sit around and watch TV or play video games until hunger or boredom inevitably set in, reluctantly throw in a workout at some point to prevent the pounds from exponentially adding up, then shower and groom and dress to impress, all in preparation for nine in the evening when the Pub would open for business.

This was his routine. Sometimes he'd walk around the city if it was a nice day out. Sometimes it was his designated day to stop in at a General Store for supplies and provisions. But it was all in preparation for that nine o'clock time frame, —the moment he could go home.

He wasn't an alcoholic, not in the sense of the word as he understood it anyway. Alcoholics, in his mind, drank continuously, and of course, the State rations were never enough to allow anyone to do that. Even at the bars, they would only serve you a couple before your quota for the night was filled.

He was a drug addict though—that he could admit. Cannabis, cocaine, painkillers. He could even get the new and improved zombie pill once in a while if he was willing to short himself food for a few days. He never had enough of any to become truly reliant on one but did enough of every to never have to feel sober if he didn't want to. And access was easy enough. You could get it all at a Store. You could get everything at a Store, everything you needed anyway.

So why hadn't he just waited?

His head had been low, but he picked it up now to look around the room. There weren't many people: the judge in robes perched at his bench, the "jury" of three to his two o'clock, the court reporter in between the jury and the judge, the "prosecutor" to the reporter's left, one guard, one news reporter, and a few of his friends behind him. All were waiting stoically for what was forthcoming: a verdict of guilty.

He looked back toward the floor, then back in his memories, back to Tuesday night, a night out with his friends. The same friends who were here supporting him now.

That was how the night had started anyway—a group outing at Pub 19. They'd all had a beer. They'd chatted for a time and then each had another. The memories were clear as day.

It was after they left—around eleven o'clock—that things started to get fuzzy. His friends called it a night because they had work the next day. He decided to stay because he never had work, because one more beer for the night was allowed by the State, because he didn't want to waste any liquid gold.

Eleven o'clock. Yes, it was around then. He could remember checking his phone before he went to use the washroom. He had gone to the washroom, then he had gone back to the bar, then …

Blank. Nothing. It was like that time never existed. Try as he might, he just couldn't remember anything until the moment he woke up with guards around him, the moment they cuffed him and spoke the words to him.

"You're under arrest, sir, for destruction and robbery of a State enterprise."

He shook his head unconsciously as he thought back. What had caused him to do that? He couldn't remember, but right now it almost didn't matter. What mattered was that he was guilty. The evidence was unquestionable.

There was video of him at the bar. There was video of him leaving. There was video of him walking toward the Store. There was video of him picking up a pipe near an alleyway and smashing the glass of the back door to get in. There was video of him inside the Store, smashing the cabinet behind the counter and grabbing all the zombie pills he could find. There was video of guards rushing in and one of them tackling him to the floor, where he fell unconscious, only to wake up and realize exactly what he had done.

It was him in the video. It had to be. The resemblance was uncanny, and the surveillance tapes showed the whole path from Pub to Store.

The only question was, Why? Why would he do that. He had grown frustrated with life—of that there was no doubt—but not to the degree that he would do something like that. He had a drug problem, but he had never stolen drugs or felt the need to, and his re-up day was coming.

Why hadn't he just waited? It didn't make any sense.

Beep. Beep.

A sound from behind the judge garnered everyone's attention and put those muted faces immediately on edge. The beginning had been the hardest because it hadn't seemed real. But it was getting real now—very real.

The Computer had made a decision.

"Deron Boyd."

The robotic voice behind the screen made his blood run cold. He had tried to remain calm throughout this whole ordeal and had done so to this point with relative success. But now he felt sick, and it wasn't just the two-plus days of forced detox that had him on the brink of throwing up his lunch. It was knowing that life as he knew it was about to take a turn off a cliff, and how long he could free fall without a crash was anyone's guess.

Why hadn't he just waited?

"The Crime Network has analyzed the evidence. Upon review of the surveillance tapes, there is little room left for any reasonable doubt. As such, the Crime Network finds you guilty on both fronts: guilty of the crime of destruction and guilty of the crime of committed or attempted robbery. Your sentence, in line with the mandates, is two years in the State Work Camp for the destruction and three years for the committed or attempted robbery, served consecutively."

There was the briefest of pauses, as if to let the sting linger, and then the Computer continued. "This concludes the Crime Network's analysis in the case of *The Utopia versus Boyd*. The review of this decision shall now be conducted by the jury, and if the decision is upheld, Mr. Boyd's options shall be read to him by the judge. That is all. End transmission." The screen went blank.

"And what says the jury?" the judge asked. But the question really wasn't necessary other than as part of due process. Deron's fate had been sealed the moment the Computer spoke.

Each member of the jury simultaneously held up a card anyway. Guilty. Guilty. Guilty.

Deron looked on with no surprise. The evidence was clear. And even if it hadn't been, it wouldn't have mattered. To overturn the Computer, all three would have needed to find him not guilty, and since the invention of the Crime Network, that had literally never happened.

"Very well," the judge continued. He looked from the jury toward Deron. Deron returned his gaze. "The Crime Network and the jury have spoken, Mr. Boyd, and the verdict is guilty. I'm sure you know what happens now, but I'm required by the process to read this statement to you anyway."

Deron nodded in understanding. The judge turned to his paper and read matter-of-factly.

"You, sir or madam, have been found guilty of committing one or more crimes against the State and/or people of the Utopia. By law you are given the following choice: you may serve your sentence in the State Work Camp, whereby upon release, you will be assigned to the guards or other field of volunteering for a period of no less than ten years, barring exceptional circumstances, including but not limited to reaching the retirement age of sixty, or, as an alternative to the State Work Camp, you may elect to be put to death by euthanasia. If you do not make a choice, you will, by default, be sent to the State Work Camp. Please make your selection now."

The judge peered over the paper and through his reading glasses as he finished his statement. And Deron felt the weight of that look like he'd been hit by a ton of bricks.

This is happening, he thought with a sense of panic. *This really is happening.*

But when he spoke, it was with an air of tranquility. It was like somewhere deep down, he'd always known this would be his fate, like from the dawn of his existence, his mantra had always been one of genuine acceptance: *it's not going to happen to me until it happens to me.*

And for twenty-seven-year-old Deron Boyd—a descendant of African heritage from centuries before, a man with brown eyes, buzzed hair, and a short beard, standing six foot one and weighing two hundred pounds in equal parts muscle and fat, who chose jeans and flannels as his State-sponsored garments, who was stoic by nature, gloomy by nurture, addicted to drugs but friendly when you got to know him, unmotivated but harmless, careful but not enough—for Deron Boyd, this was always going to happen, by his hand or another's.

"I'll take the years in the work camp. I ..." He thought of adding more but just let it pass through his mind and not his lips. *I still want to live.* "I'll take the years."

He gazed down and then back up again, and by the time he had, the judge had already spoken. "Then it shall be done." The judge banged his gavel. All rose. "The guard will take you away," he instructed. "You will be transported by guard van where you will join the others who've been sentenced. Good luck to you, sir."

Deron nodded. *He means it,* he thought. *He might care about me, he might not, but the good luck part, he means it. He thinks I'm going to need it.*

"But first, the jury may depart. Thank you for your service."

Each nodded without speaking. They formed a line and walked by his defendant's table: a white woman at the front who looked to be in her early fifties, a brown-skinned man in his early twenties behind her, and a black man in his thirties bringing up the rear. None gave him a glance, and he scarcely gave them a look either. He harbored them no resentment. They could hardly be blamed for following the Computer, especially in such an open-and-shut case.

He felt no resentment at all, in fact, toward anyone in the room. The judge read the rules, answered questions, and banged his gavel if there were outbursts, but he had no more power than anyone else in that room.

He was, like the rest of them, following the lead of the Computer.

He couldn't even hate the prosecutor. She made no arguments, didn't attack his character or threaten him in any way. Her job was simply to submit the surveillance footage. In the Utopia, the law didn't care why you did what you did, what your character was like, or whether you were a worker or freeloader, reactive or calculating, on drugs or sober. The crime was the act. The sentence was pre-determined and mandatory. There was no room for discretion. It's why there were no defence lawyers: the State had no use for them. The evidence presented tended to be overwhelming. The Utopia was blanketed by surveillance, and any tapes could quickly and easily be analyzed by the Crime Network. Witnesses were almost never necessary, and court reporting was minimal because there were no appeals. There was no need for them either. The Computer was never wrong, and the law was clear.

Most actions in the State were legal, and any minor violations were enforced by the guards outside of the courts. You couldn't rape, kill, or do other acts of violence, but anything outside the scope of the "Ten State Commandments" was basically fair game. Because of that, there were fewer trials and frivolous court actions. Because of that, you could go from crime commission to sentencing in only a few days. The efficiency was unmatched.

"Time to go, Boyd," said a voice in his ear. He had been distracted by his thoughts but didn't really need to use too much cognition to guess who was speaking to him. He looked to his right and saw the guard—a handsome man about his age with a similar physique but much paler skin and blond hair and blue eyes. He was wearing the traditional all-red guard uniform. A belt surrounding his waist held handcuffs, a tiny radio, and his holstered weapon.

"I won't cuff you if you go quietly," he said.

Deron nodded in appreciation. There were two types of guards in the Utopia: guards who volunteered after having met the personality test requirements and guards who were assigned after having spent time at the Work Camp. This man was clearly the latter.

Deron stood, took two steps to his right, and then turned right again and headed for the exit. There were three people waiting for him when he arrived: Marla, Diego, and Charlie, friends he'd grown up with since before his brain could record explicit memories of their existence. They were people he trusted and valued and loved. They had always been there for him, through his good days and bad, and this time had been no exception. Vacation time was rare for working folk (or "volunteers" as they were called in the Utopia). But each had sacrificed a day to support him through his trial.

"I'm sorry," said Marla.

"Stay safe," added Diego.

"One day we'll meet again, and it will all be the same. We'll do things together, just like old times." This last comment by Charlie nearly broke him.

It didn't though. Somehow, someway, he maintained his composure. He hugged each of them goodbye and went quietly out the door. His friends embraced behind him, tears in each of their eyes, knowing Charlie's comment was only a half-truth.

They might see him again. They might one day be able to do things together again. But it would never be the same. Not for Deron. After five years in the Camp, how could it ever be?

The van was parked out front, an old police-style one with a glass window separating the front seats from the back. The guard opened it for him, and he went in without hesitation. The doors were closed behind him, and the guard took the driver's seat. Within a minute, they were on their way, and only then did the sadness truly take over.

Why hadn't he just waited? It didn't make any sense.

CHAPTER 2

Matthew Tucker and Jim Mollin stood together in the parking lot of the Valking District Courthouse. It was a bright, sunny day with the perfect amount of breeze—a typical day in the Utopia and a typical day for them. They had skipped the weather discussion and moved on to other topics.

"Alright, that's the last of them for today. The Unglow District case is one of those battery cases that took place behind closed doors, so that one is going to take another day or two. Sometimes makes you think it's time to put surveillance inside the housing units."

"Shit, I don't know about that, Jim. Might make those cases run a bit more smoothly, but you really want a camera in your place recording you at all times, never knowing if someone is sitting there watching what you're doing?"

Jim shrugged his shoulders. "I don't know, I'm a pretty boring guy, Matty. Not much to hide ... But point taken." He smiled.

Matt smiled back. "See, yeah, I don't have much to hide either, but I think the system works as it is. Good balance to it, and even if it takes another day or two, the Computer always knows."

Jim nodded and smiled again. "This is true, Matty boy. This is very true. Anyway, how's the journey been so far? Any trouble?"

"Nah," Matt responded, taking his eyes off Jim for a moment and focusing them inside the open back of the van. "They're quiet, same as usual. Still processing it all I think."

"Good. Good to hear. I'm glad it's been quiet because in a few minutes, it might not be anymore."

"Oh yeah? And why's that? The next one coming out a rapist? Killer? Anger problems?"

"None of those, Matty, fortunately for the others. But still could be a problem. I say 'might' and 'could' because I don't know who it is yet. This next one, whoever it is, will have been chosen."

"Another one? That's my second one this week! And I only do the runs for five courthouses!"

***

DERON PERKED UP AT the raised voices, as did his comrades. He had been joined by two others, both women, over the last several hours. They had been picked up from other courthouses, and as of yet, the three hadn't spoken to each other, but there was a general intrigue amongst the group now. The guards had been speaking out of earshot, but the one that had been chauffeuring them around was clearly agitated by something now, and they all wondered why.

***

"I KNOW, I KNOW. But the Computer has to keep the balance. Something must be off. Too few volunteers. A bunch of releases from the Camp maybe. Or perhaps it's just one of those statistical oddities that you got two in one week. Who knows. All I know is that we have to trust the Computer."

"I guess so." Matt thought about it for a moment and then nodded his head. "Yeah, you're right. I can't be worrying about that kind of stuff. The Computer knows, and I guess I should just be thankful I was assigned here after my stint because if I had to live with the fear I might one day be sent back, I'm not going to lie to you, Jim, I don't know what I'd do."

Jim put a hand on Matt's shoulder and gave it a quick rub. His eyes were those of a man who understood completely. "Same here, partner. Same here."

Jim took his hand away, and just as he did, the doors of the courtroom swung open. A man stepped out with a guard close behind. The man was handcuffed behind his back.

"Let's go, down the stairs," the guard instructed. The man didn't respond but did what was asked and started to descend. To say he was tentative about it would have been quite an understatement. If it was a race around the track, a snail might have lapped him. It looked to Matt like the man was afraid he might fall.

Matt shook his head. "Those necessary?" he asked the incoming guard once the pair had finally made it down the steps. He pointed as best he could toward the handcuffs.

The guard shrugged. "Better safe than sorry," he replied.

"I see," Matt responded, in a way that made it clear he did not see at all.

The guard shrugged again. "You never know how they'll react to being chosen."

YOU wouldn't know, Matt wanted to say. He knew the guard in front of him was fresh out of school and hadn't exactly been tabbed as a potential rookie of the year. He bit his tongue though. The kid did have a point.

"True," he said instead. "That is true. But from my experience, if someone feels disgruntled about being chosen, they'll let you know it the second their name is called, all the way out the courtroom, and for at least half the van ride. Might even complain to one of the Camp supervisors when they get there until they realize the pointlessness of their objections. But a quiet man or woman—they accept the rules. And there is no need to cuff them. Am I right, sir?" His eyes quickly changed direction from the guard to his newest Camp recruit.

The man nodded. "Quite right. Quite right indeed. I'm forty-five. Have lived freely for a long time. Always knew this could happen and accepted as much. I am at peace."

Matt nodded back with a sense of true belief, belief that the man himself believed what he was saying, that he'd had lived a good life, that he knew and accepted the rules of the Utopia, that he wouldn't cause trouble—at least until he saw what life was like on the other side of the Wall.

"Uncuff him, Junior," Matt instructed.

"If you say so," the boy, whose real name was Mike, responded. He did what was asked.

"Thank you," the man said, sounding genuinely appreciative. He began to walk toward the van without being asked to.

***

DERON AND THE OTHERS saw him coming.

"I wonder who this guy is," said one of the women. She was sitting across from Deron but talking to neither him nor the other woman beside her. She was looking out the back of the van as she said it.

"Must have done something fierce," the other woman chose to respond. "Our driver was freaking out about him."

"Yeah," she replied, still looking at the man. She then abruptly turned to Deron. "What do you think?" she asked.

Deron was still looking out the back of the van, but he could tell through intuition he was the one she was speaking to. "Well …" He started but then stopped. The man was getting closer, but he was taking his time, like he was on a nice afternoon stroll without a care in the world.

Deron looked toward the women, who were now both eyeing him. He was still processing everything and didn't really feel like talking but he knew he should say something. "Yeah, maybe." It was all he could think to say. He looked back toward the man. "I guess we'll find out."

***

"VAN ALL CHARGED UP?" Jim asked, pointing at the cable sticking out of the butt-end of the vehicle.

He was still standing with Matt and "Junior," but they had shifted over some. Matt had his hand on one of the back doors of the van. The man was already inside, having taken a seat beside Deron. His fellow passengers had acknowledged him with nods as he entered but none had spoken.

"Should be ready to go," Matt replied. "These things charge quite efficiently."

"That they do," Jim agreed. "See you next week?" He stuck out his hand, requesting a shake.

Matt obliged. "See you next week, Jim." They each closed one of the van's back doors. Jim began to unplug the cable.

"I can take that," Matt offered. "Or at least have Junior do it."

"I got it, Matty. Don't worry," Jim replied. "You go." And before Matt could say anything else, Jim had already pulled the cable and started to roll it up.

Matt watched him do it with a strange feeling in his body that was somehow both pity and admiration. He was a good man that Jim. At fifty-seven years old, he was just a few years away from mandatory retirement, yet he worked harder than most of the young bucks out here. Nothing could slow him down. It was honourable. It was impressive. It was a learned behaviour.

"We going?" Mike asked, noticing Matt had spaced out.

Matt shook his head no but answered in the affirmative. "Yeah. Sorry. Just thinking about the route," he lied. "I'm used to going from Unglow District."

"You know you got GPS, right? The thing can even drive itself if you want it to. This ain't the 1800s."

Matt smiled at that. *Smart ass,* he thought. But he couldn't be mad. It was the type of thing he would have said back when he was the kid's age.

"You don't say now?" Matt said, as Mike chuckled to himself. "Get in the van, Junior," Matt ordered, still smiling. "Of course I can use the GPS, but sometimes it's still good to use your brain in this world. You'll learn that one day."

"Whatever you say, boss," the youngster replied. "Let's just get out of here before we're late." He walked to the passenger's side of the van before Matt could respond.

Matt thought of firing back, but the kid was already out of range. *And besides,* he thought to himself, *he's not wrong. It's not good to be late. The powers that be might think you aren't taking your job seriously if you are, and that is not advised.* And just for a split second, his blood went cold. *If anyone knows it's me.*

He walked to the driver's side and opened up the door. He used his ID to start the van and they drove off toward the Camp.

***

WHEN THE ICEBREAKER CAME, it was in a form unexpected. But given it was she who had opened her mouth first about the new man, it was not from an unexpected source.

"So ... how about that recession?"

And even the normally emotionless Deron couldn't help but burst out laughing along with the rest of them.

"It's killing me," said the new man in between laughs. "Almost couldn't make my mortgage payment this month." And that got them going even harder. The second woman was nearly choking. It wasn't until thirty seconds later that they all eventually calmed down.

"That's too good," the second woman said. They all nodded in agreement. For the moment, at least, the dynamic had changed. They were all still strangers, all still headed toward an uncertain future, but all of a sudden, each felt a little more at ease.

"Can they hear us?" the first woman asked. She was a larger black woman who looked somewhere between late thirties and early forties.

"I'm sure they could if they wanted to," replied the man, who had pushed Deron one spot over toward the front of the vehicle and was now sitting across from her. He took a quick look to his left as he said it, past Deron and toward the two guards. The two parties were separated by a thick layer of glass. "But I don't think they are," he said, looking back at the woman. "Otherwise, I think they would've reacted to us laughing."

"Don't think it even matters," the other woman chimed in from the seat across from Deron. She was younger. Probably around his age, Deron thought. To him, she looked what his school textbooks had termed "East Asian," though in the Utopia, technically there were no races or ethnicities. Everyone was just a Utopian. But in school, everyone still learned about other parts of the world, and it was commonplace to use this knowledge as part of a physical description. "One way or another, we're still going to the Camp."

And that statement depressed the mood a little bit again. But the conversation didn't die.

"Would it be a faux pas for me to ask why everyone is taking this little excursion?" the older woman asked. And the tasteful way she put the statement somehow managed to brighten their spirits once more. "You know, since we're on the subject of the Camp."

Each shrugged their shoulders as if to say, "To hell with it. Why not?"

"I can even go first. To be honest with you all, I really feel like I need to get this off my chest. It has been bothering me since it happened."

They all nodded in understanding. In some shape or form, they each felt the same way. But that still didn't prepare them for what they were about to hear.

"Whew, okay, here goes." She took a deep breath—in and out—and then just spat it out. "I was hiding a child."

"You what?!" shouted the East Asian woman. "How?"

They were all stunned, even Deron, who, before this whole ordeal, hadn't concerned himself with much of anything other than what drug to take next. Even he was at a loss. Hiding a child—it was unthinkable.

"I know. I know," she continued somewhat frantically, feeling the need to explain herself as quickly as she could. "I don't know what I was thinking. But when I was leaving the hospital after giving birth, I just saw my child there, and I couldn't help it. I just felt this overwhelming need to bring him home. This was my second child, my last one by law, and my first child I had over seven years ago. I always missed him. Still miss him to this day. Still wonder what school he was sent to and how he is doing. And so when I saw my second child, I had to take him with me. I knew I would be caught. And within a few hours, they had taken him back. But I just had to try."

Tears had formed in her eyes. They hadn't fallen yet, but they were right on the brink. The East Asian woman was consoling her, rubbing her back.

"I'm sorry," she continued. "Maybe you understand, maybe you don't. I know the rules and why they are what they are. I don't know what came over me, and you guys probably think I'm crazy for telling you all that, but I needed to get it out there. And saying it aloud, I actually feel a bit better." She sniffled and wiped her eyes. Her lips curled upwards and formed a smile. Her face, like her words, said she had started to accept what she had done.

The three others looked at each other, unsure of what to say. None of them had had a child (or in the case of the men, none that they knew about). None of them could know her pain. None of them could truly understand what she had felt in that moment—that moment her child was taken.

Taken by the State.

There were no families in the Utopia, at least not in the traditional sense. Any children born were immediately separated from their mothers and fathers, and after being deemed fit to leave the hospital, they were housed with other children born around the same time. They were raised by caretakers and teachers in boarding schools up until their twenty-first year. They were taught math, science, history, law, English, and other humanities, and all took a course they called "The Utopian World" up until their seventeenth year. They were then given specialization options for their final four years, depending on grades, interests, and something known as the "Statewide Personality Test." Up until their eleventh year, they were sheltered from the rest of the Utopia in development schools, during which time they only interacted with their caretakers, teachers, and classmates. After that, they were slowly integrated into the rest of society, slowly got to meet other kids and adults, slowly started to learn the Utopian way of life outside the confines of the classroom.

After they left school, those who did well were assigned a job placement, where they learned on the go. They worked that job, as long as they were good at it, for as long as they were capable or as long as they wanted to. They could apply for a different job at any time. The Computer's Job Network made all hiring and firing decisions.

Those who did not find a job or did not want one didn't have to get one. The system ensured freeloaders, as they called them, were adequately taken care of. Everyone could get everything they needed in terms of food, clothing, or otherwise from one of the many General Stores. Each week, no matter who you were or whether you worked or not, you could pick up your quota of rations from the various offerings.

And as far as housing went, the State covered that too. There was no homelessness in the Utopia; everyone was assigned a place to live, in the form of a small apartment unit, upon leaving school. Every unit was owned by the State, but citizens could move if they could find someone who was willing to trade units with them. Other than proximity to your workplace, there was no great advantage or disadvantage to any assigned spot. Each city district was essentially a carbon copy of every other. Each building unit was essentially the same, give or take a few features. And the technology everywhere was so advanced at this point that things hardly ever broke or needed fixing.

And the craziest part of all—it was run without any type of monetary system. People could trade items if they wanted to, but as far as money went, it didn't exist. That's why workers in the Utopia were called "volunteers." They were not paid for what they did. They did their jobs because they enjoyed them, because they would be bored without them, because the State had convinced them that it was honourable to work—or because they were scared. And believe it or not, those four factors ensured that there were usually more job applicants than there were openings. Because some people enjoyed their job so much, it wasn't really work. Because some people needed something to do every day or they would go nuts. Because some people believed the Utopian propaganda that told them it was a Utopian's duty to volunteer for the greater good. And because some people were simply too damn scared of the consequences of not volunteering to do anything but.

"Thank you for not judging me." Deron had been daydreaming, thinking about it all. But this last comment from the woman snapped him back into it. "I know it may seem strange, but if you were me, it would make sense. If you could feel …"

She tried to continue but was at a loss for words. They all were. Separating a child from their parents was part of the fabric of Utopian life. It had happened to all of them as kids. They learned about other forms of family in school, but to actually live like that, as a tiny, isolated unit—it defied everything they knew.

"Never mind. Maybe I'm just crazy. Or selfish. Or both. But either way, it doesn't matter. I know the rules, and I broke them. And for that, I got what I deserved. Now someone else say something before you convince me you're all ghosts." And that lightened the mood again. They each chuckled to themselves.

When the laughter died down, the East Asian woman spoke next. "Well, thank you for sharing that," she said. She still had her hand on her new female companion, but it had moved to her shoulder. "I know that took a lot. It's a brave thing to share." She paused for just a moment and then continued. "So, I guess it's my turn."

And they all perked up again at that. Deron now had a nervous energy and voices in his head that somehow screamed both *tell me* and *I don't want to know*. After hearing the first story, he was both curious and scared.

"I ..." She started and then stopped to look at each of them. Each was sitting on the edge of their seat, like it was the final game of the Utopian Soccer League season and they were going to a shootout.

Just say it! Deron thought. He was almost starting to sweat, almost as anxious as the moments just before the Computer made a ruling on his case. The *tell-me* voice in his head had completely taken over, and he knew the reason for it.

The Utopian way of life. His thoughts about that reminded him of what he'd had: friends, leisure, a safety net that was there at all times. And on a random Tuesday night, he'd thrown it all away to steal pills he didn't need from a place that was one of the most guarded in all of the Utopia. It just didn't make sense. He'd tried for three days to find some kind of justification for his actions, and he just couldn't do it. There was just no good rhyme or reason.

So now, he needed to hear something his brain would accept. He'd tried to understand the other woman, tried to see why hiding her child was a justifiable thing to do, why it was worth going to the Camp for. But he just couldn't comprehend it. He'd been raised with no parents. They'd all been raised with no parents. It was one of the rules of the game, and she herself had said she knew breaking the rule was wrong. So why had she done it? She was always going to get caught. The risk/reward just wasn't there, like it hadn't been for him.

He needed that risk/reward to have been there for one of them—this East Asian woman or, if not her, the other man. In his own mind, he needed to find a way to justify their actions. Because if he couldn't, if what they told him also seemed to lack clear rationale, it meant to him that they'd all thrown their lives away for nothing. It meant to him that they were all being banished from society simply because they were undisciplined or dumb or bad people. Or maybe something even worse. Maybe they were being banished because secretly, deep down, that's what they'd all wanted all along. Secretly, they'd hated everything this whole time. Themselves. Their lives. The Utopian way.

He needed to know that there really could be a good reason to break the law, that his actions weren't just a form self-destruction, that there was a real purpose in them that he would one day ascertain.

Today, he wouldn't discover that valid justification. Today, he would go on thinking that on that Tuesday night, he had made the biggest mistake of his life. But he also wouldn't be convinced that he had simply self-destructed either, wouldn't be convinced that he secretly hated the Utopian society somewhere deep down inside.

Today, he would simply learn it was possible to fathom why someone might break the law, why the risk/reward might be worth it in certain circumstances. That would make complete sense. And it would hurt him even more.

"I was trying to contact the outside world." And their eyes all went wide as she began to tell her story.

***

"I can't believe she didn't tell you," said the older woman. "I'm so sorry, darling." It was her turn now to be the consoling voice, and her efforts were necessary. The younger woman was crying.

Deron watched on, himself getting teary-eyed. He was not one to cry, unless he was under the influence and couldn't control himself. He hadn't shed sober tears in a few years. But he had been on the brink of sober tears twice today, and this time, he was even closer than the last.

The younger woman had just revealed to them her tale of woe. And this particular story had some aspects to it that, to him, were far from incomprehensible.

"I just wanted to know she was okay," she sobbed, harder now than she had been when telling her tale. She was crying in the older woman's arms, and it took all the strength Deron had not to go over there and hug her himself—or add to her pool of tears.

Her story centred around a friend she had grown up with since the start of her life. They'd been in all the same classes and had done everything together. They'd even found a way to get matching jobs in the same museum, working overlapping shifts.

That was until a week ago, when out of the blue, her friend announced that she was leaving the Utopia, leaving everything behind because she wanted to start fresh, because she wanted to see the "other" world.

She never saw it coming. Never got a hint even once that that was her friend's plan. And needless to say, this sudden revelation turned her entire world upside down.

The Utopia was an island, and in Utopian law, there was only roughly a four-year window where one could choose to leave: from the moment you graduated school up until your twenty-fifth birthday. All that was required was three-months' notice to the State, and they would allow you to go, no questions asked. The only exception was if you had a criminal record. In that case, you were stuck in the Utopia until the day you died.

Twice a year, a ship left and came. The first voyage was with those who had chosen to leave. The return ship carried ones who had chosen to come and who had been accepted by the Computer as "qualified individuals." The conditions were these: If you chose to leave the Utopia, you could never return. If you chose to immigrate into the Utopia, you could never leave.

The ratio of those who came to those who left varied year-to-year. Some years, more people chose to leave the Utopia than others. Some years, more jobs were available in the Utopia in certain industries, and so applicants with experience in those industries had an advantage. It was all kept track of by the Computer.

This woman's friend had been on the most recent ship, which left a few days ago. The State didn't tell you where you would land until you boarded the ship. The rumour was that the drop-off point changed sometimes, but no one—except the Computer and perhaps some of the State officials—knew what the destination would be until the ship was ready to set sail. Because of this, the young woman was worried about her friend. She knew she would never see her friend again because she had already turned twenty-five this year and was therefore ineligible to leave. She had only wanted to make sure her friend arrived at her destination safely. To do that, she had to try to contact someone who was no longer located on the island, otherwise known as the outside world. To do so was illegal

THE UTOPIA

under Utopian law. She was caught and convicted.

"I know, sweetheart. I know," the older woman replied. She looked toward the men for help, but neither could say anything. The man beside Deron was too stunned, and Deron was lost in his own head.

He took a deep breath, trying to suck the emotion back into his body. With his right hand, he reached up and tenderly rubbed his neck. Surrounding it was a gold chain. When he had finished massaging his feelings down, he pulled the chain out from underneath his shirt. Dangling in view now was the attached gold letter *K*. He clasped the pendant tightly with his bare hand and kissed it, thought for a moment more, and then returned it to its resting place underneath his shirt. He took one more deep breath and began to recompose.

"I'm sorry," he said, mostly under his breath but still loud enough to hear. The three others looked at him, knowing this story had affected him but still unsure why. "It's a tough thing, someone you care about leaving like that. It's a tough thing. I ... I'm sorry."

The younger woman nodded and released herself from the older woman's embrace. She had stopped sobbing now and took a moment to wipe her eyes. "Thank you," she said. "I believe you really feel that."

And then they all put their heads down and went quiet, each now once again resting with their back against the inner layer of the van, each now once again wrestling with the inner layer of their soul. Deron now realizing the saddest part of it all.

They had been broken already, and they weren't even at the Camp yet.

***

FOR THE NEXT FIFTEEN minutes, all any of them heard were the bumps in the road and the little voices in their heads. Deron's was speaking loudly, telling him not that everything would be fine, but the opposite, in fact—that everything had gone to shit and there was nothing he could do about it.

The idea of telling his story had popped into his head, but he wasn't sure it would help. Both women had teared up telling their tales, and he still couldn't tell if they had found the exercise therapeutic or damaging. If he had to guess, it seemed the latter.

Even if I did say it, how could I explain it? he asked himself justifiably. And he didn't have an answer.

So instead of saying anything, he started to focus all his energy inward. He was beginning to feel sick—physically, not just mentally. His brain was on the frontlines taking siege after siege, but he also felt aches and pains throughout the rest of his body and a queasiness in his stomach. For the past few years, he hadn't gone more than a day or two without some drug in his system, but lockup hadn't exactly provided him with his daily rations. He was onto day three of his detox and was feeling the effects.

"I can go next," the man beside Deron spoke.

Deron looked at him, at first with irritation, but after a second, he realized he had no reason to be upset. It wasn't the man's fault he was feeling this way. He looked at him again, objectively this time, and the word that came to his mind was *composed*. This whole time really, this man had seemed by far the most accepting of his position.

It was ironic given what he was about to tell them.

"That is, if you all still want to do this."

Given the way they all felt, some resistance could have been expected, but surprisingly, there was none. At least not from the older woman.

"Sure," she said almost instantaneously. "Why not? If you want to tell, it's only fair we listen."

The man wasn't necessarily sure he was eager to tell; he just thought it was the fair thing to do given that the women had spoken already. The constant silence was bothering him as well, but before he got a chance to express this, she continued.

"And besides, I'm not going to lie to you, I do kind of want to know. We heard our driver yelling something about you before you came from the courthouse, so it got us—me—a little bit intrigued."

He looked back at her, eyes squinting. "Interesting. Well, I don't know what that was all about, but I just feel like us all sitting here depressed isn't doing us any good, so maybe it's best to keep talking. Just a thought."

"I can get behind that," said the older woman. "I've kind of been drowning in my own thoughts since we stopped talking. What do you guys think?" she added.

She was asking Deron and the younger woman, but neither gave an immediate response. The younger woman was on the fence about it. Deron was still irritable but also wasn't sure it mattered. Talking or not talking, it all seemed to feel negative.

"Well, if no one objects, what happened was—" The man started to talk again, but this time was quickly interrupted by the East Asian woman.

"Is it something really bad? I don't want to know if it's bad," she said. "I thought I did, but all the negativity I'm feeling right now, I just don't know if I can handle any more."

Deron, as was generally his custom, offered up no opinion, but he did have thoughts, and those were that he agreed. The last story had taken a bite out of him. If it was about to be revealed that he was sitting beside a rapist or pedophile, he might just lose his mind.

He was about to say something just then, to tell them that maybe if they wanted to keep talking, it should be about a different subject. But by the time he opened his mouth, it was already too late.

"I was chosen," the man said nonchalantly. "Unfortunate, I guess, but I've lived a good life. Because of my past volunteering, I only got a three-year stint too. I'll be out with over thirty years of life still ahead of me if all goes well, which I guess is to say if this place doesn't take too many years off my ticker. They say it can do that to you. They say it can be a hell of a place, the Camp. But that's alright. Like I said, I've lived a good life, so I can't complain. I owe this duty to the Utopia for all it has given me. I owe—"

"Stop." It was Deron who spoke, with a sternness in his voice that got the attention of the others. The black woman looked at him and nodded. The East Asian woman buried her head in her hands and mumbled inaudible sounds to herself. Mentally, they had all suffered through a lot today, had heard stories grim and sad. Enough was enough.

"Please stop." Deron looked him in the eye. The man thought to rebut him, but upon returning Deron's gaze, he nodded in understanding and then turned away. Deron did as well. For the next little while, Deron sat with his hands in his lap and his head dangling toward the floor. Until they arrived at the Camp gates, not another word was spoken.

CHAPTER 3

"How was the drive, Tucker?"

They had arrived at the Camp gates—one set of them anyway; there were a few spread along the Wall. Speaking to Matt now was an entry guard, the same one who was there each time he made this trip, always with the same question.

"Fine, Stan," he replied. "And you? How has your day been?"

"Uneventful as usual. You know how it is. The economy bridges get most of the traffic. I just wait here for the regulars."

Matt nodded with no response. There wasn't much more for him to say, but even if there had been, he wanted to keep moving. They had arrived with time to spare but not much, and the area warden valued punctuality.

As if sensing this, Stan wrapped things up. "Well, anyway, I won't keep you. Know you've got to drop your new campers off. Just have 'em smile for the camera when you roll in. You know the drill."

Matt smiled and then nodded once more. To say he knew the drill was the understatement of the year. He knew all the protocols like the back of his hand. Since he'd started with the guards, he'd always done this same job. Over and over and over again.

"I'll see you around, Stan," he said. He gave the man a quick salute and then rolled up his window. Once he had, he pressed a button marked <- on the dash.

***

IN THE BACK OF the van, Deron shuttered violently in sudden surprise. Behind where his head was resting, a strip of the vehicle was starting to peel away.

"What's going on?" the older woman asked. And as if on cue, she got an answer.

"Attention passengers," said a voice, a voice they all recognized as the driver's. "As you can see, one of the rear windows is being opened. I would ask that you all move to that side of the van, place your head at the crevice level, and look outside. We are now entering the Camp, and the law requires that you look into the surveillance camera so the Computer may identify you with its facial recognition software. If you do this without complaint, I will see to it that the window remains open until we get close to the drop-off point. Thank you for your cooperation."

The driver stopped talking right as the side of the van finished contorting. What they were left seeing was an opening about one foot in height and eight feet in length, like a series of airplane windows only all interconnected and all capable of removing and then replacing themselves as part of the frame. They would have thought of it like something out of a *Transformers* movie had those existed in the Utopia.

The four looked at each other, baffled at first, but they slowly began to settle, slowly remembered the instructions and what they'd been asked to do.

Deron went first. He stood up, turned in place, then knelt on the bench and stuck his head through the opening.

What he saw looked like a form of security booth. Not many existed in the Utopia, but he could remember something similar at the entrance of the school he used to attend. It was a checkpoint of sorts, acting as the gateway between one world and the next.

He couldn't see much around it (they were too close to it), but from what he could discern, the road behind them expanded at one point and separated into additional paths. He presumed these paths led to other gates, and this would be confirmed for him in the coming moments.

For now though, he just waited for them to roll along. He couldn't see it yet, but there was a camera waiting to capture their image once they scooted forward, but only after they were all in position.

"C'mon, guys," he said, still staring through the opening. "Let's just get this over with."

Unbeknownst to him, they all nodded their heads. The chosen man immediately turned in his spot and followed Deron's lead. The child hider similarly walked over and knelt in position without vacillation. The outside-world contactor was more hesitant. She looked to her right, and only when she saw the young guard—a boy who couldn't have been more than a year or two out of school—only when she saw him staring at her through the glass with this glaring look of impatience was she sure of what she should do. She shuffled over and joined them. A few seconds later, they continued on their way.

They first passed a camera at perfect eye level: if they were looking through the opening, they had no choice but to stare into it. *Not like we would avoid it even if we could,* Deron thought. It wouldn't buy them any favours where they were going.

They passed underneath the arm barrier, and once they had, they received another announcement. "You may sit back normally now if you would like. Thank you for your cooperation."

The rebellious part of each of them wanted to go tell the driver to take his instructions and shove them up his ass. None of them did so. None of them even moved. But it wasn't in an act of defiance that they chose to keep their positions locked. They were simply mesmerized instead.

They had passed the security booth, and Deron could see now that he had been correct. There were three other gates, each separated by fifteen to twenty yards. A transport truck was about to leave through one of the gates. The truck had just passed over a thin bridge, wide enough for only one vehicle at a time. Each road had its own bridge. Deron's van had just started to drive onto one. Below the bridges was a pit at least twenty feet deep.

Deron barely noticed any of this. Had it not been for the moving truck, he probably wouldn't have seen anything in his peripherals at all. His eyes, like the rest of the group's, were glued to one thing. He was staring at the Wall.

He had seen it before. All of them had, in fact. One of the first trips

Utopian kids took was to the Wall. It was a monumental achievement of modern structural ingenuity: around three hundred kilometres wide and forty feet high at all points. It was something Utopians were taught to be proud of.

But it was also something Utopians were taught to fear because inside that wall were the ones who'd been punished for breaking the commandments, utopians who'd lost their way, who were in need of reform, who hadn't realized how good they'd had it and required a reminder.

They stared at the Wall because never before had they seen it from this vantage point, from the perspective of someone on the inside of the dividing line, from the perspective of someone who'd been judged by the Computer as no longer deserving freedom.

It was funny in a way. Technically, there was no "inside" of the Wall. The Wall did not surround any particular space. On the Camp side of structure, you would eventually hit water like you would on the side opposed. And yet the second they crossed over, it felt like something was different. The second they crossed over, it felt like something was wrong. The second they crossed over, it felt like they would never see anything on the other side of that Wall again.

One by one, they stopped staring outward and returned to their seats: first the younger woman, then the older woman, and then the man followed them. Deron stared the longest, with a thought in his mind that he just couldn't seem to make disappear: why hadn't he just waited?

He turned around, sat, and stared up toward the roof of the van. Why hadn't he just waited?

***

IT WAS EVENING BY the time Matt pulled the van over for good.

"We made it, Junior," he said, feeling pleased and relieved. The clock on the dash read 5:54. They were six minutes early.

Mike looked at him and responded. "Good thing," he said. "I was about to fall asleep."

"Watch—" *What you say*. That was what he had been about to reply, but he caught himself before he did. Inside the Camp, you did not want to speak anything controversial (which falling asleep on the job could definitely be considered). As long as they were in the van, they were probably safe, but it still wasn't worth the risk. Technology was so good that the potential was there to capture just about anything, and although he had no true understanding of how much the State could or did listen in on conversations on this side of the Wall, his paranoid mind told him you could just never be too careful. "Watch your step getting out. Sometimes your equilibrium is off after sitting for so long."

Mike smiled and laughed. "Yeah, maybe for you, old man. I'm good to go." He opened the door and got out.

Matt smiled after him and shook his head. *One day you'll learn, Junior,* he thought to himself. *And hopefully one day before it's too late.*

He did an about-face and exited himself. His smile was wiped the second he did. It was time to get serious.

The area warden was here. And he wasn't wasting any time.

"Guard Tucker," he said the moment Matt planted his feet on solid ground. He approached him without hesitation, hand extended. "Nice to see you're on time. I expected you a bit earlier seeing as how you were not bringing me anyone from Unglow District today, but on time will do."

Upon hearing that, Matt's heart began to thunder in his chest. But he did his best to keep his composure and shook the man's hand.

"Yes sir, Supervisor Reynolds. My apologies." He tiptoed with every word, careful to make sure he wasn't making any excuses, careful to make sure he was showing the proper respect. The Utopia generally frowned upon the use of the word *sir* when addressing a superior; no matter what your position on the hierarchical chain, everyone was supposed to be equal to everyone else. But with certain people, the word still held value as a sign of subordination, and Reynolds was one of those people.

The man looked up at him with a wry smile. He was a shorter man, about five foot seven, with a round face, shaved head, and thick beard. Thick was also an adequate description of his body type, in equal parts muscle and fat. Yet in spite of his perceived indifference to his bodily appearance, his skin (at least the few parts of it you could see under his blue supervisor uniform) was well maintained for someone nearing fifty and was a nice olive colour. And despite his height, or lack thereof, he was as intimidating as they came, even when he was just kidding.

"Relax, Tucker. I'm just messing with you, friend." He gave Matt a clap on the shoulder, and that allowed the younger man to force out a smile. "You know if you got here super early I'd be busy with other things anyway. No point in it. No point in it at all. In fact, sitting around waiting, I would venture to guess, only adds to a new camper's anxiety."

Matt nodded, partly in agreement and partly because it was what he knew was best. What he didn't know was what to say, but thankfully, he wouldn't have to provide any type of oral response.

"Speaking of which, let's go see the new recruits." And with that, the supervisor began to stride toward the back doors of the van. Matt followed close behind. Mike was there waiting for them when they arrived, and the second they did, Reynolds gave him the order without so much as a hello.

"Berkowitz, open it up, soldier."

"You got it, chief," he responded, and the moment he said it, Reynolds flashed him a glare that might have turned him to stone had he seen it. Sir was acceptable as a sign of respect. Chief was a bit too chummy for the good super's liking. Matt felt that old thumping in his chest again. The kid was skating on thin ice.

But he didn't know it, and so he opened the doors without a care in the world. And instead of him feeling the weight of that stare, it was the ones inside who took the brunt of it.

The first thing they saw was a blue-uniformed man glaring back at them like they were the scum of the earth. And the first thing they heard was a welcome that came out so strained, it sounded as though it hurt his vocal cords to say.

"Good evening to you all." And then suddenly, the glare softened, and the face contorted into an almost crooked smile. "Welcome to the Camp."

***

THE NEXT FIVE MINUTES went by quite uneventfully, at least in Matthew Tucker's world. There was no blow up from Reynolds toward Berkowitz. There was no argument from any of the campers as they exited the van that a mistake had been made and that they shouldn't be here. There was nothing memorable at all that happened in those five minutes, and he was

THE UTOPIA

thankful for that. And thankful even more so that he was now being given permission to go home.

"You can go, Tucker. No reason for you to have to wait here. I see the last van just pulling in now, and most of the others have gone already."

And when he heard those words, he didn't hesitate to accept the offer because he knew better than most that one day, it might not come.

"Thank you, Supervisor Reynolds. I appreciate that." They shook hands, and he was about to go before, at the last second, he was halted in his tracks.

"Oh and, Tucker, just one more thing." They were standing by the driver's side door. There was no one else within earshot, but Reynolds began to whisper anyway. "Talk to that boy in there if you don't mind." He was referring to Mike, who was sitting in the passenger's side front seat of the van. "Guard Berkowitz is young, so I don't expect him to be perfect. But I worry he's a bit too ... how should I put it ... impertinent at times. Perhaps you can mention to him that it is probably in his best interest to be a bit more reserved in his early days. Now, I am quite tolerant of the various personality types as you know, but some less open-minded individuals might mistake his behaviour for a general aloofness, and that would just be a shame. You understand what I'm saying?"

Matt nodded profusely without even realizing his head was moving. He did understand. Oh boy, did he understand. Every single word.

"Yes sir. I will speak to him. I know he means well. He just ..." He paused. He had already said too much. "I will speak to him."

"Excellent." Reynolds smiled. "I thank you for that, and I'm sure he will too." He gave Matt another pat on the shoulder and then began to walk away, leaving him with only a few final words. "Now, you have a good night."

"Thank you, Supervisor Reynolds. You too," Matt called after him. And then before he could even think another thought, he hurried into the van and closed the door behind him.

"What was that all about?" Mike asked as he entered. "He ask you to cook him dinner or something?"

And in his mind, Matt screamed at Mike to shut the hell up. But instead, his mouth formed the words, "Was just checking to make sure we had enough charge to get back." He started up the vehicle.

"Do we have enough charge? Looks like we're just over half. Maybe we should just charge it while we're here."

"No," Matt said, more sternly than he would have liked. He had already started to circle around and pull away from the area.

"Wow, okay. Sorry for asking," Mike responded, pouting a little bit.

"Sorry," Matt replied, more calmly now. "It was a fair question, and I didn't mean to be rude. It's just been a long day, and I kind of want to get home. I think we can make it."

"Yeah. Yeah, okay. Fair enough. I'm a bit tired myself. Was up early today. Actually, I'm going to close my eyes for a little bit if you don't mind."

Matt thought that was a brilliant idea. Oh, how much harder it is to say something stupid while you're asleep. "Sure thing, Junior. You get some rest." *And hopefully when you wake up, you'll see the light.*

He thought about giving the boy the speech right then, telling him that he had to be careful how he talked and acted on the job, explaining that while they couldn't fire him merely because of his personality, they could target him, and the second his work got sloppy (which it would, at some point; everyone has their off days or runs into trouble every once in a while), they would upload evidence of this slippage to the Computer's Job Network. And once that happened, it was only a matter of time. Enough complaints backed up by surveillance evidence and he would be gone.

Matt unconsciously flexed his fingertips inwards and then out again over top of the steering wheel. The tension he was feeling in his body was overwhelming because Matt could see Mike's future with the most exquisite crystal clarity.

Mike would be fired, but when the Computer fired him, Junior wouldn't just be unemployed. If it were just that, Matt wouldn't care. He could chalk it up as a learning experience for the kid, perhaps even a blessing in disguise.

But that wouldn't be his punishment. No, his punishment would be something much worse. Because in the Utopia, the competition for jobs was fierce and unrelenting. There was no room for someone to treat their occupation without its proper respect. A job wasn't just a job in this place.

It was also protection. And to take depriving someone else of that privilege lightly was as great a sin as any.

That's why if you ever get fired, kid, you aren't going home, Matt thought to himself. *You're going to the Camp.*

He knew it all too well because it had happened to him. Inhale. Exhale. He took a deep breath to steady himself.

It had been years since he'd been released, but never for a second had that experience left him. Never for a second had it not motivated him to stay on the right path. Never for a second had he forgotten what had gotten him sent there in the first place.

He had been like Junior once: an arrogant twenty-something who thought he was all that, thought he was untouchable and that nothing could ever happen if he talked back, if he showed up late or left early, if some days he showed up drunk or high.

Junior could still be saved. Mike wasn't yet close to the level Matt had gotten to. But without an intervention, one day, he would get there. Reynolds had seen it, and he saw it too. He would get lazier, his work would start to slip, until the day it cost him.

Matt looked to his right. The boy had dozed off peacefully into dreamland. Again, he thought of giving him the speech right then and there, just waking him and spitting it out, explaining what would happen if he didn't take things more seriously, describing the Camp and how it would break even the most tough-minded of men and women—how it had done so to him.

He moved his arm toward him but hesitated just before his hand clasped the boy's shoulder. He'd thought all this through. He knew what needed to be said. And if he woke the kid up to say it, Mike would understand that this was serious. He would do well to tell him now.

He nodded his head once, hesitated for another second, and then returned his hand to the steering wheel.

But we're still in the Camp, and in here, you never know if they're listening. He would tell him when they were out.

* * *

WHILE MATTHEW TUCKER HAD found the five minutes following

Supervisor Reynolds's "welcome to the Camp" address to be quite uneventful, Deron Boyd had found that particular period of time to be anything but. In just those five minutes, he had finally learned the names of the others he'd been transported with, had been separated from them, and had gotten his first look at what was to be his home for the next five years.

First came the names: Evelyn Yung, Joyce Parker, Bartholomew Winters. Each had been called out by the man who had introduced himself as Supervisor Mirko Reynolds one by one, said once in monotone and then checked off Reynolds's list, the first and only time Deron would ever hear them spoken.

Following the introductions, the other three had been assigned to a group that was destined for another segment of the Camp. They weren't told where or why, only how. A bus had transported them along with several others. They'd hopped on that bus, and Deron never saw them again.

Deron had been assigned to a different cluster, one that would remain in this part of the Camp. He had been told to stand with a group of other people—about twenty on quick count, around equal parts men and women—and otherwise given just one other instruction.

"I'll be making an announcement once I check-in the ones in the last van. Everything else you need to know will be explained then."

Since then, all he'd done was stare at his surroundings. It was a lot to take in. Behind him, from the direction they'd come from, was endless open space. To his right was the same, just dirt and grass and a four-lane road with a median running through the middle that ran parallel to the east-west direction he was standing. In front of him though was something else entirely. Beyond a connecting road was the beginning of an assembly line of factories. He could only see the makings of two from his current position: one directly in front of him and one immediately to his left. But he knew there were others. Oh so many others. And he was about to become the newest employee in one of them.

"Everyone!" The call was loud and purposefully distressing. The area warden wanted their attention. He also wanted to show them who the boss was around these parts.

Deron had been enamoured with the factories, but he now looked back over to his right and turned his whole body to face that direction. Supervisor Reynolds was standing with a microphone on a raised platform about ten feet wide and four feet high. He was behind a podium, which Deron had somehow failed to notice. There were at least seven or eight guards scattered throughout the area. The sun was just beginning to set.

"I just have a few things to say, and then you can be on your way. I know there is an adjustment period, and I would like you to be able to begin that as soon as possible. But first I must outline the rules and regulations."

Deron turned for just a moment to look at his fellow recruits. Some looked healthy. Some looked sick. Some looked tired. Some were stone-faced. Most appeared to be listening. None appeared to be thinking of protesting. Yet.

"Living conditions: Each of you has been assigned a bed in one of the designated housing complexes. Barring unforeseen changes, that will be your bed for the duration of your time here. Working conditions: This area of the Camp is limited to factory work. Each of you has been assigned a job in one of our factories. You will work there for twelve hours per day, except on your designated half day."

"Twelve hours!" The comment was said in a low voice but with great emphasis, enough to make the area warden pause for a second.

He stared hard into the crowd, tried for a second the pick out the source (it was a man around Deron's age standing near him), thought of making a general comment toward the group when he couldn't determine who had caused the ruckus, thought better of it, and simply continued on.

"We have taken religious beliefs into consideration when assigning your half day. If you don't like the day you have been assigned you can try to trade with someone else in your factory and report it to your factory supervisor if you come to an agreement. Otherwise, the day you are assigned is the day you are stuck with. Clothing and food: You will be given one work uniform and one leisure uniform. These uniforms are designated to you and you alone. Each uniform has a specific number..."

Deron's mind checked out the second he heard his stomach rumble. The mention of the word *food* had apparently reminded his body it hadn't received nourishment in some time.

"Argh," he grumbled, quietly enough that he himself barely heard the sound. He was starting to feel sick again. The lack of food. The lack of drugs. Hours upon hours sitting in a van. The stress. The sadness. It was all too much and happening way too fast.

"If you have any questions, ask someone in your living quarters. They will know the answer. That's really all I have to say. We will take the time now to hand out your first night's supplies. When I call your name, come grab your things from Guard Sanchez here, and then if your housing complex is close by, you may go. If not, you can wait for the shuttle."

He paused only for a second. He had been reading from a script and needed to flip his page. "Alright, let's get this over with, ladies and gentlemen. Appleton."

A man stepped forward almost immediately. Deron watched as he slowly but surely advanced the twenty-foot gap between themselves and the platform. There was a guard now standing there at its base. A van was backing up toward him. It stopped about five feet from the platform. The guard—Sanchez, he presumed—opened the back doors just as Appleton reached him.

What happened after that, Deron couldn't see—Sanchez had moved behind the van, and Appleton as well was now blocked out by the open door—but could deduce. Inside the vehicle were their rations for the night. Sanchez was handing Appleton his. When Appleton re-emerged with a reusable shopping bag slung over his shoulder, Deron discovered his hypothesis was true.

"Barkova."

A woman stepped forward and began to walk, crossing paths with Appleton along the way. Eventually, Appleton rejoined their group.

"What did they give you?" a voice called out the second he had. Most of the group crowded around to hear his response, figuring they might as well learn what they could. Any information would be useful. They were all in the same boat, after all.

"Haven't really looked through the bag yet," he responded. "But from what I can tell, just some clothes, food, and a book."

"A book?" a different voice questioned.

"Yeah. It's got the instructions in it apparently."

"Instructions?" the first voice repeated.

"That's what the guard said. Figured that means it tells you where you're living, what job you're doing, stuff like that. Haven't looked at it yet, so I have no idea."

"Boyd."

Deron felt a sudden jolt at the sound of his name but quickly settled. This was probably the only time when it wasn't such a bad thing to hear your name called in the Camp.

He moved forward slowly, one step at a time. His eyes darted all around, unsure of where to look. They first settled on Supervisor Reynolds, but his response stare was sharp and unwelcoming; Deron didn't want to look there. His next gaze was toward the Barkova woman, but her eyes were sad and distant; not exactly the face he was looking for to cheer him up. He finally settled on staring at the ground. It was safe and uncontroversial. He watched his feet crawl forward until he was eventually at the van.

"Boyd?"

He looked up with a nod toward Sanchez. Only from this close up did he realize the size of the guard. Deron's height was above average, but he felt tiny next to Sanchez. He was a nice enough man though.

"This is your stuff for the first night." He handed Deron a pre-stocked bag. A number—7629224-0809551—was written in some type of ink on the strap. Deron recognized it immediately as his Utopian ID number. "There's a leisure uniform in there. You can wait until you get to your housing complex to change into it, but you must do so when you get there. There's a factory uniform in there as well. You can change into it tomorrow morning before work, or you can wait until you get to the factory to change into it. Either way, make sure you bring your leisure uniform to work so that you can shower at the facilities before you go home. There are no showers in the housing complexes. We've also given you a meal for tonight. When you want to eat it is your choice, but it is the only food you are getting until tomorrow so keep that in mind. Do you understand?"

Deron nodded. He was about to turn away but was caught before he did.

"Last thing. There is a book in there with instructions written on the first page. It'll tell you where your housing complex is, where you are working, and all that other stuff. In the front cover is a card. Bring that card everywhere, and do not lose it. I don't have enough time to explain everything now, but you'll learn as you go. The rest of the book contains empty pages. You may write in them as you choose. There is a pen in there for that. Any questions?"

Deron shook his head no.

"Good, because I don't have time to answer any. If one comes to you, as the supervisor said, ask someone in your living quarters. They will know the answer. Otherwise, just work hard and follow orders. If you do, you will be fine. Good luck, Boyd."

"Thanks." He said it out of instinct, almost stuck his hand out for a shake even. But he restrained himself just in time. *This man seems like a good guy, but this is not that type of place,* he reminded himself.

Deron turned and walked away. Blank was his stare. Empty was his mind. The group saw him returning but didn't speak a word to him. He didn't to them either. They were all in the same boat, but that boat was capsizing, and each was only concerned about saving their own skin. Never in his life had he felt so alone.

He stopped a few feet short of the group, turned to his right, and walked a few feet more toward the street. When he was far enough away that no prying eyes would catch him, he reached into his bag and fetched the book. *Might as well see what they have in store for me,* he thought. Only it didn't quite work out like that. Not at first anyway.

No way.

His eyes widened the second he saw the front cover. Instantly, a smile lit his face, a comedic type of grin in the darkest of moments.

He'd never been great at finding the humour in things. When the kid who had called him slow on the playground in ninth year challenged him to a race and faceplanted after fifty metres, that was annoying, not funny, because he didn't get to beat him fair and square. When he'd accidently put cocaine in his pasta water and not salt, that was a waste of precious resources and not something to laugh at. There wasn't much room for irony in his world.

He shouldn't have found this amusing either, but he did. For some

THE UTOPIA

reason, he did. He found it amusing in the same way he had when the woman had asked how they were handling the recession. It was just too absurd.

Printed on the front cover, under the title *Laws of the Land,* were the Ten State Commandments.

No Work Below Standard

No Robbery from the State or the People

No Assault/Battery/Harassment

No Rape/Pedophilia

No Killing (with the exception of State-ordered euthanasia)

No Destruction of Any Kind

No False Witness

No Hiding of a Child/Birthing More than Two Children

No Contact with the Outside World (unless sanctioned by State orders)

No Rebellion Against the State

One by one, he read each of them, his smile widening every time he hit one of the ones he'd been found guilty of. What was he supposed to do with that list? Preach them in the mirror and tell himself that the Lord will smite thee if thou dost not obey? Like he hadn't already been smitten? Like he didn't know the laws? Like being in this place wasn't enough to convince him not to break any of them again.

Absolutely absurd.

He flipped over to the back cover still smiling, expecting to see perhaps a list of ten things he could do to improve upon himself. What he saw instead was a map of their segment of the Camp. His smile quickly faded as he remembered what he'd been told.

There is a book in there with instructions written on the first page. He turned the book back over and flipped it open, and sure enough, there they were.

CHRISTIAN JERRY MARCHIONI

Resident:	Deron Boyd
Housing Complex:	M-1 Bed 377
Workplace:	4F
Occupation:	Sawmill Labourer
Shift:	8 a.m. – 8 p.m.
Rest Period:	Sunday Afternoons

Note: Use the map to find your housing complex and your place of work. You start work immediately. Be on time or there will be consequences. Your card is in the pocket inside the front cover. Keep it on you at all times.

There was a flap in the inside front cover. He reached into it and, as expected, there was a card. It had his name on it, his ID number, and the same picture of his face as his Utopia ID. The identical information from the first page of the book was on the card.

He stared at it for a moment, flipped it over (there was nothing on the back but a barcode), reversed it one more time, and then stared at it some more. When he got tired of looking at himself, he put the card back in the front flap and then glanced over at the group. Another woman was being called. Gafferty was her name. Nothing new to see.

His eyes moved to the street. There was a bus waiting there, one different from the one he had seen his van-mates get on. That one had left some time ago. He wondered where they were headed, and what would happen to … What were their names? He had already forgotten.

He looked back at the group. There was a thought of rejoining them, but what was the point? He was tired, he was hungry, and there was nothing to gain by waiting. He flipped over the book again and stared down at the map. M-1. It was just a few blocks away.

One step at a time, he began to walk away. After ten yards or so, he came across a guard. He expected her to say something, to ask him where he was going or tell him to wait for the others. But she just stared right through him like he didn't even exist.

If only that were the case.

Step by step he marched, on a journey to a place he would never wish to find, every single pace leaving a part of him behind. Disgust and disgrace were the only feelings in his mind.

Every single face was screaming the whole time. Welcome to the Camp.

***

THIRTY MINUTES AFTER HE had first passed the woman guard with soul-snatching beady eyes, he felt as though a little part of that soul had been returned to him. He was still at the Camp, still on the precipice of a half-decade-long struggle, still under the well-reasoned impression that the worst was yet to come, but he had also accomplished his first task without incident, had gotten an initial lay of the land during a relatively quiet and cool evening stroll, had filled his stomach while he was at it with a ham and cheese sandwich and banana from his supply bag. And in this part of the world, those were the wins you needed to not entirely resign.

He looked up at the building now before him, a large "M-1" painted on its surface. It was different from the various factories he had passed. There were no smokestacks or chimneys, no guard vans or delivery trucks, no ominous auras emanating from it at all.

It had a smaller, more communal feeling to it, at least from the outside. And Deron desperately hoped the inside would match because it was his new home.

He looked up even farther, now toward the sky. It was a beautiful skyline. The sun was on its last legs for the evening. The clouds hung above ever so delicately. Even this place couldn't destroy a scene so picturesque.

He enjoyed it for a moment longer, stored it in his memory for recall at a later time, and then looked back down at the building. There was really only one thing left to do now. He'd been standing by the sidewalk, but at that moment, he took the chance to head toward the complex. It was time to go inside.

Within a few seconds, he arrived at the front doors. They were made of frosted glass. Only once he'd shielded his eyes like a visor and peered through the glass up close did he realize what was behind them.

He pulled one open and stepped into a foyer area about six feet by ten. Directly in front of him was another set of doors. Unlike their predecessors, these were made of metal and were completely impenetrable by the human eye. Concrete walls surrounded them. He couldn't see what was beyond.

He tried to open them for the sake of it, but he knew it wouldn't work. To his left was a scanner. You needed access to get in. And he figured he had just the card.

He reached into his bag, grabbed the book, opened the front cover, and pulled out what he'd start referring to as his Camp ID. He tapped it to the scanner and sure enough, presto. The lock mechanism clicked, and he was able to advance to the next stage.

The lobby was empty when he entered it. There wasn't even a single couch or a painting, let alone a person. It was just empty space, walls, and a few omnipresent cameras. It was like the building was abandoned.

Deron shoved his card back into the book and then the book back into the bag. Something about this lobby was creeping him out, and he wanted to get out of there. So much for that communal feeling.

He walked as far forward as he could (which was relatively far considering he was in an unfurnished lobby) and then looked both directions. There was an opening in the wall on both his left and his right. Each led to a hallway. The left side looked like stairs. The right side looked like a wheelchair ramp. He chose to go left, thinking he might as well take the stairs while his legs were still working.

The stairs veered forward and then back. When he got up the first flight, he noticed that unlike on the main floor, this entryway had a door guarding the passage, another metal one that didn't let him look inside. A number "2" was painted on it.

I guess I'm the next one, he thought to himself, remembering the information on his Camp ID. *Building M-1, Bed 377. That must be the third floor.*

He climbed the additional floor and entered through the door. On the other side was a sight to behold.

"Wow," he said aloud. The second he entered the room, he was hit by a wave of astonishment. It took a moment to get his bearings.

He looked left and right, up and down, studying the whole space. The room was massive. He'd thought the lobby was commodious, but this area reminded him of a small warehouse in size and components.

Shop lights lit the room from above. There were no windows at all. Like the lobby, the walls were all concrete. And they were almost as barren but for a single clock, an air conditioning unit, and cameras, of course. The floor was where things changed.

Beds. If this warehouse specialized in anything, it was beds. There were rows on rows of them, equally spaced apart like tombstones. All were perfectly made, the sheets and covers perfectly tucked in, just waiting for the bodies to return to their resting places.

This is unbelievable, Deron thought. And he felt that too. But at the same time, he couldn't say at all that he was surprised by what he saw. What else had he expected?

"You new?"

Had it not been for the question, he probably would have stood there unattuned for a bit longer. But the voice snapped him back into it.

He'd known there were other people in the room (two to be exact) the second he'd entered; his mind had just so far chosen to ignore them. But that was all about to change. He looked to his left.

"I am," he replied. "How did you know?"

His entry point from the stairs had brought him to the middle section of the room. The man speaking to him was at his ten o'clock.

He replied with a smile. "You get used to seeing the same faces," he said. "Haven't seen yours before."

Deron nodded. That made sense. You spend enough time somewhere and you probably recognize just about everyone there, even if there are— he looked left to right and quickly counted—one hundred beds.

He thought to say something back but realized that they might as well continue this conversation in closer proximity. He hugged the wall, looking down at the beds as he did. Each was labelled with a number (go figure, what wasn't in this place?). He passed 361, then 371, and stopped for just a moment when he hit 381.

"Hey," he said. There was a man in a yellow jumpsuit lying on the bed, not the one who had spoken to him, but a different sort of man, a man probably in his mid-thirties. He was pale-skinned with long black hair down past his shoulders. He had a round face and goatee and was thin in a way that made it look like he barely ever ate. He was staring up at the ceiling with eyes so distant they might as well have been on a different planet.

Deron stood over him for a moment, wondering first, who he was; second, if he'd respond to him; and third, where he could get some of the stuff that this guy was on. When it became clear that no answers were forthcoming, he moved on.

The original speaker was six beds over—387. He was sitting at the toe end of his mattress.

"Don't mind Merlin," he said in a voice that sounded more constructive than consoling. "He's not well."

Deron looked down at him from his upright position. The man was on the shorter side, with brown skin and bushy hair. He was an older man as well, Deron thought, at least by Utopian standards. He had a few wrinkles on his face and hands. He wore the same yellow jumpsuit Merlin was in. His only accessory was a silver ring around the fourth finger of his left hand.

"You mean physically or mentally?"

"Both. But more so in the brain. There are days where he is lucid but others where he is just a shell."

Deron glanced over toward the other man. He was still lying in his bed and staring up at the ceiling. He hadn't moved an inch.

"Does he get medication for it?"

"He does. Some days he takes it, some days he doesn't. Some days it helps, some days there is no change. It's the same here as the other side of the Wall. The Computer's Health Network can analyze your symptoms and narrate your condition. It can prescribe you pills for treatment. But even with how far the science has advanced, there is no perfect cure for any type of mental illness. So whether or not you take the pills, whether or not they work, it is all totally irrelevant. Any way you slice it, it is up to you to live with the consequences of your actions. It is always you."

Deron looked back at him and nodded in understanding. He hesitated for a moment, but in the end decided to continue the conversation. There was something interesting about this man. Deron could tell he had been here for a while.

And despite everything that had happened before with the others, despite how that had made him feel, he kind of wanted to know why.

"And what choice did you make that led to these consequences? If you don't mind me asking."

"I killed a man." There was zero hesitation. He didn't even blink.

"Really? You? You don't seem—"

"He attacked my wife."

"Your wife? But—"

"Yes. I know. There is no marriage in the Utopia. But I loved this woman, lived with her, slept with her, stayed true to her. There is no marriage in the Utopia, but she was my wife, you understand?"

"Yes." Deron didn't even have to lie in response. A part of him knew the rules and knew that, by definition, having a wife in the Utopia was impossible. But a larger part of him knew exactly what he meant.

He was starting to feel sad again, the same way he had when the others had told their stories. But he'd never really been one to learn from his mistakes, so he kept talking anyway.

"I think I know what you mean."

"I didn't mean to kill him. Truly I didn't. Up until that point, I even considered him a friend. But that day, his judgment was clouded by all sorts of drugs, and he made a pass at my wife, in her own home, with no care or regard. She told him no, but he wouldn't listen, so I had no choice but to react. Suffice to say, things went too far, and he ended up dead. I was sent here three days later."

Deron nodded, feeling every word. His emotions were heightened, but he managed to remain calm because this man was calm. His voice hadn't broken pitch or stride at any point. His voice said he'd accepted what he'd done and had accepted his fate a long time ago. But that didn't mean he accepted everything.

"The system is rigged. I know you've seen it firsthand. They don't factor in the circumstances. If you do the crime, you do the time, plain and simple. There is no room for reason. It didn't matter what that man had done. It didn't matter that it was an accident. I killed a man, and that was all there was to it. And the fact that it was in our unit, the fact that there was no camera evidence of what happened, that made it even worse because if I hadn't confessed to the crime I committed, if I had tried to fight it, they would have charged my wife as well. If she'd tried to protect me, she would have been charged as a false witness. Or perhaps even worse, they might have charged her with the killing too. And for the past twenty-one years, she could have been stuck in this place right along with me."

"But because you admitted it, they left her alone," Deron stated matter-of-factly. He was starting to see where this was going.

"Correct. That was our gentlemen's agreement, so to speak. I would admit guilt, and in exchange, they wouldn't charge her. Because as long as she's not charged—"

"The Computer can't make a ruling," Deron interrupted.

"Yes. Exactly. The Crime Network only makes judgments on issues logged as crimes. If the information is never uploaded, there is no case to judge. So I admitted my guilt, not because I felt I had done something unconscionable but because it had to be done. I was sent to trial anyway since the only plea in the Utopia is not guilty. Not that it mattered for me or matters in general. They say it's so people can't just be coerced into admitting guilt and sentenced without a ruling from the Computer. They say it's to be fair, but it's not. Nothing about it is fair. The jury, as they call them, hear the Computer's ruling first and then make their decision. What group of humans is going to overturn the all-knowing Computer? None. You might get one on your side. Maybe even two. But not all three. Never all three. Especially when you have admitted your guilt."

"Yeah," Deron agreed. He thought of speaking more but didn't really have anything else to add. He just simply agreed. With all of it.

"Anyway, it doesn't matter for me. I did what I did, and I can't change it. I care about these things more for future generations, so people who really shouldn't be here aren't sent. Perhaps people like you."

The man stared at Deron hard. He'd been intense the whole time, but this was the first time Deron felt the power in his eyes. It was almost like the man had x-ray vision and was looking inside him.

"I'm not so sure that's true," he responded honestly. His head tilted to the side; his gaze slanted away. He was deciding whether or not he should tell this stranger his story. Eventually, he reasoned there really was no choice. "I robbed a General Store. On a Tuesday night, I just broke through the glass and tried to grab my fill, which makes it tough for anyone to say that I shouldn't be here. I literally did one of the dumbest things anyone could ever do. And the worst part of it is, I don't even know why I did it. I just …"

Deron's hands started to shake. He could feel his heart rate beginning to quicken. He took a deep breath.

"Are you okay?" the man asked.

"That depends on your definition," Deron responded. He closed his eyes and took one more deep breath. After a few seconds, his heart rate began to slow again. When he reopened his eyes, the man was still seated in front of him, only there was something different in his facial expression. He was smiling. Genuinely. And something about that smile helped put Deron further at ease.

The man stuck out his hand. "Hakeem," he said.

Deron obliged. Despite the man's wrinkles, his skin was soft and comforting. "Deron," he replied softly.

Their hands stayed connected as the man spoke his next words. "You'll be okay, Deron. The first stretch is the toughest, but after that, you'll find that this place isn't that much different from the other world you knew. And once that happens, you'll be able to move forward. In one way or another."

Deron nodded in response, their hands still together. Hakeem had made him feel better. The man was wise, there was no doubt about that. And experienced too. But for the first time since they'd met, Deron wasn't so sure that he necessarily agreed. He pulled his hand away but continued to look down.

"But have you truly moved forward? Aren't there still times where you wish you would have done something different? Or feel sorry about what you did?"

"No one is ever truly sorry for the things they have done, for if they were, they wouldn't have done those things in the first place."

Deron snapped his head around. Hakeem looked on and continued to smile. It was Merlin who had spoken. Still staring at the ceiling like he was lost in a trance, he'd been listening the whole time. Deron looked back at Hakeem.

"The boy is lost, but he is intelligent," Hakeem said. And he felt that way too, that the ones with the mental illnesses had something special inside them, something that allowed them to perceive the world in ways others could not. On another day, he would have explained this idea to his new friend Deron, but there was no rush. They would see plenty of each other. And now wasn't the time.

Hakeem looked up at the clock and, for the first time, moved from his bed. He faced the wall toward the east, the farthest wall from his bed.

"It has made me happy to talk to you, Deron, and I look forward to doing so more in the future. But now, my son, I must pray."

"Pray?" Deron responded with a bit of disbelief. "You're religious?"

"Since my youth, yes, I have sought help through patience and prayer. And through the teachings of Islam."

Deron's open mouth accurately depicted his feelings of surprise. There were some religious folks in the Utopia, but the percentage of those who took their religion seriously enough to go to church every weekend or pray at the designated times was negligible at best. Holy scripture was not banned by the State, but it wasn't taught either, so most simply ignored it. The only way to become religious as a youth was through independent study during one's free time, and for the few that did that, Christianity was most often their religion of choice. Deron himself had dipped his toes into the biblical tales but hadn't even gotten his feet wet before he quit.

A part of him wanted to ask why Hakeem had chosen Islam, but for a reason unknown to even himself, he said something else instead. "The area warden mentioned taking religion into account when scheduling our half days, but to be honest, I thought he was just saying that for show. I'm surprised they even allow people to practice religion here."

"You shouldn't be," Hakeem responded, so quickly that it was like he knew the comment was coming. "Religion is good for them. Belief in God means you will not give up hope, and they don't want to break you completely, for the broken are a dangerous opponent. Both here and on the outside."

Deron wanted to ask him right then what he meant by that, but the man wanted to pray, so he just nodded his head instead. He could ask him about it later. There were other things for him to do right now anyway.

THE UTOPIA

He looked to his left. Along the west wall and past the 390 section of beds was a washroom. He went to use that instead.

He sighed as he entered. The bathroom was spacious and quite clean, all things considered, but he realized in that moment that he hadn't had to share a washroom since his school days. Just another X on his list of lost liberties.

He sat down in one of the stalls, thinking about it all. His day. His life. Something along the road had led him to this place, but what exactly it had been, he just couldn't pinpoint. For some time he stayed, hoping for something, but nothing ever came. The only conclusion he drew was that maybe it didn't even matter. Maybe Hakeem was right. Maybe he just needed some time.

Eventually, after he had finished his business and had enough of thinking, he cleaned himself up and headed for the sink. He washed his hands there, and after he had done so, reached into his supply bag for his change of clothes. They had told him to put on his leisure uniform when he got here, and he had no reason to disobey that order. The clothes he was wearing felt dirty and heavy anyway.

He changed quickly then grabbed his water bottle (one had come as part of his melange of supplies) and filled it to the brim using sink water. It was cool and quite refreshing. He refilled it once more and was about to head back out when he saw something else in his supply bag, something he hadn't noticed before. And it made his heart race.

It can't be! he thought. *Why would they?*

But it was exactly what he thought it was. Previously buried, he'd unearthed the most ironic item in his care package: a tiny little prescription bottle holding only a single tablet. And he didn't need the label to tell him the type of drug. It was a zombie pill.

This has to be a joke, he thought. *They're just fucking with me.*

And most of him believed that. Most of him really did believe this was some type of replica placebo or some other form of test. They'd ask him for it tomorrow, and if he couldn't give it to them, there'd be some sort of consequence. In this place, thoughts like these were anything but irrational.

He opened up the bottle. Close to his eye, it looked even more like one of those little tablets he had thrown his life away trying to acquire. If this pill was a fake, it was one hell of a doppelganger.

He shouldn't take it. Every rational bone in his body was telling him not to. Even if it was a real zombie pill, and even if it wasn't a test, there was absolutely no reason he had to take it now. He could wait and ask Hakeem if it was standard that they received them for the first night jitters. He could ask if they got them daily. If they didn't get them daily or often, he could save it for another time when he would need it more.

That would have been the smart thing to do—the rational choice. He had nothing to gain now and a whole lot to lose. But when you're someone like Deron, and it comes to drugs, rationality doesn't work the way it is otherwise supposed to. When you're someone like Deron, the rational choice is to take the drug no matter what the circumstances.

It was overwhelmingly likely the drug was put there on purpose. It was overwhelmingly likely the drug was put there either as some type of test or as an additional supply. But on the off chance it wasn't, on the off chance it was put there by accident, on the off chance they might ask about it, not as a form of test, but simply because he wasn't actually supposed to have it, on the off chance any of those fictions were reality, then he would have to give it back. He wouldn't get to take it.

And what a waste that would be.

He popped the tablet and washed it down with some water. The second he did, as had often been the case in his life, he immediately regretted it. But it was too late now. He had to hurry before the effects kicked in.

Couldn't have even just done half, he thought to himself. *Couldn't even limit yourself to that, could you?*

A part of him was genuinely upset, but his feelings of self-loathing would have to wait. For now, he had to get to his bed. He grabbed his supply bag and burst out of the washroom with vigour, so much so that it even made Merlin stir. It was Hakeem who spoke though. He had finished his prayers and was back to sitting on the corner of his bed.

"Nice to see you've joined the club," he said, pointing to Deron's uniform as he approached.

"Yeah, thought I'd try to fit in first day," he replied, a pretty friendly response considering the stress he was feeling. He hustled past Hakeem and, for the first time, sat down on his own bed. Each mattress was on a bed frame, which was elevated just enough to store supplies underneath. He stuffed his bag under the bed.

"Anything else you would like to ask me?" Hakeem said. "Probably best to now before everyone else shows up. It can get a bit hectic then."

Deron looked at him and smiled—a fake smile that he figured Hakeem would probably see right through, but at least it was better than telling the man who had been so kind to him to screw off so he could get high in peace.

"Thanks," he said. "I appreciate that, Hakeem. If I think of anything, I'll let you know. But I actually just realized how tired I am. It's been a long day. I'm going to try to get a bit of rest I think."

Hakeem smiled back, seemingly unattuned to any paranoia. "Fair enough, my friend. That is probably a good idea. You get some rest. You'll probably need it for tomorrow."

"You're probably right," Deron said back. He would have said more, but he wasn't entirely sure that he hadn't slurred the words. He had meant it sincerely when he had said that he was tired. And he wasn't about to feel any more awake any time soon.

He tucked himself into bed and lay on his back. The lights overhead were shining in his face, but in five minutes or less, it wouldn't matter one bit. That thought made him smile, and for just a moment, he felt genuinely happy for the first time all day.

Welcome to the Camp, he thought to himself, still smiling. For the next minute, he thought this over and over until he passed out.

And he didn't think anything again until he woke up the next morning.

CHAPTER 4

*R**ing!*
　　His eyes fired open in stunned surprise, like he was in one of those horror films and the demonic spirit that had taken out his friends had just revealed itself to him. Only he wasn't shrouded in darkness in some haunted house. He was looking up at those damn lights instead.

　　He blinked a few times to try to get his bearings. He felt disoriented. He knew where he was and what he had done to get here. What he didn't know was anything else.

　　He sat up in his bed, blinked a few more times, and started to look around. The beds, previously empty at the time he had passed out, were now filled with men, some stretching and rising to start their day, some sitting up and shaking the cobwebs loose like him, some still lying with their eyes shut, trying to catch just a few more minutes of sleep.

　　Where had they all come from? And how hadn't he heard them come in? They must have made noise. One or two must have even tried to talk to him. How could he possibly have slept through all that? No human being would be able to. There was just no way. He had all but convinced himself this was all just a dream, then he remembered taking the pill. Suddenly, it all made sense.

　　He breathed in and out, put his hands to his face, and wiped the sleep out of his eyes. All things considered, he felt pretty good, which, now that he thought about it, wasn't a surprise. The pill had this strange way of refreshing you once you remembered what planet you were on, especially if you slept—he looked toward the clock reading 6:32—for almost eleven and a half hours.

He stretched once and prepared to stand up when he felt a tap on his shoulder. He looked to his left and saw Hakeem.

"Good morning, my friend. Nice to see you are awake. I was a bit worried about you last night. You would not wake for anything."

"Really?" he responded, throwing a fake puzzled look on his face. "Strange. I must have just been exhausted. I really haven't slept at all since I got arrested." That was true at least.

"Exhausted is putting it mildly," Hakeem replied. "I've seen dead people harder to wake up. And you didn't even have your earplugs in."

Deron chuckled at that for a moment until he realized that maybe Hakeem wasn't joking. He had probably seen dead people, maybe even in this room. Deron's face went stoic again.

"Anyway, just thought I would say good morning and check in. Do you know where you're going?"

"I believe so, yeah. 4F. The sawmill. I saw it on the map yesterday; I just have to figure out the best route."

"Good. Very good. And what time do you start?"

"Eight o'clock."

"Excellent. You have plenty of time then, which is good. Just one word of advice?"

"Sure, please. I could use all the advice I can get." It wasn't hyperbole; he really did mean it.

"Get there early. Especially on the first day. It's not worth being late. Trust me, it's just not worth it."

"What happens if I am?" He was genuinely curious.

"Depends how late and how often. First time, if it's only a couple minutes, you probably just won't get breakfast. But if it persists and becomes a pattern, or if you're extremely late, the consequences can get much more severe."

Perfect, Deron thought. *Just great. Not feeding you is a light penalty in their eyes. Wonder what they consider a serious punishment.* He thought of asking but decided maybe it was best to just never find out.

"Thanks, Hakeem," he said. "I'll keep that in mind. Honestly, I was thinking I might even leave now just get the route down and ... I don't know ... See what there is to see, I guess."

"Sounds wise," Hakeem said with a smile. "I will see you later then, my friend." He stuck out his hand. Deron shook it.

"See you later, Hakeem."

And he would see him later, at the end of his first workday, where their discussion of punishment would come around full circle.

But before that conversation would occur, Deron would learn a lot in the hours in between. He'd learn the ropes. He'd learn about the peaks and valleys that made up the Camp's landscape. And before any of the chaos and turmoil, he'd learn that at times, the Camp could be a pretty innocuous and mundane place.

Deron left that morning having spoken to no one else. The opportunities were there, but no one seemed to notice (or care about) the new guy. Even the men on either side of him in beds 376 and 378 paid him no attention. Cliques had been established long before he'd shown up. It would take him some time to carve out his niche.

He walked out the door around 6:45. The streets were the busiest he had seen them, mostly with foot traffic—campers marching to work, and the odd guard stationed here and there to ensure compliance with the rules. The only vehicles he could spot were guard vans, busses, and the odd transport truck.

Deron roamed the streets with his supply bag slung over his shoulder. He hadn't been sure at first whether or not to bring it, but once he'd seen others leave the complex with theirs, he'd decided to follow suit. It had made sense to. He wanted his water bottle, he'd been instructed to bring his work uniform, and he needed his ID and the map on the back of the book.

So far, he'd followed that map for about twenty-five minutes. It was an easy read. Everything was labelled, and all the streets ran exactly parallel and perpendicular to each other. The Camp, this part of it anyway, was an entirely rectangular grid.

And he was just about at where X marked the spot.

He waited for a bus to go by (it was filled with people being transported somewhere) and then crossed the final street leading to his destination. A left turn and a couple hundred metres later, he was at the gates of 4F.

"Present your card, please."

There was a guard standing there, but it was an automated voice who made the request. Beside the main vehicle entryway was a smaller gated path. The same type of scanner that was at his housing complex was built into the wall beside it. A camera was staring him in the face.

Yes, master! He felt an overwhelming urge to yell this for some reason, but that wouldn't have been wise. He checked himself before he wrecked himself and instead just flipped his book over and grabbed his card from the inside flap. He then presented it to the scanner and the smaller gate opened for him. The guard had just a few words for him before he entered.

"Hope you're not with the seven o'clock group," he said. "If you are, you're late."

No, sir! Again, he thought of yelling this (he even thought to throw in a salute), but again, he did not. Something had come over him, and he wasn't sure what to make of it. He hadn't been up this early in a long time, and yet for some reason, he felt wonderfully energetic.

"I'm an eight o'clock start actually," he replied politely. "This is my first day, so I came early to learn the ropes."

"Smart," the guard replied. "That's a good idea. Your forewoman will appreciate that." The man turned and pointed. "Go through that door and tell anyone you see that you're looking for Agatha. She's in charge and will get you set up."

"Thanks," Deron replied. *You've been a grand help!* He thought to say more, but there wasn't really more to say. The guard was holding the gate so it wouldn't close, but there was a beeping sound starting to emanate from somewhere, likely indicating that the gate was not supposed to remain open for long. Either way, it was time to move on.

He tipped his invisible cap to the guard, crossed a dirt strip, and made his way inside.

***

DERON'S FIRST DAY AT the sawmill would be an experience he would never forget for as long as his heart continued to pump blood. There were a great many reasons for this. As a man who had never worked a labour job (or any job for that matter), the sheer size and efficiency of the operation was a sight to behold. The positive way he was treated was something he would remember not to take for granted. On and on, there were lessons aplenty, but mostly, what he would carry with him from then on was this.

Everywhere, he had to follow the rules. Everywhere, he had to play his role and do what was asked so the larger system could function, but more so here, at work, than anywhere else. Here, his behaviour was most determinative of his chances of survival. Here, above all, he had to be a well-greased cog in the machine. Here, above all, there was no room for wasted breath.

And when you learn something like that, you tend not to forget it.

His entry through the door had led him into a dining area of sorts, complete with long tables, garbage bins, and various appliances. The space was segregated from the factory equipment, but large glass windows allowed him to view the inner workings of the operation. Peering through the frames, he was astounded from the very start.

Even from this tiny corner of the factory, he could see wood being transferred from one machine to the next. What was happening in that second machine, he couldn't tell, but he ventured to guess the wood was being sliced and diced to certain specifications. He'd find out in a minute he was correct.

Right as his interest was at its peak, he heard a tapping on the window. A woman was motioning for him to come to her side of the glass, and he heeded those instructions without needing to be told twice.

But before he could, there was another scanner to get through the dining hall. He presented his card, and the door opened without delay. He then rounded the corner and approached the woman.

Agatha was her name. Factory forewoman was her game. And she was a tall forewoman at that—about his height with a slender frame and long blonde hair. She wore the same red jumpsuit as the guards, and Deron approximated her age at about forty. Her smile was so bright and cheerful, it almost made him forget where he was.

Only not quite. Instead of forgetting, in the thirty minutes that followed, Agatha showed him what his life would be like for the next five years, loading him with information, which he would have struggled to retain under any other circumstance.

Their tour started outside, where he was shown a collection of tens of thousands of ready-to-use logs. A crane was picking them up a few at a time and dropping them onto a deck where a debarking machine then removed their outer layer of skin. Once that occurred, the stems were transferred along the machine back inside through the open wall on the north end of the building. Scanners then determined the quality of the log and how it would be cut by the saws.

He could basically recite her words in his head.

After the initial cuts are made, a log is transferred either to the carriage saw or the double-length infeed. If it goes to the carriage saw, lasers are used to determine the best way to use the log. Next, an operator manually runs each log one by one along a track and slices off strips with the vertical bandsaw. The sliced pieces are then automatically transferred along the track to the resaw— we call it the horizontal bandsaw—while the larger pieces, called cants, are manually tossed onto a different track where they can be reprocessed.

For pieces that are cut vertically, the resaw is used to trim the piece horizontally, and any extra waste is collected in the machine. The waste is then automatically sent to the chipper, while the now suitably cut log is sent on a different path.

Logs sent to the double-length infeed are similarly cut into usable sideboard pieces by the reducer twin. The remaining cant goes to the curve saw gang, where it is cut into different sized boards. The sideboards go to the edger automatically. Rounded boards cut by the curve saw gang eventually make their way to the edger too. Flat boards go straight to the trimmer. This decision of what is flat and what is curved is made by the machines.

Curved boards are recut into viable rectangular shapes. The waste goes to the chipper. The recut boards then make their way to the trimmer as well, as all rectangular boards eventually do, where any boards that are too long are cut to specification.

All boards then go to the sorter where they are automatically sorted by their length, thickness, and width. The dimensions vary based on which saws they were cut by and the decisions of the scanners. The boards are then dropped in their appropriate bins, where they collect and pile up. Once a bin is deemed full, an operator drops the pack, and the pile is transferred to the stacker outside. A pack is next taken by forklift to the green yard, where it sits for about a week until it is ready to be dried in the kiln. After a pack of boards is dried and planed, they are ready to ship.

Simple, right?

"And that's it! Any questions?"

Yeah. About a thousand, he wanted to say. His brain was hurting just thinking about it all. To him, this was all just one giant Rube Goldberg machine only with actual practicality.

But he also wasn't sure if asking any of his questions would actually be beneficial. There was really only one thing he needed to know.

"Just one, I guess. What's my role in all this?"

"Excellent. Eager to get to it; that's what I like to hear," she said with a smile.

Deron couldn't tell if her intention was for that smile to be comforting or if it was the smile of a madwoman, but for some reason, he felt it was the former.

"You will be what we call a bottleneck breaker along the assembly line. You make sure that no boards fall off the track at your station and that they are separated enough so they can pass on efficiently to the next machine."

"That's it?"

"That's it; that's all. For now anyway. Your job could change eventually. We've got about 150 workers at this plant, all with different roles. Some are data entry, some work the forklifts or the crane, some are cleaners, some are planers, and some handle the woodchips. There are a variety of other jobs as well, and some people transition through stations throughout the day, but for now, all you need to know is the life of a bottleneck breaker. If that changes, we'll let you know. But before that, why don't we get some breakfast." She smiled.

Before he could respond, she turned and began to lead him back toward the dining space. He followed behind closely, past this saw and that saw, his heart beating a bit faster with each one they passed. There was no reason yet to be afraid. That would come later. Right now, he still felt quite good. No withdrawal symptoms, and he believed his new boss's smile to be genuine.

But the inevitability of it all was becoming more real with each passing step. In just a few moments time, he'd complete his first walkthrough. In twelve hours, his first day's work.

He looked back at the saws. It was all a cycle, just like that beating heart in his chest. Pump this to that until the end product was alive. There was only one difference: his heart would stop working long before the machines did.

***

THERE WERE OTHERS ALREADY in the dining area when they arrived, about fifty or so, he reckoned. Most were sitting down at the long tables, and the rest were quickly filing into their spaces. A few employees were beginning to serve breakfast. The clock on the wall read 8:02.

Deron sat at the end of the nearest table. There were others in close quarters, but no one asked who he was or how he was doing. This, apparently, was not the place for chatter. The mood throughout the room was somber and quiet.

Eventually, he was served his plate. A banana, a ham and cheese sandwich, and this packaged treat he recognized as a filler bar. It was tasteless and odourless, but as the name implied, it did a good job of ensuring your hunger was satiated.

The meal was eaten with profound efficiency. By 8:14, they had all finished, and at the stroke of quarter past, they all stood up, almost in unison, leaving their waste behind for the cleaning staff to deal with. One by one, they presented their cards to the scanner and exited the room.

Most immediately left for their posts the second they returned to the work floor. Deron, however, did not. There was one thing he had to do first.

He made a beeline across the floor to the other side of the room. Directly opposite the doorway that led to the dining area was another doorway of sorts. This one, as had been described to him during the tour, led to the washrooms and shower facilities.

He scanned his way into a small room. That room had two additional doors, one on the left and one on the right. These didn't require card access, only a choice. The left was marked with a ♂ symbol, the right with a ♀. Tempted he was to go right. It would probably smell nicer. But he was expected to go left, so left he went.

What he saw when he entered was something he could only describe as a Utopia Gym changing room of yesteryear. A short hallway led to a series of lockers with a few benches for sitting. A connecting room had a large showering area with dozens of nozzles. Attached to that was another room with about a dozen toilet stalls and half as many sinks. Nothing was new, but like their housing complex, everything was just adequate enough so that you really had no complaints—not that he was about to start a revolution anyway.

Which reminds me, he thought. *Let's hurry the hell up.*

He placed his supply bag down on one of the benches—he'd been carrying it around all day up to this point—and took a peek inside. He needed two things: his water bottle, which he'd refilled during breakfast, and his work uniform. He was the only one who hadn't changed yet.

He slipped out of his leisure clothes and into his factory attire. The colour was black instead of yellow and the lining was a bit thicker, but otherwise, the fit was the same. Once he had changed, he found a locker to stuff his belongings in, set the combination lock (there was a safe-like code bar on each locker, the standard locking system in the Utopia), grabbed his water bottle, and threw his leisure uniform in a hamper, which he'd been instructed to do. After that, he returned from whence he came, scanned out (you didn't have to in order to open the door from this side, but he'd been told to do so for time stamp purposes), crossed the floor, thought of grabbing a hard hat from the bin near the dining hall, thought against it since they weren't required, and eventually made his way through stairwells and railways to his station. There, another man was already sorting.

"You the new guy?" he asked. The man had sensed his presence but looked toward him for only a second. The machine's conveyor belt was in motion, and he couldn't afford to look away.

"Yes. I'm Deron."

"Ronald," the man replied, taking another quick moment to turn away from his work. He was a short, pudgy fellow with long curly hair. "Nice to have you aboard, Deron."

Deron wasn't sure if he meant that sincerely or not, but he guessed it was at least partially true. Any added labourer meant less work for everyone else.

"You understand what you're supposed to do?" He was back looking at the machine. A few pieces of wood had piled, and he spread his gloved hand across the top of them to spread them apart.

"I think so, yeah. Just make sure the boards aren't too clustered together and spread them out if they are. Or if one falls, put it back on the track."

"You got it, brother. Ain't exactly rocket science, but don't take it too lightly either. Machine clogs cuz of us, they won't take too kindly. And you know they'll have the evidence."

Deron did. That was one thing about the Utopia he'd always understood. They always had the evidence, and this place was no exception. He'd seen plenty of cameras on his tour.

"Anyway, don't worry too much about it. That's why they have two of us here. If you miss something, I'll catch it before it passes to the next track."

Deron nodded to himself as he looked down the line. The wood was flowing from his right to his left, with Ronald about eight feet away downstream. Any clutter he missed, the man would have to bail him out.

Deron had to trust him on that, and he did. He'd just met the guy, had no clue what he'd done to get himself sent to this place, had no knowledge of his character whatsoever, but he knew he could count on him to clean up his mistakes.

Whether he wants to or not, he'll do it to survive. Like we all will. It's our most basic instinct, and they've created the perfect system to bring it out. For as long as we can take it.

He turned back toward the track and got to work.

***

IN THE NEXT EIGHT hours, Deron would come to discover what life in the Camp was truly about. That concept of grinding for survival would no longer be just an idea in his mind. The time for theory was over; it was time for action. He was now on the job. This was the real world in motion.

And like it always seemed to be in every walk of life, the practical component was not quite the same as how he'd envisioned it.

THE UTOPIA

He wouldn't be yelled at. He wouldn't be belittled or told he was worthless. He would get washroom breaks and a surprisingly appetizing pasta and bread lunch. He would be able to talk when he felt like it, and Agatha would even come by and compliment his efforts. He wouldn't be battered or bruised by any of the guards at all.

But he'd be worn out a different way, both physically and mentally. He'd be on his feet constantly, the only opportunity to sit down coming during washroom breaks and lunch. He'd get wood splinters in his hands because he hadn't thought to ask for gloves (he'd since rectified this problem over lunch), and the flutter of sawdust in the air would agitate his eyes and nose. Even having rolled up the sleeves of his work uniform, he'd sweat constantly in the dense factory air. And none of these discomforts were even the worst part.

Worst of all by far was the monotony of the work. For the first thirty minutes or so, he'd been able to imagine this as a challenge of some kind. He'd always loved Tetris, and if he convinced his mind enough, he could envision this as some sort of play on the game. Fit the wood on the conveyor. Make sure none of the blocks spilled over the edge. It was simple yet effective. But only for a short while. After that initial time frame, after becoming drenched in sweat and feeling the aches and pains that came along with the work, it became a lot harder to convince himself that this was fun. It became a lot harder to convince himself this was anything but a job, and a laborious one at that. And the hardest part of it was that he couldn't even let his mind wander off to somewhere more peaceful. If he did, he risked making a mistake, and even if he never actually did screw up, he risked *looking like* he was going to screw up. And with the cameras always rolling, that was a risk he just couldn't take.

He sighed quietly to himself as he wiped some sweat from his brow with the back of his dirty glove. It had been eight hours since he'd brushed aside his first piece of wood. For more than seven of those, he'd been standing in the same exact spot doing this same task over and over with no end in sight. The only reason he even knew how long it had been was because they announced the time every hour. There were no clocks that he had seen outside of the lunchroom, and of course they were not given phones or watches.

Eight hours. That's all it had taken to chip the first cracks in his foundation. He had walked in this morning feeling wholesome, feeling refreshed, feeling ready for the challenge, not having accepted yet *what* he had done but having accepted that it *had been* done and that there was nothing he could do about it now.

Already that perspective was starting to change. They had treated him as well as he could have hoped, and he was already wondering how long he could last. Hard work. Perseverance. Mental toughness. These had never been words that were synonymous with Deron Boyd. On the best of days, his effort was minimal. On the worst, he was a downright sloth. He got by because it's harder to let yourself die than it is to make yourself live.

But then again, he was still here. And that thought, for the first time in hours, allowed him to crack a smile.

While he had never been one to take the bull by the horns, he had also never been one to just quit either. He'd lost a lot in his life, most recently his freedom. It was okay to find this hard. It was okay to have some doubt. This was never going to be easy.

Survival instinct. He didn't have it in spades, but he had it somewhere deep inside—where even the leeches and parasites that prodded at his brain, that sucked all joy and happiness out of him, where even they wouldn't traverse. It was locked away, only showing up in the darkest of hours. He had a will in him to live that wasn't strong, but it was there. It was why he had picked this place over death. It was why, in spite of how hard he was already finding this, he would be back tomorrow. And the next day. And the day after that. Until the day came where he finally couldn't take it anymore, and what he would do then was anyone's guess.

But that day wasn't today. That day wasn't tomorrow. That day might come before his sentence expired, but it wouldn't come anytime soon.

There were already some cracks in his foundation. Some from now and some from a time ago. But he was also nowhere near collapsing yet. Especially not after what happened next.

"That's it! I'm done!"

The shout was loud and clear, even over the humming and rumbling of the machines. What was unclear was where it had come from or who had said it. Both Deron and Ray (Ronald had been reassigned about halfway through the day and another man had taken his spot) instinctively turned to get a glimpse of the action but could spot nothing out of the ordinary from their positions. Deron especially was intrigued by the yell (anything to break up that monotony he had been brooding over gloomily), but after a quick second of wonder, he frantically returned his attention to the machine. The conveyor belt was still running, after all.

But the shouting didn't stop either. "No! I will not calm down! I have had it! Four years of this shit is enough! I am finished! Cleaning this same factory every day for four goddamn years! I will not stand for it any longer!"

Now Deron was really intrigued. This didn't just sound like defiance anymore; it was a full-blown mutiny. A part of him wanted to take a washroom break to see what was going on, but that would've been too obvious. He asked Ray instead.

"What's happening?" he said to his companion, who Deron thought kind of looked like an older, heavier version of himself. The resemblance was uncanny actually, now that he was seeing him more closely.

"That? Oh, that's just Murphy," he said, shuffling his eyes back and forth between the conveyor belt and Deron. "He gets loud like that every three or four months or so."

"Really?" Deron questioned, genuinely surprised. "Won't he be punished for that?"

"You're letting me the hell out! Today! Today, Greg! Or I'll fucking break you!"

"He will be, yeah. Insubordination isn't taken lightly in the Camp. Most people who act like that around here would've had the book thrown at them already, but he's got some ... let's call them psychological issues, and when he's doing his job properly, which is about ninety-nine percent of the time, he's actually the best damn cleaner they got. That's why they've never switched him to a different role, and that doesn't help either. Drives a man crazy doing the same thing over and over."

"Yeah," Deron concurred, nodding his head. "Yeah, I'll bet."

The conversation could have ended there, but Ray continued. "Anyway, he's just lucky it's Agatha on the rotation and not Edwin. Because if it was Edwin, he'd make him scrub all night till his hands bled for carrying on like that."

"Whose Edwin?" Deron asked instinctively. The conveyor belt was still rolling, and he shuffled a few pieces of wood apart before he looked back at Ray.

"Edwin? Why, he's the other foreman. They rotate them guards. Six months on, six months off. It's the only way they can stand to do this job."

"Makes sense, I guess."

"Murphy, that's enough now! Stay where you are; I'm warning you! Do not approach me!"

Impulsively, Deron took a peek over his shoulder. His sightline was blocked out by the machines, but he still couldn't help but wonder what was going on. And he wondered about Murphy.

"What did he do to get sent here?" Deron asked. Every time he asked this question, it seemed to only cause him pain, and yet for some reason, he just couldn't resist. It was like he was cursed with curiosity.

"That's the thing," Ray replied. He'd been serious the whole time, but this was the first time he really stopped what he was doing to take a good look at Deron, like what he had to say next was especially important. "He didn't do nothing."

"Wait. What? What do you mean he didn't do nothing?" And then it clicked. "You mean he was chosen? But didn't he just yell that he's been here for four years? I thought the max for that was three!"

"No, sir," Ray replied, wagging his finger back and forth like Dikembe Mutombo after a highlight reel block. "That's a common misconception. It's a three-year maximum if you've volunteered for ... I want to say at least three years, but that might have changed since I've been in here. Regardless, yeah. Murph never volunteered. Even in those cases, the Computer will usually only stick you with three max, but technically, up to five is allowed, and five is what he got. Rarely happens as far as I know, and when it does, you feel for the man or woman. So if you want to know the truth, that's probably the reason they've let him get away with so much, not just because of a mental illness or even the fact that he's a good worker. Just those factors alone, he probably still would've gotten the needle at some point, but I think they feel sorry for him. Even Edwin. Man's a hard-ass but not heartless."

Deron was listening, but not with the same vigour as he had been before. His whole life, he had been taught that the maximum sentence anyone chosen could receive was three years. Every law class he'd enrolled in—up to age seventeen when he stopped taking them—they had mentioned that point at some time or another. When had that changed? And more importantly, why didn't he know about it?

"Yeah," he replied. His mind was still spacey, but he wanted to say something. It was he who had started this conversation, after all. "Yeah, that makes sense. Who wouldn't feel sorry him?"

Ray nodded and patted Deron on the shoulder, sensing he was a bit lost—not understanding why, just knowing it was the case.

"It's okay though. He's done most of his time already, so he'll be out in a year or so. After that, he'll probably be put in some low-leverage volunteer job for the next ten until he can retire. In a few years, the guy will actually have a pretty easy life." Ray looked back to the conveyor belt for a second and spread a few pieces of wood. "Speaking of life, I think you and I should be getting back to focusing on the here and now for the time being, wouldn't you say? Wouldn't want people to get the wrong impression. Wouldn't want—"

Bang!

"Holy shit!" someone yelled.

"What was that?" went another.

And then a voice, the loudest of them all, screamed, "STOP THE MACHINES!"

When Deron heard that, his mind woke up instantly from its catatonic state. The bang was a jolt, but the scream was the orchestrator of the response in his amygdala—the orchestrator of fear.

Stop the machines. Something serious must have happened. In this place, he doubted the machines stopped for just about anything.

He had turned his back to the conveyor belt at the sound of the shriek. He didn't need to turn back around to know the track had stopped moving. He could hear it, the sound of silence emanating through the factory. This lasted for a few moments, then all he heard was footsteps.

"C'mon." He looked to his right. Ray was talking to him. "Let's go." And although his mind was telling him that maybe that wasn't such a good idea, his feet moved anyway. Curiosity had killed the cat, and it seemed determined to kill him one day too.

He followed Ray along the catwalks and up and down stairs, until eventually, they were near the dining area and close enough to see. A crowd of over fifty had already gathered, but they were spaced out enough so that the entire scene was visible. On the floor lay a man saturated in a pool of blood. He was face down and his body was immobile. A guard was standing over him, weapon drawn, his face drenched with sweat and panic.

"I just … He came at me … I … Oh God." He collapsed to his knees and held his head, his weapon, still in his hand, looking like a bull's horn sticking out of the side of his face.

The crowd stood by stunned. More and more people ran over to join, and the second they got close enough to see what had happened, they halted in their tracks and ceased to make noise. For the time being, only one person spoke.

"Erin and Darnell, I need you to take Greg out of here." Agatha was at the controls, standing in the middle of the chaos, speaking in a tongue that was forthright but composed, like she'd been preparing for this all her life and knew exactly what to do.

"Yes, Forewoman Jones," a shorter woman in a red jumpsuit replied. Her voice was just loud enough in the silence for all to hear. A taller man in the same attire didn't speak but acted with her in unison. Together they approached the shooter and whispered something in his ear, and the result was compliance. The shooter returned his weapon to his holster, placed his arms behind his back so the woman could cuff him, and the three of them began to walk toward the door leading to the dining hall. The crowd formed a tunnel so they could proceed untouched.

"What happened?" someone whispered beside Deron. A young woman in front of him turned to respond, a woman with piercing brown eyes and short wavy black hair. He couldn't help but notice she was particularly attractive.

She whispered, "Murph lost it. He …" She paused for a second, noticing Deron for the first time. Her look toward him was inconspicuous and, if anything, stiff, but for some reason, he sensed a salaciousness in it too, enough to make him shiver, even though it was over in a flash.

"He usually just yells and then calms himself, but this time, he took a run at Guard Zimmer. Greg panicked and shot him."

"Everyone!" The shout came from Agatha again. Any whispered conversations immediately halted, including there's. The wavy-haired woman turned back around to face the front, but there was something strange in her movements. Deron could swear that while she was now looking forward, she was purposely inching backward toward him ever so slightly.

She settled right in front of him, far enough away that they weren't physically touching but close enough that he could feel her presence anyway. He tried to ignore her as Agatha continued.

"As the overseer of this factory, it is my duty to speak in times such as these ... It is my job to keep you all safe, and today I have failed."

The Forewoman had a presence now that seemed so juxtaposed to her earlier demeanour, and yet in spite of this, Deron couldn't sense any unnaturalness to it at all. She could scrap that happy-go-lucky attitude any time she wanted. She could go alpha dog at any moment and command the respect of the room. She was a leader by nature, by nurture, and by everything in between. No wonder she'd earned this job.

"I don't need to tell any of you how terrible this is. Murphy was a good man, and he didn't deserve this. None of you deserve this. The Camp is a place people come to grow and to learn, to overcome the past, and to provide for the future. The people here are the backbone of the Utopia. They'll never tell you that, but it's true. You all have value, each and every one of you. And to see someone taken away from us too soon, it stings. You may not believe me. I am here by choice, after all, and none of you can say the same."

Her voice cracked for just a moment. She took a deep breath, clenched her hand into a fist, and steadied. Others in the room could feel the emotion. Deron might have too had he not been distracted by his own confused feelings.

"But it's true. I am hurt by this like you all are. And there will be repercussions. I can promise you that. And I guess ..."

She paused. Again, there was some emotion behind her voice, this time more noticeable, even to Deron, who'd decided right then he needed to take a step back both literally and figuratively. But again, Agatha held it in, held it in like whatever else she had been thinking of adding.

"I guess there's nothing more to say. If you have any questions about what happens now, this is the time to ask."

"What happens to Zimmer?" came an instant shout. Deron could feel the tension in the room skyrocket, as if there wasn't enough of it already. That did not seem like the type of question she had been inviting.

Deron expected some potential backlash from this new version of Agatha, that she would tell the shouter to pipe down, that it was none of his business, that if he wanted to find out, he could join Zimmer wherever he was going. But there wasn't any of that at all.

She answered him straight, as if she too believed it was a perfectly reasonable thing to ask. "The guards have put him under arrest. He will be brought to jail tonight and tried sometime early next week. What happens to him then is up to the Computer."

She waited for a response from the man, but there was none. The answer seemed to suffice. Another question came.

"Do we have to go back to work today, Forewoman? Some of us just saw one of our comrades literally shot in front of us. The powers that be have to understand that it isn't fair to ask us to just pretend this didn't happen and go on with our day."

Another boldly framed but reasonable question. Also answered respectfully and rationally.

"It isn't fair, Ishan. It isn't fair at all. But I don't make the rules. I only follow them, like we all pledged to do by remaining in the Utopia past our twenty-fifth birthdays. Most, if not all, of you are here because you chose not to follow those rules. You can make that same choice again now, and I wouldn't even blame you. Heck, down three of my guards, until I radio this in and backup comes with Internal Affairs and whoever else they send along, until that happens, I'll be powerless to stop you. But there will be consequences. Not from my hand, but from the hand of the State. If the risk is worth the reward to you, then you and anyone else can go right ahead and walk out that door, but if it were me, I'd stay, use the work as a distraction, and if you want to pour one out for your friend after that, I'll make sure you're all uploaded a freebie by the time you walk out of here. It won't get you your friend back, and I won't pretend it equates to even one percent of your loss, but it's the least I can do."

Ishan nodded, satisfied. Deron thought this woman should be queen of the Utopia.

"Anything else?" The room was silent. "Okay then. Let's start up the machines and get back to work. You'll all be out of here at your normal times. Goran, call this in."

The guard answered something that Deron couldn't hear. The crowd had started to disperse back to their posts. Deron was about to leave to his but was bumped just before he could.

"Sorry," a voice said. A smiling face was behind it, that of the woman who had given him the look earlier, the one whom his brain had told him to take a step back from, but the rest of him had desperately wanted to stay near. Instinctively, he smiled back. She slid by him without another word, but as she did, she slipped her hand over his so gently that it almost made his hair stand up—and another part of him as well.

He watched her as she walked, hips swaying in a way that made him fantasize what was under that work uniform. That wavy black hair cut off invitingly at her neck. He felt a sudden lust and then shook his head to snap out of it. This was no time for such thoughts. A man had just died. His feelings should be remorse, pity, and sorrow.

Get your shit together, he told himself. And a part of him truly believed that he should. But at the same time, he couldn't deny that this was the best he had felt since this morning. Maybe even better. He shook his head once more, with only one final thought before he picked up his feet and went back to work. *What a world,* he thought. And it would only get better.

But not right away. In fact, for the remainder of the workday, it was business as usual, as if nothing had happened, as if no one had died.

Internal Affairs came, but that hardly changed a thing. No one was interviewed or questioned in any way. There was no need. Like just about everything else in their world, it was all caught on video. And like just about everything else in their world, their opinions on the subject didn't matter. Only one was influential: the Computer's.

Deron didn't see any of the supposed order-keeping guards. He didn't see Murph's body being removed or the cleanup of the blood. He only noticed it was gone when he passed by the dining area for dinner. After finishing his dinner of bread and stew, his body was finally granted the opportunity to leave as well.

He followed a group of employees into the washroom area. Before he left for the night, he, like everyone else, wanted to wash the grit and grime from his body, to eliminate the stench of sawdust, woodchips, and death.

There were towels laid out for them at the entrance to the showers. He picked one up, undressed, tossed his work uniform into a hamper, and then returned to the locker room once he had cleaned himself off. There was a large clothing rack present there with a multitude of hangers. His leisure uniform, freshly washed, was dangling from one of them. He grabbed it, put it on after drying himself off and tossing his towel aside into a separate hamper, then collected his things from his locker. He was about ready to leave for the night when a familiar face caught him just before he could.

"You want to come?" Ray questioned.

Deron's instinct was to ask where, but intuition told him the answer. Ray had told him about some of the amenities the Camp had to offer during their conversations and a lot about one place in particular he and his pals liked to frequent.

"To ye old watering hole?" he said.

Ray laughed. "A watering hole is a very apt description for it," he replied with a smile. "But yes, I did mean the bar."

Deron thought about it for a quick second. A part of him was exhausted from his long and arduous first day. A part of him was distracted by other things. A part of him loved drugs and alcohol and wasn't sure of the next time he would get a taste.

"Sure," he agreed. "Yeah, why not?"

"Great," Ray responded with another smile. "I just have to grab my things and gather the troops, so why don't you just wait in the dining area, and I'll meet you there."

"Sounds good, Ray," Deron said with a smile of his own, half fake and half real. Then he exited the washrooms without another word, making his way across the floor and into the dining area where a certain someone was waiting for him there. That's when business started to transition into pleasure.

***

HE DIDN'T TALK TO her at first. In fact, he tried his damnedest not to even look at her, telling himself there was something off there, something he

THE UTOPIA

didn't trust, that she must be a spy planted by the State, that her job was to flirt with new recruits, gauge their tolerance of their newfound position, and report back if there was a problem. It was all just a test, like that zombie pill had been. And he'd failed on part one, so he had to play it coy and hold his nerve for part two. Two strikes in a row would set him dangerously close to the edge, especially this early on in his sentence. At the rate he was going, he'd be next week's Murphy.

That's what he told himself, and in this place, he could even convince himself there was some logic to the thought.

But what he was really feeling was a schoolboy crush: the kind where he'd spend hours (like the last four hours, for example) thinking of something to say, only nothing felt appropriate; the kind where he wondered if his beard was too messy or if she'd prefer it shaved off entirely; the kind where he hoped she would indulge him and at the same time prayed she would stay far away; the kind where he didn't know anything about her but was sure that he wanted her.

He peeked over toward her. He tried to do it subtly, but there was no point. She was on the opposite side of the kitchen, talking to a co-worker (another not-so-unattractive female), but at the moment he gazed over, she looked him dead in the eye. He recoiled out of instinct, but it was already too late. She had caught him. And unfortunately for this schoolboy, there was no math textbook to bury his head in and hide behind.

He made the decision in that moment to go over and talk to her—it would be more awkward not to at that point—but that wasn't necessary. She had waltzed over to him almost before he even had a chance to think it through.

"Hey," she said. Her tone was somehow delicate and raspy at the same time. Cigarette seductive is how he would have branded it. She sat down next to him and turned her body to face his.

"Hey," was his response. He wanted to add more but didn't know what to say. She had entered his life so suddenly and at such a strange time. His feelings were apparent, and somehow that made them all the more confusing.

"You okay?" she asked. This time, when she spoke, the rasp was gone and the spirit behind the words was genuine concern.

Depends on your definition, he thought to respond. That was what he had told Hakeem the previous night. It felt like an apt description then, and it still felt like one now. This was all happening so fast, and he still hadn't had time to process it yet.

But he smiled and said, "Yeah, I think so. Just been a crazy first day with what happened to Murphy and all."

His smile drained at once, and for the first time, he felt it—the reality of what had happened. He'd been able to distract himself with thoughts about other things, but the magnitude of the event was finally starting to hit home. A person had been killed. Not right before his eyes but close enough. And who was to say that wouldn't be him one day soon. It could happen in a flash.

"I'm sorry," she said. His hands were in his lap, and she reached out and caressed them in her own. Her touch was warm. And inviting. And surprising. He had looked away from her to think but now had no choice but to return her gaze.

"It's awful," she continued, her face drooping to match the somberness of her tone. "Things like that, they don't happen as often as you might expect around the Camp, but they do happen, and every time they do, it's just sickening. Especially on your first day. I just couldn't imagine."

"Yeah," he replied. "Yeah, it's tough." He looked down for a moment. Like so many times in his life, he thought of just leaving it at that. He had never been one to open up much about his feelings, not to strangers or even the ones he trusted most.

But when he looked back up at her then, something came over him, something he had resisted in the past with varying degrees of ease but which he now felt powerless against for some reason: an urge to reveal his truth and everything that came with it, to really explain what was on his mind in that moment.

"I've lost someone close before. It was hard then, and honestly, to this day, I think I still struggle with it sometimes. It can weigh on me when I think about it deeply."

He felt another insatiable yearning right then. To clasp the chain around his neck. To grab it and show her and explain to her what it meant to him. But he couldn't do it. His arms held back, and that was the moment when his mouth started to as well.

"But not like that. I've never seen something like that. Or heard. The desperation in his screams is what will haunt me the most. It's ... Yeah, it's just tough."

And that was all they would say on the subject that night. It was the closest he would come to revealing the biggest sorrow in his past. It was far from everything he had. He would have to travel miles and miles to get all the way down that road. But it was a start. He felt a little bit better.

"It's okay, sweetheart," she said with a smile, a smile that somehow made him feel like everything indeed would be okay. "You're not alone. I'm here for you."

She stood up with her arms outstretched to the sides. He followed her lead and did the same. They hugged, and he got an inkling they might have done even more had they not been standing in the middle of their work's kitchen area.

"Now, what do you say we get a beer, help take the edge off?" She smiled that grand smile again. He returned it with his own.

"Sounds like a plan to me," he said. "I just promised Ray I'd wait for him is all." He turned to look for the man, but he was not yet in sight.

"Keeping your promises—what an upstanding gentleman," she teased. "Well, if you don't mind, I'm going to run along ahead. My girl Donna has been anxious to go because she doesn't want to stay out too late."

"Of course, yeah, don't let me hold you up. I'll see you there ..." He stretched out the last word so she would offer her name. She took the hint.

"Carla." She smiled.

"Deron." He grinned back.

"I'll see you there, Deron." She made off with a wink. He stood in place and watched her go, shook his head and chuckled as feelings of bliss flowed through his body. His heart was full. For the first time in what felt like ages, for the first time in a long time, he thought maybe there was a chance.

He had been with other women since *her*. He was no Wilt Chamberlain (nor did he even know who Wilt Chamberlain was), but he had not exactly gone celibate either. He went to the bar almost every night, and it wasn't always just to hang out with his friends or to enjoy his own company. He had gone with more notorious intentions plenty of times, and on more than a few occasions, he had succeeded in his exploits.

But those other women, none of them had appealed to him the same way she did. Those other women, they had jobs and lives. They had hobbies and their own friends. They needed him a lot less than he needed them. He had a void in his heart, and they couldn't fill it.

But Carla? For some reason, with her, he believed there was a chance. She had sought him out, comforted him when it was the farthest thing from her duty. Shown him her desires without hesitation or fear of what she might find. There was something powerful in that, something he could grasp on to, something that wasn't just blind hope and a prayer.

Those other women, they had jobs and lives. This woman had a life without him too, but for twelve hours a day, they were stuck in this factory. For at least a little while, they'd know the Camp and nothing more. Maybe she was the light to balance out the darkness. Maybe he truly hadn't thrown his life away for nothing. Maybe there was some sense to this madness after all. He'd try to believe that for as long as he could.

"Hey, Deron." He snapped out of it when another hand took hold of him, this one a lot larger and not quite so soft to the touch. It was Ray. "Sorry that took so long. A few of the guys had to wait to shower, but we're all set now. You still want to come with?"

"Yeah. Yeah, absolutely," he said, truly meaning it this time.

"Excellent," Ray replied. "Great to hear it. In that case, why don't I introduce you to the guys. This is Deke. That's Yuri Yin, but we call him Wise Guy."

"And we call you fat man," Yuri interrupted, and they all burst out laughing. Deron chuckled along as well.

"See, Wise Guy. It works on all levels." And they all laughed some more as Ray gave Deron another pat on the shoulder. The humour temporarily distracted him from his thoughts.

Deron met them all then—four in total not including Ray, or Ronald who was there as well—and was fairly happy to. They seemed like decent guys, and in this place, he figured there was strength in numbers.

They walked out the door together, them chumming along, him chiming in every once in a while but mostly just laughing to himself. He felt good, but his schoolboy-crush nerves were starting to kick in again the closer they got. There was a certain someone waiting for him at the bar. He wanted to talk to her about something that wasn't sad or depressing, but the ruckus they were causing wasn't allowing him to think. He'd been waiting for them to settle down a bit; their friend was dead, after all. That was the whole reason they were out here, was it not? He'd expected that to sink in at some point, but it just wasn't happening. It was starting to get on his nerves.

"Suck it, old man."

"You'd like that, wouldn't you?"

More laughs and carrying on. Deron was on the brink of saying something, of calling them out for their perceived indifference toward the situation but stopped himself before he did. *I guess I should enjoy the positivity while it lasts,* he thought to himself somberly.

At some point, they'd get quiet, would remember why they were there and what the occasion was, would note that there was more to this journey than simply a free beer. The mood would change then, and it might not change back.

Enjoy it while it lasts, he reiterated to himself. *Because it won't last forever. Maybe this is just their way of dealing with the pain. Or even if it's not, even if they don't actually care at all, it's not like your motivation for being out here is really in homage to Murphy either.*

He nodded to himself, genuinely believing the points to be valid, especially the first one. Smiling and laughing. He doubted much of that occurred in the Camp. He might as well soak it all in. Who knew the next time he'd be feeling this way.

Enjoy it while it lasts. He thought it one more time, hoping it would stick. Enjoy it while it lasts.

***

THE BAR WAS EVERY bit the watering hole Ray had said it would be. Dim lighting couldn't disguise the paint chips or, in some cases, fully fledged holes in the walls. There were spills everywhere, some large enough you could comfortably refer to them as puddles. Even the space itself, while impressively large, lacked the same discipline in its layout as the rest of the

Camp. Long tables took up most of the floorspace, but unlike the tables in their factory dining area, there was no pattern to their placement. They were strewn about like landmines, and even their quality was of a second-class rate. They weren't dirty per se, but they were old and wooden instead of metal. Some even went so far as to have displaced nails sticking out of their grooves or entire chunks of wood missing in certain spots.

When Deron saw the room, his first instinct was to leave. He didn't feel threatened exactly, it was more a feeling that he was out of place, like he had just crossed an imaginary line of caution tape into somewhere that he wasn't supposed to be.

He stayed because he knew he was just being paranoid. Likely the setup was just part of a dissuasion tactic. Make this place ugly so people are less enticed to come. Give the criminals somewhere nice to hang and they'll be here all the time. Broken windows theory be damned.

Deron mostly stayed though because he had come here on a mission: to continue flirting with Carla. He hadn't seen her yet, but that was okay. There were steps to this here game. And step one was to grab the fattest cold one they would allow.

They each got a stein (the choice of beer was limited to Utopia Lager, Utopia Pilsner, and Utopia Stout; the same as everywhere else) by tapping their cards for the bartender at the back of the room. The process was relatively quick and painless. There were people here, probably over one hundred, but most had already been served and weren't in the habit of lining up for seconds. Ray had explained to him in line that, barring special circumstances such as theirs, one beer a month was all you were rationed.

They sat at a table in the back corner of the room. There were others sitting at it when they arrived, but the table was large enough that each group was still segregated. Deron didn't recognize any of their faces. He was pretty sure none of them worked at the sawmill. In fact ... He peered around the room overtop of Ray and Wise Guy across from him. There were a few familiar faces he could spot now at other tables, but not many. And still not the one he was looking for.

"Gentlemen." He snapped back to attention as Deke—an older man, probably the oldest one in the crew, Deron reckoned—began to speak up from the seat beside him. His voice didn't boom, but it was loud enough that nearby tables probably could have heard him if they'd wanted to.

"Thank you all for being here in these unsettling times. I don't need to tell any of you twice the purpose of this sojourn. We all know the tragedy that occurred today. We lost Murph, a sawmill legend. Ruthlessly gunned down by the infectious regime that plagues this land."

"That's right," agreed Shawn, another of their squad. He sat farther down the table and, like the rest of them now, was listening intently.

"Killed like so many others before him. For civil disobedience. Disobedience against the oppressive forces, whose answer to any backlash is to work us revolutionists to the bone until we're too damn tired to fight back any longer. Until the work is just part of a daily routine. And for what, I say. I'll tell you what. So those bureaucratic assholes can sit up in their ivory towers and look down on us with an evil eye. So they themselves can grow strong while we suffer."

"Exactly," agreed Ronald this time.

Deron thought that a rather convenient opinion for someone who was stuck here, but he also didn't necessarily believe the opinion to be wrong. He continued to listen and found himself starting to agree more and more with each passing word.

"There was a time, gentlemen, before any of yours, before even mine, where freedom ruled the day, where you weren't given a position of power simply because you scored optimally on a goddamn personality test, where those who worked hard got rewarded with payment, and where that payment could be used to buy whatever one wanted, not simply what we were told was okay for us to have.

"Those days are long behind us. It was a gradual transition by all accounts, but once the current system was in place, the money was slowly phased out. The choices were slowly gone. And what we were left with was this: an island that can produce all the goods it needs to function for all the people that inhabit it. But at one hell of a cost. The cost of our freedoms.

"A century ago, those with sense left this place in the Great Transition. The unenlightened stayed and were joined by others from afar, people who'd been oppressed in their own lands, people who thought anything would be better than what they had come from, who thought they had nothing to lose. Little did they know—little did they know that when they came here, they'd lose everything and more.

"Today, the death of our brother reminds us of that stinging loss, reminds us of the oppression we currently face, reminds us of the freedom we lack. But it also reminds us that there is a will inside of us to one day fight back, to one day step up and make this place our own again." He lifted his stein out in front of him over the table. "And to that I say, cheers to you, Murph. Cheers to what you stood for. You will not be forgotten."

"To Murph," shouted Ronald, raising his glass.

"To Murph," echoed Shawn, doing the same.

Ray followed, then Yuri, Carlos (the last member of their current group), and finally, Deron.

"To Murph," he said, raising his arm. And in that moment, he felt a surge of energy course through his body. In that moment, if they had given him a gun, he could have been convinced to take out the nearest guard. In that moment, he felt the gravity of the situation, felt the oppression, felt the Utopia had robbed him of his life.

Glasses tapped. They all sipped. The moment passed.

"Hell of a speech there, Deke," said Ray, his stein still by his mouth. "Could really feel the passion." He took another swig.

"Ahh, it was nothing," Deke responded modestly. He had finished off half his glass with his "sip" and was now returning it to the table. He hiccupped, then said, "Just the words of a bitter old man."

"Is that all true?" It was Carlos speaking this time. The boy sat diagonal Deron, and if it wasn't for the facial hair and the fact that he was a Camp attendee, Deron would've thought he was twelve. "I mean, I know about the Great Transition; I remember that from school. But is it true everyone only came here because they had nowhere else to turn? And that people here left because they preferred a system using money?"

Deron wondered about this as well. He too remembered talks about the Great Transition, how there was a five-year period where people had to decide whether they wanted to stay or go, back when money still existed, at least in some capacity, before all the current rules were set as law for good.

He thought back to those lessons, and immediately, something struck him as odd. He could vividly remember being told why people had decided to leave. The reasons were so repetitive, they were almost quotes.

Some people left because they didn't want to give up their kids at birth. Previously, they hadn't had to. The school system at that time was year-round boarding school, but parents knew their children and could see them as they wished. For the next generation though, the State would act as parents and guardians from day one.

Some people left because the thought of labour camps disgusted them. The Camp hadn't yet become what it is today, but jails had almost completely been eliminated. Believe it or not, some people thought jail was a more appropriate form of punishment. They'd rather criminals be given a free ride than contribute to the good of the rest of society. Most believed in the Camp, but these people did not.

Some people left because they were in the sweet zone of what the historians call the Lost Age. The euthanasia law was not yet in effect, but in five years, it would be. It would be grandfathered in, so people over sixty at the time the law was implemented could live for as long as they were in good health. They could retire and live their dwindling years free to do whatever they pleased, as long as they didn't break any laws of course. But those who were under sixty, they would be subject to the new law, a law that put them to death once they hit age eighty regardless of their health. The Lost Age refers to those who would have been between fifty and fifty-nine at the time the law came into force. Many of those left, hoping to live beyond their eightieth year. Those who stayed faced the same rules as today. They were able to retire at sixty and live their remaining years in peace until they hit that magic number.

There were other reasons too. Some people didn't like that from then on, a Computer would be making all the significant decisions. Some people wanted to travel the world and knew they wouldn't be allowed to leave once the new laws were in place. Some people were out of work and didn't think they'd get the job they wanted under the new regime. There were dozens of reasons Deron had been taught as to why people might have left. But what struck him as odd, what he couldn't seem to get out of his head, was that money was almost never mentioned as one of those reasons. No one left because of money, except for those few greedy souls at the very top who just took, took, took. They realized they wouldn't be able to take any longer and had to go find another land to pillage. For the rest of the Utopia, the elimination of money was seen as a monumental achievement—a true step toward equality. No person below the top felt sorry to see it go. That was exactly what they'd said. Wasn't it?

Something about this conversation was making Deron question his sanity. He took a large gulp of his beer.

"Who knows, honestly. Everything they tell you is bullshit, so there's no way to really tell one way or the other."

That at least isn't true. His mind seemed to be shouting it as a defence mechanism, but this time, he was sure he was right. This time, Deke was taking it too far.

Most of the things he'd learned in school did seem to have some practical application, or at least some solid logic behind them. He even figured the news broadcasts were pretty legit because they didn't cover up the bad stuff. If a fire happened somewhere, you heard about it. Any type of shooting, from one of the guards or otherwise (people in the Utopia were allowed to have guns, although there was really nowhere in the law where using them in any way was appropriate other than at the firing range), it would make the coverage. Heck, even his break-in at the General Store had been a footnote during their program. He was sure this thing with Murphy would make it on there too, if not right away, at least in the near future. There were no news crews allowed in the Camp, but that had never seemed to stop them from getting the story.

Although I guess they never did report the change to the Chosen Law, he thought to himself. *Come to think of it, they never seem to mention ANYTHING about someone being chosen. Ever.*

"But logically, it makes sense. Rich people here, if they weren't going to be guaranteed power or promised something better than the life of a commoner, it makes sense that they would have left. Makes sense for those that had any type of savings really. Otherwise it would have all just gone to waste." Deke took another sip of his beer, a humbler one this time, then continued.

"And the people who came in, makes sense that they would have come from nothing. Why would you leave somewhere where you were thriving to come to a place where you get nothing out of your work but a chance to survive? You wouldn't. You'd have to be some kind of desperate to come here, especially if you weren't even guaranteed a job. Might have seemed nice at first, getting fed and housed without having to contribute. That would have seemed like the dream." Another swig. "That is, until you ended up like Murph, sentenced to this hellhole labour camp having broken no laws and done nothing wrong. Doubt those people were pleased they had made the journey over then."

"True," Carlos said, nodding his head. "That's very true."

Deke gave a half-hearted shoulder shrug. The old "it's up to you if you believe me but I know I'm right" look. His mouth moved along with it.

"Anyway, it was before my time, so who the hell really knows, I guess. All I know is there are people out there enjoying their milk and honey and I'm in here sweating my bag off for twelve hours a day, and it's pretty goddamn unpleasant."

"Amen to that," Wise Guy chimed in. He had mostly been focusing on his almost finished beer during the conversation. He took another swig. "And fuck the guards."

"Fuck the guards is right," Deke agreed, pointing at Yuri with some intensity. "You'd think that since many of them used to be us, they'd treat us with some respect, but all they care about is making sure they don't end up back in here. Even worse are the ones who've never been here. They think we're their goddamn slaves."

"Speaking of the guards," interrupted Ronald. He'd been sitting back in his seat but had perked up the second the guards were mentioned. "I heard a rumour …" He stopped speaking for a moment and took a look around the room to make sure no one was in earshot—no one who shouldn't have been anyway.

"What is it?" asked Carlos.

Ronald signalled for them all to lean in close. He whispered, "Rumour has it that a couple of them have been sanctioning fights for the area warden."

"What?!" exclaimed Carlos, a bit too loud for Ronald's liking. A few people farther down the table turned their heads and looked.

"Pipe down, kid, if you want to hear this. And shut the fuck up about it after I tell you. You didn't hear this from me." Carlos shut up. "Apparently, there's this building near the brothel—"

"Wait, there's a brothel?" This time it was Deron's turn to interrupt. He'd been in his own head for much of the recent conversation, questioning everything he knew or thought he believed, no longer sure what was true or what wasn't. But the mention of the word *brothel* had brought him back to life.

"Yeah. We got a brothel at the Camp," Ronald answered more respectfully (Deron's interruption had been a lot less flamboyant than Carlos's). "That's what I call it anyway. They call it the adult fun house, which I guess makes more sense now that I think about it cuz there's no sex workers or nothing. Basically, it's a place you can go once a month with a lucky lady and bang her brains out for an hour with no one watching."

The table laughed. Deron questioned. "They allow that here?" he asked, astonished.

"Sure they do, kid. Think about it. They got all these people here working twelve hours a fucking day. They need to give 'em something to keep 'em going, something to look forward to. It's the same reason we can get a beer here once a month or a zombie pill down at the pharmacy. Without these releases, we'd be a lot harder to tame."

"Wow." Deron nodded. "That's kind of nice, I guess," he said reservedly. A part of him thought they had to be fucking with him and that there was no way this "brothel" was real. Another part of him thought that explanation sounded absolutely reasonable and was probably the least conspiracy-laden thing he'd heard since he sat down. After the next few words, he decided to agree with the latter part.

"Fuck yeah, it is," Wise Guy said excitedly. "Love that place. You get your own little room and everything. Been trying to set something up for a couple weeks now. Think I finally got the girls to cave."

"Girls?" said Carlos. "As in, plural?"

"As in, one can't handle the Wise Guy on her own, so she needs to bring a friend." There were laughs around the table.

"Get any more conceited, Wise Guy. I fucking dare you." This joke was Shawn's. More laughs followed.

"Who are they?" Carlos asked once they'd finally settled again, sounding genuinely curious.

Wise Guy gave him the slimiest of smiles and said slowly and methodically, "Well, one is—"

"Can I finish my goddamn story?" Ronald was the one to interrupt this time. "Who the fuck cares who they are? If they're going at it with Wise Guy, you know they've been with half the Camp."

And the group of them laughed pretty hard at that. Even Deron chuckled a bit. The only one who didn't was Wise Guy, who Deron noticed was not only not laughing but also had a pretty serious scowl on his face, as if what had been said had cut him a little bit.

"Yeah, whatever you say, Ron. At least I actually get some, unlike you, dirtbag."

"Oooooooo," went the table. There were smiling faces all around, except from Yuri, who was still scowling, and Deron, who was still trying to determine if Yuri was actually upset or not. He wouldn't get to find out.

"Yeah, yeah, yeah, fuck you all," Wise Guy said, in a voice that actually sounded less divisive this time despite the vulgarity. "Tell your goddamn story, Ron."

"Thank you, Wise Guy," Ron replied with a smile. "Real stand up of you to let me finish my piece. Don't even mind you calling me a dirtbag anymore cuz of that." There were a few muffled chuckles before he continued. "Anyway, so what I was saying was this. Apparently, some of the guards, don't know which ones, have been finding people with beefs with each other, asking if they want to scrap, and if both sides agree, they go down to this building near the brothel—don't know which one—and duke it out."

"That's nuts," said Shawn.

"If it's true," chimed in Wise Guy. "Don't know what guards. Don't know what building. Sounds like some made up folk tale to me. How would they even get away with that? There are cameras everywhere. They allow a lot of things here but that sure as hell ain't one of 'em."

"Could be," Ronald admitted. "Could be just a rumour, yeah. But it's not impossible." He took a sip of his beer. "Wouldn't be the craziest thing we've seen."

It went quiet for a bit after that. Heads went down, and for a short time, the bantering stopped. There was no more yelling, no more jokes or puns. They all took a moment to reflect on the events that had transpired, on the fragility of life.

Deron did as well, his mind passing from subject to subject. He thought of Murphy, of course, and how he had died, but he also thought about other parts of their conversation. Their talk had made him think deeply about the world he knew, and his questions would remain long past the expiry of this night.

The past, the present, the future. If he took only one thing out of their discussion, it was that they were all intertwined. Some day he would see how.

The silence also brought back a few more shallow thoughts too. His mind once against wandered to Carla. Where was she? He took another look around the room and couldn't find her.

Eventually, the conversation picked back up again, but this time, Deron wasn't into it. He was feeling gloomy. The sips of beer had given him a jolt of life at first, but he'd since finished his stein and was starting to grow sleepy.

At one point, he excused himself from the table and went to use the washroom. In the process, he made a deal with himself. He'd do one lap looking for Carla, and if he couldn't find her, or if she wasn't here by the time he exited the facilities, he would go home. He played out the scenario, and she never came. At this point, that was kind of a blessing, he figured. He really did just want to go home now.

"Hey, guys," he said to the group once he had returned to the table. He didn't sit back down. "I think I'm going to head out. For some reason, I made the brilliant decision to come in early for the first day, and it's starting to hit me now."

"That's what you get for trying to impress, rookie," Wise Guy said. "They don't give a shit about you around here. Word of advice, just do what's asked. Anything extra doesn't net you a company car."

They all laughed. Deron smiled too through his hazy, tired eyes. "Duly noted," he said. "I'll see you all tomorrow then." He picked up his supply bag from off the ground and waved them off. They each said some sort of goodbye to him. The clock on the wall, he noted, read 9:31. He realized in the moment that this was the latest he'd been out since the arrest. He stepped outside a bit fearful of what would happen, but he made it home without incident.

***

THE FIRST THING HE did when he stepped onto his floor was brush his teeth. He spent five whole minutes at the sink, scrubbing away until his gums were nearly bleeding. He checked the mirror a few times to make sure he had gotten every last morsel of food and plaque there was to remove. Even then, he wasn't entirely satisfied.

He had never been one to take particular care with his personal hygiene. On the outside, he would go weeks without washing his sheets. If he wasn't leaving his apartment, he could go days without even washing his body. But the one thing he consistently did was clean his teeth, at least twice a day and sometimes more if he felt he needed to. He just always seemed to have this bad taste in his mouth, and he was desperate to get rid of it.

He spat, washed his face with some sink water, then returned to the main room. It was a serene atmosphere here for the most part. The majority of the campers were lying in their beds, some reading books, some with their eyes closed. The ones who weren't were huddled in small groups, chatting amongst themselves. It was strange in a way, seeing the harmony in the room, everyone appearing to get along without conflict. It almost made you forget that the tenants of this building were a bunch of criminals, almost made you wonder how everyone was kept in line, until you remembered your workday, how tired you were, and the cameras that were always watching. Then suddenly, it didn't seem so farfetched that no one wanted to cause trouble. Then suddenly, it made some sense, at least on the surface.

He made his way over to his bed, thinking about it all, again realizing how tired he was. It had been a long day, and an emotional one at that. He was drained and more than ready to pass out. He would be KO'd, he thought, the second his head hit the pillow. There was just one thing he wanted to do before he slept.

"Hey, Hakeem," he said, approaching the man's bed. He was behind Hakeem's head, so Hakeem didn't see him coming at first. Once he did though, he put down the book he was reading, sat up, and faced him.

Deron expected a smile, a "nice to see you survived your first day" or some other type of banter, but there was nothing of the sort. Something was different.

"Deron," he said. The way he said his name, the look in his eyes, both showed real concern. His next words were confirmation. "I heard what happened. I'm terribly sorry. For that to occur on your first day, you must be one of the unluckiest souls in the world."

Deron's eyes went wide with shock and surprise. *How could he possibly know that already?* He asked as much once he had regained composure.

"News travels fast in these parts. Of course, sometimes that news turns out to be incorrect, but the look on your face tells me this story is true. Please." He made a gesture welcoming Deron to sit down.

Deron hesitated a moment—he was still processing how that information had travelled that quickly without phones or internet—but eventually obliged. It had been his plan to talk to Hakeem, after all. And this was part of the story. The only problem was how to tell it.

"I uhh …" He looked toward Hakeem, who was staring back at him now with an almost frightening intensity. "Sorry, I'm a bit buzzed." He chuckled. Hakeem did not. His face never broke. He had mentioned that as a defence tactic and both of them knew it.

Eventually, Hakeem spoke. "Understandable given the circumstances. It is a rational way to deal with the pain of a trauma such as this."

Deron thought about this. Was he in pain? At times it seemed like he was, and at times it seemed like he didn't give one damn. But perhaps that was a defence mechanism too. He nodded to himself.

"Yeah. I … I don't know. It was tough seeing something like that," he reflected. "Seeing him just lying there, knowing he would never get up again. I mean, I didn't see it happen, and I didn't know him at all, obviously, but I don't know. Just makes you feel … vulnerable, I guess."

"I can understand that," Hakeem replied. His face still hadn't broken, but Deron could sense a compassion in his tone. Hakeem put a hand on Deron's shoulder. "You'll get used to it. That feeling, I mean. One day you'll wake up and you won't feel that vulnerability anymore. The things you see, they'll just be a normal part of everyday life. It's sad, but it's true."

Deron nodded in response. He didn't know what to say. The idea of not feeling vulnerable sounded promising; the idea of death being normalized did not. "Do you see it a lot out here?" he eventually asked. "Death, I mean."

"See? No. Hear about? Yes. People die all the time in the Camp, but the vast majority of those deaths are a lot less dramatic than the one you experienced. Occasionally, someone will suffer a stroke or heart attack from being overworked. Accidents happen in the factories once in a while. But most deaths are from illness. Modern medicine can do wonders, but it can only go so far. The viruses are always adapting. It's kind of ironic actually. One of the reasons the Utopia claims it's necessary to be cut off from other civilizations is to avoid the worldwide pandemics, but I can guarantee there is just as much illness here as anywhere else. Maybe not in the same forms, but the viruses here, they do the same jobs."

Hakeem smiled for the first time, an ominous smile that might have given Deron a sudden chill had it come from anyone else. Instead, he just ignored it, accepted the information, and looked around the room. The clock on the wall read quarter past ten. The chatter around was even lighter than before. Most everyone was now cemented to their beds. It was about time for him to follow suit, but he had just one more question for Hakeem before he did, the same question he'd originally had on his mind when he'd first decided to enter this conversation.

"Hakeem, can I ask you something?"

"Of course, Deron. What's on your mind?" His smile had faded, but Deron hardly noticed.

"Well, it's just that, everyone here that I've seen so far, granted it's only been one full day, but still, they seem pretty ... I don't know, decent. Nobody really strikes me as the notorious criminal type." He paused for a second, trying to find the right words. Eventually, they came to him. "I guess what I'm asking is, Why is that? I mean, I figure it's partly because people are too tired at the end of the day to cause trouble, and partly because the cameras are always watching, but is that really all there is to it? Or is there something more?"

He was nearly out of breath by the time he finished asking. There were people around, and he was pretty sure at least a few of them had overheard his question about them, but right now, he didn't care. If they wanted to chime in their input, he'd be happy to hear their opinions too.

He looked inwardly toward the trenches of his mind. In some ways, the Camp was exactly what he'd expected. In other ways, it wasn't anything close to what he'd anticipated at all. He'd decided somewhere along the line he needed to know more about the Camp's inhabitants to get a real understanding of the dilemma he was facing, to truly know if he'd be able to survive for five years, to gauge soundly what he was up against.

Was this really all some elaborate conspiracy? Or were the people here truly deserving of their places? The conversation in the bar had him questioning the entirety of the regime and, perhaps more importantly, questioning himself.

Conspiracy theories. Questions about the State. These were things he had thought of before and weren't just things that had been mentioned to him in passing by some of the people he had met.

He'd just always blown those notions off as entirely improbable. Of course there were lies. Of course there was some corruption here and there, some oversights, some people who got lost in the cracks, some who escaped punishment when they shouldn't have or, vice versa, were rewarded unrightfully. But the idea that they'd always been and forever would be entirely oppressed, it just hadn't made sense. The Utopia had raised him. The Utopia had taken care of him even when he'd provided almost nothing in return. That didn't seem like oppression to him. It seemed like the opposite, in fact. And people who thought otherwise were either misguided or simply distasteful individuals. He'd always believed that. He would've left when he'd had the chance if he'd thought otherwise.

But now—now his circumstances were beginning to make him wonder. Now he'd seen the Camp, and the way things were seemed just a bit too perfect, just enough work to make you too tired to fight back, just enough freedoms to make you not want to, just enough hope to keep you from risking it all.

Was it psychological warfare? Was it the perfect set of circumstances to tame even the most hardened? Or were the majority of people here not really hardened at all? Were the majority of people actually innocent? Or perhaps they'd been pushed into breaking the law by some form of entrapment. It seemed so unlikely, seemed like such a crazy idea, so impossible to pull off. And yet here he was, having no recollection of what he had done or why he had done it. Perhaps he was not alone in his story.

He looked outwardly toward Hakeem. Something inside him was telling him this man would have the answers. He didn't know how or why, but for some reason, he was just sure of it. For better or worse, this man knew the truth.

He was on the edge of his seat as Hakeem began to talk.

"The State will tell you that the average Utopian is more docile than others around the world. They will say this is because of the community schools, because people learn to grow up harmoniously in large groups. They will say it is because of equality. Everyone is treated the same, and this leaves little room for any vindictive hatred. They will say most crimes are slips of the moment rather than large character flaws, slips that must be punished for the system to function, but still actions that can be redeemed. I say that's all bullshit."

He stared hard at Deron again, this time with even more blazing intensity, almost like he was looking into his soul to see if he understood.

"Utopians are no more or less collaborative than anywhere else in the world. The reason people in the Camp are tame, for the most part, is because of the things you've mentioned: the exhaustion and monotony of the work, which make rebellion seem like an unmanageable chore. The cameras are always watching, leading to the idea that you will get caught if you act immorally, no matter who your actions are directed toward. But there is another aspect too."

He left the thought dangling there for a moment, like the cliff-hanger of a TV episode asking you to tune in next week to find out what happened. Thankfully, Deron only had to wait a few seconds.

"The most aggressive, they do not come to the Camp. Or if they do, they do not last very long. They are killed off before they have a chance to cause any sort of mutiny or trouble." There was a slight pause as he let that sink in, then he continued. "And I'm not talking about just rapists and psychopathic murderers. There are some of those as well, but what I'm mostly talking about are the ones who are the most vocal, the ones who do not play the game and who stand up for something greater. Those rebels, as they call them, are killed before they have a chance to revolt. Either that or they cover their tracks well and bide their time in hiding."

Hakeem's face twitched then, and if Deron didn't know any better, he would have sworn that twitch had been a wink, some kind of signal with a hidden message underneath, like he had a firsthand understanding of the words he was preaching. To Hakeem, it seemed, they were more than just words.

But Deron couldn't be sure, so he didn't bring it up. He just answered instead. "That's a very good point ... Thanks, Hakeem. I think I get it now."

And he did get what Hakeem was saying; he just wasn't really sure if all his questions had been answered. *But I guess that's asking a lot,* he thought to himself. *Trying to understand everything the first day. That's probably not realistic.*

He thought about asking more, but he was really tired now and pretty sure he wouldn't be able to properly analyze any new information anyway. He decided to save the conversation for tomorrow. God knew there'd be plenty of time in the future for discussion.

"I think I'm going to go lie down," he said.

Hakeem smiled at him, a different smile than the one Deron had seen before. This one had a real cheerfulness behind it. "I can appreciate you would be tired," he said. "Get some rest. Lights go out in a few minutes anyway."

Deron looked up at the clock and then back at Hakeem. "Good night," he said. Hakeem returned the words in kind, picked up his book again (a book with a beautiful cover, having some type of symbol or writing in the middle surrounded by a pattern; Deron had never seen anything quite like it before), and lay back in his bed. Deron returned to his.

He sat at the base of his bedframe and wiped his hands across his face. He was unbelievably tired, and it was time to get some rest. His supply bag hung from his shoulder. It had travelled with him all day and proven useful many times. He reached into it now to grab his earplugs, but his eye caught something else instead. It was the book, the one with the map on the back and the laws of the land on the front.

It shouldn't have meant anything. He had seen that book enough times already that he had practically memorized its features. But when he saw

THE UTOPIA

it right then, he got a sudden urge, like the one he'd had earlier in the day with Carla: an urge to tell the truth.

Only this time, he would tell the whole truth.

He grabbed the book and opened the cover. On the first page were the instructions, but beyond that, the pages were empty. He grabbed the pen that came along with it and just started to write.

Log Entry: Day 1

Today was my first full day at the Camp, and already I feel tired. The work is taxing both mentally and physically. It will take some time to adjust.

Something bad happened today. Well, something worse than bad. I guess I can count on something bad happening pretty much every day, but this day was different. A man died at our factory. He was executed by a guard. Not right in front of me, but I saw the result: a body strewn out with blood all over. His name was Murphy. A good man by all accounts, and a loss to both sides. We lost a soldier. They lost a cog in their machine. What this will mean for the future, we'll just have to wait and see.

I've met some people here, and they all seem okay. Hakeem sleeps nearby, and he seems to be the best of them. I think he is very wise, someone to listen to and bounce opinions off of at the least.

My workmates seem decent too. They are a rowdier bunch, but hopefully, if nothing else, their energy will be infectious. I will need as much of that as I can get to survive in this place.

There is one other person I met today as well. I was supposed to see her at the bar (that's right; they have a bar and apparently some form of brothel house as well!), but she never showed. I'm sure there was a reason. I'll ask her tomorrow. There is something about her that I really find intriguing. Perhaps she is the one who will make this place bearable. I guess there is only one way to find out.

Until next time,

Deron Boyd

He smiled as he wrote the last line. It had been one hell of a day. Every emotion he could think of, he had felt at one point, and a lot of them were negative. He still felt a lot of fear and confusion even now. But he had survived. And that meant something.

He put the book and the pen back in his supply bag. This time, he did grab his earplugs and fixed them in his ears. The warning bell rang right as he did. In a couple minutes, the lights would go out. And the second they did, Deron's body shut down for the night as well.

CHAPTER 5

Sixteen hours later, Deron still didn't have any answers, but he did feel a hell of a lot better.

It was near two thirty in the afternoon, and he was standing in the shower facility at factory 4F, singing his heart out. He'd completed his first half day without incident, and an afternoon off was cause for celebration. The water running across his bare skin was warm and therapeutic.

He had slept through the night quite peacefully and had woken up this morning feeling relatively refreshed. He'd had a few bouts of mild nausea and some shaky hands early on (which he'd attributed to his withdrawal symptoms returning after the day-long effects of the zombie pill had worn off), but the symptoms had been minor and had gone away and stayed away once he'd started work. He thought he was pretty much clear on that front for the rest of the day and hopefully beyond.

At lunch, he'd eaten heartily (more pasta and bread) and had returned to his work feeling bright about the day's prospects. He'd gotten a chance to briefly talk to Carla, and she'd apologized to him for flopping on going to the bar. Apparently, she had an explanation that she would tell him later. Today was also her half day, and there was something she had planned that, since it was his half day too, she wanted him to be a part of. That proclamation had gotten him excited, and when he got excited, he sang, old tunes especially.

The Utopia was cut off from the rest of the world, but of course, there was a time that they hadn't been so segregated. A vast amount of music, food recipes, games, and the like were imported in those times, and of course, many other cultural imprints were brought by immigrants during the Great Transition. Even today, the odd art form trickles in when someone decides to make the pilgrimage here from another land.

"I'm Gonna Be" by The Proclaimers, the song he was singing now, had been around, by Utopian standards, since the dawn of time. And while it wasn't exactly Mozart's Symphony No. 40 in terms of beauty, it had survived, like most music here did, because there wasn't a whole lot of new music produced in their world. Musicians were not considered essential in the Utopia, so the only way to make it as one was to start playing as a hobby and then be granted Exceptional Status by the Computer's Entertainment Network. At that point, as long as you were creating up to certain standards (in terms of quantity and quality, though how those were measured for art forms had always been a mystery to Deron), making music became your career, and you were then ineligible to be chosen.

The same rules applied for things like traditional art and fiction writing. Similar rules applied to things like sports and acting, though these involved tryouts. Entertainment was not considered a need by the Utopia, and having too many people get credit for unneeded jobs would be a loophole in the system. It was so much more efficient to just recycle the past or ask people to create art on their own time. Because job or no job, fear of being chosen or not, the State knew people would do it if the art was their true passion. And if the art was their true passion, and they worked at it hard enough, one day, eventually, they'd get good enough to be granted Exceptional Status. Everything tied up nicely in a neat little bow.

Deron wasn't sure if The Proclaimers would have survived in this land. They might have been forced to work as welders or plumbers at the same time they made music if they didn't want to risk being chosen. Was their music good enough that they would have been granted an exception? It was really tough to tell. But either way, Deron was glad they'd made this song. He really liked this song.

He started to shout the chorus but then, for two reasons, quickly shut his mouth. The first was he realized he was a verse early on his chanting of random noises. The second, and more practical reason, was he realized that maybe it wasn't wise to make so much racket.

He turned off the nozzle and stood silently for a moment as he looked around the shower area. There had been others here before who also had a half day (including Yuri Yin, a.k.a. Wise Guy), but they had already showered and departed. He alone was left in this room, suddenly remembering where he was and the situation at hand, suddenly wondering to himself what would happen next, not worrying—he was still feeling refreshed and confident—just genuinely curious.

Eventually, he got tired of wondering and decided to just let it happen. He dried off, changed into his leisure uniform, grabbed his supply bag, and departed from the washroom. He walked across the factory floor with a certain swagger in his step that he hadn't felt since some time well before he ever got to the Camp. There would be dark days ahead. His questions were still unanswered. But for the next little while, his focus was singular. He was eying the beautiful woman straight ahead, with her short black hair and lustful brown eyes, beckoning him in, daring him to show how badly he wanted her. And at some point, he would, but he would start off playing coy.

"Hey," he said to her, at about the transition line between the factory and the dining hall. Inside, he was smiling brightly, but his face held firm. He was still supposed to be a bit upset with her for not showing up to the bar, after all.

"Hey, hot stuff," she spoke back. He nearly broke but was able to contain himself just barely.

"Wow, trying to butter me up already," he said (mostly) straight-faced. "Think that'll make me forget how you ditched me last night?" He crossed his arms in "disgust" and raised one eyebrow.

"Oh, stop," she said playfully, attuned to the sarcasm. "Donna reminded me of something as we were walking there, and I couldn't back out. I could've let her go alone, but that wouldn't have been fair. You don't feel safe going there alone. Not as a woman."

And the instant she said that, the suave persona he had been presenting immediately disappeared. "What do you mean?" he said, almost instinctually. But the question he really wanted to ask was, What or where is there?

"You'll see," she replied. She gave him another flirty smile, one that made Deron feel strangely nervous. But he had grown conscious of the fact that he had broken character and so did his best not to show it.

"Whatever you say, girl," he replied, returning to the facade. "Whatever you say." But it didn't come out with the same confidence as before, and he was pretty sure she could see that. If she did though, she chose to ignore it.

"But first," she said, "I think I owe you a drink."

She extended her hand out, her back half-turned, ready to lead him away. Deron still didn't understand what was going on, but he had no thoughts of declining a beer or anything that came after. He linked his hand in hers, and they made their way to the bar.

***

HE WOULDN'T BE SERVED the quota of drinks he would have been allowed outside of the Camp, but he wouldn't have to use up his monthly allowance either, and that was almost as good.

As they entered, Carla said, "How 'bout you find somewhere to sit, studdle bunny, and I'll get us some drinks."

Studdle bunny. He had almost burst out at the seams at that. But he was still playing his game and trying to act as indifferent as possible. He agreed to her terms with a simple but effective, "Sure."

Not ten seconds later, she was at the bar ordering, and he was posted up at a table close to the front. Today, in contrast to the night prior, the bar was near empty. There was a group of three women at the back-corner table where he and his fellow sawmill workers had sat yesterday and a couple men sitting a few tables down from them, but that was it. He didn't find this surprising. The vast majority of people were surely still working, and even for the minority that weren't, it didn't make sense for them to waste their only beer of the month on a random Sunday afternoon.

Carla returned to the table with a stein in each hand. For a second, he was about to ask how she was able to get two beers, but then he remembered the one-a-month rule plus the freebie she hadn't yet used from last night. *And one plus one is two. That's quick math; very good, Deron!*

"Got you a lager. I hope that's alright," she said, sitting down in the seat across from him.

"As long as it's made with love," he replied. He nearly facepalmed himself after he said that, but it worked out just fine.

"The guy behind the bar looked a bit grouchy. Not sure he mixed a whole lot of love in there, but he might have mixed in something else for all I know. Take a sip and find out." She pointed at it and winked.

Deron smiled and leaned back in his seat. He had a reply to that, but on second thought, he considered it might sound a bit too chauvinistic this early in their relationship. He went the safe route instead.

"Strange how the bars here are open in the afternoon and the ones back home don't open until late in the evening."

"I've thought that as well. Maybe it's their way of recruiting," she joked. "If the degenerates know the alcohol party starts early on this side of the border, then maybe they'll be more enticed to come play."

"Except, sadly, you can only play once a month." He did a fake pout, which she laughed at.

"Not you apparently. You're at a beer a day and haven't even used up your paycheque yet. You are one smooth conman, I tell ya. My oh my."

Deron chuckled. "I guess I am," he said. He leaned forward again and picked up his drink. He held it halfway across the wood table, his elbow acting as a fulcrum on the surface. "Cheers to the Camp and all of its charm. A place where the worker's always towing and the liquor's always flowing."

She laughed heartily at that and picked up her glass as well. "Cheers," she smiled. They both took a generous sip of beer and then placed their steins back on the table.

"So tell me some things," she said, wiping a bit of foam from her lip.

"What kind of things?" Deron asked. He grabbed for his beer again and took another sip. His exterior was still relaxed for the moment, but his interior was beginning to feel that all-too-familiar rush of nerves. He was really hoping she wouldn't ask how he had ended up at the Camp. He'd felt cheery and blissful almost the entirety of the day. He really didn't want to go down the dark path again. Not right now.

"About you, silly." She smiled with that same vivacity that seemed to appear every time he looked at her. It was an extraordinary smile, so bright and mesmerizing, so blatant and alluring. But there was also something about it, he started to notice, that he just couldn't put his finger on, something he didn't trust. It was a smile that made him feel mostly warm, but a small part of him felt uneasy as well, like there was some kind of secret hidden behind that smile and that secret could be anything. He decided in that moment to find out what it was.

"Not much to tell," he replied. He put his beer down again and crossed his arms. "They sent me to school in the Valley where I produced average grades across the board. Did carpentry for my final four years. Had a few close friends that I remained in touch with after we graduated. Lived in Wexin District before this whole thing went down."

He paused. She looked at him to continue, but when she realized he wasn't going to, she spoke. "That's it?" she asked, sitting back in her own seat and crossing her arms as his female mirror image. "That's your story?"

"I mean, yeah, kind of," he said. He scratched the back of his head with his left hand. For the first time, he felt genuinely uncomfortable. No, that was not *it*. That was not *it* at all. His story wouldn't exactly make the tabloid headlines, but there was a lot more to it than that. He just didn't feel like going into details at the moment.

Something about that smile, he thought. Even now, there was still a form of it on her face, not the upbeat, flirtatious one, but a teasing grin, like what he had shared couldn't have sounded any more pathetic.

He didn't want to reveal more. Yesterday he'd had an insatiable urge to tell her his truth, but yesterday he had been vulnerable. Today he was not. Today he was in his element and thinking with a rational mind, that mind telling him that in a place like this, it was probably better to keep your cards close to the vest, especially when the cards in your hand were weak. But he also realized he needed to give a little to get a little.

"My childhood was boring for the most part. Didn't get into a whole lot of trouble. Had a few hobbies here and there but never stuck to or got particularly good at any of them. Mostly, I'd just hang out with my friends and do what I was told." He took another large gulp of beer, thinking to himself that he could have spiced things up with a story or two (like how he had tried to land a backflip off the monkey bars and had severely sprained his ankle, or that time where he had fallen asleep in the woods during a field trip and had to find his own way back), but for the most part, what he was saying was the truth. His childhood really had been quite boring, the same way it was for most kids who grew up in the Utopia. There wasn't a whole lot of room for troublemaking or exploring.

He put his beer back down. "And I never ended up working in carpentry after school ended. I never ended up working at all actually. I graduated, was placed, and spent the years following doing just about nothing …"

He hesitated for a moment almost too short to notice. He probably would have for longer if he wasn't almost half a stein deep now and starting to feel more impulsive, but either way, he would have ended up saying what he said next. It was true (sort of; the timeline was off, and the reason he would give for starting the habit was utter bullshit, but the thesis itself was accurate), and, well, give a little to get a little.

"… Nothing but a bunch of drugs." As if to confirm this, he took another giant gulp of his beer.

When he put it back down, she was smiling at him again with that grand old smile. "See, there you go," she said. "I knew there was something. Everyone's got something."

"I guess so," he said, feeling more confused about that smile than ever. It was as if she was genuinely pleased he had been—had been? Who was he kidding? Once an addict, always an addict—addicted to drugs, like that was some great part of him that made him more interesting than the rest of these dopes, and she was proud of herself for successfully coaxing it out of him.

Unconsciously, he began to pinch his fingers together, began to feel a heaviness in his head unrelated to the alcohol, began to reflect that this woman across from him seemed a far cry from the woman who had been comforting him yesterday.

Had that all been just an act? And if so, why? What was her game? To gain his trust, hear all his secrets, and then … Do what with them? This was all starting to feel very troubling. This was all starting to feel like some sort of mistake. But he was already in it so couldn't back out now.

"I just, I don't know, I guess I just had a hard time adjusting to life outside of the school structure. Too much time on my hands. Zero motivation to do anything with it. And drugs were just fun, just a way to not worry about stuff."

He sunk his head low like he was thinking deeply, but in reality, he was just waiting, waiting to see how she would react and what she would say. Did she remember what he had said to her the day before about losing someone close? Would she put two and two together (that's four!)?

In the end, consciously or not, she didn't bring it up. "Makes sense," she said. "I had my own little flirtation with some substances at one point in my life."

"Did you?" Deron asked. He stared hard into her eyes, trying to read them. Her grin was still present, but it was much less pronounced.

"Yeah, for a couple years," she said almost nonchalantly. "I was trying to make it as an actress, and I just couldn't get a gig. And while I was trying out for shows and movies, I was also doing this boring as hell administrative job for the State, and it was all stressing me the fuck out. Needed a little pick me up every now and again." Her smile broadened, the same smile as before, only this time, when Deron saw it, he didn't feel the same worry. He felt relief instead.

She'd been one question away from really putting him on the spot, one connection from backing him into a corner that he couldn't escape from. If she'd asked him about *her*, he wouldn't have been able to lie. She would have seen it on his face the second he tried, and he'd either have had to rip the mask off or accept that she'd always know from then on he'd been wearing one in the first place.

She'd had him on the ropes and very nearly had him pinned. But he'd managed a reversal at the very last second. Now she was the one talking. Now he was the one directing the conversation. Now he was the one in control. And he planned to keep it that way.

"Fair enough though. You were stressed out actually doing things as opposed to sitting around doing nothing like me."

"I guess. But I feel like you probably handled yourself better doing them. I would get angry and lose my temper. Actually how I ended up here." She smiled to the point where she was actually chuckling.

"Really?" he said. A classic probing question meant to keep her talking.

"Yeah." More chuckles. "I guess I shouldn't laugh, but it is kind of funny looking back. I had this tryout for this character, Mavis Marine. I—"

"Wait, you were going to be Mavis Marine?" Deron interrupted, sounding as perplexed as he felt. For a second, he forgot everything else and just let that sink in.

Mavis Marine. He knew Mavis Marine. She was one of the leading characters on this detective series he sometimes watched, this hotshot badass type who was getting reamed out by her superiors about as often as she was catching the criminal. Decent show. A bit unrealistic (in her fantasy world, they actually had to track the bad guys using old-school methods; there weren't cameras everywhere to catch all the action) but well-made, all things considered. And Mavis, along with Argod Zenobiel, the series' main villain, were definitely the two most interesting characters.

"That's awesome."

"Yeah, well, I didn't get the part, clearly," she joked. "And that's kind of what led to this whole episode. I was high on coke during my tryout. Thought it would help, and honestly, it probably did. For that character, you needed to be a bit on edge." She expected some type of reaction, but Deron was just staring at her blankly in stunned silence. When she realized his gaping mouth wasn't going to emit sound, she made hers keep moving. "Anyway, that's not really important. I only mention the coke because if I hadn't been high, maybe I wouldn't have, whoopsie me, kicked holes in the wall and destroyed one of the video screens when the Computer didn't pick me. Maybe I wouldn't have punched the guard stationed there square across the nose when he tried to arrest me for destruction of property. Got myself an extra rebellion charge for kicking him in the stomach while he was down."

She looked at him deeply then, for once, no grin of any kind on her face, and Deron felt it immediately. Everything she was saying was the truth—there was no question about it—every single word.

"Or maybe I would've done all that shit anyway. Maybe coke or no coke, I finally reached my breaking point. Who the hell knows, and who the hell cares, really. Moral of the story is I ended up here, and that's all that matters."

"Wow," Deron replied quietly. He was leaning back in his seat, and his eyes were so wide, they looked like they may very well explode. He was speechless. Her story had hit him in a way that he'd failed to anticipate. It had made him feel guilty. "Wow. That's just ..." His eyes narrowed and dropped to the floor. He couldn't bear to look at her. He felt a little sick to his stomach, and it wasn't the alcohol that was the problem.

How could I have been so stupid? he thought, beginning to wallow in his own pity party. This whole time, he'd been sitting here asking himself what secrets she had stored, questioning her integrity, wondering if she was someone he could trust.

But now—what he was realizing now was that if anyone was dishonest, it was him. Whatever secrets she had behind that smile, she was ready to reveal them without any hesitation, without any fear of judgment, without any fear he would do her any harm. He was the one who had been sitting here this whole time with something to hide. He was the one who feared judgment. He was the one who feared harm. He was the one deceptively trying to get inside her mind. Her smile was genuine. It had been the whole time. It was his expressions that were fake, his words that were lies. He couldn't look at her because he felt terrible for that.

But mostly, he couldn't look at her because after all she had revealed, he thought he might very well love her.

"I'm sorry, I don't know what to say." Emotion was gripping him now. He'd tried to play it cool this whole time, and for what? So he could woo her with some false confidence he didn't have? So he could get into her head and trick her into admitting some dark secret that wasn't there? What was he doing?

Just tell her, he thought to himself. *You've been holding this in for too long. Maybe she can be the one to help you.*

And a large part of him truly did believe that, a very large part, but not all of him. And until it was all of him, he wouldn't crack. In the end, he held it in the same way he always had.

"You okay?" she asked. She could see him rubbing his eyelids and staring toward the ground. She hadn't seen him tear up, but she could sense the emotion.

"Yeah, sorry," he said. "I get emotional when I drink. And hearing that story just makes me sad." Except even that wasn't true.

"You're sweet." She smiled and reached across the table. He presented her his hand. "But you shouldn't feel sad. Because I don't feel sad. At first I did. At first I thought coming here would be the end of the world."

She slowed down and gazed deeply again, only this time within. This time her eyes were distant and reflective, her head nodding to itself in understanding of her own truth.

"But it wasn't. If anything, coming here saved my life, Deron. I am so much happier here than I was out there. I know how crazy that sounds, but it's true. Here, I know what I have to do every day, and I actually like the work I do. Insane, right? This girl, who wanted to be an actress her whole life, working at the sawmill and enjoying it. But I do. I really do, and it's not just that. It's the mindset. There's no worrying anymore about whether or not I'll make it. There's no worrying anymore about what anyone thinks of my performance. I don't have to act anymore. I can just be me, and there's something beautiful in that."

She smiled again. Deron looked into her eyes and thought he had only seen a smile so beautiful one other time in his life: the day *she* had told him she was leaving.

He nodded and said he understood. In reality, he couldn't remember anything she had just said at all. He took another glug of his beer, and she did of hers. They sat there silently for a while, deep in their own thoughts.

In the end, it was the clock that brought them back to the real world.

"Oh shit! Deron, we have to go," she said, sounding a bit panicky.

"Why? What's up?" he replied automatically. The alarm in her voice almost immediately spirited away his sadness. Funny how even your emotions can get scared.

She chugged her beer with reckless abandon (there was about half a stein left) and then grabbed his hand. "C'mon. Finish your beer if you want but do it quick."

Deron felt confused. This was the first time he had seen her seem worked up in any type of way. But he did what he did whenever he felt confused: he drank. He polished off his beer and they hustled outside.

"Where are we going?" he asked back on the streets.

"You'll see."

"Okay, but why the rush?"

"You'll see, Deron," she said, sounding mildly annoyed. When she looked back at him though, that flirty smile had returned to her face. And for a reason even he couldn't understand, his first reaction was to not trust it again.

Not this again, he told himself, now feeling annoyed. *This is nothing bad. It has to be part of the thing she had planned, the one she was talking about earlier.*

And he was pretty sure that was true. The only question was, Why couldn't he seem to shake the nervous feeling from his body?

He would see soon enough.

***

AND WHAT HE SAW, he would remember for the rest of his life.

What is this place? That would be his first thought the second they got close, and he would never forget it. Over and over, the words would repeat themselves inside his head like some type of dark lullaby. Over and over, he would recall the swelling-like bulge in his eyes as he took his first glances at the sight now before him. Over and over, he would remember that feeling of his stomach tossing and turning, like he'd just taken a bungee dive over the biggest cliff in the Utopia and all that was left for him now was to see if the rope held. No matter how many times he came back here in the future, he would always remember that.

Because those feelings would end up being an omen of what was to come, a premonition of the uncomfortable situation he was about to find himself in. And no matter how hard he tried, he couldn't disassociate those feelings from such a novel location. The stimulus in front of him would forever produce that response. Time after time, no matter how much he changed, those feelings would return.

But that problem was for a future Deron, who didn't yet exist. Right now, he just knew he had never seen anything quite like this. Right now, he just wanted answers. Only he was afraid to ask.

What is this place? This hadn't been the first question dancing around in his head on their journey over here. In the twenty minutes of brisk walking that had passed, he'd had many more. *Why are we walking so fast? How can she remember all these twists and turns without looking at a map?*

THE UTOPIA

Why does something feel so off about this?

All these questions were valid and completely rational. But he'd kept them to himself, convinced it was best not to upset the apple cart any more than he already had. Carla had grown increasingly on edge since they'd left the bar, and he surmised that since he'd already misjudged her once, the wise move was to just keep his mouth shut.

And for a time, that *had* seemed like the correct move. Other than the racewalking, all had seemed normal. They passed factories big and small. They passed what he was pretty sure was another housing complex. They passed guards and cameras and work and progress, all centred around a theme that seemed to fit the general mould of the Camp: clunky but effective.

That was, until they got to this place.

This place was different. Deron felt like they had crossed over an invisible barrier into another dimension. The barricade was the same (a gated fence that you had to scan your way into). There were guards stationed just beyond, and that wasn't abnormal either. But it was what they were guarding that he couldn't quite comprehend. Even in the Camp, this seemed like something too strange to be real.

Standing before them was a giant circus tent. It must have stood at least fifty feet high, with a width and depth of at least double that. The fabric looked smooth and was army green in colour. The poles were shiny and strong, reflecting the light of the hanging sun. There was a single entrance slit at the front of the structure, large enough that four people could comfortably walk side by side through the plastic-strip curtains that hung above. He'd never seen anything like it before in the entirety of his life.

What is this place? That age-old question wouldn't seem to go away. As if the circus tent wasn't enough, there were two beach-style huts that couldn't have felt more misplaced stationed just in front, one off to each side of the entranceway, only instead of serving piña coladas, they appeared to Deron to be some kind of check-in booths. *Checking-in for what,* he wondered. Each had guards stationed within and a computer on the front counter. The only tangible difference between the two was that one had a lineup and the other did not.

"What—" He almost said it, but before he could get it out, Carla was dragging him toward the booth with no line. His anxiety would be prolonged for a bit longer.

"Are you checking in, camper?" The question came from behind the counter and was posited to Carla as they approached.

"Yes," she answered. "Carla Cortez. Should be for four o'clock." They had made it to the counter now. Carla hunkered particularly close, almost leaning over it to look at the computer screen inside the hut.

The guard woman, a pretty lady of about thirty-five, made a few clicks from her seat behind the counter, then said, "You know it's already 4:05, right?" still clicking away.

"Yes, we got held up," Carla replied calmly. Her voice indicated no open concern for being late, something Deron took note of only because he had come to associate tardiness with the deadliest sin of all in the Camp.

"No problem. As long as you understand you won't get extra time." Carla nodded. "Okay. Well, in that case, you, Carla, are all set." The woman smiled at her.

"Thank you," Carla said, smiling herself. There was a scanner attached to the counter, and without even being prompted, Carla tapped her card.

"Deron, get out your card," she said to him then. Again, he could hear some anxiety in her voice, although he suspected her stress was nothing compared to his own.

He hesitated for a moment. His brain was telling him that maybe he should ask a few questions before he used his card for ... whatever this was. Maybe going into this completely blind wasn't the best idea.

For what felt like the millionth time, he scanned the scene with bloated eyes. Tent: still there. Carla: still anxious. The woman at the counter: waiting for him patiently. The other guard beside her, whom Deron was really noticing for the first time, was male, older, and looking far less impressed. His face seemed to say, *Just get on with it already.*

Deron pulled out his card and tapped it on the scanner.

"Great," the woman said. "Deron Boyd, you are good to go. Enjoy yourselves. The others are already inside. Tent eighteen."

Others?

"Great, thank you!" Carla said. A moment later, she was dragging him again, this time with so much force that it might have taken off a small child's arm. They walked between the huts, passing a man and a woman on their way out of the tent, both smiling profusely.

What the hell is going on? Deron nearly shouted it in his head. He had so many questions. Where the hell were they? What were they doing? Who were these *others* they were about to meet up with?

And as his mind was rambling, he came up with perhaps the most interesting one of all. *When did she decide to make me part of this?* She hadn't known he had a half day until just a few hours ago.

He glanced one more time at the woman beside him. Her smile was back, and in that moment, it felt like her anxiety had left her, like she'd been labouring through a project and it was finally on the brink of completion, like the sweet taste of victory was about to make all that effort worth it.

He could have questioned her about it, but at this point, he figured it was only a matter of seconds before all his questions would be answered. He glanced toward the plastic strips they were just about to pass through and decided to just enjoy the show. For better or worse, the circus was in town.

***

FOR DERON, PASSING THROUGH the overhanging plastic strips was an experience that could only be described as metamorphic: visually, from the brightness of the sun to the reduced glow of overhanging lanterns; aroma-wise, from the fresh-smelling outdoor air to a musty indoor stench. But most of all, it was the temporary transition of a twenty-seven-year-old man back into a ten-year-old boy, a boy who had first laid eyes on those plastic strips during a trip to the Utopian Zoo, during a trip from another life, a life of blissful innocence, before captivity or animal rights were on any child's radar, before drugs and alcohol and questions about people became a part of any routine. It was a trip that was simply a rite of passage for his cohort and a learning experience blended with some fun.

At age ten, Deron hadn't been much of an animal lover, but he had enjoyed that day, and later on, he had seen it as more and more special. The Utopian Zoo was the only one of its kind on the island, and it was only accessible by the public for a few weeks per year. The rest of the time, it served its purpose as a laboratory of sorts so that researchers could study the different species, to learn what the animals could teach them about how to survive.

That day, he hadn't cared a whole lot for the tigers and snakes and lizards, but he still looked back on it fondly as a shared experience with his friends, one that he had never replicated—some of his friends had been back since they'd turned twenty-one, but he had not—and that had always seemed fitting. That day was special to him because it was different, because it was a new experience. And it probably would have dampened his opinion of that day had he tried to recreate it. Past events tend to draw more affection in retrospect than as they are occurring, and any amateur psychologist could tell Deron that that day couldn't have been *that* wonderful. He didn't remember very many specifics about the animals or otherwise.

But there *was* one thing about that trip he could recall now, clear as day. It was an association that in any other scenario would have remained locked deep within the crevices of his mind. It was about those plastic strips, and a question from his friend Marla. He could see the moment in his mind's eye like he was standing in it presently.

"Why do they have those, Teacher Applebaum?" She had pointed as they entered one of the reptile exhibits. And their teacher had responded.

"They are used here partly because they help keep the temperature and humidity steady for the animals, but mostly they're actually for people. They are easier than having to open and close a door every time a new person wants to enter or an old person wants to leave."

"Oh. Neat!" she had responded the way a child does, with an enthusiasm that comes from gaining new knowledge, which adults can rarely summon. And then she had walked back and forth through that gateway as if to test that theory. She must have done it at least four or five times until their teacher had instructed her that it was time to move on.

That was what he remembered. Not what the tigers ate or why the lizards shed their skin. Not the date they had gone or who he had sat beside on the bus. He remembered those plastic strips and their practical utility, remembered it like it was the most important information he'd ever been told. But there was one thing Teacher Applebaum had forgotten to tell them. They were also a barrier for sound.

What are those...

Noises. What brought his mind back to the present were the noises coming from his left, his right, and all throughout the space. From outside, they were inaudible, but in here, they seemed to grow louder with each passing step.

They walked in a straight line through the dimness, their shoes softly tapping the fabric floor. To his left were more tents, and to his right, the setup was the same. Three rows of six in each direction, spaced equally apart with military precision, green and sleek like their parent-tent incubator. He felt like he was trapped in some sick Camp version of a Russian doll.

Only Russian dolls didn't make sound.

"Mmm."

"Ahh."

The noises. He could hear the noises coming from inside the tents. No audible words, only sounds. Panting. Grunting. The thrusting sound of skin against skin. A bed creaking. Steadily. More thrusting. A moan. His mind became dizzy with sensory overload, until suddenly, the lightbulb switched on and it all became clear.

The brothel. Holy fucking hell. She brought me to the brothel.

And for just a moment, his face lit up with delicious glee. His spine tingled with thirst as the blood rushed to regions mostly in his core, as his mind conjured up thoughts of him and her alone in a tent, bare-fleshed and lustful, with him shouting in pleasure, "This is the best surprise ever!"

And then he remembered the *others*, and all he felt were nerves. All he felt was a sickening sense of disappointment forthcoming. *Others.* It could have just meant other people in the room, in their own tents filling their own sexual desires. But it didn't. His rational mind wouldn't let him believe otherwise. She hadn't known he had a half day until today's lunch. He had never originally been part of this plan. She was coming here whether or not he was with her. And his rational mind was right.

When they arrived at tent eighteen, the last tent on the left, courtside from the runway they had gradually ventured down, Deron could already hear noises coming from inside. There were no sexual overtones, no "ahhs" or shouts of "yes!" It was just a simple conversation between two fellow hedonists. And that was somehow worse.

A male voice: "That slut better get here soon or we've gotta start without her, babe. I ain't wasting my once a month. If she wasn't so hot, I wouldn't even let her in at this point."

A female voice: "Stop it. She'll be here. You don't have to be such an asshole about it."

And in that moment, feelings of possessive jealousy overrode his senses. He could feel his blood begin to boil, his carotid begin to bulge, his hands turn into fists, his mind empty of all coherent thought except for one. He could swear the male voice sounded familiar.

The tent was zipped closed. Carla sunk down to her knees, and Deron watched her unzip it in a methodical, almost sexual way, a way that at almost any other time would have turned him on, a way that he might have (wet)dreamed about her unzipping his uniform. And when she had finished doing that, when she had finished sensually making her presence known, she announced herself like a reality star diva, like the real meaning of the word *slut* was that she was the star attraction.

"I'm here, bitches," she shouted with a smile.

That goddamn smile. Deron was standing beside her crouched body and could see it in full view. And, oh, how badly he wanted to wipe it off the face of the planet in that moment.

His eyes veered left. From beside her crouching body, a body he once lusted for but was now growing to hate, he tried to see into the tent. When he found he couldn't do it, as she had only unzipped it about halfway, he finished the operation himself, equally dramatically but with much more aggression.

And what he saw inside was somehow shocking and, at the same time, exactly what he expected. There was a sheeted mattress lying on a bedframe that barely hovered above the ground with two naked bodies sitting stretched out on top of it, their upper halves held up by the face-down palms of their hands. The illumination was minimal, but there was no question he was perceiving correctly.

It was Donna and Yuri Yin.

"Wooooah, hold on. How'd the rookie score an invite?" Yuri spoke first, in a tone that was more conversational than disapproving, like he was actually interested to know.

"Cuz he's hot," Carla replied, still on her knees, still with that impregnable smile on her face.

There was something about the way she said it, like that was the only part of him she had cared for this whole time. Something about that almost made him lose his mind. He'd never hit a woman before, never even come close, not even when he was eleven and Mary-Jane Castelle had spit in his face, not even at twenty-three when that drunk lady had punched him for no reason at all at the Pub. He'd never even blinked. But if there was ever a time, he thought, this might be it.

Carla began to get undressed. Unzipping her yellow leisure uniform slowly from her neck, past her breasts, and down beyond her abdomen.

"Speaking of hot," Yuri the Wise Guy said.

"Yeah, you like that?"

"Fuck yeah I do. Donna, give me a tug would you." And she did, on command like some kind of sex slave, reached one hand over and started to stroke him off.

Carla had almost her whole uniform off now. She was naked to the knees, hadn't been wearing a bra or panties or anything, leaving nothing to be imagined. Deron could see the racy curve of her backside as she began to crawl on all fours toward the mattress.

"Oh fuck, that's hot," Wise Guy said. His face looked fierce, concentrated, a sick sense of pleasure behind it that was just waiting to blow like the seed in his genitals.

"Donna, throw a condom on him, sweetheart. I think it's time to get serious."

With her free hand, Donna managed to grab a condom, tear the package open with her mouth, and begin to work it on. Deron watched on from the edge of the tent in a trance-like state, unable to move, unable to speak, watching Carla crawl, the swaying of her hips like a hypnotist's pendulum.

The rage hadn't left him. If anything, it had grown exponentially in size. A fireball of hate, just waiting to explode. It was just waiting for the magic words, just waiting for the spell to release its hold.

"Deron, baby, help me get out of these shoes will you." She looked back at him as she spoke. His glare was firm, but it was like she didn't even notice. She smiled, winked, licked her lips.

"I want you, Deron. I want you to punish me for the bad girl I've been. I want to feel every inch of you, and once I've had my fill, I want you to watch—"

"No."

It was one simple word, stated matter-of-factly like he was checking a box on some type of questionnaire, a word they had all heard or said thousands, maybe millions, of times. He himself used it often.

Hey, Deron, do you want to go for a walk? Maybe hiking? Bring some food and have a picnic while we're up there? No.

Deron, you think you should turn down the stove heat maybe? I think you're going to burn the chicken. No.

Yo, Deron, your mood is miserable, man. Think maybe the drugs are hurting more than they're helping? Think maybe you should cut back? No.

Hey, Deron, can you do this? Hey, Deron, can you stop that? Hey Deron. Hey Deron. HEY DERON.

No. It was a word he was used to saying. Sometimes for the better and sometimes for the worse, sometimes to be tolerant and sometimes to be petty. But never in his life had he meant it more seriously than he did now. Never in his life had he been so sure his word choice was appropriate.

No. He did not want to be here. He did not want any part of this situation at all. He had not been privy to this plan, and this was not something he would have willingly gone along with. And when the three of them saw his face, they understood all this instantly.

"Deron, sweetheart—"

"No," he repeated, this time with real force. His face was a scowl that would have intimidated the boogeyman. His anger was burning through his pores like a five-alarm fire. Never in his life had he felt so humiliated. Never in his life had he looked at someone with such contempt, not a guard, not a rival, not even himself.

"No. I'm not going to be part of whatever the fuck this is."

"Deron," Carla spoke slowly. Her face was without emotion, but her voice revealed mild concern. She could see Deron was distressed. What she didn't know was how distressed. Or what he might be capable of. "I see you're upset, and I'm sorry for springing this on you without telling you. I thought it was a surprise you might like, but it appears I was wrong."

"You thought lulling me into trusting you, tricking me into believing you cared about my feelings or well-being just to use me for your sick fantasies, you thought that was something I would enjoy?" he said heatedly. He was still standing at the edge of the tent, an invisible forcefield keeping the demon within him at bay. For the moment, at least.

He stared at her and shook his head, the resentment building with each passing second. Her eyes dropped away, but he could see them beginning to tear up. For once, there was no smile, just an unrelenting lip quiver and a puppy-dog frown. Her face said she knew how badly she had hurt him, and it was affecting her deeply in her soul. But he wasn't falling for it this time.

"Fuck you. You disgust me," he said with beastly disregard. And he probably would have said more had he not been interrupted.

"Hey, chill the fuck out, rookie," Yuri snapped. He hadn't moved—he was still sitting upright on the bed, naked and exposed—but Deron had known since the beginning that he'd simply been biding his time, waiting for a chance to step in. He was Deron's size, muscularly toned, and Deron knew his type: the alpha asshole who would never pass up an opportunity to prove you were a class below. "You're not even supposed to be here, so either be grateful or get the fuck out."

And in a parallel universe, Deron crossed into the dark side, struck his opponent across the face, and began to ring his neck. In that alternate world, Deron showed Yuri Yin what you got for being a wise guy. But in this current iteration, on this planet, in this world, he stayed right where he was, not because he was afraid, not because his anger had in any way subsided, but because he still had a few rational bones left in his body, and those bones were telling him that Yuri was right. He was not supposed to be there, and the fact that he was wasn't on Wise Guy. It was on himself, himself and Carla, a woman who, not an hour ago, he thought he might just love, a woman he now hated more than anything in the world.

He turned to leave.

"Deron," Carla called in a voice that was not hysterical but was not steady either. He hadn't turned fully, and he could still see her face. Tears were running down her cheeks. "I'm sorry if I hurt you. I truly am. But I just met you, sweetheart. I don't know what you expected. How I went about it was wrong; I realize that now. I should have told you what was happening. I just truly believed you might enjoy this as a surprise."

She wiped the tears with her arm, and for just a moment, Deron felt something like remorse, like maybe he had gone too far, like maybe it *had* been just an honest mistake. Maybe there was no malicious intent. Maybe it was just a misguided attempt at welcoming him into their social group from an unorthodox brain. And then he saw her smile and that theory was put to rest.

"Just stay," she said, sitting on her knees. She put her hands on her breasts and began to flush with colour. "C'mon." Her tears had dried up and her voice was getting raspier. "This might not have been the way you had envisioned it, but don't think I haven't seen the way you've been looking at me. You want this too." And then the most teasing smile of all. "C'mon, Deron. It's just sex. I'm sure a stud like you has been with other girls where that was all it was. It's because you're new to the Camp. You want this all to mean something, but it doesn't. It doesn't mean anything at all. The truth is in here, and even out there, none of it really matters. So just come over here and play."

And for the first time since the tent had opened, since he'd first looked inside, there was a voice in his head telling him to do it, telling him that maybe she was right, that he was taking this too seriously, that he should just have some fun, that he should at least get *something* out of this. He had been with other girls where it was nothing more than sex, girls he'd shooed from his apartment the next day and had never seen again.

The voice was asking plainly what made her any different than any of those girls? He had only known her a day. How could she have possibly made him feel so crushed, so cheated? How could she have possibly invoked in him this type of indignation?

There was one key difference. Those girls had never led him to believe there was something more, had never asked him to reveal his deepest secrets, had never offered him a lifeline when he was at his most vulnerable.

Carla had done that. She had done that purely for her own gain. She

THE UTOPIA

didn't care about his feelings. To her, he was just a pawn in her sex game, and though he once doubted that, she had just revealed the truth to him.

None of it really matters. She had said that, and if she wanted to use that to feel better about herself, she could go right ahead.

But she had made him feel like *he* mattered, made him feel like he mattered at a time when he was scared and alone and *needed* to matter. And to blow that off like it was nothing, to tell him to just ignore that betrayal and come back to bed—that was not something he was about to stand for. Not now. Not ever.

He turned and walked away, back toward the entrance with a thunder in his step that would've made the skies proud. He only looked back once. As he approached those damn plastic strips that made for the cleanest of doorways, he looked back to see if Carla had come after him.

But there was no one there. She had chosen to stay. *And why not?* he thought. *After all, none of it matters.*

He left the animals behind and returned to the other side.

***

THE AIR WAS COOL when his mind finally reverted to some semblance of normalcy. For four hours, it had felt like there was a giant wall of bricks where his brain should have been, and only now, sitting here at the corner of the M-1 building, leaning his back against the concrete structure, did it finally feel like he'd been able to chisel away some of that blockade. Only after he had set up the dynamite and nearly lit the fuse had he made the determination that the foundation was still salvageable, even if some of the old construction would have to be replaced.

He remembered walking out of the circus tent, but from there, it was just a blur. From there, he was just a wounded beast operating on defensive instinct, battle-tested and worn, harmless if left to his own devices but savage in the face of adversity.

He was pretty sure he had nearly fought a guard on his way out. The man—or woman, he couldn't remember which—had instructed him to scan out on his way to the exit, and his first instinct had been to brawl, to shout "fuck your scanner!" at the top of his lungs and crack the lucky man or woman's head in like an uncooked egg, to show them he wasn't just some pet they could order around.

But then he remembered Murphy, and his will to survive proved stronger than his emotions. He was a wounded beast, but he was a wounded gazelle, not a wounded lion. He would fight if he had to; otherwise, he would run. His jaw locked before he could do something stupid, and he scanned out as instructed, hustling away as fast as he could while the predators' appetites were still satiated.

From there he had gone back to the bar (shocker) and had downed his monthly beer without even tasting it. Within seconds of receiving it, it was flowing through his throat like a tidal surge until the last drop was gone. That memory he was sure about. Someone had even congratulated him on "the fastest chug they had ever seen."

Things unsurprisingly got hazier after that. Had he talked to anyone there? Probably, but he couldn't remember what they looked like or for how long. Had he puked? Possibly. He wasn't immune to the odd spew, that was for sure. And he had definitely used the washroom at some point. He had lingered around there long enough that he would have had to.

And after that... He looked down and consulted his notes. Sometime within the last half hour, he had decided to write down everything he could remember in his log book in hopes it would jog his memory, and this strategy had actually proven somewhat effective.

That's right, he thought. After that, he had gone to the pharmacy with dreams of scoring a zombie pill. The pharmacist had been a bit unnerved by his demeanour, but she had eventually given in and given him the pill. He was entitled to one after all. The first day's had been a freebie.

But had he taken that pill? It would make sense that he would be this woozy if he had taken a partial. A full one knocked you out almost instantly, but a partial turned you into, well, a zombie. Dazed and confused but still physically functional. It would make sense that he couldn't remember much after the pharmacy if he had taken it right then. All he could recall was watching the sun go down and then sitting by the corner of the M-1 building.

But as he looked through his bag, he realized it was still there—still there, intact, and untouched, like it had been the other five times he had checked.

THE UTOPIA

"What's happening to me?" he asked himself under his breath. He put his head in his hands and shook it in the darkness. It wasn't a complete blackout. The moon was bright, and the stars twinkled overhead in the cloudless night. There was a streetlight nearby illuminating the sidewalk, showing him that he was not alone. But God, did he feel alone.

He hadn't felt this depressed since the day *she* had left.

He stared out toward the street. Plenty of people had come and gone since he'd begun sitting there, most of them in the past half hour as he was writing out his thoughts. returning from their workdays, ignoring him completely. And why shouldn't they? In a world of dread and drear, who takes notice of another lost soul?

"What's happening to me, Merlin?" he called out, louder this time. A man had been pacing back and forth on the sidewalk for the past fifteen minutes, and although Deron had yet to see his face clearly, he knew it was Merlin. It was something about the mannerisms, the hunched-over stance, the way he flicked his wrist like he had just shot a three-pointer every time he was about to turn around. It just fit the persona.

Merlin stopped his pacing for just a moment, looked over, stared hard in a way that was not a glare but simply a strained effort to see into the darkness, and then went back to pacing. On another day, Deron might have found this reaction amusing, but that day was not today. Today, he kind of wished that Merlin was more normal, that Merlin would be his friend.

Deron looked up at the moon and began to reminisce. He'd been trying to avoid these memories at all costs, hiding behind his anger to keep them at bay. But anger wasn't helping in this case any more than anger ever seemed to. He might as well just think them and get it over with. It would hurt, but it wouldn't kill him. He had contemplated it all countless times before, and yet he was still alive.

He clutched the gold chain around his neck and brought the K up to eye level. There had been times in his life when he'd considered just tossing the damn thing. Every time he thought about her, it only seemed to bring pain, and maybe if he relinquished this talisman, some of that pain would go away. There were times when that seemed like a reasonable assumption.

But he could never bring himself to do it, and in his heart, he knew why. It was partly because she had used her once-a-year value item on him and he didn't want it to go to waste and partly because it brought flash to his otherwise bland wardrobe and was a sleek accessory. But for the most part, those were just facades for a truth that he couldn't deny. He couldn't get rid of it because he refused to let her go.

He stared at the chain with vibrant intensity, knowing it represented the thing he missed the most in his whole life, knowing it represented perhaps the biggest mistake he'd ever made, knowing that if he could do it all over again, he would have done it differently.

But he couldn't. He was here, and he wasn't going anywhere. He could only hope to make the best of a bad situation. But he had tried to do that today, and he had gotten hurt again.

Maybe that's just the way the world works, he thought to himself somberly. *Maybe it's all just meant to be a struggle.*

"The snake never remembers like the one who got bitten!"

Deron believed these words to be a strange addition to his thoughts until he realized it wasn't *his* thought at all. He glanced up and saw Merlin. He was no longer pacing. He was standing motionless on the sidewalk and shouting in his direction. Shouting at him.

"The snake never remembers like the one who got bitten!" he shouted again. His face was stern, his eyes piercing with raw emotion. It was like a demon had taken control of him and was using his voice to give the world one final warning.

"The snake—"

"Merlin, that's enough."

A second voice came from Deron's left, and he had to glance just slightly in that direction to catch Hakeem. He was approaching slowly over the concrete slab that separated the sidewalk from the outer wall of the building. His tone was authoritative but non-threatening.

Merlin never even looked at him. He stared at Deron a moment longer, opened his mouth but closed it without sound, and then went back to pacing like Hakeem had just spoken the Lord's prayer and the evil spirit had been exorcised.

Hakeem, meanwhile, approached. Deron expected him to stand before him in his line of sight, but he instead took a seat beside him against the wall. Together they stared off into the abyss.

"Never really got used to sitting on concrete," Hakeem spoke after many moments of lingering silence.

Deron said nothing. He continued to stare, now following the pacing Merlin with his gaze, back and forth, back and forth, like a model train on an endless loop, no station to call home, only destined to stop once its power was drained.

"Nope, never did," Hakeem continued, like Deron was his shadow and being ignored was perfectly acceptable because that's what shadows did: come out when things were bright; stay hidden otherwise, in the darkness of the night, whenever they'd lost the fight.

"On my knees before the Lord, I feel nothing. But on my ass, the concrete is much less forgiving. Guess it would've done me some good to hit the squat rack every once in a while."

Deron muffled a chuckle. He was listening. When Hakeem talked, he knew better than to not. It was just what to say back that his mind couldn't propagate.

"For some reason though, I don't think the ass pain is what is troubling you, Deron. No, I think it is something much deeper than that. Something perhaps to do with that chain you're holding."

For the first time, Deron's eyes moved into near focus. He had the chain in his left hand, gripping it softly in his half-closed fist. He hadn't even realized he was still holding it.

"That's part of it, yeah," he said, still looking forward. "This chain was given to me by my girlfriend. Well, ex-girlfriend, I guess. She left on a boat almost four years ago now. Her name was Kimmy."

Hakeem looked at him but gave no response. Deron thought he might, but Hakeem was simply waiting for him to continue, to reveal his story, a story he had kept so secret to all but those who knew him best. And even to them, he had never admitted how deeply he'd been hurt. They probably sensed it, could probably see it in his eyes or tell by his issues with addiction. But he'd never spoken it aloud until now, where it flowed so easily, it was almost like it had never been a secret at all.

"I loved her, Hakeem. I really, really did. And a part of me still loves her. I try to tell myself otherwise, but it's true. And today—today I thought that maybe, for the first time since she'd left, I'd found someone who might be able to fill that gaping hole in my heart, who might be able to make life feel livable again. And it blew up in my face."

"And how did that make you feel?" Hakeem asked, his eyes once again forward with Deron's now.

"I don't know. Angry at first. I know there's no point in feeling angry. It won't help. But at the same time, I don't know how else to feel. It's all so confusing. I just … I don't know what to do, Hakeem. I just really don't know anymore. What should I do?"

In that instant, Hakeem rose from his seat, slowly and painstakingly, his knee cracking and his mouth giving off a half grunt of strained effort. He didn't even look at Deron, but he said in that moment the exact words he needed to hear.

"Laugh or cry, brother." He nodded his head like he was agreeing with himself, looking into the beyond, like the answer was out there and he was just a puppet reciting a divine message. "Laugh or cry. But one way or the other, release yourself from this tension. It won't make you whole, but it's the first step to recovery."

For the first time, Deron's eyes shifted to Hakeem, but the older man was already beginning his march away. "C'mon, Merlin," he called. "It's time to go inside." And like a dog, Merlin followed, snapping out of his spell. Deron watched until they went into the building, and once again, he was alone.

He dropped the chain and put his head down by his knees. He was alone. And he felt alone. In a world full of trials and tribulations, in a world full of pain and suffering, he felt like he had entered the last frontier, only instead of finding a land of milk and honey, he'd found a barren wasteland. He felt like he'd built the most comforting fire, only instead of heating him through the night, it had burned down his home. He felt like what he'd felt like on many a day since she'd left. Beaten. Broken. Alone and afraid. He felt like if the gorge was large enough, he could cry a river of tears.

And this time, he didn't try to hold them in.

It came slowly at first, a few sniffles and then a few drops, until suddenly, he was weeping in uncontrollable sobs, years and years of emotions pouring out of him unrelentingly like an overfilled glass, for all the loss, all the pain, all of the mistakes. He cried and cried for what felt like hours until his tear ducts had been drained. And when he was done mourning his losses, he kissed the gold *K* and felt a sudden surge, a sudden euphoria, as goosebumps rose from his flesh like nature from the earth. Time stood still as he savoured what he would one day recognize as the most bittersweet moment of his existence.

Never in his life had he felt so powerful. Never in his life would he feel so powerful again.

CHAPTER 6

At five thirty on Monday morning, a time during which Deron Boyd was peacefully asleep, having cleansed himself of years and years of harboured emotions, Matthew Tucker was restlessly tossing and turning in his bed.

"Argh," he grunted, looking at the clock on his nightstand table. He'd been in bed since ten o'clock Sunday night, but he'd barely slept a wink. He'd barely slept this entire weekend, in fact. He'd been plenty tired enough to, he just hadn't been able to get his mind to stop racing, not tonight and not the night before either, not since he'd been given his Monday assignment.

He took a deep breath, transitioned to his back, and stared up at the ceiling, thinking, for probably the hundredth time, about the call he had received, knowing it would do him no good to keep dwelling on it but feeling powerless to stop himself.

The call had come in at around nine thirty Saturday night, just as he was settling in with a nice glass of wine and preparing to play some online chess. The regional blitz tournament was next weekend, and he really wanted to go on to nationals. He'd been something of a prodigy in his youth, had lost some love for the game as he'd gotten older, had abandoned the game entirely when he was sent to the Camp, but had rediscovered his passion in the past couple of years. Sometimes you don't know what you've got until it's gone, and for him, chess filled the role of tactical de-stressor, something that could help keep his mind sharp for work in the guards but with a lot less pressure than his real-life occupation. If he made a mistake on the chessboard, he could laugh it off, learn from it, and be better for it the next time. If he made a mistake on the job, he could have hell to pay or worse.

That was why the phone call had scared him half to death. As soon as he saw the caller ID flash "Commander Martins," he knew something bad had happened. For the commander to call him at nine thirty at night on a weekend the matter had to be serious.

On the first ring, he nearly dropped his wine glass as his mind scrambled to come up with potential reasons for the call. *Had* he made a mistake? He couldn't think of one. Unless—

Ring!

Unless it had something to do with Mike "Junior" Berkowitz. Had the supervisor decided to report him after all? Is that what this was about?

Ring!

Or, his mind flashed, *maybe it's even worse! Maybe they overheard me talking to Junior about keeping his mouth shut. Maybe they thought I was talking bad about the Utopia, saying he could be punished for speaking how he did. I didn't speak until we left the Camp, but maybe they have the vans bugged. Maybe they have our fucking minds bugged for all we know!*

Ring!

He only had one left. And there was no question of not answering.

"Hello?" he said delicately, a little afraid of the voice on the other side.

"Hey, Tucker, it's Commander Martins. Sorry to call you so late on a Saturday, but I'll get straight to the point. There's been an incident."

Incident! Incident? His first reaction was the incident must have involved him, but that didn't quite make sense. He couldn't think of anything he had done that could be perceived as unorderly besides the conversation in the van, and he didn't think a talk like that could be classified as an incident. Maybe this didn't have anything to do with him at all. He started to feel a bit encouraged, although he was far from at ease. Whatever this was, he was still sure it was bad news.

"I'm sorry to hear that," was all his jumbled mind could think to say.

"Yes. It's bad, Tucker. I'll spare you the details, but the crux of the story is a guard shot a camper at one of the sawmill plants this afternoon. He's been locked up, pending trial, and as you know, murder trials get expediated. If all goes as expected, he'll be on the stand Monday morning."

"Jesus!"

"Jesus is right, Tucker. I'm not a religious man, but according to the reports, this man would need Jesus, Moses, and about six or seven miracles to save him now. Cameras caught it all, and if they hadn't, about twenty witnesses saw everything, including the plant's forewoman. This is about as open and shut as a case can be." Matt was starting to see where this was going. "Anyway, I'm calling you, Tucker, because the trial is going to take place at the Wexin District Courthouse, and I know that's your assignment. Just wanted to give you a heads up that this could be a tough one."

"I appreciate that, Commander," he said, hoping *that* was the punchline. It would be tough to watch a fellow guard get convicted, especially having been there himself, but if that was all it was, it was nothing compared to what he thought this call could have been, something the equivalent of a fried Junior burger with a side of Tucker fries. At least he didn't know *this* guard. "That won't be easy to watch, but I appreciate you giving me the chance to prepare."

"Yeah, well, you're going to appreciate me a lot less in a minute, Tucker, so hold your horses before you go about thanking me too much."

And that was the moment the fright truly set in, the moment his stomach dropped and his blood began to run cold. He'd been hoping that was all, but somewhere inside, he'd known that it wasn't. The Commander wouldn't have called him at nine thirty on a Saturday night just because a guard was being tried, even if it was for murder. He'd seen that movie a few times before already. It wasn't a noteworthy script.

He'd only call if he, Tucker, was about to be a main actor in the saga.

"What?"

"The guard—his name's Gregory Zimmer. He's thirty-eight years old, and he's already done a ten-year stint in the Camp. The victim rushed him apparently, but he was a smaller man with known mental health issues, and he didn't have a weapon. He knows he's going to be sentenced until he's sixty, and he also knows he's not going to last in there for that long.

He's going to choose death, Matt. And you've been assigned to watch over his execution."

Matt's mouth went dry, and his hand started to tremble. His head felt light enough that it might just float away, and as things stood right now, he wouldn't have minded that one bit.

"Tucker? You still there?

"Yeah," he replied. He sat down on the couch and shook his head in an effort to regain his composure. He put his wine glass down and started to rub his eyes. Suddenly, the red liquid seemed far less appealing to his unsettled stomach. "Yeah, sorry. Just trying to process. I've never been involved in a ... you know, euthanasia before."

"Understandable, Tucker, that's why I called you. Executions are tough, especially if it's your first."

Execution, he thought. God did he wish Martins would stop using that word. He much preferred euthanasia. It sounded a lot more civilized.

"I hope I didn't ruin your weekend."

"No, not at all, Commander. Thank you for letting me know ahead of time."

"You're welcome."

The commander then gave Matt a few administrative instructions that he could only bring himself to listen to out of fear of being punished if he did not follow them exactly. He then hung up the phone after asking Matt how his chess game was looking. Matt told him it was going fine, but he hadn't played particularly well that night. His focus just wasn't there.

As he finished recounting the closing minutes of his Saturday night, Matt rolled across his double mattress from one side to the other, hugging the sheets, twisting and turning them under his body so he was trapped in a cocoon. The air conditioner chilled his apartment to the optimal degree. His blinds were thick, blocking out any light that might try to sneak through the window. Physically, the conditions couldn't have been more ripe for sleep.

"Just relax," he said, closing his eyes. "You can still get a few hours if you just relax."

But he couldn't fall into a deep sleep for more than twenty minutes at a time.

THE UTOPIA

***

AT SEVEN THIRTY, HIS alarm went off, and it was time to get up for real. His previously shut eyes flashed open with the same jolt of fear he felt every weekday morning when the blaring sound of the alarm heightened his already hyperactive senses.

Beep! Beep! In many ways, he hated that noise, telling him the time for rest was over, telling him where to be, reminding him that he was subject to the will of the Utopia, reminding him he had to be on his toes at all times. Many a morning he had wanted to take that alarm clock and fastball pitch it against the wall, but today was not one of those days.

Today, he rolled over and lightly tapped the off button. Today, the alarm was less of a burden and more of a godsend. Today, he was happy for it to finally put him out of his misery.

He rose from his bed and headed toward the kitchen. His apartment was a typical Utopian style setup, the layout, in the dynamics of Fibonacci's key, crafted and connected to fully optimize the space.

He heated up a pan and cracked a couple eggs. His breakfast of champions usually consisted of eggs plus some toast and maybe a smoothie of some kind if he was feeling a bit frisky. Today, the eggs and toast would do just fine. He wasn't particularly hungry.

He sat down at the kitchen table after he had prepared his meal, eating quickly and constantly checking the clock. He had plenty of time. Technically, he didn't have to be in the courtroom until the session started at nine o'clock. But he liked to be at least ten to fifteen minutes early, and in the Utopia, no matter how much time you had, you always felt like you were running late. At least he did, anyway, knowing what the punishment could be for tardiness.

"X-12, start the shower," he yelled as he stood up to clean his plate. "Medium heat."

"Starting shower," the automated voice responded. He heard the water start to run in his bathroom.

X-12 was his apartment's home operating system, a standard feature of all Utopian homes. You could program the voice and even the name; Matt chose X-12 to remind himself he was talking to a computer and not a person. It could control basically anything in the home if you gave it instructions. It was convenient as hell and also highly suspect. Matt was pretty sure, almost positive actually, that the computer kept a recording of everything you said. Key words likely alerted the State to monitor your conversations, maybe even activated a hidden camera so minute it could be concealed anywhere on the premises. He wouldn't put it past them, and it was something to always remember, but he had also developed an immunity to caring over the years. He didn't have people over often and never spoke any pejoratives or slander against the State. Plus, there was nothing he could do about it even if he wanted to. He could turn the program off, but that itself would have been suspicious.

He showered efficiently, dried himself off, and then changed into his finest red guard uniform. He added his holstered weapon, his handcuffs, and his radio to his belt, and once he was satisfied with his look in the mirror, he commanded X-12 to turn off everything before he headed out the door. It was only 8:12. He would be at the courtroom as much as half an hour early, but there was no point in waiting. He would just grow more anxious sitting around his apartment.

He took the stairs from the third floor down to the first and exited through the lobby. Outside, the sun was shining, and the streets were at their typical level of congestion. The extended bike lanes were packed with riders, the car lanes less so with only busses, service vans, trucks, and emergency vehicles.

In the Utopia, there were four main forms of on-road vehicle, and none of them were your typical private car. Personal-use vehicles were not a thing in this world; therefore, the only cars on the roads were ones that provided services to the greater community. Busses took people to and from certain central locations (and to outskirt travel spots occasionally, like the zoo or certain museums), service vans went around fixing issues or providing other useful functions such as collecting garbage, and trucks dropped off goods. The purpose of emergency vehicles is self-explanatory.

Otherwise, for short distances, people got to where they needed to go either by electric bicycle—a staple of Utopian travel and Matt's personal favourite—or walking, which was very possible in the Utopia; the weather was almost always nice, and the Utopia tried to place you as close as possible to where you are starting your first job out of school. Of course, you could end up changing jobs, but even then, a lot of times, you could trade apartments with someone to move closer to your workplace.

On each main road, there were two bike lanes on either side of the street. Electric bicycles, which actually looked more like tiny carriages than bicycles, were fastened into the road like horses on a carousal ride, spaced at equal distances apart. They moved along the bike path automatically at any green light. People could hop on or off any time the carriages stopped. If someone was going north and needed to transfer west, they hopped out of the carriage, walked to the nearest west-travelling bike lane, and hopped on for a ride.

Travelling this way could get you pretty much anywhere you wanted to go in the big city. In a worst-case scenario where your workplace was on a smaller side street or in a less-populated area, you could still take the electric bikes most of the way, then either walk the remaining duration or scan your ID to borrow a real bike—a traditional bike stand was present at the end of nearly every important arterial road—and ride the rest of the way. It was a one-of-a-kind system not seen anywhere else in the world, or so the Utopia claimed.

For long distance travel, which was almost never necessary because most meetings could take place through video conferencing and the same stores and goods were present in each and every city, there were two bullet trains that ran loops through every major city and district in the Utopia. Each train started on an opposite end, and each could do the full loop in less than half a day. If an overnight stay was required, each station had hospitality beds for that exact situation.

If you physically could not walk due to old age, injury, or disability, your electric wheelchair could get you most places via the sidewalk. Accommodations were made so that you could work from home or somewhere nearby, and there was always a General Store in every metropolitan neighbourhood. If you were blind, there were special phone applications that allowed you to do a job regardless and could lead you around town as if you had a seeing-eye dog in a pinch. If there was any other problem that would prevent you from potentially working or leaving home, you could comfortably bet your soul that the Utopia had thought about it and found a solution.

Matt stared through the road traffic, considering whether or not to try to hop on a bike. He loved the relaxing feeling of lying back in a carriage, the chill of the slight morning breeze flowing through his blond locks as he rode toward his destination. His prospects for the day always felt a lot brighter after that.

Today, however, he decided not to ride. He was on the north side of the street, needing to head east, and from his vantage point, he couldn't spot a free bike. He could cross the street to get a better look, but there wasn't much of a point. The courthouse was only a few blocks from his apartment, and it was also on the north side. Today, it made more sense to walk. Today, no matter how comfortable the carriage or how nice the breeze, he wouldn't feel relaxed.

He strolled along the sidewalk at an economical pace, half his body wanting to get there as quickly as possible, and the other half wanting to avoid the place for as long as he could. In the end, he guessed it made no difference what his body wanted. The result would all be the same.

On his route, he passed the typical Utopian storefronts: a Pub, an office building, another apartment complex, a General Store (that one almost took up half a block by itself, which was not uncommon; they did supply just about every good you could think of, after all), a gym, a medical clinic/pharmacy, and a grooming salon. The only shop that was out of the ordinary was a tattoo parlour, the employees of which had been given special designation for their rare artistic talents. Matt had frequented the place and could attest to such. Chanda had done the half-sleeve consisting of a dove, a lantern, and flowers as filler on his upper right arm, and over a year later, he was still enamoured with it.

Of course, that became the last thing on his mind the moment he arrived at the courthouse.

"Today's gonna be a bad one," he muttered to himself under his breath, looking at the judicial edifice in front of him. Normally, he didn't mind climbing those steps. The courthouse designs were probably the most aesthetically pleasing in the Utopia, and there was this odd comfort he had gained walking into that building, knowing it was someone else that would be up on that stand and not him, knowing that other being would be on the receiving end of any punishment.

It was selfish, a bit immoral even, but it was a developed defence mechanism, and he preferred it to being perpetually afraid. It was the only way to do this job and still go home at night with some level of sanity intact.

Today, that line of thinking wouldn't work, however. Today, he was afraid, afraid for a fellow guard and the decision he would make, and afraid for himself and what he would have to do. But there was nothing he could do about it.

He climbed the steps the same way he had since he'd first been assigned this job, and when he got to the revolving front door, he entered without hesitation. Fear was a weak enough emotion when it was hidden. Showing fear outwardly was a strike against your competency as a guard. And he knew very well what happened to the incompetent.

"Morning, Matt," said a woman as he entered.

"Morning, Elle," he said back with a smile that was a lot faker than her own. It was partly because of his anxiety but partly because of her. There was something about her he just didn't enjoy.

"Beautiful day out, isn't it?" she exclaimed, bits of the candy bar she was munching on flying out of her mouth.

Every time he saw her eating, it was always a candy bar or some other junk. And sometimes the chocolate stains on her lips would remain there for hours.

"Indeed," he replied with another fake smile. *Same as every other day.*

"I just love this weather! I'm going to go to the park later and enjoy the swing set!" And she began to chuckle to herself, this time at least making a half-hearted attempt to cover up her mouth.

"Sounds like fun," he said, indifferently.

"It is! And it'll be great exercise!"

He didn't respond. Instead, he just approached her station. She was seated behind a monitor in the middle of the front foyer. To her right was a glass barrier with a single set of doors. It acted as the exit. To her left was a conveyor belt set up with bins like security in a western-world airport. Attached to that was a full-body x-ray scanner, and just beyond was another glass barrier without the set of doors.

Just in front of the conveyor belt was an ID scanner, and Matt tapped his card. This was the only part of the operation he considered necessary, a way to prove to the State that you had signed in for work or had showed up for your arraignment if you were on the other side of the law. No one was going to dare try sneaking in anything suspicious, and even if they did, the plethora of cameras abound would catch them anyway. The x-ray machine was overkill, but c'est la vie.

He walked into the x-ray machine without dropping anything in the bin (the conveyor belt was only necessary if you brought in a backpack or other form of package), extended his arms as instructed, and waited for the word.

"You're all good, Matt!" Elle said with vibrant enthusiasm.

Matt exited the machine, turned with another fake smile, and gave her a thumbs up. He didn't feel like speaking. Something about Elle was just off-putting, and it wasn't solely her lack of table manners.

Mostly, he found her just too damn bubbly for someone who worked all day around criminals and authorities.

"Have a great day!" she yelled with a wave. "I'll see you later!"

"You too." Matt waved back. He smiled a bit more genuinely this time. He was happy to leave her behind along that proverbial dusty road. But his happiness was short-lived.

The anxiety returned as that dusty trail became a tile-laden floor. The courthouse consisted of only one long hallway with four rooms attached. The first two rooms were for morning sessions, the latter two were in case the morning sessions ran late and were not available for the afternoon or in case of other administrative or technical issues. Rarely were more than four cases total heard daily. The system was maximally efficient so there was essentially no backlog, and the scare tactics generally led to an unprecedently low crime rate. The fact that the Ten State Commandments essentially made up the entire criminal/civil code helped as well.

Right now, none of that mattered to Matt at all.

Halfway down the hallway, TV monitors flashed on both the left and right. He chose to view the left, but either would have provided him with the same information. It was the list of cases on the docket, the first line of which read "Courtroom #1 – Utopia vs Zimmer" with a start time of nine o'clock. In the top righthand corner it showed the current time. It was 8:37. His body began to shiver.

THE UTOPIA

"Settle down," he told himself lightly under his breath. There was no one around to see him sweat, but if a tree fell in the forest with no one around to hear it, he was pretty sure it still made a sound. "There's no reason to be nervous. It's not you on the stand. You're just doing your job. This is just a normal day." But his words were a hard sell. This was not a normal day. He was going to have to watch a man die today. And it was hard to accept that as just part of the course of business.

He looked at the double doors just left of the monitor. To the left of those was a bench. He had two options. He could sit outside and wait, or he could enter now before the others arrived. Neither option felt great, but he guessed he preferred the second. At least that way there'd be no chance to meet the defendant beforehand. It was best not to get acquainted.

"Okay," he sighed under his breath. He grabbed the door handle with an unsteady hand. His nerves were acting up, but at least he could go inside and try to settle down.

He pulled the door open and headed into the courtroom, the same courtroom where just a few days earlier, he had watched a stoic fellow named Deron Boyd get convicted on all charges. It was the last case he'd witnessed—and, oh, how much better he had felt on that day. He needed a few minutes alone to remind himself that no matter how this went, it wouldn't be his fault.

But when he stepped inside, they were all already there.

And for a split second, so short that if the moment had been any quicker, it would have ignored the rules of time, Matt felt complete and utter panic when he saw those faces, like they were the faces of macabre ghosts, readying to drag him down into the underworld, an underworld filled with a collection of lost souls, left to roam eternally in the sound of silence, none of them ever to see the light of day again.

All simultaneously turned to look at him in eerie synchronization as he stepped into the courtroom, all with the same stare, all with the same look of impending doom on their faces, all possessed by the same thought.

The thought hung in the air for just a fraction of a moment, and then just like that, it was gone. Just like that, it was over. Their eyes transitioned back to their previous indulgences, and they went back to being human.

Only later would he realize that *he* was actually the ghost—a blond-haired reaper in an all-red robe, the harbinger of death and the gatekeeper of freedom, collecting the souls of both the living and the dead.

He walked behind the back row of seating and only turned when he arrived at the far wall. He could have walked down the middle aisle, but that might have once again garnered their attention. He was much more keen on sliding silently into place.

He studied the room on his journey and discovered, unsurprisingly, that the familiar players were all here: Judge Sanderson with his shaved head and reading glasses; Prosecutor Winthrop in her same skirt and suit jacket; Court Reporter May, one year from retirement; and Guard Witsel, who transferred the prisoners and took care of them until Matt arrived. Seeing them all now, no longer as ghosts but as co-conspirators in the cause, he started to feel a little more comfortable.

As he approached his familiar spot (a folding chair just off to the right of the defendant's table), the other guard stood up to meet him. They shook hands and whispered quietly.

"Hey, Matty. I'd ask you how you're doing, but I think I know the answer."

"Yeah, let's just say I haven't exactly been looking forward to this all weekend, Marshall. What's with everyone being here so early?"

"Not sure to be honest. I guess folks were just antsy to get this over with."

"I guess so."

"Anyway, all the best to you, Matty. And I hope this goes without saying, but any choice this man makes is not on you. Remember that."

"I'll try, Marshall. I'll try."

"Alright then."

They shook hands again in conclusion, and then Marshall Witsel made his way out of the courtroom. Matt watched him go and thought that never in his life had he seen the man move so quickly.

He took one last look around the room before he made his next move. It was quiet at the moment. The jurors were sitting in their box, all staring separate ways. The judge had his head buried, as did the prosecutor. There were no news reporters fussing about, and despite the gravity of what was about to take place, he wasn't overly surprised. Things that happened at the Camp had a tendency not to leak, at least in the short-term. And of course, no crews were allowed to actually enter the Camp and monitor for breaking news. No, what happened here today would likely remain unknown for at least a little while, unless somebody here talked. And he could think of only one person who might.

His eyes glanced down, toward the only source of noise in the entirety of the room. Less than ten feet away sat a woman in the middle of the first-row bench on the defendant's side. She was whispering quietly to Greg Zimmer, who was staring at her blankly, seemingly lost in his own thoughts.

On another day, Matt would have told her she couldn't do that, that if she kept speaking to the defendant, she would be escorted from the courtroom. But today, he didn't say a word. He just passed through the gateway separating the action from the audience and sat down in his chair.

And that's when it started.

"Ladies and gentlemen." The voice was Judge Sanderson's, a deep, booming voice that echoed throughout the room. "It appears that all of the necessary parties are in the room. As such, I'm proposing we start early if there are no objections. That way"—*We're not wasting our remaining hours,* the voice in Matt's head screamed—"we are not all just sitting here anxiously waiting for something to happen. Any objections?"

"Yes!" spoke a voice, the only one in the room whose opinion didn't matter. It was the woman sitting behind Zimmer. She stood up and raised her hand like a schoolchild who just couldn't wait to tell the class the correct answer.

"With all due respect, Miss," the judge replied calmly, "that is not how this works. If the defendant himself objects, then we will sit here for the next twenty minutes or so collecting our thoughts, but you yourself are not a party to this process. That decision is his and his alone."

"Well, fine then. Tell them, Greg," she ordered commandingly.

Greg, who had been looking at her with an expression bordering on reproach since she'd stood up to speak for him, turned toward the judge and said only a few words. "I'm good to begin."

"Greg!" she shouted exasperatedly.

"Miss, please." Judge Sanderson slammed his gavel for order. "If you cannot keep yourself in check, I'm going to have to ask you to leave this courtroom."

"Don't bother," she scolded. Her voice was still defiant, but emotionally, she had changed. She was now close to tears. "I'm leaving. You hear that, Greg! I'm going! I'm not going to just sit here and watch you give up!"

Now the tears had started, and she didn't try to hold them in. She rose from the bench and headed for the exit.

"Belinda," Greg called after her, but she was gone, burrowing down the aisle like a thoroughbred at the Kentucky Derby, all the way down the back row until she was out the door.

Greg looked down, dejected, tired and broken and close to tears himself. It was the look of a man who had just lost his last glimmer of hope, the look of a man who had come up short in his life just one too many times.

When Matt saw that look, he nearly broke himself. He wasn't one to cry often. He hadn't when he himself had been sentenced to the Camp, hadn't when he had broken his arm falling off the playground, hadn't when his favourite teacher had passed suddenly because of a stroke.

But now he was on the brink, for reasons unknown. Perhaps the world had finally worn him down enough to crack him. Perhaps he saw his own future in this man before him. Perhaps it was just happenstance and there was no reason at all. He would never know why, only that he felt it. He had to bring her back.

"I'll get her," he said, rising to his feet. Greg looked over, blankly at first, but then he simply nodded. Matt knew to seize the moment and started to make his way.

"Guard Tucker?" the judge spoke up questioningly.

"I'll be back, Judge," he replied, not looking back. "Just want to make sure she doesn't stir up any trouble. Don't worry about me; I'm not needed anyway. You can start without me."

He paused at the doors and looked back just long enough to hear the judge's response. "Very well," he said. "We'll start without you."

"Great," he said appreciatively. "Thank you, Judge. I'll be right back, I promise. You won't even notice I'm gone."

He hustled out the door, and when he saw her, she was in tears, sitting on the bench just outside the courtroom. Her face was covered by her flat palms, but drops were falling through the cracks of her fingers. Her sobs echoed through the hallway. She looked like a broken wreck.

Down the hall, the numbers had increased since his little detour, and they appeared to be enjoying the show. A few were openly staring, and a couple more were looking on with more illusory glances. They weren't very good magicians.

"If you folks have somewhere to be, get to it," he called out. He wasn't sure why he said it, his mouth just kind of *did*. But if his purpose was to redirect them, his command did the charm. People didn't always respect the guards as humans, but they respected their authority. Growls from a red uniform did wonders to herd the sheep.

Matt sat down next to the woman and started to stare forward. He didn't know what to say, nor was he sure he even *wanted* to say anything. He hadn't felt this much confusion since his days before the Camp.

He thought back to those times. He had worked as a landscaper taking care of city parks, always showing up a bit late and heading out a bit early, leaving an uncut patch of grass or a tree half trimmed. He'd had a backwards hat and an anything goes, party-like-you-mean-it attitude. He'd chased girls and struck out, but that was alright because you couldn't hit the homerun if you didn't swing for the fences. He was carefree in those days. Some would call him careless. But he'd been happy then. He hadn't been sure of much else, like what he really wanted to do in life or how he was going to get there, but he had been sure of that. He'd been enjoying his life and all that came with it. Until they'd sent him away, sent him away and taught him that life was not all fun and games and rainbows and sunshine, sent him away like they wanted to do to that guard, only the man had other plans.

"It's not fair," the woman said. She sniffled her nose and began to wipe her eyes with the cuff of her long-sleeve shirt. "I know what he did, but it never would have happened if they hadn't forced him to become a member of the guards in the first place. He was never cut out for it."

She didn't look at Matt, and he didn't look at her. He thought about her statement and recognized her point. When he had first been assigned, he himself had questioned if he would make it in the guards, if he could handle the responsibility, the authority, the pressure. For someone like him, the challenge seemed monumental.

He had survived, but not without hiccups. And even to this day, some five years later, he still wondered what would have happened if he'd been given another role, one that wasn't just picking up prisoners and bringing them to the Camp, one that was consistently like the role he had today.

His life since his release hadn't been easy, but it had been simple: drive from A to B and then back to A, enjoy some wine in the evening, read or play chess, go on a date once or twice a month, and surf on the weekends. This lifestyle hadn't brought back his same youthful bliss, but it had brought him comfort, major feelings of relief, and a minor sense of purpose. And at thirty years old, that was really all he wanted.

But what if his role had repeatedly been the one he had today? What if for five years, his job had been to sit back with some popcorn and watch people die, listen to them beg for their lives as he stood there and did nothing? Would he have been able to adjust, or would it have shattered his very essence? He'd seen many convicted, and he'd seen a few choose death. But never in his life had he been the one to watch over that process. Never in his life would he have envisioned himself capable of that. But what choice did he have? Maybe that was the answer.

"We don't get to choose," he mumbled, mostly to himself. He had forgotten where he was and his purpose for being here. "We have to do what we have to do."

For the first time, she looked at him, seeing his words through her own lens, as an answer to her paradigm, not the words of a lost man.

"And what if you *could* choose?" she said. "Would you still be here? Watching people make the hardest decision of their life in their lowest moment? Watching them suffer? Is this what you would do?" Fresh tears were in her eyes, hanging on her eyelids like raindrops off the banister. The initial storm was over, but the earth had yet to dry, and the clouds were still threatening.

He looked at her for the first time. *He killed someone,* he thought. *You can't possibly just ignore that!*

But his mind was coherent enough to know she wouldn't hear it.

Whoever this woman was, she clearly loved this man.

His gaze on her held firm, analyzing her being. She was a skinny woman with a round face and wiry black hair. Her tears weren't helping, but even without them, he could see she wasn't pretty. He didn't care for the way she berated him, nor the way she insistently passed judgment on his character. This wasn't his fault. He hadn't made Greg pull the trigger, nor had he charged him with the crime. To treat him this way was fundamentally unjust, and yet he couldn't help but like her.

"We don't get to choose," he repeated. His eyes were sad and distant. He wanted to say more, but he couldn't bring himself to further justify his case. Somewhere deep down, he knew there was always another option, always another choice. But, oh, it was so much easier to tell himself there wasn't, to blame someone else instead.

"But *you* do," he said, bringing his eyes back into focus. "If this is his last day, you get to choose: either be there for him or have his last memory be of the one who loves him most leaving him behind."

At that, she exploded into tears, and he felt no remorse. What he said was unfair, but none of this was fair. The truth is almost never fair, but someone had to say it. If she didn't go back in, she would regret it for the rest of her life. He was saying it for her.

"I don't want to lose him," she sobbed. "I don't know what I'm going to do without him."

The words came out strained, and then she cried even harder, perhaps the hardest Matt had ever seen anyone cry before. For fifteen minutes, she cried, by herself at first, until eventually, she needed comfort and grabbed onto Matt. He let her sob into his uniform until the last tears were dropped.

"I'm sorry," she said, after finally regaining some measure of composure. "I know this isn't your fault, but it's all so overwhelming."

"It's alright," he said back. "You have every right to be upset. I wish things could be different."

She nodded her head as she looked into his eyes. "But they're not," she whispered with a certain air of acceptance she hadn't previously shown.

"That's right," he agreed. "So why don't we go back in there and see what happens. I can't promise a miracle. In fact, I'll tell you right now it won't happen. But maybe if he sees you, he'll choose to go to the Camp. It's not the result you want, but it's better than the result you expect. At least that way, you can be together again one day."

"Yeah. Yeah, okay. Thanks." She forced a smile and stood up. Matt did as well. "I'm just going to run to the washroom quickly, but I'll be right back."

"I'll wait for you," he said.

"Okay."

She left. He watched her go, and as he did, his mind inevitably wandered to her question. What would he do if he did have the power, if he didn't have to be a guard? Since the day of his release, he had never really thought about it because it had never been an option.

One day it will be.

But that day wasn't today. Nor was that day any day soon. And until it was soon, he decided it was probably best not to think about it. The *what ifs* would drive him mad with longing.

After ten minutes of her being gone, he started to get concerned, but just then, she reappeared, looking a little refreshed. To him, she still wasn't pretty, but her eyes had a bit of a sparkle in them that he hadn't previously noticed. Perhaps she'd been crying again.

"Okay. I think I'm ready," she said. She looked anything but, but he wouldn't disagree.

"Let's go," he said.

And they both did together.

***

WHEN THEY STEPPED BACK into the courtroom, everything was quiet, and Matt knew right away exactly what that meant. The evidence had been presented and uploaded. The defence had refuted (or likely, in this case, abstained from doing so), and all that was left was to hear the decision—the decision of the Computer.

That was bad news in the age-old adage. The good news for Greg was that Belinda had returned, and when he realized that, he smiled. Despite his stubbornness, his love had not abandoned him, and there was something beautiful in that, perhaps enough to let his soul rest in peace.

Belinda, for her part, smiled at him too—a much more forced smile but a smile nonetheless. It was a smile that said, *I'm still mad at you Mister, but this isn't the time or place*. It was a smile that showed she was with him to the end.

It was a heartwarming moment that might have affected even the most calamitous of souls. Matt's was not one of them. He saw the magic of the moment, but his mouth formed no grin. He, for one, was not in the smiling mood.

Belinda returned to her seat in the front row; Matt returned to his chair, the same chair he had watched many a trial from, watched as men and woman alike were condemned to years of hard labour, watched with zero care or concern or sense of responsibility.

Oh, how things had changed.

"Gregory Zimmer."

The robotic voice sent a chill down Matt's spine, so deep that it had him literally shaking in his shoes. He knew the next words. He had heard some variation of them repeated a thousand times, only this time, they would have a distorted overtone, a bit more bite and a little more sting, like even though they were directed at Greg Zimmer, they were really meant for him. He felt how he had when the Computer had said his own name, only this was somehow worse.

"The Crime Network has analyzed the evidence. Upon review of the surveillance tapes, there is little room left for any reasonable doubt. As such, the Crime Network finds you guilty of killing a fellow Utopian. Your sentence, in line with the mandates, is life until age sixty. Thus concludes the Crime Network's analysis in the case of *The Utopia versus Zimmer*. The review of this decision shall now be conducted by the jury, and if the decision is upheld, Mr. Zimmer's options shall be read to him by the judge. That is all. End transmission."

"And what says the jury?" the judge asked. He sounded lethargic, like his voice had a daily word count and he felt sorry to waste any of his quota on such an asinine bit of procedure because he knew there was no point.

All three held up their guilty cards to the surprise of no one in the room. Even Belinda didn't gripe (she had started to tear up again, but her mouth remained stapled). They had all known this was coming.

It was what happened next that was the moment of truth.

"Very well," the judge spoke. He then turned to Greg. "The Crime Network and the jury have spoken, Mr. Zimmer, and the verdict is guilty. I believe you are aware of the decision that comes next, but I will read the statement anyway as is required by the State."

Zimmer nodded. The judge read. "You, sir or madam, have been found guilty of committing one or more crimes against the State and/or people of the Utopia. By law you are given the following choice: you may serve your sentence in the State Work Camp, whereby upon release, you will be assigned to the guards or other field of volunteering for a period of no less than ten years, barring exceptional circumstances, including but not limited to reaching the retirement age of sixty, or, as an alternative to the State Work Camp, you may elect to be put to death by euthanasia. If you do not make a choice, you will, by default, be sent to the State Work Camp. Please make your selection now."

The whole room was on pins and needles. The tension was so thick that the knife would damn well need to be a katana if it wanted to even make a dent let alone a cut. If Bruce Buffer had lived in the Utopia, this was the moment he would've yelled his most famous catch phrase.

It was time.

"Greg," Belinda whispered. She was starting to sob, but so far, she was keeping the hysteria out of her voice, not that it really mattered. It was doubtful the judge would have disciplined her for this.

Greg turned to look at her.

"Please," she said. "Just take the years. I know it will be hard, but it won't be forever. And when you get out, we can still be together. We've made it through this once before, and we can do it again. Please, Greg."

Her speech was valiant, and just for a moment, Matt allowed himself to think it might work. Greg himself began to tear, the first real sign of inner struggle anyone had witnessed since his arrest. Maybe there was a chance. Maybe he wouldn't choose death after all.

But it was more blind hope than anything. This was always going to be Greg's choice. Matt had known it from the moment he saw the man. He was not going back.

"I love you, Belinda," he whispered. Now tears were falling, streaming down his face. "I never meant to hurt Murphy, and I never meant to hurt you. I'm sorry."

"It's okay, Greg," she sniffled back, her own tears flooding her face. "It was an honest mistake. Everyone knows that. It's okay. There's still time to make up for it."

When Matt reflected later, he realized that if there were a single moment he could have changed, that would have been the one. He would have rewound time and interfered with the sequence in any way he could—thrown his chair, told her to leave, smacked Greg across the face, anything to change how Belinda felt in that moment.

Because in that moment, her lips curled upwards, and she actually smiled, genuinely smiled, smiled with an honest belief that he might actually choose the years. But that was never going to happen.

"I love you, Greg."

"And I love you, Belinda. I'm sorry."

He stood up, turned and faced the judge, then matter-of-factly spoke the words that ended his own life.

"Death," he said.

And somewhere, a dark genie granted him his wish.

***

WHAT HAPPENED NEXT WAS a tumultuous series of events that would have put a Deron Boyd blackout to shame.

It started with Belinda going into fits of anguish and rage, releasing long, agonizing sobs that penetrated the hallway and put the entire building on notice, her shouting unintelligible screeches that would haunt their eardrums long after she became just a footnote in their lives.

Matt had tried to calm her, but for Belinda, there was no coming back. A single word had set off a series of emotions that would be difficult for any human to conquer. Although she would have to learn how to if she wanted to survive.

Sometime during the howling, backup security was called. Later, Matt wouldn't remember who had called them or for what reason; all he would remember was Guard Ellen "Elle" Thomas—*Of course it had to be her,* he thought—and another guard named James Norfolk entering the room and trying to settle Belinda down.

For Elle, this meant using the brilliant line, "Oh, cheer up, it's a beautiful day out!" They were meant as words of solace, but that was right about when Belinda snapped.

"Beautiful day?! Beautiful day?! My Greg is about to be put to death and you call this a beautiful fucking day?!"

Had Greg not been there, that probably would have been the end of her. She probably would have socked Elle across the face—*God, that would have been a sight for sore eyes*—fought with no regard, and ended up the victim of a guard shooting in a plot twist so ironic, Matt wouldn't have believed it if he hadn't been there to see it.

Fortunately, he *wouldn't* see it. Right as the tension was mounting to its peak, Greg spoke up with a venomous ferocity that shocked them all back to their senses.

"Belinda! Calm down NOW!"

And she went from uncontrollable bursts of emotion to stunned silence in a matter of seconds. Her mouth clamped shut, and her tears drained almost instantly, like some almighty hand had just turned off the faucet.

"But—"

"No. This is my choice. And I'm sorry that it hurts you, but you cannot act this way. If you do something foolish, you'll end up right here with me."

"Well, maybe I want that!"

"No, sweetheart, you don't."

Time seemed to stand still as Greg then paused to assess the situation, looking to each of the three guards in the room with calculating eyes, asking himself what each of the bemused faces would do if he made his next request, deciding the answer was nothing at all.

"I'm going to go hug my Belinda," he said in a powerful voice that shook Matt to his core. It was a voice that, ten minutes prior, Matt would not have thought the man capable of producing. Belinda had said that Greg had never been cut out for the guards, and for a while, Matt had believed her. Right then, he thought he might well have made a good commander.

"I'm a man on death row with nothing to lose. I would ask that you respect that."

THE UTOPIA

And what was there to say? He simply nodded yes, and that was enough. "Thank you."

Greg went over, hugged her, and they both began to cry. There were no manic sobs, just a steady release of the remaining emotions left in their bodies. When the moment was over, Greg whispered something in Belinda's ear and began to walk away. Belinda followed him with her eyes but not with her body, and when she wept again, it was controlled and quiet. There would be no need to arrest her. Only Greg would end up in handcuffs on this day. He was chained right before Matt put him in the back of the guard van, after they had made the walk to the underground and exchanged meaningless words of thanks. Matt was thankful to Zimmer for calming the situation; Zimmer was thankful to Matt for allowing him one last hug. Neither was truly that thankful for each other.

Those were the last words they spoke before they hit the road. They drove for about fifteen minutes—though it felt more like fifteen seconds to Matt, who had been reflecting on the events that had just transpired—and were just about at Wexin District Hospital: Gregory Zimmer's final destination.

Wee-woo-wee-woo!

A siren blaring behind them is what brought Matt back to life. In his right side-view mirror, he could see it: an ambulance hard-charging with thoughts of overtaking.

Matt had already pulled onto the main hospital road but stopped his van so the vehicle could get around. It did so efficiently and then drove under an archway about fifty yards up. From where Matt was stationed, he could clearly read the acrylic sign posted over the arch. The letters made out the words Intensive Care Unit.

For a moment, Matt forgot the world as he watched the driver and a passenger scramble out of the ambulance and head for the back doors. They opened them quickly and then, along with a third person from the inside of the cabin, lifted a stretcher and brought it down onto the pavement. The person on the stretcher had some type of breathing mask on and was hooked up to a machine Matt couldn't make sense of.

Only after they had hustled the stretcher into the building did it connect with him why he was so drawn to the scene. Those people were trying to save someone who was dying. He was about to kill someone who was healthy. How to make sense of such a paradox was far beyond his scope.

God help me.

He shook his head to get rid of the thought and instead remembered the instructions Commander Martins had given him on Saturday night.

"If the man chooses death, you'll have to take him to the euthanasia section of the hospital. There's a secret entrance to get there, so you won't have to walk him through the building. I suggest you take it. Hospital staff and even some of the patients, if they see a guard with a handcuffed prisoner, they'll put the pieces together, and I doubt very much you would enjoy walking through a swarm of those accusatory glances."

Really? You sure? Sounds to me like a trip to the carnival.

"To get there, tap into the underground parking with your card and proceed to P3. There will be a guard down there who is blockading the entrance. I'm not sure who will be on duty, but whoever it is, talk to him or her. He or she will tell you what to do next."

Grand.

He looked around and studied the road. His only immediate option was to continue straight, but in about thirty yards, he'd be given a choice of left or right. Left would take him by the intensive care unit and other entrances beyond. Right would lead around the side of the building into parts unknown. His instincts were telling him the road just did one large loop around the building (the hospital had its own block in a less populated area outside the downtown core, and these streets were exclusive to it), but there was only one way to find out. He put the vehicle in motion and began to putter along.

He chose right, and about a third of the way around the loop, he found what he was looking for. A ramp led down to the underground garage, and he rolled down it to the doorway.

The garage door opened automatically as he approached. Beyond it was a median, dividing the traffic in and out. A barrier arm blocked his path but only for a moment. He tapped his ID to the scanner and passed through without a hitch.

Now came the hard part.

From P1 to P2, to his chest began to tighten. From P2 to P3, he physically began to sweat. He tried to distract himself with other thoughts like questioning why a society that had eliminated private vehicles would continue to waste so much space on parking; the spots here were sporadically filled mostly with ambulances plus a few other service vehicles sprinkled in. But distraction was hardly an effective strategy. This was just one of those things he would feel anxious about until it was over. And perhaps for a long time after that.

On P3, the layout of the floor changed. Previously, he had been given the option of left or right after descending the north-facing ramp, but here, left was the only option. He followed the path, making a left at each right angle, until he reached an arm barrier surrounded by concrete walls on both sides, dividing the room in half. Unlike the garage gate at P1, there was only one lane in and out, and unlike that gate, this one had a tollbooth occupied by a guard. The setup reminded him in some ways of his typical drive into the Camp. And, oh, how appropriate.

He rolled up to the booth, and the man inside looked back at him so stone-faced that had you asked Matt in that moment, he would have sworn the man was a prop, just some type of mannequin done up to the nines, there to frighten away any trespassers. It would have scared him half to death if he hadn't already been so afraid. And so wanting to avoid death.

"You Matthew Tucker?" he asked from the booth.

"I am," Matt answered in robotic confirmation.

"Heard you might be coming. You've never been here before, have you?"

"I have not." *Nor do I want to be now.*

"Well, here's hoping this is your first time and your last. I don't envy you, let's put it that way."

Matt said nothing, but his already worried heart was beginning to thump in his chest. If it didn't slow down soon, he would stop resenting the fact that he was here and start being thankful instead. The hospital was the exact place he would need to be.

"Here's what you're going to do. Inside is a single door leading to an elevator. Take that elevator. From this level, it's automatically programmed to go to the fifth floor. It will do so without stops. Once you get to the fifth floor, wait in the hallway for the doctor. That's all you have to do. Understood?"

Matt nodded without speaking. What was there to say, really? *Nope, don't get it, boss. Guess you're going to have to take over for me!* For some reason, he didn't think that would fly.

"Good. I'll radio the doctor and let him know you're here. You just go up to the floor and wait like I said."

Matt nodded again that he understood. The guard wished him good luck, a statement he almost scoffed at but didn't, and then Matt tapped his card and proceeded through the gate. The area he entered held just columns and empty space, and it took him but a moment to find the door he was looking for: a metal one smack dab in the middle of the east wall. He pulled up close to it and parked.

His heart was still thumping, but he did his best to ignore it and got out of the vehicle straight away. The longer he waited, the more anxious he would become. He walked to the back doors of the van with only one real thought: *I hope he doesn't try anything. Oh God, please, I hope he'll just come along.*

And despite his failure to follow scripture, God answered his prayers. When he opened the back doors, Greg was calm and serene, so much so that Matt had an inkling to remove his handcuffs but not enough jam to do it.

Greg exited the cabin and Matt shut the doors behind. Wordlessly, they then walked to the metal door, and Matt opened it for his guest. He let Greg pass through first and followed in behind. They were now standing in a ten-by-ten room with only a single elevator as décor.

Matt pressed the button, and immediately, the doors opened, almost like the elevator had been anticipating their arrival. They stepped inside.

"Fifth floor, going up," the robotic voice said.

And they turned to face the doors in that conditioned way everyone does without really understanding why—a habitual response passed down through generations for no apparent reason—just before the elevator started to move.

If only they had been conditioned on how to handle what happened next instead.

THE UTOPIA

***

WHEN THE ELEVATOR DOORS opened, the floor revealed wasn't the dungeon Matt had expected it to be. The walls were not made of cobblestone. There were no torchlights of fire or chains hanging from the ceiling. The hallway was drywalled and well lit, like a typical hospital wing, and perhaps that was appropriate. After all, no dungeon in existence sees more death than a hospital.

They stepped off the elevator and Matt looked left and then right. The setup on each side was a mirror image down to the paintings. Each corridor owned a bench, a floral arrangement, and three separate doorways. Matt had an impulse to seek out what was behind doors A, B, and C, but he didn't dare defy his orders. He would find out soon anyway.

"Sit?" he propositioned. Greg responded with a head nod. His face was stoic and, in many ways, unnerved. Looks can be deceiving, but if Matt didn't know any better, he would have sworn that Zimmer was less nervous than he was. They sat down on the metal terminal-style bench to the right of the elevator, each occupying one seat out of the three.

For a long time, they just sat there staring off into space. Matt thought this eerily similar to the way he had sat with Belinda but an hour and a half ago, back when there was still hope (a tiny glimmer of it, but still some) that this moment would never come. Now it was almost here.

A part of him wanted to talk to Greg, but what was there to say? Tell him he was sorry? What good would that do? No good at all that he could think of, and even if he said it, would it even be true? Was he really sorry? He wasn't sure he was. The man had made his decision, and that was no one's burden but his own. What was there to be sorry for?

He looked over at Greg. He was sitting with his head down, staring at his open palms, as if questioning their integrity, questioning their choices. His stare said those hands had been the bearers of his misfortune, that they had acted beyond his will and triggered his demise.

Matt looked down at his own, flexing them in and out, admiring the creases, feeling their shape and texture, wondering to himself what those hands were capable of, asking himself if their will was good or evil, if aiding produced pleasure, if destroying caused them pain.

Those hands, with one quick motion, could release Greg from his shackles, give him the freedom to continue to roam the earth. But with another motion, they could summon his weapon from his holster, pull the trigger, and end the man's life on the spot. So much power was in those hands, and yet so powerless they felt. What choice did he really have?

He looked back at Greg with unrelenting confusion. A part of him wished he could let the guard walk; a part of him wished he was already dead.

"You know, it's funny," Greg spoke, and the moment he did, Matt flinched, like he had forgotten the man could talk and this rediscovery was frightening.

Greg didn't see it. He was staring forward when he started, no longer looking at his hands, focusing on the wall in front of him instead, staring through it like it wasn't a solid surface but a window of transparency. Only instead of looking out, he was seeing inward instead, seeing into his own soul.

"You would think I would feel terrified right now, but I don't. I don't feel angry or sad either. I just feel ... relieved."

He's losing it, Matt thought. *He's trying to rationalize what he's done.* Suddenly, he felt more terrified than he'd felt at any other time that day, maybe more terrified than he'd felt at any other time in his life. *You don't want to hear this.*

"I think a part of me always knew something like this would happen. I was never cut out for the guards. Belinda knew it, and so did I. But it was the guards or the Camp, and I made a promise to myself I would never go back there. No matter what the cost, I would never go back."

Please stop. He could feel it getting worse. Sitting here quietly, he had started to feel a bit better, but now he was beginning to physically feel sick. He was about to hear a dying man's thoughts, and the spirit of those words wouldn't ascend on once this was over. The ghost of them would live on in him forever, prodding around his brain at the framework of his mind. He would never be the same.

But he didn't try to shut him up.

"And ... I guess, I could never admit this to myself, but it really is the truth. I always thought it was the Camp I was so afraid of, but it wasn't just the Camp. It was all this, this whole way of life. I'm just not cut out

THE UTOPIA

for it. If it hadn't been for Belinda, I would have given up some time ago. She made this place bearable, although a part of me also wishes I'd never met her. I know that sounds terrible, but why hold it in now? Because if I hadn't met her, maybe I would have left when I had the chance."

He turned to look at Matt. Matt had turned his head away and was now staring forward, but he could feel that gaze upon him, studying his being, analyzing his soul. He was absolutely terrified.

"You're a good man, Matt. Don't let this break you because this is not your fault. Know that I'm okay; understand that I'm at peace. Truly. I bear you no grudge. In fact, I pity your position. Truthfully, I would rather be me right now than you. I'm not scared to die."

Matt's frantic brain wanted to yell at Greg to stop it, to tell him that none of that was true and that he had lost his mind. But inside, he didn't believe that. This man had not gone crazy. This man had not lost his ability to think. This man had mined for years, through deep fog and muddy waters, to discover this wealth of knowledge. He was speaking now only because it was in his will to pass it on.

Matt turned with sad eyes, met Greg's gaze, and heard his truth.

"I'm not scared to die; I just pray to God I don't return."

In his mind, Matt turned and ran toward some unknown destination, panicking and crying and begging to be left alone, repenting his sins and promising to do better.

In reality, the elevator opened, and the endgame drew upon them.

***

WHEN THE DOCTOR FIRST hopped out of the elevator, he said only a few words: an apology for being late (even this traumatized version of Matt managed to find some amusement in that) and instructions to follow him. They didn't even get his name, and perhaps that was for the best. Matt wasn't exactly planning to invite him over later for dinner.

He led them into the nearest room, and the setup inside was simple: a single operating table with leather tie-down straps and a machine for anesthesia. Matt recognized it from the time he had been put under so he could receive surgery on his broken arm, a surgery that had been a success; his arm had mended quite well.

Today, there would be no healing.

Greg sat on the table without prompt and the doctor handed him a pill. He described it as zelderpin, but Matt recognized its appearance and knew it by a different name. He, like others, had colloquially termed it the zombie pill.

Greg swallowed it down, and the five minutes they spent waiting for him to sleep were the most awkward of Matt's life. The doctor ho-hum chatted like he hadn't a care in the world, and until the moment he passed out, Greg responded back like he was making a new friend, chatting about the weather, sports, and even their favourite meals. The most ordinary of conversations under the most extraordinary of circumstances.

When Greg finally passed out, Matt was grateful, but not for long. Now he was the target of conversation instead, the doctor describing the procedure in excruciating detail.

"We give him desflurane through the mask now just to be safe. There should be no suffering at all during a procedure like this, and adding an anesthesia ensures he won't feel a thing."

"That's good," Matt said, having no clue if he actually believed that to be true. Maybe it was a commendable precaution. Maybe nothing about this was commendable at all. His mind was in shambles.

The doctor put the silicone mask over Greg's breathing ports and then flicked on the machine. It came to life with a hum like a high-voltage power box. When Matt heard that sound, all he could imagine was an electric chair and currents of electricity firing through Greg's body, which would seize uncontrollably until his heart stopped for good. It wouldn't happen that way, but the result would be the same.

Reaching into his lab coat, the doctor pulled out a syringe.

"Now we just inject belkital, which is an improved version of the outdated pentobarbital. This will stop the neurons in his brain from firing, and when that occurs, the rest of his body will shut down within a few minutes. After that, it will all be over."

Thank the stars, Matt's brain screamed, and he didn't even admonish himself for thinking it. He was too terrified for that, too overwhelmingly anxious. And the thought made too much sense.

Thank the stars this was over. Thank the stars he could leave this place. Thank the stars every day for the rest of his life if it meant never coming back.

"Okay. Here we go."

The doctor stabbed the needle into the thickest vein in Greg's arm, pressed the top of the syringe down, and injected him with poison. As the life left Greg's body, the thoughts left Matt's mind. The inner chatter was gone. No more questioning of his moral compass. The deed had been done, and there was no going back. He drifted into a place far away, where no pictures could be seen and no words could be heard, where he felt no fear or anxiety or compassion or relief, where there was no judgment of character or assessment of choices, where everything just *was*. He went into that place because it was the only way to survive.

And he only returned to earth after he knew it was safe.

"Guess that's all," the doctor said, looking back. "Another crew will come for the body, so don't you worry about that. You get to go home early, it looks like. What are you going to do with your day off?"

Anything, he chose, as long as it was far away from here.

CHAPTER 7

Log Entry: *Day III*

It's hard to accurately depict my feelings about what happened at the Camp today. I have the words: serenity, concern, drive, contempt, tedium, isolation, appreciation. What I don't have is a way to connect the web. Each feeling seemed appropriate in the moment; none felt especially fitting as a theme. Even as of writing, I have yet to determine whether today was a good day or a bad day. I guess I'll start from the beginning.

The feelings started before I even woke up. I slept like a baby, and that in itself is a blessing, but even more so was this dream I had sometime in the night. It was one of the most beautiful I can remember having in a long time. Even thinking about it now is making me smile.

I dreamed I was standing within a lighthouse gallery. It was sometime in the night. The moon was shining brightly. The stars lit the endless sea below. The waves were crashing restlessly against the rocks. The wind was still. The lantern split the night, lighting the blackness of the natural beyond.

I had no clue where I was; no idea why I was there. But I felt an aura of peace in that moment, protected from the world at large. I was the only living soul but for a bird that crossed silently before my eyes. I followed its path through the skyline across this incredible backdrop and only lost interest when I saw the orange light dancing across the horizon. It might have been the most magical thing I have ever laid eyes upon. Never in my life have I seen a colour scheme so stunning. I just wish I could have stayed there forever.

My real day was far less appealing. The antagonists in my Sunday story were, of course, present, and although I avoided them well, I know that is something I cannot do forever. Eventually, I will have to engage in a conversation, if for no other reason than to not become a target. I know Yuri was talking about me today with the other guys at lunch. I didn't sit near them, but sometimes you just know.

Today, it was the right decision though to keep my mouth shut. The emotions were too raw. I might have done something I would have regretted, something that would cost me in the long run.

Anyway, it didn't happen, and the rest of the day was quiet and uneventful. The only other thing worth mentioning is the card game I just finished playing with Hakeem. It's called Link. I had never played it before but found it quite enjoyable. A nice way to end the night. Maybe next time I'll even win. I'd say I could sure use one of those right about now, but I'd rather end this on a positive. Hoping for more good dreams tonight and better days ahead.

Salud,

Deron Boyd

Log Entry: Day VI

No dream again today. I've been hoping to see the lighthouse again, but it's not coming naturally. I can force it into my mind, of course, but it's not the same thing. The same magic just isn't there.

Of course, that's really the least of my worries at the moment. I'm almost sure the guys at work have it out for me now. I'm still working with Ron in the mornings, but he no longer speaks to me. Ray talks to me in the afternoons, but I can sense something is off. There's no charm behind his words; I think he just wants to avoid a confrontation. I don't know what they see in Wise Guy, but apparently, he's got them hooked. Maybe it's just as simple as him being a part of the group first. I can imagine loyalty is in high demand around these parts.

I guess I'll just have to see what happens when I finally make my move. Yuri openly smiles around me now. I would love to wipe that smirk off his face, but that isn't the smart play. I know that, and so does he. I just have to do my best to keep avoiding them until I can determine what to do.

Figuring it out,

Deron Boyd

Log Entry: Day IX

Shit hit the fan today. Every pot has their boiling point, and I guess this was mine. I tried to avoid it for as long as I could, but inside, I always knew she would eventually say something. I could just see it in her eyes. She's one of those people that can only exorcise her demons by confronting them. It's her fatal flaw, the same way it is my own.

I probably didn't have to snap at her like I did, but I just didn't want to hear it: how terrible she felt, how sorry she was. I wanted no part of it. You don't put someone you've just met in that position. You don't ask them to open up to you and then drop that kind of bomb. It's not right, and it's not fair, and there's no apology that can erase the sin. She made her choice that day when she decided to stay behind.

I can admit to feeling bad for yelling at her though. I didn't mean to make her cry. I think she feels sorrier for herself than she does for me, but that still doesn't make it right. I hate what she did, but she showed some nobility in at least trying to make amends. That deserves some respect, I guess.

Anyway, hopefully that part of it is done with at least. We can be cordial when required but walk our separate paths otherwise. I think that is for the best. If I can put this behind me then there may yet be a chance for me. Whether it's true or not, I have to believe that.

CHRISTIAN JERRY MARCHIONI

One down, one to go,
Deron Boyd

Log Entry: *Day X*

Okay, shit REALLY hit the fan today. I don't even want to be writing this, but I'm angry as hell right now, and this therapy worked the last time and it's all I can think to do. If I don't distract myself somehow, I'm going to do something bad. If Hakeem hadn't given me that suggestion, I probably would have already. I'm surprised I even made it home. I guess I have to thank Agatha for that.

Today, it finally happened. Today, that asshole finally made his move. I let those scumbags leave first like usual, anticipating they would mosey on back to their compound together like they always do, only today, they didn't go. Today, they waited for me to leave, and when I stepped outside, Wise Guy ambushed me out of nowhere, just shoved me to the ground while his cronies stood around holding their dicks and laughing.

I lost it on him, of course, and we started trading insults. The heart of what was said was irrelevant until he spoke a particular name: Carla's. He was crying about how she was basically an unenthusiastic sex doll after I hung her out to dry, how I had ruined his threesome and he had barely gotten off. HOW FUCKING PSYCHO IS THIS GUY? I should have clocked him across the chin and stomped mercilessly on his throat. I should have gouged his eyes and ripped his tongue out of his mouth. I should have beaten his head into the ground until the dirt was painted red. I should have ... I digress. Somewhere in this stream of consciousness, I should probably say what has me so enraged.

It was not the shove to the ground; I had been expecting something like that to come eventually. It was not his mention of Carla. At least not at first. His mention of her hesitation made me feel a bit worse about blowing up on her, but in the end, she had still ceded to his advances by her own free will. No, it was what he mentioned after that has me running on fumes.

THE UTOPIA

When he told me he had hit her after for "wasting his time," I nearly lost my mind. Doesn't matter what she did to me; doesn't matter her other sins. You don't do that. Ever. And if this guy thinks he can get away with that, he has another thing coming.

And as far as Ronald, Ray, Carlos, Deke, and Shawn, I swear to God I would have fought them all if she hadn't shown up then, hadn't asked what all the ruckus was and demanded we go home. I almost lost it anyway, but intelligence prevailed. When Agatha speaks, you listen.

Same goes for Hakeem. Like I said before, if it wasn't for him, I would probably be seeking out Yuri right now instead of sitting here with a pen. When I told Hakeem about my rivalry with Wise Guy, his advice was to drop it. He said the old line about time healing all wounds; I replied that the only thing time did in here was kill you, and when he heard that, I think he got the memo that I would never let this go. If I'd told him all the details, he probably would have understood better, and I will tell him everything once I'm in a more rational frame of mind, but either way, he came up with another plan instead.

Apparently, the rumours about the fight club are true, and Hakeem says there's a guard who works at my factory who helps sanction the scraps for the area warden. He says if I drop him the code "braised salmon," he can set me up with a fight. How he knows this stuff fascinates me, but it's not my place to ask. It's probably best I don't know anyway.

I'm going to do it. Yuri deserves it, and this needs to be settled. If it doesn't happen in the ring, it will happen outside, and at least this way, I can take him out with no fear of any repercussions. His judgment day is coming, and this time, I'm the one with the gavel.

Fuck this,

Deron Boyd

Log Entry: Day XI

Tides began to turn today. I had the dream again. Still don't know where I was or why I was there, but that orange light seemed a little brighter this time, as if whatever was causing it was closer than before. I couldn't see the source, but it was probably just the sunset. Doesn't entirely make sense because in the dream, the moon is full and bright, but I guess that's the allure of dreams. They don't have to make sense, and when they don't, that might make them even more beautiful.

Ironic, I guess, that the dream reappeared last night. In the dream, I was so at peace and everything in the world felt right. In real life, I feel none of that same concord. In real life, I feel that just about everyone is against me, but at least today, I started to fight back.

I found the guard. His name is ... I'm thinking now that maybe mentioning names the way I have been doing is unwise; if someone in the Camp finds this log book, that could lead to serious complications ... But on second thought, what the hell? It's not like all the events I'm writing about haven't been caught on camera anyway. This is the Utopia we're talking about, not exactly a place where privacy rules the day.

His name is Guard Thornwell, and when I asked him if we'll ever see the day where braised salmon replaces stew on the dinner menu, his eyeballs nearly popped out of his head. He didn't threaten me though or tell me to shut up. He just quietly asked if I was sure about this, and when I responded in the affirmative, he said he'd speak to the relevant parties about my request and get back to me in a few days. I can only hope now that "getting back to me" means setting up a meeting and not charging me as a proprietor in this whole conspiracy—or worse.

I'll try not to think about that and just hope this plays out well. Life is hard enough without constantly reminding yourself it's hard.

I will survive,

Deron Boyd

Log Entry: Day XIV

It's happening. Thornwell finally got back to me today with the news. Tomorrow night, I'm meeting with Supervisor Reynolds to discuss the matter. Wasn't told where to go. Wasn't told what time. Wasn't told what to wear (ha!). Wasn't told anything. All I know is tomorrow is the day this shit starts to get straightened. I'm tired of Yuri's snarky grin every time I walk past him. I'm tired of the awkwardness of working with Ron and Ray, knowing they're talking about me behind my back every time they're with the group. I'm tired of having to look over my shoulder every time I walk home. It's time to put a stop to it all.

There will be blood,

Deron Boyd

Actually, no, there's one other thing. I'm embarrassed to write it, but these are supposed to be honest. Correction: they NEED to be honest. Putting my thoughts on paper is the only thing keeping me sane. If I leave them inside, I know I'll drown in them. So, I guess with that said, here goes nothing...

I've been talking to Carla these last few days—not about what I am planning (although I think she senses something is up) but just about life in general. I play it off like I'm uninterested, give short answers to her questions and rarely prompt her back, but inside, and I hate to admit this, I'm actually enjoying it. It even feels strange to write, but it's true.

I haven't forgiven her, at least not completely. But I do feel sorry for her. She didn't deserve what Yuri did to her (and may have done to her again, for all I know; we haven't talked about that). I can feel she's afraid of him, and I get the sense they—Yuri and his band of hairy men, I mean—are talking about her the same way they're talking about me. It's sad because she was such a carefree spirit before all this, and now I sense the same fragmentation in her that I feel within myself. It's not right, and I guess I feel partially responsible for it. If I hadn't done what I did, she probably wouldn't be so sad. Although I don't regret doing it either. I still think it was the right thing. It's all so confusing.

Anyway, I'm getting off topic. The point here is simply this: we seem to be enjoying each other's company, and even if I can never completely trust her again, perhaps she doesn't have to be an enemy either. Perhaps we can help each other feel better about where we're at, and that can be enough to form a functional kind of—dare I say—friendship. Only time will tell, and *while a part of me is hesitant after what she put me through, another part of me thinks it is worth it to find out. Maybe there's still some light at the end of that tunnel.*

Now I'm actually done,

Deron Boyd

***

HE FINISHED OFF HIS shift the same way he had every night since the shoving incident: by letting Yuri and his gang shower well in advance of him, only taking his turn once they had all exited stage left. It was a brutal waste of his precious free time, but in here, survival came first. In here, you would cut off an arm if it meant saving the body.

Plus today, there was another purpose.

He stood in the factory by the dining hall door. He wasn't the only camper left (those on clean-up duty were always the last to leave), but he was the final remnant of his shift, the last grain of sand from the eight o'clock hourglass, stuck on the framework until gravity pulled him through. He was waiting for Thornwell.

Stand by the dining hall door at the end of your shift. Do everything else normally. Shower. Take some time to collect your things. And then come out after your whole shift is gone. Don't come out immediately, but don't wait too long either. If you stand by the door too long, people will wonder what you're waiting for. If you stay in the washroom too long, people will wonder what you're doing in there. If you don't see me after a little while, leave the building. I'll find you outside.

Deron hadn't asked what all the precautions were about, but he could guess it had something to do with the cameras' omnipresence. And if Thornwell was worried about the cameras, that meant the fight club was a highly exclusive secret operation.

A highly exclusive secret operation has but a few select members, members who are usually paranoid they will one day be discovered. Those who are paranoid are often quite dangerous. Dangerous people don't often like surprises. When he connected all the dots, the message spelled out was loud and clear: Be careful, and do exactly as you're told.

He had been standing by the door for maybe three minutes before he made the decision to leave. There was no sign of Thornwell, and while "a little while" wasn't exactly a specific timeline, he figured three minutes was just about the upper limit of that spectrum. A part of him thought this might even be some kind of test to see if he could be trusted.

He tapped out for the night, exited the building, and when he entered the darkness, his first feeling was fear. Every time he departed from here, it was the same story: a constant worry that tonight, Yuri would strike, attack him from the shadows like some haunting apparition. *Return of the Wise Guy*, now available for streaming.

He wasn't there though, and neither was anyone else. Deron was alone in the darkness, kicking dirt and pacing, knowing he was being watched but not knowing who was watching, sensing the world around him but not quite seeing it clearly.

He had come a long way in the last two weeks. Despite his misfortunes, he had managed to settle in. He'd made a good friend in Hakeem, who he could trust with his secrets and play cards with at night. He'd grown accustomed to the work, appreciating its simplicity, especially in the moments he was plotting his revenge. He didn't even hate that part. Anger was useless as a problem-solving emotion, but this whole vendetta at least gave him a purpose, at least made him feel like there was more to his life than the daily routine.

He'd been sober since the Monday morning after "the incident," and had felt no withdrawal symptoms in well over a week. His body was sore, but it was a good type of sore, the type of sore that let him know he'd earned his rest for the night, that he'd accomplished something. And even if that accomplishment wasn't the type he had hoped for, it still gave him a sense of pride.

These last two weeks, he had contributed to something, had stood up for himself, had battled and clawed and learned he could survive. Only when he stood out here alone did it seem like the world could swallow him up at any moment.

Only in moments like these did it seem like the darkness was here to stay.

He stopped his pacing when he saw the flash of headlights. They came from a moving target headed straight toward him.

He froze but stayed calm. The headlights were partially blinding, but he could see just well enough to deduce it was a guard van. They might ask him why he was still here, but he was doing nothing wrong. He would tell them he was just waiting for a friend. Most would find that explanation credible.

This guard would not, but it also didn't matter. When the van pulled up, it was Thornwell.

"Hey, I thought—"

"Quiet you," Thornwell said through his open window. He opened the driver's side door and got out aggressively. "We have to make this look right. Guards and campers aren't friends, ya hear, and if someone is watching, they're gonna wonder what the hell is going on." He grabbed a handful of Deron's jumpsuit and started dragging him to the back doors. "You sit back here. Don't worry, nothing's wrong. Just precautions, like I said."

Before Deron could even get a word in, he'd been tossed into the cabin and the doors had been shut behind him. It was a bit of a shock to his system, and his mind flashed back to the time of his initial arrest, but for the moment, he wasn't overly concerned. The idea that this was all just a precaution did seem to have some merit.

Better safe than sorry, I guess. And he really wanted to believe that. *But then again...*

Did safe mean playing the act or taking out loose ends? Did sorry mean all of them going down together or them pinning it all on him? Doubt was starting to creep in.

Maybe I should... But it was already too late. Thornwell hopped in the front seat and began to drive away.

***

WHEN DERON SAW WHERE he'd been transported, he felt his chest tighten.

In and out. In and out. It took a few of the deepest breaths he had ever taken to settle himself down, and even the fresh influx of air didn't entirely do the trick. Of all the places Thornwell could have brought him, he never

THE UTOPIA

would have expected here. Outside of a giant circus tent.

"C'mon," Thornwell commanded, "it's just around the corner." But Deron just stared, stared at the place that had caused him so much mental anguish, the source of all his troubles, the reason he was here.

Over the course of the ride, with each passing turn, he had sensed within himself increased trepidation, all the while blowing it off as budding anticipation, as fear of the unknown, as understandable paranoia given his position. But now?

Now he was starting to think those feelings were something more like intuition, that his mental state had been induced by clairvoyance, that his body had somehow known it was about to be taken here.

Suddenly, he wasn't so sure this was a good idea.

"C'mon!" Thornwell ordered, more boldly this time. And that got Deron moving, whether he wanted to or not. He was no longer sure this was such a good idea, but there was one thing he *knew* was a TERRIBLE idea: disobeying a guard's orders.

He followed Thornwell around the corner. They had exited the van near the northwest corner of the tent, and Thornwell was now leading him around the side. Once Deron lifted his head up, he noticed something he had been oblivious to before.

At the northeast corner of the property, still within the gated fencing, was a building that looked like a warehouse of sorts. Its size was strange (if it *was* a warehouse, it was on the smaller side), but stranger still was its location: cramped in the corner and inaccessible from the adjacent streets. It looked like it had no business being there.

Kind of like how I feel.

Deron tried to ignore the thought, but his anxiety was increasing with each passing step. As they approached the building, he became acutely aware they weren't the only ones there. He could see the outline of two figures standing in the darkness.

Closer they crept, closer and closer, until they were close enough that Deron could finally see the faces. One was a mystery, but the other he knew instantly. It was a hard face to forget. It was the face that had been there to welcome him to the Camp: the face of Supervisor Reynolds.

Now he REALLY wasn't sure if this had been a good idea.

"Sorry to keep you waiting, Supervisor Reynolds," Thornwell said once they had gotten within spitting distance. "Agatha asked for my help with something, and I couldn't tell her no."

Reynolds's reaction in that moment was one that Deron would never forget: he glared at Thornwell with a look so hot, it was a surprise that lasers didn't come shooting out of his eyes; a look so sinister, a viper would have backed away for fear the beast was poisonous; a look so vile, it would have turned the wicked Medusa to stone.

If you could have frozen the frame and asked Deron in that moment what he thought would happen next, he would have expected the end of Thornwell's life. He would have thought Reynolds would pull his weapon and shoot him in cold blood, or maybe grab him by the throat and strangle him with his bare hands, or maybe hang him from a cross and laugh while he bled out. The look was that indignant.

And then the face cracked, and it became a grin so quickly, it was like the person behind the mask had transformed into someone else.

"Not to worry, Thornwell," Reynolds advised. "You did the right thing. And it's nice to see you remembered not to flash your headlights at me this time."

"Yes sir, Mr. Reynolds," Thornwell said softly. He had heard the sarcastic jab, and the scowl had resonated. Deron thought the man looked like he wanted to cry. He honestly felt bad for him.

"Oh, cheer up, Thornwell. I'm just kidding." Reynolds smiled, a more honest-looking smile than the grin he had flashed. Thornwell managed to smile back, but his was more of a yearbook photo smile than a Christmas morning one.

"There you go, Thornwell, much better. I know I'm a stickler for punctuality, but sometimes things are outside of our control. I understand that good and well, and besides, you've done a fine job. This lad Boyd here is exactly as you depicted him. He looks like quite the fighter."

He didn't look at Deron then, but Deron felt the attention on him anyway. It made him feel cold and somehow more uncomfortable than he had already been. There was something off about this man.

Probably should have figured that when you heard he ran a fight club. Thank God for hindsight.

THE UTOPIA

"Let's bring him inside, and we'll talk."

Reynolds turned about-face, and the other guard, the one who had been waiting in the wings with him and had yet to say anything, pressed a button on the remote control he was holding, and the warehouse's garage door began to roll up. The area warden took the lead, followed by Mr. No-Sound, with Deron and Thornwell bringing up the rear.

What they walked into, to Deron's absolute amazement, was, in fact, a warehouse. No-Sound flicked a switch, and the place lit up in fluorescent illumination. After taking a moment to let his eyes adjust, Deron scanned it all.

From front to back, piled high, were boxes. Many were labelled "pasta," some "books," and others had no clear labelling at all. In the southeast corner were stacks of lumber; in the northeast, steel; and between the two, a forklift good for at least ten thousand pounds. But in the middle of it all was the grand prize.

No way, Deron thought. But what he actually meant was *yes way*. What he was looking at wasn't a mirage, but rather something very real: a thirty-foot octagon, raised perhaps two feet off the ground. There were various weights laid upon it and a treadmill in the centre, but its real purpose was clear: it was a cage-fight battleground.

Behind him, the garage door was closing. He turned instinctively toward Reynolds, trying to remain stoic, but his face showed stunned surprise, and everyone could see it.

"Now, I know what you're thinking, but let me explain. We leave it out in the open like that because it's impossible to hide anything in this god-forsaken world. If someone comes by for a little routine inspection, well, we wouldn't want to seem suspicious now would we?" He smiled that grin again, then Deron watched it vanish like it was never even there. "But we do take precautions. There are no cameras in this building, at least not as of yet. There will be. The State will make sure of it, the bastards. But this building is new, and my reputation is strong enough that the board will give me another month or two before they start asking any questions. After that, we'll have to switch locations, but that won't be a problem. We've done it twice already."

Deron opened his mouth as if to say something, but there was nothing on his mind. The area warden continued.

"This works because the building itself has a legitimate purpose. We put it up because we needed the extra storage space, and that's exactly what it provides. The ring in the middle, that's so the guards have an extra spot to work out when they're off-duty. There's no gym in the Camp, and its patently unfair to our brothers and sisters who want to maintain fitness. It's our duty to do better, hence the treadmill and the weights."

In that moment, he unleashed his broadest smile yet. He seemed to be enjoying showing off his genius. Deron, on the other hand, was enjoying it a lot less. Sweat was beginning to seep through his jumpsuit.

"You see, Boyd, everything is accounted for. We tell people our adult fun house is not operative due to maintenance purposes on certain nights so that we can stage the fights. The cameras in the surrounding areas can catch you coming in and out, but if you're a guard, you can just say you were going for a workout. If you are, well, *you*, we'll give you a box so any voyeur will think you were here to help organize supplies. Everything's accounted for."

He said it so confidently, it almost forced Deron to believe him, to believe this stubby man with the bald head and thick beard knew exactly what he was doing.

I know he's really staging fights here, that he's not lying to me or tricking me just to give me more years.

Check.

The logic in his plan is sound, and there's just no way he would do this if he honestly believed there was any way he would get caught. It's just too much risk for such little reward. He must have a plan for just about every scenario.

Check. Check.

If this was a game, he would win. If it was a movie, he'd pull it off. But ...

Deron still had doubts because this was not a game. This was not a movie. This was the present-day Utopia, and in the present-day Utopia, you just didn't get away with things like this. In the present-day Utopia, you just didn't get away with anything.

As if sensing his reservations, Reynolds's face turned cold. The fake grin disappeared, and he no longer looked at Deron like he was some eager student. He looked at him much more like some type of disgusting insect that just wouldn't leave his space.

"Now, that's enough information. What I need to know from you is this: are you going to fight?"

"Yes." He said it instantly. It didn't come out as assertively as he'd hoped, but it was enough to do the trick.

In reality, seeing that cold look again made him more doubtful than ever. He was almost sure, in fact, that this was a terrible idea. But after seeing all this, was he really in a position to turn down his request? To say *nope, sorry, just kidding* and walk away like this conversation had never happened? Somewhere, the voice of Matthew Tucker was whispering he had no choice.

"Good. And who is it that you would like as your opponent?"

"His name is Yuri Yin. He works in factory 4F with me. He seems to have a personal grudge against me, and I would like to settle it."

"That's fine. I don't care about your reasoning. I just need to know if you are in, who your opponent is, and what you want to happen if you win."

"What I want to happen if I win?"

"You heard me, Boyd. The winner gets to pick a punishment for the loser or a reward for himself. Nothing insane, of course. You can't have him killed and you can't ask for your freedom, but you can ask for anything within reason."

"Well, in that case, I guess . . ." He had to think about it for only a second before the answer became clear. "I would like him gone. Not killed, just transferred somewhere else. If that's possible."

Reynolds's continued scowl gave him the impression that it wasn't, that he had just made one of the ridiculous requests Reynolds had just said he wouldn't tolerate, that his greed was liable to cost him.

Then Reynolds's face broke into a smile so bright, it was like it had its own outlet. It was categorically terrifying.

"Why, of course it is. I thought you were going to ask for a day off a week or something. What you want is no issue. Transfers happen with some frequency around here. No one will bat an eye if ole Yuri Yin takes a permanent trip out to the farms. It's a deal."

Deron breathed the largest sigh of relief he had ever breathed in his life. The area warden looked at his watch.

"Now, it's starting to get late. There's another event on the cards tonight, and you mustn't be here for it. So, what I need from you now, Boyd, is to grab one of these boxes of pasta and take it to your factory. Thornwell will drive you, and if you have any other questions, you can ask him en route. Otherwise, you will receive further instructions in the coming days. Understood?"

"Understood," he stated, probably more confidently than any other word he had spoken this whole time. By some miracle, he was going to make it out of here with a positive outcome.

He walked over to the nearest box pile and picked up a load of pasta. Thornwell gave him a nod, and together they walked toward the exit door beside the garage. Only when they were moments from freedom were they halted in their tracks.

"Oh, and just before you go, Boyd," Reynolds called out. Deron looked back, but the area warden was facing away from him, looking at the ring. "This should go without saying, but do not tell anyone about this. If you do, well, let's just say there will be some serious consequences."

"Understood," he called out. But his confidence had left him again, and this time, his voice shook. Reynolds was right. He didn't need to be told to keep his mouth shut; he had assumed that was a given. But something about hearing the instruction put it all into perspective for him.

They'll blame me if word spreads, he recognized in that moment. *If they think they might get caught, they'll shut down, and they'll blame me for that.*

He let that sink in as he emerged back within view of all the cameras.

CHAPTER 8

Sakura Saito lay supine on her mattress in her Zeeble District home. It had been a few hours since her last pick-me-up. Her eyes were closed, and she could have slept had she given in to fatigue, but there was no point. They would be here shortly, she could feel it in her soul, and when they came, she would go with them. It wasn't worth it to fight back, and she couldn't argue with their premise. It was what she deserved.

This wasn't the first time she had stolen drugs from the General Store. Unlike Deron Boyd, she was something of an expert, had practiced her routine many times before making her first attempt, and even then, she'd had the wherewithal not to go through with it when the circumstances had proven precarious. She was disciplined like that. In other aspects, not so much, but patience was not a problem.

When they requested she come in early to help restock the shelves, she did so without complaint. When customers asked questions, she calmly explained to them what items they could return so they could stay below their quota. When Guard Paulus asked her out, she refused him kindly every time and never lost her temper. Only that one had been a mistake. Because maybe if she had said yes, even just a single time, there would have been a chance. Funny how it was all connected.

As a little girl, she had been shy, almost cripplingly so. She had talked only when spoken to, and even then was often asked to repeat herself because her response had been so timid. While other kids played in groups, she played by herself, hopscotch or jump rope or games on the computer. Solitaire was her favourite because it required no interaction. Doctors had discussed the possibility of social anxiety disorder.

Adolescence had brought her out of her shell, and the external concerns lessened. She made friends, none that she was especially attached to, but they were more than just peers she was forced to interact with. She actually enjoyed their company, for the most part, anyway. There were times when it got overbearing and she needed to be alone, but generally, their presence in her life enhanced her well-being and helped with her transition into the real world.

She'd graduated school with a degree in chemistry but had never planned to pursue any relatable occupation. She'd just needed to study something, and the experiments were fun. The only time she had tried to apply her knowledge was later in life when she had tried to make her own synthetic cocaine, and that had turned out how most home experiments with harsh chemicals do—it had nearly killed her. She had taken the stuff and spent the night between stages of profuse sweating and vomiting. That had ended her chemistry career for good.

Now she just stole drugs whenever the rations weren't enough and she needed a fix. It wasn't particularly hard. She had picked up employment as a General Store clerk out of school, and after seven years on the job, she had learned the ins and outs. For the last three of those seven, she had stolen basically any time she felt like it. All she had to do was slip a baggie into her sleeve when a customer placed an order. The drug counters were down low, and if she crouched and angled her body just right, her act was invisible to the world. There were cameras, of course, but all systems had blind spots, and she'd figured out where they were. The Utopia was good, but they weren't omniscient. A missing baggie here or there would go undetected or be chalked up to a data-entry error. That was until today.

Today, for the first time, she had slipped. Well, no, that wasn't true. Her first mistake had occurred four years ago when she had started using drugs in the first place. Then she'd made another a year later when she stole for the first time. It was all connected, after all, and you couldn't have one event without the others.

But today had been her first literal slip. She had always been able to tuck the baggie in her sleeve and hide it there until her break or ask to go to the washroom and stuff it in her shoe if she ever started to get anxious. One way or another, she had always been able to concoct some type of plan. And on the days when the elements had been against her, when the lineups were long or her boss was unwilling to let her venture off, she had always been bailed out by some type of blind luck. It was the theme of her life. She'd always been able to just get away with it.

It happened when she was a kid and forgot to (or just didn't care enough to) study for a test. She could always cheat off her neighbour and would never get caught. She could have even had the answers sticking out of her backpack if she'd wanted, and the teacher wouldn't have noticed.

It happened when she was fresh out of school and looking for a job. She was afraid of being chosen, and so her only choice was to apply. There was lab technician work, but she didn't want that kind of job, and the labs were located far away from the epicentre of the city. Those jobs would have meant a lot more travel time and a lot less convenience.

Her alternative was this clerking job. The shop was located in a beautiful area, and she was sure if she got the work, they would give her an apartment somewhere in the heart of town. The situation was ideal.

She was probably one of three to apply for the two lab slots, the field of her study, and probably one of ten to apply to be the clerk, a job you could qualify for with literally any degree. The Store followed up with her; the labs did not.

She could think of countless examples of her luck throughout the years. The time the truck would have hit her crossing the street had she not turned around, only doing so not because she had realized she was walking across a green light but because she had started panicking, thinking she had lost her phone.

Or the day she had gone to the beach and enjoyed a nice surf, emerging from the water at just the right time. A minute later and there was a very real chance she would have been a victim of the shark attack.

Or when an ex-boyfriend started becoming too possessive, and he just so happened to get asked to take over a new position, a new position that was his dream job and also happened to be located halfway around the island.

It was like some mystic force had been there at every turn, watching out for her, making sure she was okay no matter what elements tried to intervene. It was as if she wielded some magical shield, had some mysterious purpose that she had to fulfill, and the puppet master wouldn't let her fail no matter how badly she seemed to undermine him. Only today had been different.

Today, after years of surviving by the skin of her teeth, the enamel had decayed and the dentist had finally had to rip that sucker out. Today, all those years of good fortune had finally caught up to her, and now Ms. Fortune was threatening not only to surpass her but to leave her in the dust. Today, she had slipped, and that slip was liable to wash away a lifetime of caution.

She had done the hidden baggie trick same as she always did. Only today, that baggie had fallen out of her sleeve as she was making her way to the washroom safe zone. It dropped right on the floor where a set of prying eyes caught wind of it instantly—those belonging to Guard Paulus.

He hadn't said anything to her, but she had seen his eyes and known instantly what would happen. He would call it in. It was his duty, after all, to call in any suspicious activity and then let the cameras decide. And in this case, their decision would be simple. She was quite sure—no, she was absolutely certain—they had caught her little misstep.

After that, she had thought of just waltzing out of the shop and never coming back. If today was going to be her last day of freedom for a while, she might as well enjoy it. She had stayed only because if her past had shown her anything, it was that if anyone could get away with this, it was her. Objectively, she knew she had no chance, but subjectively, her belief had yet to die.

She sat up in her bed for what felt like the first time in hours. On her nightstand was a plate, a white powdery substance lined up on its surface. She took a reusable straw and sucked the powder back until it disappeared up her nose. The boost of energy that came after was exactly what she needed. She'd been fading hard and fast.

She put the plate down and lay back in her bed, thinking of what it was exactly that had gotten her to this point and struggling to find an answer. She had started doing drugs for no obvious reason and had continued doing them for many she found hard to justify.

She'd never even had a drink before she met Ronaldo, but he had introduced her to substances of all textures and colours. Never forcefully, never even through suggestion. On their first date, he had simply ordered a beer, and so she figured so should she. Sitting down with someone she had only met over the island dating app had her agonizingly nervous. If nothing else, she thought that maybe it would help take the edge off.

Tragically, it had worked, and that was probably the main reason her drug use continued to evolve. Alcohol and cocaine vanquished any nerves. Cannabis helped her relax and recover. All were useful around Ronaldo because until the very end, she felt butterflies when he was near, not because of fear but because she really liked him, and she thought if she acted shy and quiet then he would lose interest one day.

In the end, she had lost him, but not due to her own misgivings. They saw each other for some time and his infatuation never waned. He loved the way her glistening black hair fell softly down her back. He loved how the curvature of her narrow eyes enhanced her broad, dimpled smile. He loved the smooth texture of her skin and the playful way she jested with him and shushed him when she was angry.

Never in her life had anyone taken notice of her the way he had. Never had anyone appreciated her the way he did. And never had anyone since.

His accident had been her first real stroke of misfortune, had taken from her the only thing she had unequivocally trusted in this world other than herself.

She had done drugs before to bring out her personality. But she had started stealing drugs to cope with the sudden loss, to take away the pain of knowing he was gone, to eliminate the sadness she felt within her heart.

Years later, the pain had mostly subsided, but she defended her continued drug use by telling herself it was for its original purpose: to make her more outgoing and help her meet new people. Because if Ronaldo had shown her anything, it was that somewhere deep down, she didn't want to be alone, that some part of her had developed a dependence, that she didn't need anyone, but she did need someone.

Had it helped? Maybe. She had met other people, done other things, and continued to survive. She rarely even thought of Ronaldo these days, but she could admit that since his accident, she had never quite felt the same. Maybe she never would. Maybe love like that was fleeting and she should have cherished those moments because they were not meant to last forever. Maybe this was the moment comfort became good enough instead.

Knock! Knock! A rapping at her door made her flinch, but she didn't stir.

"Sakura Saito. Can you open up, please?" came a muffled voice through the door. "It's Ashlyn Dunst from the guards. I'm here with my partner, Carey Dunlop. We would like to speak with you."

Sakura moved only her arms, bending them backwards and clasping them behind her head. She would open the door—she had no plans to cause a scene or resist what was coming—but only when she was good and ready.

She stared at the ceiling of her apartment for what would be the final time. She felt no nerves. The cocaine was a reason for that surely, but not the sole one. This was only the second time in her life she had gotten unlucky, and something was telling her that just like the first time, this wouldn't do her in, that the forces of nature still had something planned—not because she was special in any way but rather the exact reverse, because she was unremarkable, and non-essential people had this weird way of surviving, this odd resilience that the privileged did not possess. They could see the world in a way that always gave them a chance. And if what she believed was true, then this wasn't the end.

If everything was connected, this was simply a new chapter.

CHAPTER 9

Log Entry: *Day XVII*

Well, it's officially on. Today, I learned that Yuri has accepted my challenge, and I can't say I'm too surprised. People like him have a tough time walking away from a fight, and I think he wants to get me as badly as I want to get him. Maybe even more so.

The fight is scheduled for just less than a month from now. Thornwell said the area warden wants to give us ample time to train so that we can put on a good show. After working twelve hours a day, I'm not sure I'll regularly be in the mindset to get a good pump in, but I can at least practice some technique. As much as I hate to admit it, I think Yuri will be a tough opponent. I know he's strong, and he seems like the type who might have some experience in this realm.

I just hope he doesn't try any funny business before the bout. I don't expect him to. In fact, I believe the area warden might just cut his balls off if he did. I think the guards, the ones who are aware of what's going on anyway, will keep a close eye to make sure there's no foul play. I don't expect trouble, but at the same time, I wouldn't put it past him. He's proven more than once that he's capable of taking even the most malevolent approaches.

I'll plan what I can, and do what I plan,

Deron Boyd

Log Entry: Day XIX

Finally got the rules today, and I've got to say, I'm pleasantly surprised. I was expecting a no-holds-barred cage match, possibly with baseball bats or swords or, I don't know, fucking nuclear missiles maybe. But it turns out, our only weapons are our fists. Gloved too, not even bare-knuckle. Turns out Reynolds was a boxer back in the day and is a huge fan of the sport. Our fight is just a boxing match! Albeit, with one major difference ...

Okay, two major differences actually. The ring is an octagon, which is a bit weird, but since neither of us are trained in the sport (at least, I hope Yuri's not trained; if he is, I'm likely in trouble), that little nuance shouldn't change much. A well-versed boxer might notice, but it is doubtful we will.

The real difference is that there are no scoring rounds. The fight just continues until one person drops the other for a ten-count. The fight could go for hours (unlikely; what is much more likely is that one of us will get winded within the first ten minutes and be unable continue. NOTE: WORK ON CARDIO) or, well, I guess a bit over ten seconds.

At least now I can devise a strategy. I remember reading online once about this legendary boxer. His name was Muhammed Ali, and he had this title fight one time against this guy—Foreman, I think his name was.

He knew Foreman had the power advantage, so he defended himself until Foreman tired, and once he did, Ali was able to knock him out! Maybe I'll try something similar. I can consult with Hakeem and see what he thinks. He still thinks this is a bad idea (and he's not wrong), but since I've committed, he has promised to help me. I am thankful for that because, let's be honest, I could use all the help I can get.

Keeping on keeping on,

Deron Boyd

THE UTOPIA

Log Entry: *Day XXIII*

Minor incident today. Nothing game-changing, but it has forced things to progress a bit more quickly than I would have liked.

It was Wise Guy who provoked things—surprise, surprise. The real surprise is that this didn't come sooner. He'd been actively avoiding me the last few days, and none of his posse had chastised me either. For a second, I actually thought he might have gained some respect for me; that he was actually capable of that. Should have known better. It was all part of his mind games.

He was avoiding me hoping I would let my guard down. Whether I did or not is up for debate, but the one thing he was able to divulge by studying me for the past week is that this fight is mostly about Carla and what he did to her. I think that previously, he'd assumed this was just an attempt at revenge for the shoving incident. But the lightbulb finally turned on, and now he knows the truth.

If I had to venture a guess, I would assume he deduced this (after many strenuous hours of racking his microscopically small brain, I'm sure) based on how much time Carla and I have been spending together recently. I have not fallen for her again! I promised myself I would not make that mistake, and thus far (I don't like those words, but honestly, I have also promised), I have kept my word. I have forgiven her though, not only for her sake but, selfishly, for myself. I really do enjoy spending time with her. I can't pinpoint why that is, but for whatever reason, she just adds a brightness to my day. Maybe it's because she's always smiling. It's infectious, I guess.

With that aside, the main reason for bringing her up is that when Yuri put two and two together, he decided to throw a wrench into the equation. He assumed (rightly, I'll give him credit for that at least; although I kind of figure it was Ray or Deke who actually figured it out) that if she was smiling and happy, I probably hadn't told her about the fight, and he figured he could stir up a little controversy if he let that gossip spill. Unfortunately, he was right.

Suffice to say, Carla was not pleased to learn this little tidbit. I tried to explain, but she seems certain this will not end well, and I guess I can't blame her for thinking that. She said it was selfish to put myself in that position, and while I'm not so sure I agree, I didn't fight her on it. I don't like to see her upset.

I didn't tell her I was doing it for her because I don't think it would have helped. I just hope she'll one day understand my motivation and why I couldn't let this go. At least now that the cat's out of the bag, I won't have to worry about that secret weighing me down. I can just focus on what I have to do and on doing it well.

Nothing can stop me,

Deron Boyd

Log Entry: Day XXXII

Training went great again today. Between work and my daily runs, I think I'm in the best shape of my life. It only took being sent to a labour camp and declaring war against the scum of the earth to make it happen. If I was still on the outside, there's no way I'd be this healthy. Funny how life works.

Also had a good talk with Carla again today. She's still not thrilled about what I'm doing, but she's being as supportive as she can be. I'm beginning to understand why this is bothering her so much. With each passing day, the idea that I'm doing this more for me than I am for her is gaining traction in my mind. She seems to have put the altercation behind her; I'm the one that can't seem to let go.

In any event, it's irrelevant because I have to go through with this one way or the other. If Yuri pulls the plug, that's one thing, but I cannot back down, not because of pride but because I get the feeling Reynolds isn't the type of man you want to disappoint. He expects a fight, and I'm going to give him one. The training continues …

Harder, better, faster, stronger,

Deron Boyd

THE UTOPIA

Log Entry: *Day XXXVIII*

Less than a week before fight night, and the nerves are starting to grow. I see Yuri in the changing room, and as much as it pains me to admit it, he looks like a Greek god. I have no clue whether he'll be able to walk the walk when push comes to shove, but if this was a bodybuilding contest, I'd have to concede.

I can tell he's nervous too though. He hasn't said a word to me in over a week, not even a taunt or a backhanded comment, and even his friends have stayed away. Speaking of which, I feel like there's something funny going on, but I can't say exactly what.

Last week when Ronald was moved to a new position, I thought it was just coincidence, but today, Ray was moved as well, and that gives me pause. Would Agatha really have endorsed such a request? I guess it's possible; she does seem to utilize a more liberal form of leadership. But what would they have said to her if she asked why they were both all of a sudden so eager to switch positions? They wouldn't have discussed the fight, of course; that wouldn't make sense. But might they have suggested to her something about me? That I am not working hard or that I'm abusive in some way? This all seems so paranoid, but in our world, is it really?

Hoping it's just the nerves,

Deron Boyd

Log Entry: *Day XL*

Three days in a row now, and that can't be an accident. What's the old line? Once is happenstance, twice is coincidence, but three times—three times is a pattern. And I don't like the look of this particular configuration.

The guards at the factory are watching me. I can feel it. Every time I turn to look, they swivel their beady little heads away, but I know they're watching. There used to be gaps in time where I wouldn't see a guard for hours, but now, they're always there, just waiting for me to make a mistake.

I'm certain this is Yuri's doing. Ronald and Ray MUST have said something, and now the guards are trying to corroborate their tales, trying to see if I'm a bad worker or am abusive toward my partner or whatever else they might have said.

What worries me is that no matter what I do, they'll see what they want to see. People are much quicker to confirm their hypotheses than to deny them, and if that happens here, I may end up being punished for something I didn't even do. Insane how this all works when you really think about it.

Of course, this could all just be paranoia talking. The fight is in three days, and I'm nervous as hell now. This could just be my mind playing tricks on me, me letting Yuri get into my head.

The argument can go both ways, but either way, I must be careful. Bad things are on the horizon if I am not.

Scared but alive,

Deron Boyd

Log Entry: Day XLI

Received final instructions today. After my shift ends on Saturday, I am to walk toward the adult fun house, and someone will pick me up just beyond the gates. I am to come alone, of course, and to tell no one (although I have already broken that condition). When I get there, everything will be set up and the match will begin promptly. God, I'm nervous.

I have told Carla all the details because I think she deserves to know. I brought her into this against her will, and she at least deserves to have the ability to prepare. I can tell she's frightened about what will become of me, maybe even more than I am. She seems to sense that Yuri will try something to get the upper hand. I've tried to convince her that the guards will protect me because of their own vested interests, but she appears unconvinced. I guess I can't blame her for that. Putting trust in authority is never easy, especially in our world.

The only thing I'm thankful for is that in a few days, this will finally be

THE UTOPIA

over. One way or another, closure is coming, and I can finally stop living life looking over my shoulder. What a blessing that will be.

Worn out but not broken,
Deron Boyd

Log Entry: Day XLII

Had the dream last night. First time in a month I've seen the lighthouse and the beautiful colours dancing across the sky. There was a breeze this time, but it was gentle, and the waves showed no ill will. There was one thing in the dream that did scare me though.

The bird is a raven. Before today, I had only tracked the bird, but this time, I really saw it for the first time. It had never clued in with me that the bird is black, so it couldn't be a gull or any type of seabird that I've ever seen. The raven blended into the background the first two times, but this time, I really noticed it, and when I did, I felt afraid.

It didn't look at me. It didn't chirp or say anything in its language. It just gave me a bad feeling. I felt cold when I saw it, like its presence was some type of warning. I just hope it's not a bad omen of things to come. If the bird has any symbolism, I would imagine that is it.

Tonight, I have no thoughts about the fight; I have done all the preparation I can, and it's time to just let the chips fall where they may. This ends tomorrow.

Good luck,
Deron Boyd

***

HE WALKED THROUGH THE valley of the shadow of death very much fearing evil.

It was sometime just after eight thirty in the evening, and the sunlight had long since given way to the darkness of the night. There were streetlights around, but not enough to dissect the blackness that surrounded, not enough to allow him to see any hope of emerging from the end of this tunnel. And that wasn't even the worst part.

Worse still were the people. He had left Carla only ten minutes prior, but since he had been alone, he'd had this unshakable feeling that not only was he being watched, but that one of those watchmen was actually a night stalker on the prowl, waiting for the moment the collective eyes wandered or the second he took a turn down the wrong alley, ready to steal away his already fleeting spirit, to burn him down to hell before he could even step foot in the ring of fire.

He looked to his left, and across the street, there were no green pastures. To his right, he saw no rivers of flowing water, and the influx of people leaving that factory were anything but quiet. The streets were bustling with men and women headed home after a long day, the commotion around him making his soul feel anything but refreshed. Yet he continued along the path.

At the spot where the sidewalk sloped into road, he was given a choice. He could continue straight for another block and then make the right turn, or he could turn right immediately and later follow up with a left. Dissecting his options, he noticed that the former path was a lot more occupied than the latter. He chose the calmer route, praying it was safer.

But all roads lead to Babylon, he reminded himself. *Doesn't matter much which path I take because all roads lead there.*

His fractured nerves were descending into panic. His head was throbbing with worry and his muscles ached with apprehension. This upcoming battle was not David versus Goliath (although he would have gladly played the role of David if it was offered), and he had genuine belief he could emerge victorious, but what he feared most was the unknown. What would happen to him if he lost? For that matter, what would happen to him if he *won*? Was it possible that would just be the end of it?

He doubted the area warden would let him off so easily. He was unsure, in fact, if the area warden would let him off at all. There were so many variables his rage had shaded from him when he'd made the decision to venture down this road, so much he had put aside in the name of blind hatred. He had let his emotions get the best of him, let them put him in this precarious position. And perhaps the worst part was that now, in the moment he actually could have used that emotion, the moment he could have channelled it into some type of advantage, now that passion was nowhere to be found. It had gone into hiding, cowering in fear like the rest of him, cowering in a fear that was threatening to swallow him whole.

"C'mon," he mumbled, trying to psych himself up, trying to reinvigorate some positive energy. He shook his body like it was made of rubber, trying to force the tension out of it, thinking that maybe he should jog the rest of the way to work up a sweat and get the juices flowing. He had almost started running when the shout came.

"Deron, watch out!"

In a panic, he spun around like a ballerina dancer, lacking the grace, but achieving the velocity. He held a fighting stance as he stood and faced his counterpart.

Looking back at him, maybe two feet away at most, was a man he had never seen before, a tall man, with a wiry frame and messy hair. This reaper wore no hood and held no scythe but had another weapon instead. In his hand was a plumbing wrench.

Before Deron even had time to think, a van pulled up beside them.

"What's going on here?" The question was threateningly stated, and Deron knew instantly who it was stated by. Supervisor Reynolds was demanding answers through the passenger's side window.

Deron's scrambled brain provided none. He himself was still processing what had happened. His heart was jumping in his chest, and things weren't about to calm any time soon.

Because jogging toward them was the absolute last person he wanted to see, the person whose voice he had recognized instantly when she'd called but who his brain had consciously tried to block out, hoping she would turn around before she was seen.

Don't! he thought. But it was already too late. Carla had caught up to their little standoff, passing the weapon-wielder and approaching Deron's side. The confused faces turned to her, searching for answers. She provided them excitedly.

"He had a weapon! He … he … he was going to hit Deron with it!"

"Woah! What?" the man shouted.

Accusatory eyes all transitioned to the man with the wrench. He took a couple steps back in conditioned reflex as he began to get defensive.

"Lady, what are you talking about? I'm just walking—"

"Why do you have a wrench?" She pointed at him accusingly. Beneath the glow of the nearby lamppost, they could see her every gesture, the look of real fear affixed on her face. "And why were you bringing it up like you were ready to take a swing?"

"Yes, I caught that as well," Reynolds chimed in. "It was subtle, but I agree with the young lady here. It did look like you were about to raise that thing with some vile intentions."

"No sir!" he yelled. Now the man was panicked. It was one thing to have a fellow camper accuse you of something. It was another thing entirely to have the area warden agree with that opinion. "No way, I swear to you! I raised my arm because I was about to itch my nose! When I heard the girl yell, I got spooked, and maybe then it looked like I was about to do something, but I swear to you, I was not! What would I have to gain? I don't even know this man!"

"Still doesn't explain why you're holding a wrench," Carla fired back.

"I was working on the plumbing at factory 12F, the auto parts factory. But then I got told there was a problem at the power plant and was sent to go help with that. I swear to you, it's true. Guard Maurice Levesque sent me. He told me to bring the wrench just in case they didn't have one. I swear on my life."

He was panting by the time he had finished getting the statement out, and Deron thought he looked absolutely terrified. With good reason too because if that whole thing was a lie, that "swear on my life" offer might just be accepted.

Deron's heart was still pounding, but he at least now had some understanding of the situation. Unbeknownst to him, Carla had followed him, probably to look out for this exact scenario, probably thinking Wise Guy might just try to send one of his henchmen to soften up his opponent before he faced the boss himself.

Apparently, Reynolds had believed the same thing or, if not, had thought of some other reason for following him. There was just no way he could have reacted that quickly had he not been lurking in close quarters.

He too must have been trailing Deron the whole time, ready to react in Deron's defence, or perhaps act as an incentive if Deron had thoughts of backing out.

He understood all that. The only question was, What happened now?

Deron looked over at Reynolds, who was staring at the man with his best Medusa face. The man was looking back at him with terror in his eyes, fully comprehending what would happen if Reynolds said the magic words. Deron still didn't know whether this man had actually intended to harm him or not, but in that moment, he didn't care. In that moment, he felt sorry for him.

"Alright," said Reynolds. "I'll have to call Levesque later to remind him that we do not let campers around here leave with any potential weaponry, no matter what the circumstances, but I believe your story. I can smell a lie from a mile away, and you may stink of something rotten, but you don't stink of that. Move along, soldier, you're free to go."

And you could see an almost erotic relief splash on the man's face when he heard those words, like he had never heard a more harmonic sequence of sounds in his entire life, likely because he never had.

"Thank you, sir. I promise I'm not lying. I promise." And he left with that without waiting for a response, passing Deron and Carla without so much as a glance in their direction, no words of ill will for almost sending him to his grave. He left before Reynolds had a chance to change his mind.

Deron watched him go by, wondering to himself whether the man had truly been a part of a larger scheme, eventually realizing it really didn't matter. His problems ran a lot deeper than that. And his problems were still here.

"Now," Reynolds continued, and that reverted Deron's eyes instantly back to him, returned him immediately to the state of fear he had previously known. Only this time, it wasn't just for himself. "It seems we have a bit of a predicament here."

Deron shuddered. Those were not the words he wanted to hear. And this was not the face he wanted to be looking at: stone cold and evil.

"I believe I told you, Boyd, that you were not to tell anyone about this little arrangement we've got going here, and it seems you have failed me on that. What to do about it is the question."

"He didn't tell me, Mr. Supervisor." Reynolds's face didn't break, but his glance shifted over to Carla. "I swear it. It was Yuri who told me because he wanted to get under my skin. And Deron didn't tell me to follow him today either. I did that on my own. I was worried someone might come after him."

Reynolds studied her while Deron's fear heightened. What she had told him was the truth, but what if he didn't believe her? Or what if he didn't care?

He glanced at Carla with desperate, sad eyes, wishing he had the power to make her invisible or teleport her away. She had risked everything for him, and leading up to this moment, what had he done for her in exchange? Tell her she was disgusting. Hate her with passionate vitriol. Oh, how he regretted those actions and feelings now. She had been the one to keep him sane throughout this whole ordeal, this ordeal that could have been avoided but for his unwillingness to let go. If anything happened to her because of him, he didn't think he could live with it.

He was not *in* love with her. After what happened, he would never allow that again. He did love her though. And now he felt a part of him always would. He just prayed he would see her again after today.

"I'm not sold, lassie, but my instinct is telling me to believe you, and my instinct is never wrong," Reynolds said. Deron's eyes flashed toward him. His face was still stone, but the bitterness was gone. He looked ... human again. "I guess it doesn't matter now anyway. If you know, you know, and I've got to admit, it was brave of you to watch over Boyd like that. Reckless, but brave. Hop in the back. The both of you. We're all going to drive over the rest of the way together. That little skirmish has me thinking it's best to eliminate all risk."

"You mean I can come?" Carla sounded shocked, and Deron felt the same way.

Why would he allow that?

"That's what I said. Now, get your asses in the van before I change my goddamn mind or before more people come down the street."

Carla and Deron looked at each other with wide eyes. Both were astonished by this sudden turn of events. Both were feeling it wasn't right and that something may be amiss. But what was there to say?

They walked to the back doors, let themselves in, and locked themselves in the cabin, praying the vehicle was acting as a cargo truck and not as a hearse, saying nothing to each other but feeling the same thing.

No matter where they were headed, it wasn't the house of the Lord.

But it wasn't a death house either, at least not yet.

When the doors of the van opened up for them, they emerged in a place foreign to Carla but recognized instantly by Deron. Boxes were piled high. The placement of the wood and steel hadn't changed. The only thing that was different was that the treadmill and workout equipment had been removed from the octogen. And there was someone standing in the middle of it, someone nicknamed Wise Guy.

"'Bout time you showed up, Bitch Boyd!" he yelled, reigning down his favourite insult the second he saw Deron. He was already gloved up, shirtless, and in trunks. A light sweat was exuding from his muscular physique. At a normal time, he was Deron's height, yet standing elevated on the ring platform, he seemed to tower above him. But Deron didn't fear.

"Ohhh, and what the fuck is this?" he shouted. Carla had been cut off from his viewpoint, but as she joined Deron beside the van, she came clearly into focus. "What is that skank doing here? I didn't request another threesome."

And when he said that, Deron felt his fists clench so hard that his fingernails began to cut into his palms. He'd been scared walking here; he'd been scared during the van ride. But seeing his rival in the flesh, knowing this was his chance to finally put things right, he felt a yearning for revenge instead—until Carla grabbed his arm.

"Don't listen to him, Deron," she spoke softly in his ear. "He's just trying to rile you up and get you off your game. You need focus to beat him, not anger."

But for the moment, his fists stayed locked, the emotional part of him not wanting to hear that, figuring that anger was exactly what he wanted to feel because if the anger dissipated, the fear might return.

But the rational part of him knew that wouldn't be the case. The fear had stemmed from the unknown, and the unknown was gone. He could see his opponent. He had some semblance of belief that if he won this battle, promises would be kept. And whatever came next, he would be able to handle because he would no longer be facing it alone.

His fists slowly unclenched, and his muscles released their tension.

"Alright, Boyd, we don't have all night here. Time to suit up."

Reynolds pointed him in the direction of the ring, and he went without delay. Carla held his arm for a moment longer but let go without struggle. She had done all she could, and the rest was up to him.

Deron removed his jumpsuit shamelessly and changed into trunks. A guard, one that he did not know, wrapped his hands and helped him with his gloves. The whole time, the same message repeated in Deron's head: *I will be victorious.*

After a few minutes of warmup, he stepped into the cage alongside another nameless guard, this one not his trainer but the referee for the bout.

"Biggest mistake you ever made, Boyd," Yuri taunted. "Biggest mistake you ever made."

Deron ignored him as the referee explained the rules. "Alright, this is a boxing match, gentlemen, not a cage fight. That means no kicking, no screaming, no biting or any other type of psychopathic bullshit you crooks can come up with. Is that clear?"

Both nodded.

"Good. Now this battle is for as long as necessary. The first person to knock the other down for a ten count wins. You may not hit someone who is already on the ground. Respect that rule or you will be disqualified. Is that clear?"

Both nodded.

"Good. The final conditions of this match are as follows. If Deron Boyd wins, Yuri Yin will be sent to another part of the Camp where he will serve out the remainder of his sentence. If Yuri Yin wins, Carla Cortez will be sent to another part of the Camp where she will serve out the remainder of her sentence. Is that—"

"Wait. What do you mean Carla will be sent to another part of the Camp? What does she have to do with this?" Deron panicked. All that focus he had spent the last twenty minutes or so building up left him at the sound of a few words.

Yuri smiled. "That was my request. We each get one, and that was what

THE UTOPIA

I chose. Bet you didn't see that one coming, did you?"

Deron was stunned. Of all the tricks Wise Guy could have pulled, of all the things he could have done. Somehow, Deron had not foreseen this.

"But ... But why ... Why would you ..."

"Because fuck that wench is why. And fuck you, Deron. You picked this battle for no goddamn reason. I had no problem with you, thought you might even make a good part of our group. Until you bitched the fuck out and ruined the one good time out I get a month. Even that I could have let go. But you started this crusade against me, and when you play with the Wise Guy's fire, you get motha-fucking burned. I'm sending her away because I know it's the last thing you would want. I could've reduced my hours, gotten an easier position. But I'm sending her away because I know that's what will hurt you both most. I could have sent you away, but this is much better. This way, I can see your pathetic face every day and get to continuously enjoy that same priceless expression you have on right now, the one that says Yuri Yin the Wise Guy just got the best of me. Now, let's do this already."

His mouth contorted into a psychotic grin, and for a second, Deron was too dumbfounded to react. How foolish had he been. He had taken this upon himself in order to stand up for Carla, and if he lost this now, it would result in her being unjustly punished instead.

He looked toward the audience and saw seven people: Reynolds, Thornwell, his trainer guard, and three others whose names he didn't know. The last person was the only woman and the sole person in the group he just so happened to care very much about. He looked into her eyes and saw the sad look of longing on her face, longing for this to be over, longing to get out of here, longing for them to just enjoy each other's company and think of nothing else.

He looked at her and felt like he had already lost.

"Alright, when the bell rings, you can touch gloves if you want, but I get the feeling that's not going to happen, so just be prepared to defend yourself."

Deron's eyes flowed back to Yuri, whose smile had disintegrated. He looked all business now, bouncing up and down and preparing for the battle. Deron himself raised his arms, but his heart wasn't in it. He felt limp and powerless.

"Okay, Supervisor Reynolds. Whenever you're ready, sir, we are here."

"Thank you, Guard Thompson. Everyone, this bout will start in five, four …"

Deron started to bounce around. His heart still wasn't in it, and he thought he might just get knocked out by the very first punch, but he knew he had to try. He had come too far to just throw in the towel, and there was too much on the line. There was never a thought of calling off the bout.

"… Three, two, one!"

Ring!

"Fight!"

All that was left to decide was for whom the bell tolled.

***

AND WHEN THE FIGHT began, it looked like that someone was quickly going to be Deron.

One. Two. One. Two. Yuri came out like a house on fire, and all Deron could do was stand in and eat the punches. He had his hands up, guarding his face, but then came the body shots.

"Oof," he cried out after a particularly strong blow to the gut. He had shed quite a few pounds since arriving at the Camp, and for the most part, that was a good thing. But it also meant there wasn't a whole lot of padding there to soften the blows.

He threw his first jab and missed, and as Yuri sidestepped, Wise Guy hit him with another left, this one connecting with Deron's shoulder. Deron turned and threw again, but that shot missed too, and Yuri countered with a straight right to the sternum. Adrenaline blocked the pain, but the punches were adding up already. He began to back away.

"C'mon, Boyd. You've gotta have more than that. I know you're a nice guy, but you're making this too easy." Wise Guy didn't even break stride as he reigned down the taunts. He threw punches left and right until Deron was backed all the way to the cage.

You've got to land something! his brain screamed at him. And his brain was right, but instead of barking orders, what he really wanted it to do was tell him how. He threw a left-right combination, which Yuri blocked

THE UTOPIA

easily and then returned, almost like he actually knew what he was doing, like he had maybe even trained in this sport at some time in his life.

What had he gotten himself into?

He got a chance to think about it when he was knocked to the ground for the first time. He stumbled over backward and fell on his backside. There was a small roar from the sideline. The referee began his count.

"One! Two! Three!"

Deron sat and tried to regain his composure. Physically, he was alright, but mentally, he was in trouble. He needed a strategy and fast.

"Four! Five!"

From the seat of his pants, he looked at Yuri, who was bouncing up and down like he was overtop a trampoline. He had barely broken a sweat.

"Six!"

At seven, he stood up, and Yuri advanced to pounce before the referee intervened. "Fight starts again when I say so!" he instructed.

Yuri halted his movement but didn't take his eyes off Deron. "Not much of a fight if you ask me," he teased. "But your rules, chief."

He then turned his attention to Deron. "This is what you get for trying to be the nice guy, Boyd. Should've just let the wench handle her own shit. Hasn't anyone ever told you nice guys finish last?"

Deron ignored this and tried to take advantage of the brief reprieve, but it hardly made a difference. When the ref yelled "fight," he was far from fully recovered.

Yuri came at him with unrelenting pressure. Jabs. Hooks. One-two combinations. It was less than a minute later when a straight right knocked Deron down again.

"One! Two!"

This was bad. *I'm in trouble,* he thought as he sat there on the canvas. *Oh God, I'm in trouble. What have I done?*

"Three! Four!"

"C'mon, Boyd, you wanted this fight. You've got to do better than that!"

The shout was from Reynolds this time. He wasn't sure whether it was a taunt, words of encouragement, or words of frustration since he was proving such a feeble form of entertainment, but whatever the words were, they weren't particularly helpful.

"Five! Six!"

And neither were any of the other words in his head.

I never had any chance. I was so sure I would beat him, but why? What gave me that impression? Because he's an asshole and he deserves to lose? That's not how life works. And it's not like I'm some hero who deserves any better. I deserve to lose too; it's karma for my pride.

And he believed all that too until he heard another voice, one outside his head, one a lot more inspirational.

"C'mon, Deron, you can do it!"

He looked to his right immediately and saw Carla, expecting to see concern, perhaps all-out fear. But what he saw was belief. She actually still thought he could pull this off.

When he saw that face, he wanted to cry, cry for what he had done to her and the position he had put her in, cry for the way she felt for him and how she continued to believe even in a spot where anyone with half a mind could see he had no shot. He wanted to cry, but he felt a surge of energy instead.

"Seven! Eight!"

He stood up feeling a new wind, like this was one of those video games he used to play back at his apartment and someone had just injected his character with the magic health potion. He felt ready to fight again.

"Go!" the ref shouted. And this time, when Wise Guy stepped forward, Deron clocked him with a right.

"Oh!" the crowd yelled as Yuri stumbled backward. He hadn't expected to be hit like that.

Go! Deron's mind shouted. And this time, he listened to the advice, throwing lefts and rights from a barrage of angles. It wasn't technically sound, and it was anything but pretty, but it seemed to be effective.

"Oof!" This time, it was Wise Guy crying out in pain. The blows were doing damage. Everything was going well. And for a second, Deron actually started to believe this could be the moment.

And then he was hit with a counter right out of nowhere and went down like a sack of potatoes. Yuri charged him and threw at him again just as he hit the floor, narrowly missing his chin by a matter of inches.

"Hey!" the ref yelled, intercepting Yuri just as he was about the throw another. "What did I say about hitting on the ground? You do that again and you're gone!"

"Like fucking hell I am!" Yuri snapped. Those shots from Deron had set him off. He was fuming.

Unfortunately, Deron was in no position to enjoy it. His head was starting to spin, and all his focus was on himself.

No, he thought. *No, please. Not now. Not now that I can actually win this.*

"I'm warning you," said the referee. "Do not do that. I gave you clear rules, and that was one of them."

Their eyes locked for a moment in a war of attrition, but eventually, it was Wise Guy who backed off.

"Yeah, whatever. I don't need to hit him again anyway. Fucking Bitch Boyd is buried. Start your goddamn count."

The guard-ref looked like he was about to lose his cool but held his nerve and did his job.

"One! Two! Three!"

Deron could hear him counting, and each passing number was like an added exponent on his panic meter. He was seeing stars, and there was nothing he could do.

"Four! Five!"

C'mon! But there really was nothing he could do. He was pretty sure he would be able to stand up, but if he had to battle feeling this dizzy, it would only be a matter of time.

"Six! Seven!"

He let it get all the way to nine before he stammered to his feet.

Yuri smiled when he saw that. "Bad decision, Boyd. Should've just stayed down. I'm coming for you now."

Deron heard the words coming at him from different angles. Part of Yuri was blurring in and out. He was seeing double. And then he was seeing punches. Boom! Boom! And then down he went again.

"One! Two!"

"Just give up, Boyd. It's over, and you know it. You had your chance, and you missed it. Remember that when you're thinking of Carla touching some other man's dick in another part of the Camp."

In anger, he stood up, but within a minute, he was back down again.

"This is pathetic, Boyd. Just quit!"

Up and down again. His head and muscles were feeling lighter, worse, slower, weaker. The only thing keeping him going was a single voice in the background.

"You can do it, Deron! I know you can do it!"

He wanted so badly to prove that voice right. He wanted so badly to believe in himself the way that voice believed in him.

He stood up and stumbled back against the cage, and Yuri came at him again.

"Told you to stay down!" Yuri shouted. "Eat this, nice guy!"

Deron went down again, stayed down for a few seconds, then got back up.

He's going to tire, he thought. *He has to. He can't keep throwing like this.*

Yuri threw at him once more. Deron blocked his face, knowing if he took another big shot there, it was all over. Eventually, he gave in to the body blows and sat down again.

"Just ... stay ... down!" Yuri shouted.

But Deron wouldn't. He got back up almost immediately.

He's going to tire. I can hear it. He's starting to crack. I can see it.

He took lefts and rights from all angles, everywhere but the chin. For over a minute, he just stood there against the cage, absorbing blow after blow after blow until eventually, he sat down. In the meantime, Yuri walked toward the centre of the ring. But this time, Deron noticed something different, and he was sure that even in his current state, it wasn't his mind playing tricks. Yuri was doubled over with his hands on his trunks.

"Nice guy ... Bitch Boyd ... just ... lose ... already." He gutted out the words, but this time, there was no conviction in his voice. This time, he wasn't even looking at Deron when he said them. This time, the sentence sounded less like a taunt and more like a plea.

And when Deron heard that, he felt a surge of adrenaline that might have lifted him through the roof had he not had a job to do down on earth. Suddenly, he didn't feel quite so dizzy. Suddenly, he didn't feel quite so beaten up. Suddenly, he was sure he was going to win.

"Is that ... is that all you got?" he mumbled.

When Yuri turned, what he saw was a wreck. Deron's left eye was already starting to swell. His chest and stomach were bruised. Sweat was pouring out of him like a waterspout.

But he also saw a man in a fighting stance with a smile on his face. And that made him irate.

"Argh!" He shouted some unintelligible noise and charged his foe. Deron stood and protected the same way he had over and over and over again. Only this time, when the punches landed, they felt like a cool breeze against his skin. This time, when he looked through his arms, it wasn't just with a prayer that the punches would stop. This time, he was looking for an opening.

And when he found it, he connected.

"Oh!" The crowd rose in united ecstasy as he landed the finest right hook he had ever thrown. When he hit him, Yuri's knees buckled, and he went down almost instantly. It was the only time in the match he had fallen, and it was the only time he would need to. He was knocked out cold, his head tilted to one side, his body visibly shaking. Only when he awoke some thirty seconds later would he hear the news.

He was going to a place where he would never harm Deron or Carla again.

Deron fell backward against the cage and sat down in a heap. When he had finished thanking the world, the gods, and whoever else he could think of, he looked back at his downed opponent with only one final thought.

I guess that's what I get for being a nice guy; maybe I did deserve to win after all. Because Wise Guys finish last.

***

"CONGRATULATIONS, BOYD, THAT WAS one hell of a fight. One of the best I've seen."

Deron stood near the garage door facing Supervisor Reynolds. He had an ice pack held against his swollen eye, and his legs were wobbling like jelly. The adrenaline rush was over. He could feel every cut, every bruise, the sting of every blow that had landed. He wasn't sure if he had ever been so sore in his life, and yet he couldn't have felt better.

"Thank you, Mr. Reynolds. I'm just glad it's over," he said softly. He coughed a few times but then regained composure.

"What happens now?" the voice beside him cried. It was Carla, rubbing the back of his neck through his now-restored jumpsuit. She had cried after Deron won but had since settled and was now playing the role of tending partner. Deron couldn't appreciate it enough. Or appreciate her more.

"Well, our resident villain will be shipped out tomorrow."

Reynolds's back was to the ring, but he turned now to look. Carla and Deron were already facing that direction and were privy to the sight. Yuri was sitting in the middle of the ring with his head down by his knees. Was he crying? They couldn't tell, but really, what did they care? He was gone from their lives and that was all that mattered.

"He'll stay the night with us so no funny business happens. But the papers have already been drawn up, and the approval is just a formality. He'll be sent up to farm country in the north, just about as far away from here as you can get."

"Good riddance," Carla said.

"And how about us?" Deron asked. He was a bit concerned about the answer, but if there was a time to ask, it was now, while Reynolds was still revelling in his success and appreciative of the show. The area warden turned back around to answer.

"Well, first off, you'll both have the day off tomorrow. I've already called Agatha and told her your services are required by the area warden, and when I make that call, that's the end of discussion."

"Really? That's so nice of you, Supervisor Reynolds."

"It is. Thank you." Deron felt internally there was more to it than being nice, but he let it slide. This was the most laid back he had ever seen the area warden, and he really didn't need to see that Medusa face again.

"My pleasure. You've both earned it. Now, as far as after that goes, everything will return to normal. You'll go back to your jobs, and if anyone ever asks you anything about if you know what happened to Yuri or why you were absent for a day, you don't say a goddamn word about this. You were helping me shuttle boxes, and you don't know anything about Yuri, got it?"

They both agreed vehemently.

"Good. Now." He looked at his watch. "It's almost nine thirty. That gives you both about an hour before you need to be home in your beds. So if you two lovebirds want to use our little adult fun house in the meantime to celebrate this here victory, well, let's just say I won't stop you."

"Oh, that's okay, Mr. Reynolds," Deron fumbled out.

"Yeah, you don't have—" Carla began to add.

"If you're worried about the cameras catching you, don't be. If you break in somewhere around here, even if some overseer sees you, I'm the only one who can take action, so you shouldn't be worried about that. Nothing will happen. Unless you don't trust me."

"No, it's not that, Supervisor," Deron scrambled. "It's just ... we have a bit of a complicated relationship." He had forgotten all about his swollen eye and bruised body. His adrenaline had begun to pump again.

Reynolds looked at him straight-faced, looked at Carla the same (for her part, she looked uncomfortable as well), then began to laugh.

"Whatever you say, Boyd," he chuckled. "Whatever you say. Either way though, it's time for you to get out of here. So there's the door."

He pointed with his open palm, and when Deron and Carla saw that, they didn't hesitate. They thanked the area warden for whatever they could think to thank him for, headed out the door, and emerged outside into the warm windless night. They walked in silence under the stars, side by side, avoiding contact for fear of what it might lead to. Only when they had rounded to the entrance of the tent did some mystical force seem to stop them in their tracks.

"Deron." It was Carla who spoke first. He looked at her, barely able to see her face in the shadows that surrounded. "Do you want this?"

"Carla, I—"

"I know I hurt you, Deron. I know I hurt you badly. I know we'll never be together, and I accept that because quite honestly, as much as I like you, I don't want to be with you." Her voice was shaking slightly, and there were tears in her eyes. "But when you look at me, I don't want you to see Yuri anymore. I don't want that to be the lasting memory for us. So maybe ... maybe we need this just to have some closure."

Deron looked at her, and his eyes began to mist. She couldn't see it in the darkness, but she felt his emotion, and he felt hers. He knew her truth the same way he knew his own. She didn't want to be with him, but she really did like him. She maybe even loved him. In his own way, he loved her to. He knew that if they spent the night together, maybe it would help them to leave the past behind.

He looked toward the tent. He would never get used to this place. He would always get a sick feeling whenever he saw it, would always be reminded of a certain incident that had nearly broken him for good.

But tonight, he would enjoy it.

CHAPTER 10

Log Entry: *Day L*

It's been one week since the fight, and I think it's probably about time I stop looking over my shoulder. Things have been quiet around the factory since Yuri departed, and at this point, I don't expect that to change. For a while, I thought I might see some retaliation from the rest of his gang, but none of them have even approached me, let alone uttered a threat. I get the feeling they actually might be scared of me. I'm sure they know the reason Yuri is gone. Maybe they expect me to usher another challenge to anyone who defies me. Come try to slay the king if you dare! Yeah, right. Fat chance of that happening, but I'll take the respect if that's what it is.

A week in and I also feel pretty secure that Agatha doesn't suspect a thing. Or at least, if she does suspect something, she knows it's in her best interest to keep quiet (and honestly, this scenario might be even better). Either way, she hasn't questioned me or Carla on why we were absent that day, and if she hasn't by now, I don't expect her to at all.

This leads me to my next point. Now that I'm comfortable Agatha isn't onto me, I'm thinking of asking for a change of positions. The bottleneck breaker job is easy, but man, is it boring. For a while there, I could distract myself with thoughts about my vendetta against Yuri, but that chapter has finally been put to rest, so now all I have to focus on is the monotony of the work. Things are back to normal, and I'm starting to remember that normal around here isn't exactly a good thing.

> But at least I'm not afraid,
>
> Deron Boyd

Log Entry: Day LVIII

Got the official word today that I won't be switching jobs anytime soon. Agatha said she looked into it (and for the record, I believe she did) but that there are no open spots currently available or workers looking to switch. It's a disappointing outcome, to be sure, but there's nothing I can do. I guess I'll just have to wait for something to open up. Hopefully, it'll happen sooner rather than later because after two months of this shit, this job really is starting to weigh me down.

Times like these make me truly thankful for my friends. Carla and I have been getting along great since ... well, I guess I don't need to write it out. Let's just say I think she was right about what she said that night. I think giving in to our desires really released the tension out of our relationship. At times like these, it's tough to think how I was ever even mad at her in the first place. I guess it's best not to dwell on that.

Hakeem and I have also been getting along well. There was a period of time there where I think he disagreed with a lot of my decisions, but for the past week or so, we've been back to chatting about all sorts of topics. I think it's been good for my psyche. I learn when he speaks, and I get to think on topics more deeply when we have our discussions. Helps me not think so much about the rest of this miserable existence.

> Signing off,
>
> Deron Boyd

Log Entry: Day LXI

Another rough one today, but what else is new. I feel like I've said this a lot recently, but the novelty of this experience has really worn off at this point. The first couple weeks were okay because the work was something new and I felt like I was contributing to something for once. The weeks leading up the fight actually weren't so bad either because the grind of the workday was the least of my worries. But now, pretty much all I notice is the grind, and I don't know what to do about it.

I envy Carla. We're still on great terms; it's nothing like that. But I envy how she is able to put on a smile every day, how she always seems happy. I don't get how she does it, but I wish she'd share her secret. However my mind works, it is not like that.

There has to be some way to improve my mental fortitude though. Maybe I'll ask Hakeem for some advice. He's been here over twenty-one years, and he's still surviving. And he almost never smiles.

Curse this place,
Deron Boyd

Log Entry: Day LXVIII

Interesting day today. To say it was a positive day might be a stretch. I think it's too early to tell if that will be the case. But it was definitely a day that at least broke up the monotony a little bit. At least the bookends of it.

I had the dream again last night: the one with the lighthouse and the flashing colours in the sky. It's the first time since the night leading up to the fight. I still can't say at all what it means, but I have noticed one thing. Each time I have this dream, it seems to evolve.

I saw the raven again, only this time it landed on the safety barrier of the catwalk, glided to a halt just beyond the glow of the lantern and instantly became still. I could almost reach out and touch it, it was so close.

I expected to feel scared, but there was no fear this time. In fact, I felt a certain relaxation looking at the bird, like it was a long-lost companion there to comfort me, not to cause harm. I think it felt the same way because when my eyes locked on it, it didn't move. It just stared over the horizon like it was waiting for something, for something to appear, for something to happen. I'm not sure what exactly, but I'm sure that it was waiting. There is something over that horizon that I can't see yet, but I know it is coming.

The other reason this day was more interesting involves a lot less mystery, but ironically, it also has to do with companionship. I made two friends for the price of one today: twin brothers! If I ever reread this in my later years, I might think that's a misprint, but no, future Deron, it is not! They actually are twin brothers, and they KNOW they're twin brothers. If you remember what they look like, future Deron, you won't question whether or not they were pulling your leg. One has glasses and the other does not, but otherwise, they're identical. And before you question how this is possible, future Deron, I will give you the explanation.

But first, I'll start from the beginning. Steve in bed 385 was released yesterday, and today, his replacement showed up. Nothing unusual about that. We've had a few people come and go since I've been here. But what was strange this time was that it wasn't just one new guy who came in and claimed the vacant bed; it was two! Both with round faces. Both with brown hair styled as a crew cut. Both a little bit chubbier than the average Utopian. I swear, if it wasn't for the glasses, I would've thought I was seeing double.

Hakeem saw it too, and together we went over to introduce ourselves (investigate, really; let's call a spade a spade). They noticed our blank expressions (well, mine; Hakeem was straight-faced, as usual), and after a good chuckle and a few jokes, they began to explain. This is where it gets interesting, future Deron, if you're not interested already.

Turns out Randall (he's the one with the glasses and the one who really has claim to that bed) and Andrew (he's set up on the sixth floor apparently) are twins who were born outside of the Utopia! That's how they know they're twins, future Deron. It's all so damn logical when you think about it. Because here, if a pregnant woman has twins, the kids are sent to different schools so that they don't grow up in conditions any different from other kids. But outside the Utopia, they don't have this policy! Outside, twins can grow up together in the same household, and that's what

THE UTOPIA

happened with these two. They grew up outside of the Utopia and only moved here three years ago after deciding they wanted to try something different. Sounds crazy, right, future Deron? But trust your younger self; you can't make this shit up!

Anyway, after that, both Hakeem and I were super intrigued to hear their story, so we invited them to play a game of cards. They happily obliged, and I'm glad they did. I've got to say, future Deron, if you don't remember them, your brain is probably not in a very good place because their story is something else. And, well, so are they.

They came here from America. They said they were from a small town, grew up poor, and decided to apply to come here for a chance at a better life. I remember learning in school about how bad some people had it in other parts of the world, and I've got to say, before I met these two, I never really believed it. But the way they talked about their situation—having no food some nights, abusive father and drug-addicted mother, evicted from their home multiple times. I'm telling you, future me, even if you end up hating the Utopia, you have to admit that what we have here can't be worse than that. Even the Camp might not be worse than that! Crazy to think, but it really might be true.

I asked them if there was anything they missed about home, and they said only the freedom of choice. As they grew older (they're both thirty-three now), they started to make a bit more money (not much, they said, but enough to struggle by), and what they appreciated about it was they could spend that money on whatever they wanted. If they wanted to go to a ball game, they could go. If they wanted to splurge on a meal, they could do it. It might cost them in the long run, but short term, they could do whatever they wanted, and that is something that just doesn't exist here.

It was quite interesting to hear their perspective. And honestly, future me, I'm not so sure what current me thinks about it all. Sometimes I think I hate the Utopia, but sometimes, like right now, I think that for the most part, it actually might be a decent place, that it was really me who caused my own downfall, and if I had just found a way to see past the darkness, things might have turned out different.

All I know is, I think these two might end up becoming good friends. I'm not sure what it is about them I like so much, but they just seem to have good hearts. Speaking of which ...

All this talk of companionship is reminding me of my friends. Marla, Diego, and Charlie. I miss you all dearly. I wish I was with you or that I could at least speak to you all, even if it was only for a few moments. And of course, you too ...

No, that is in the past. Marla, Diego, and Charlie I will see again. Kimmy I will not. I have done well to accept that, and I cannot relapse now.

Although I still love her all the same.

Cheers to good people,

Deron Boyd

Log Entry: Day LXXXI

Got some news today, and it doesn't sound too good. Apparently, Agatha's tenure with us is coming to an end for the year, and I don't think that's a good thing. I remember Ray mentioning Edwin my first day on the job, but he never got into specifics. Listening to Carla talk about him though, this guy sounds like a real hard case. Needless to say, I'm not looking forward to the switch. This place will grind you down no matter who is at the controls, but at least with Agatha, the treatment is fair. This guy sounds like he might be a different story.

On an unrelated note, I played cards with Randall, Andrew, and Hakeem again this evening. Actually, even Merlin joined in today. I still don't know what to think about that guy. He never says much, and when he does, it always sounds like he's speaking in parables. I guess it's not his fault. He does have some mental demons he's battling. But at the same time, his face just always makes me nervous. He stares at you hard, like he thinks you're some kind of monster he might one day find lurking under his bed. I just hope he thinks I'm a friendly monster and not one he has to kill.

I should probably get back on track because Merlin actually has nothing to do with my original point. That seems to happen to me a lot when I'm writing these, but anyway, what I wanted to say is this. Randall told me today that people who "look like me" have it tough where he's from. At first, I didn't get it, but he explained that what he was talking about was the colour of my skin. I asked him why that was, because here in the Utopia, I've never felt like I've been treated differently because of my skin tone (I've never even considered one might be discriminated against because of that before), and his response was that he honestly didn't know. He just stressed it was something that happens in his old country and other parts of the world and that it has been happening for centuries. He said every time people of my complexion build some type of momentum, something would interfere and stop the progress before true changes could be made. I don't quite understand it, but he seemed adamant it was true and adamant it was important. I guess there's a lot about the outside world I have yet to learn. I wonder how Kimmy is handling it.

Signing off before this gets too deep,

Deron Boyd

Log Entry: Day XCIV

It's official. Edwin is here, and Holy Mother of God, this guy seems like a psychopath. I was expecting bad, but I still had some faint hope, remembering Ray had described him something to the effect of being "not completely heartless." Well, I'm not sure what heartless looks like in Ray's book, but if today was any indication, this guy has a heart the size of a pharaoh ant at best.

Most people in a position of power introduce themselves by calling others to attention, giving a shout and asking for quiet so they can speak a few words. Not Edwin. This guy's idea of rounding up the troops is to blow this whistle that ... I don't even know how to describe it. I literally thought my ears were going to bleed, that's how abhorrent the screech was. And the headache it gave me lasted half the day.

The scariest part of it all, though, was what he said, yelling at us that play time is over, and it's time for real work. Like what we've been doing this whole time isn't real work? Like twelve-hour days resulting in unfathomable amounts of lumber isn't production enough? It seems crazy to say, but I think I'm more scared now than I was when I was about to fight Yuri. At least that situation I had some control over; this I can do nothing about.

Something tells me the last few months were only a warmup, that hell hath fury, and now we are really about to face the fire; that the Devil isn't a horned beast with a tail but a fat man with a whistle; and that maybe not all of us will survive his wrath.

God help us,
Deron Boyd

Log Entry: Day CII

It happened today. We'd been teetering on the edge since he started, everyone doing their very best to keep production at a maximum and complaints to a minimum to keep the boss happy. But today, someone finally slipped, and I got my first taste of what a mistake could lead to.

It was Carlos who made the mistake. How poetic is that? Even in keeping their distance and their comments to themselves, Yuri's gang still manages to torture me. Only difference this time was that it wasn't me alone who was left to suffer from their transgressions. It was everyone.

No dinner. That was our punishment. All of us. For Carlos's mistake, we all felt that wrath. It's Edwin's way of trying to scare us into perfect performance.

And the icing on cake is all he did was drop a skid of wood. Didn't jam a machine, didn't mess up any cuts and waste precious product. All he did was tilt the forklift too much and make a bit of a mess, a mess that we had cleaned up within ten minutes. We're all going to bed hungry because of that one small error, and it makes me terrified to think what the consequences will be when a real mistake is made.

Man, I hate this place,

THE UTOPIA

Deron Boyd

***

AS HE PUT HIS pen down to go to bed that night, Deron closed his eyes and began to truly reflect. He had taken some time to reread some of his recent entries, and the only summary of those tales that his mind could conjure up was that he was living in a house of horrors. Although he had managed to rid himself of Yuri Yin, Wise Guy was just one of many evil spirits he would have to fight along this journey, and this realization made his victory over Yuri seem much less monumental.

He sighed to himself as he restlessly tossed and turned. The thought was a bit depressing. But at some point, his brain reminded him that perhaps it wasn't all bad. If he could take out Wise Guy, perhaps he could take out the other evil spirits as well.

"I can, and I will," he whispered to himself softly. And that mantra finally gave him some positive hope of what was to come, finally reminded him that perhaps not all those spirits would end up being evil.

Finally allowed his body to shut down and find a moment of peace.

CHAPTER 11

On a Thursday evening some two-plus months after Deron Boyd had vanquished his mortal enemy to another region of the Camp, Sakura Saito sat facing Samantha Conway at an indiscriminately located table in the derelict Camp bar thinking that not much had changed but that something felt different.

"Zeeble," she said absentmindedly, still staring straight ahead behind her friend and toward the far wall; the one with the holes in it and the paint chips; the one that complemented their splintered, brittle wood table perfectly; the one that might as well have had a slogan spray-painted on it reading Home of the Outlaws. No, not much had changed about this place since the first two times they had been here, but something definitely felt different, something in the atmosphere. And only now was she recognizing what it was.

It was livelier tonight, more vibrant and uplifting, so much so that even Sakura, who didn't put too much stock in clichés, was starting to think that in this case, maybe the third time really was the charm. If nothing else, she was certainly enjoying herself more than she had at any point since coming to the Camp. It had been a rough first three months.

"Zeeble District, huh. Cool. I would ask you what that was like, but I'm sure it wasn't a whole lot different than anywhere else."

The comment came from her left, and she flashed a gaze away from

Sam and the wall just long enough answer. "I wouldn't imagine much." She smiled and took a sip of beer. She had an inkling to say more but nothing was coming. Thankfully, there was Sam.

"Zeeble District sucks, but Starside District though, where I'm from, that's a different story," said the comely blonde from across the table. Her hazel eyes twinkled, and her subtle lips formed a sardonic smile. "Up there, my local Pub was 245, so that's gotta be what, over ten times better than the Pub 19 you used to go to there, bucko."

The table of six shared a wholesome laugh. Sam brushed her silky layers back behind her ear in a gesture that said *I know, how funny am I, right?* And the woman to her right cackled even louder.

"I like that," said the man beside Sakura. "That was a good one."

"Yeah, except it would actually be over twelve times better," added a voice from another seat over. "Just under thirteen times to be more precise."

The five others looked at him curiously.

"Gee, thanks for that scintillating observation, Randall. Don't know how we would have ever continued the conversation without that little tidbit."

There were a few chuckles at that, then Randall responded. "Well, Andrew, it's funny you say that because if your thick head was better at calculating mathematics, maybe we wouldn't have ended up in the Camp."

"What does calculating math have anything to do with stealing a utilities van?"

"Plenty! Because if you had calculated that—"

"Okay, okay, enough, guys."

The man beside Sakura waved his arms to get the other two to calm down while the woman across from him just broke into laughter. Sakura looked to Sam, who gave her a shrug, then both women started to laugh along as well. Sakura couldn't remember the last time she had laughed this much. She certainly hadn't since she'd started her sentence.

Her first three months in the Camp had been anything but easy. The long workdays. The crowded spaces. The vitriol of the people. The almost complete lack of freedom. The Camp challenged her with so many negatives at all times, so many battles she had to fight every single day. She'd tried to adjust as best as she could, but even to this day, she was still having trouble.

It had all started her first night. From the moment she'd entered the Camp, she'd felt exceedingly uncomfortable. Hearing Supervisor Reynolds's speech about all the rules, seeing the eyes of the guards on her as she tried to find her new home: it was all terribly unsettling. But it was really the moment she'd stepped onto her housing floor that reality truly hit her.

Seeing the rows and rows of beds, it sunk in with her just how much she would miss her little Zeeble District apartment, miss her personal space. There were only four other women in the room when she walked in, but there were ninety-five more coming, and that was ninety-nine more than she had been used to living with since her seventeenth year. And for a quiet girl like her, a girl who liked to keep to herself, a "don't bother me and I won't bother you" type of creature, this setup would not just be a burden. This setup would be hell. She had known it then, and she still knew it now.

She hadn't slept well that first night. The anxiety was a factor, but more so than anything, it was the noise that had bothered her the most. Her keen sense of hearing had often been a blessing (like when it warned her that someone might be heading in her direction when she was trying to steal or allowed her to know the answers when classmates discussed assignments), but in this case, it was a curse. Because even with her earplugs in, she could hear almost everything: the snoring, the tossing and turning, the sound of footsteps when someone went to use the washroom. It had kept her on edge all night, kept her fearful that those footsteps might just be headed in her direction, kept her thinking that she might just end up like one of those victims in a slasher film. Even now, she still had that fear. Even now, it still took an agonizingly long time for her body to find sleep.

And that wasn't even the worst part.

"Sorry," the man beside her said, mostly addressing her but Samantha as well. "I would say they're not usually this rowdy, but that would be a lie," he joked.

The girls laughed some more. "That's alright; they're funny," Sam responded. "I like them. You guys are definitely some of the better people we've met here."

"Well, I appreciate you saying that," he replied. "Although I guess being best in show at the Camp is kind of like a bambino cat winning a beauty contest. The competition probably isn't so strong if that's happening."

Very true, Sakura thought.

"What's a bambino cat?" Sam asked.

"Here I'll ... Wow. Almost went for my phone to show you a picture. Can't believe I've been here almost four months and still make that mistake sometimes."

"That's okay. I've been here over a year, and I still sometimes forget. I guess there're some things you just never get used to in here," Sam replied.

"I think you're right," the man responded. "And honestly, I feel like that might be a good thing. When you get used to it in here is when you stop caring about ever leaving, and I don't know if I ever want to get to that point."

"Good point," Sam agreed with a head nod. "They can take away our freedom, but they can't take away our memories. We must never forget there is a world outside this place."

"Exactly," the man agreed. "Exactly." It seemed for a second like he wanted to say more, but then he just took a swig of his beer instead.

For her part, Sakura had zoned out and hadn't even caught the last of that. She was thinking about the bambino cat. She wasn't sure if this man was maybe being modest or perhaps had said that as a joke, but in her mind, the analogy seemed spot on. There weren't a whole lot of commendable characters she had met up to this point.

Her factory boss, for example, had had it out for her since day one, and the other employees weren't exactly angels either: always criticizing her, telling her to hurry up even though she had no experience in the job they had assigned. It really wasn't fair.

She worked in the textile factory, and even though she had never sewn anything in her life, they had her working one of the sewing machines. Her job was to sew the seam of the sleeve cuffs, and she just couldn't get the hang of it. She was constantly holding up the assembly line, and instead of switching her to a new position or teaching her proper technique, those around her just complained about her pace and threatened her with mistreatment if she did not improve.

It was a toxic culture, and she had known from the very beginning that this was going to be the case. When she had first walked in, her boss didn't even enquire about how she was, let alone ask if she had any experience sewing or if she wanted a tour. He just directed her toward a machine, and she was thrown into the fire. No tutorial. No training manual even. The only instructions were to sit down, shut up, and do the damn job.

A job she found horrible, by the way. Not just because she wasn't very good at it, but for other reasons as well. The rattling of the machines hurt her delicate ears. Clutter always seemed to invade her space. And of course, she was constantly ridiculed.

It all added up to perpetual feelings of anger, of sadness. It led to days of dread and drear. And at times when she wasn't thinking about how bad she had it, she was thinking of her losses: Ronaldo, her freedom, everything in her previous life she had taken for granted. It made her want to curl up and cry, and even as a child she hadn't done much of that. That's how badly this place had threatened to break her.

But then there was Sam.

"Hey, Sakura, you hear that? This dope says he fell asleep on a field trip one time. Didn't you do that?"

"I wish," she responded, like she had been part of the conversation the whole time. "No, I fell in the creek."

"Oh, that's right! I knew it was something."

"Ouch," the guy said. "And I thought I was clumsy," he added with a smile.

"Wasn't my fault," Sakura fired back. "Our teacher made us cross this log. It was slippery, okay?"

"Hey, no judgment," the man said through a grin, throwing his hands up in fake protest. "I took a snooze, you took a cruise; seems like poetry in motion if you ask me."

Sakura laughed. Sam reached across the table with a closed fist. "Well said, sir, well said." The man obliged with props, and Sakura continued to laugh, mostly at Sam's antics. She had a way about her, that girl. And a big heart too.

As the man talked more to Sam, she reached her hand over and placed it in Sakura's. It was a simple gesture, one that would go unnoticed by the rest of the table, but to Sakura, it meant a lot. It was Sam's way of making sure she was still here, enjoying her time, unbothered by the world around.

Sakura hadn't thought much of Samantha Conway the first time they had spoken. It was an innocuous meeting, her first morning in the Camp. This tall blonde woman, who she was sure couldn't have weighed more than 130 pounds despite her height, had simply smiled at her and asked her how she was. There was nothing more to it than that. And they didn't speak again for another few weeks.

Sakura would have never predicted in that moment what this woman would end up meaning to her, what she would do, the way she would stand up for her when their boss berated her to the point that she was almost in tears (Sam also worked in the textile factory; not in the same area, but on this day, she just so happened to be walking by). She didn't have to do that. She risked her own safety and security by doing so for someone she didn't even know. But she had stood up for her anyway because that was who she was.

After that, it became easy to be her friend, easy to trust her with whatever was haunting her at any given time, because Sam wouldn't tell, and Sam wouldn't judge. Sakura would have thought of her as a sister had she known what that was like.

She smiled at her friend, the one she had done just about everything with since that one fateful encounter, the one who had given her some hope that maybe these three years wouldn't be all hell after all. It had been a rough first three months in the Camp, but at least she had found someone to help alleviate some of her misery.

Sam smiled back. "Should we go?" she mouthed, having exited the discussion for the moment.

Sakura thought for a quick second but then nodded her head. She'd had fun tonight, liked these new people they had met, but she was also drained and ready to go home. There was another full day of sewing tomorrow she needed to prepare for.

"Hey, guys," Sam interrupted the others chatting. "Sakura and I are going to go. It's been a long day, and it's getting late now anyway. I think we both could use some sleep."

There were a few friendly protests, but little effort was made to convince them to stay. The group was tired too and would soon be departing themselves. They said their friendly farewells one at a time, Sakura and the man beside her the last to say goodbye.

"Was really nice to meet you, Sakura," he said with a smile. "And I mean that sincerely. You don't get to say that much around here."

Sakura laughed quietly to herself. She didn't find the statement particularly funny, but when she didn't know how to react, that was what she did. It was safe and easy and comforting in its way.

"Really nice to meet you too," she said back. And looking up at him, this handsome man with a dark complexion and broad smile, she really did feel that way. He seemed like a good person, one she would be happy to see again. "Maybe we'll run into each other again sometime."

"Maybe we just will," he said back, the smile still on his face. "Maybe we just will. You have a good night now."

"You too," Sakura smiled. She walked away then, and Sam took her by the hand and led her out the door. Normally, she felt scared at night when she walked out in these streets, but today, she felt good. She had made some new friends, and one in particular she was very much fond of, even if they had only spoken a few words.

Wonder what he thinks of me, she thought to herself.

Little did she know, when he went home, he would write about her in his journal.

CHAPTER 12

Log Entry: *Day CXI*

Been a few weeks since I've written something positive in here, but tonight was really ... fun. Seems crazy to write that given what's been going on the last few weeks, what with Edwin and all, but it really is true. Tonight, I was finally able to block all that negativity out and just enjoy myself without worry or care.

I went for beers with Carla, Randall, and Andrew. I invited Hakeem of course, but as usual, he turned me down. I understand he doesn't drink because of his religion, but he could still come hang out with us. Hell, Carla and I have been without drinking twice now because our quotas had been reached. But to each there own, I guess. Now is not the time to write about such things anyway. I should be focusing on the positive.

We made a couple new friends today—two women named Samantha and Sakura. Sam is this beautiful blonde lady, and man is she funny. She had me and the gang cracking up at every turn. I like her a lot. And Sakura is great too. She's super quiet, and I can tell she's uncomfortable around new people, but I feel that in spite of that, I got to know her pretty well. It's hard to put in words, but it's just a sense I have. I feel like we connected. I think inside that shelled exterior is a beautiful soul. I just hope she feels that way about herself.

I hope we see them again. You never know in this world of ours, but I really hope we do. I feel like they would make great members of our team. They seem like great people, and in this place, those aren't exactly a dime a dozen.

>Thankful,
>
>Deron Boyd

Log Entry: Day CXVII

Another miserable one. Today, one of the saws broke down, and you would think that would be a blessing. You would think that would mean work was cancelled for the day and everyone could go home. You would think, at a bare minimum, we would get a break until the machine was fixed. But that's not the way life works in here, at least not when Edwin is your boss.

Instead of waiting for a repair person to show up, Edwin had us working everything BY HAND. I wasn't on saw duty, but I was part of the "transfer team," whose job it was to carry the sawed logs from one part of the track to the next. I don't think I've ever been so tired in my life, and the worst part of it is, the machine isn't even fixed, meaning tomorrow, it's the same thing unless the problem gets rectified overnight.

I'd ramble on with more complaints, but I'm just too damn tired to write anymore. Night, night.

>ZZZZZZZZZ,
>
>Deron Boyd

Log Entry: Day CXIX

Saw was finally back up and running today, and I don't think I've ever been more thankful for something in my life. Funny how that works. Any other time, I would be bitching and moaning about my sorting job, but today, I couldn't have been more thankful for that task. Any more carrying logs and I think I would have collapsed.

Even Hakeem commented today on how worn out I look. I explained to him a little bit about our recent troubles with Edwin, but we didn't talk for long. I'm just not in a good mood, and I don't want to take it out on him. It's only nine o'clock, but I'm going to bed. Lights on, people talking, don't even care. My mind and body need it.

Sighing off,

Deron Boyd

Log Entry: Day CXXV

I'm losing it. I've had just about as much as I can take, and I'm honestly about to break. Maybe if the end were in sight, I would be able to last, but I'm barely a third of ONE YEAR INTO A FIVE YEAR SENTENCE, AND I'M ABOUT TO FUCKING SNAP!

Edwin called me out personally today. First time he's done that, and what's hilarious about it is that I literally wasn't doing anything different from any other day. Guess he just made his mind up in the morning that I would be his target, and that was enough to draw his ire. That seems to be how he works.

When he turned his back after he'd finished berating me, I cocked my fist and even took a step before I realized where I was. That was stupid. If a guard had seen me, or if Edwin had decided to turn around in that moment, I don't even want to think about what could have happened. For all I know, there could be a camera angle of it, and if it gets reviewed, I could still find myself in hot water. And the worst part of it is, I almost don't care at this point. That's how sick I am of this. The work, the fear, everything. My friends are starting to see the worst of me (Hakeem was telling me not to worry about Edwin because Judgment Day will come for him soon enough, and I nearly snapped at him). I don't like that either. This is what it was like when Kimmy left, and we all know what that eventually led to. I've got to get myself under control and fast, but man, how much easier it would be to just chuck the grenade and pick up the pieces when the smoke cleared.

Maybe I'll ask the area warden if I can challenge Edwin to a fight. I'm sure he'd get a kick out of that.

Only half joking,
Deron Boyd

Log Entry: Day CXXXV

Deke was released today. We had a big cake at lunch to celebrate, and then he and Edwin danced a goodbye salsa while everyone watched on and clapped. I'm actually smiling right now imagining that. Good to know I'm at least still capable of that expression.

In actuality, I only knew they were releasing Deke today because he told me himself. We've had minimal interactions since the fight, but he said he wanted to apologize to me for everything that happened with Yuri and the way he and the guys treated me. Not sure about the sincerity of the apology. He picked a real convenient time to tell me, what with him leaving and all. But I accepted it and said it was fine. And if that helps him sleep a little bit better at night, well, good for me for being the bigger man, I guess.

Anyway, none of that is really important in truth. It's just nice to write something other than my usual daily thoughts. I can sum those up in one line nowadays. I woke up angry, the day sucked, and we played cards at night. What a goddamn life.

Whatever,
Deron Boyd

Log Entry: Day CLVII

Miserable day. Edwin yelled at Carla until she was almost in tears. I tried to talk to her after, but she was still upset and didn't want to speak. I almost lost my temper with her for no goddamn reason, but I managed to hold it in. She's still my only real friend at the factory, and the last thing I need is to get into a fight with her.

Didn't speak much to Hakeem or Randall today and didn't even see Andrew. Randall and Hakeem went up to visit him on the sixth floor, but I just wasn't in the mood. I haven't been in the mood a lot lately. I think the guys understand, but it still feels shitty. Weird how I'm very self-aware about all this stuff and yet, for some reason, can't seem to do anything to fix it. Story of my life, I suppose.

I need help,

Deron Boyd

Log Entry: Day CLXXXV

Had the dream last night, only this time it felt more tumultuous than peaceful. I guess that makes sense given the circumstances, but I digress.

I followed the raven again. It perched itself on the veranda railing, and I followed it with my eyes. I was about to follow it with my legs as well, until it turned and looked at me.

I nearly jumped out of my skin when it set its gaze upon me. It was the swiftness of the gesture that did it, and the look of intensity in its eyes, like it was challenging me to come closer—come closer and see what would happen. I woke up in a sweat, and it must have been an hour before I got back to sleep.

Other than that, the day was quite normal—a.k.a. shitty. I guess the raven couldn't think of any new ways to torture me. Perhaps I'm in a time warp and only when I kill that bird will I be set free of my misery. Perhaps ... oh, who cares? Let's just see if Hakeem and Randall want to play Link.

Misery loves company,

Deron Boyd

Log Entry: Day CXC

Saw Sakura and Sam after work today. Wasn't planned or anything like that, just complete happenstance. I was walking with Carla toward the pharmacy (she still hasn't gotten over that cold yet), and they just so happened to be crossing our path.

We chatted for a while, and it was really quite nice. I love Hakeem, Carla, and the twins, but it was pleasant to hear some different voices and opinions for once, even if, in Sakura's case, that voice only said a few words. It's kind of cute, actually, how quiet she is. Makes me smile just thinking about it.

I invited them to hang out a bit longer, but they said they were tired and wanted to get back, which is understandable. I seem to recall Sam saying their boss was a bit of a terror as well. Although perhaps they have a new boss now? I guess that's irrelevant. If they say they're tired, who am I to say they're not?

Anyway, they said they would love to hang out another time though, so I suggested we play cards a week from tonight. They said they would love to, and you know what? From the looks on their faces, I think they seemed genuinely excited. That made me happy too.

I'm not sure why I picked a week from today. It's not like any of us have any big plans before then. But I guess it gives me something to look forward to, and that's sure something I could use. The plan is to set up a game at the park near the pharmacy. There's usually a bench or two open in the evenings. If not, we can just play on the grass. Either way, it will be nice to hang out as a big group.

I'm starting to smile too much, so I should probably finish this off. Don't want to lull myself into a false sense of security. Edwin still lurks, for the moment at least. One more thing to look forward to: the countdown to him leaving. As of today, I've officially survived one hundred days of his bullshit. That's got to be worth a medal or something.

Wear it,

Deron Boyd

THE UTOPIA

Log Entry: *Day CXCVII*

Been a tough week, but today was a good way to end it off. I guess technically, there's still Sunday, but I try to see those half days as their own entity. Sundays are the Lord's day, after all. I think that's what it says in the scriptures anyway. Not that that's really relevant to the point.

Tonight, the group of us enjoyed a nice card game in the park: myself, Carla, Randall, Andrew, Sakura, Sam, and even Hakeem left the housing complex for once. It was the first time all seven of us have simultaneously had the pleasure of each other's company, and I've got to say, it felt great. The circle felt, just, complete in some way, like how it used to feel when Kimmy, Marla, Diego, Charlie, and I were together.

We taught Sam and Sakura to play Link, and by the end, they were loving it. Sam sucked, but Sakura I think had the strategy pretty much down pat by the end. She's really smart that girl, and she opened up more today, which was really nice to see.

I think the seven of us will be seeing a lot more of each other in the future. We already have a plan for another game next week, and I'm looking forward to it already.

                             Guess maybe there is some good left in the world,

                                                                              Deron Boyd

Log Entry: *Day CCXXII*

It was a tale of two days that can be divided very simply.

The good: spent time with Sakura, Sam, Carla, and the boys.

The bad: everything else.

This seems to be a common theme of the last few weeks, and I'm not sure what to think of it. Some moments, I am honestly in bliss. I have a great group of friends who I enjoy spending time with. With Ronald having been released last week and Shawn switching to a new factory, I have zero fear of retaliation from that gang. Ray and I have even started to talk a little bit, and although I still hold a bit of a grudge, I'm no longer truly upset with him or the others either. I have my one beer a month and have been stalking up on zombie pills because I figure they might make good currency one day, but I haven't used one since that first night. Physically, I feel probably the best I have ever felt.

But then there's always Edwin, always the work, so many hours doing the same shitty job and fearing the worst if we slip up. It's taxing beyond belief. Some days, as much as I love hanging out with my friends, all I want to do is go home, put my head down, and get some respite. And I think the worst part is that ... I feel like I've said this before many times, but it bears repeating. The worst part is knowing I still have so much time to go. It feels sometimes like I'm walking in a desert, and I know there's an oasis somewhere, but what I'm not sure of is if I will find refuge before I succumb. It's there, but I can't see it, and it's really unsettling.

Sometimes, I see good. Often, I see bad. The world is a double-edged sword, and it's hard to get a handle on it.

Mired in mediocrity,

Deron Boyd

Log Entry: Day CCXL

Was another tough one, but at least a little bit of good came out of today, and I'll try to focus on that while I can. There hasn't been a lot of positivity in my life lately, so I'll take what I can get.

I finally told the whole group about my arrest. Hakeem and Carla knew, and I've told the others the story in bits and pieces, but today was the first time I went through the whole night: drinking at the bar, waking up next to a pipe and a team of guards with no recollection of what I had done or why I had done it. It was an embarrassing story to tell, but it was something I had to do. The others had all shared, and it was about time I did as well. They're my friends, and I owe them the truth.

And honestly, I felt better after I told them, like I had lifted some weight off my chest. Not the whole barbell, but at least a disc or two. I felt I could have kept discussing it if they'd had any questions.

And for a second, it seemed like Andrew did have something to say. I think he was about to ask about the whole lapse of memory. He started into some semblance of a question, but Hakeem interrupted before he could finish, and that was the end of that. I'm not sure if he did it on purpose or not, but if he did, I would guess he was just looking out for me. Typical Hakeem.

If he ever wants to ask again though, I'll be ready to answer. I may not know why I did it, but if I'm speaking the truth, I would rather know my friends don't judge me for it than understand the reason why. They are more important to me at this point.

Oh, little victories,

Deron Boyd

Log Entry: *Day CCLXXVI*

Agatha is back. Praise the Lord. I honestly thought the room might break into applause when she stepped in. It didn't happen, but you could feel the energy pick up around the place, like we finally had a reason to think that things would be okay.

I was on my last legs. I think if someone reads through this in the future, they won't need me to spell that out for them, but to whoever is reading this, I want that to be clear as day: these last six months were hell. The effort it took to get through them is impossible to explain. Even when Kimmy left, at least I had my freedom. At least I could lie in bed all day or use drugs to cope. But here, there is none of that. Here, there is the work and the people around you and that is all you have. And when one of those people makes it a point to do whatever he can to break you, and there's nothing you can do about it, the weakness that you feel is absolutely sickening. It's like you're some bug, and if you get squashed, no one cares because there are millions of other bugs who can replace you. And those other bugs, they don't care if you get squashed either because they themselves are just trying to survive. I've never felt anything like that, and honestly, I'm not sure how I'm going to do it again the next time around. I guess if you can do something once, you can do it twice, but at the moment, that feels like a farfetched idea. I suppose I should try not to think about that right now.

Agatha for queen of the Utopia,

Deron Boyd

Log Entry: Day CCCX

So Carla and Sam are officially a thing. If you have been reading along and that seems out of the blue, well, it's not. I could tell there was something there from the moment we all met, and I guess it's just been building ever since. Those two really like each other, and I can see why. They're similar in a lot of ways: fiery and passionate, but at the same time, always smiling. They really do make a cute couple.

Funny story actually: I'm pretty sure Andrew was into Sam. He never said as much, but he always seems to choose the seat beside her when we're playing cards. He looked a bit flabbergasted when the girls made their announcement, but not in a judgmental way. I'm pretty sure in America, most relationship types are generally accepted, maybe not in the way they're accepted here by just about everyone, but I think most people are at least indifferent these days. I think I remember Randall saying that in passing once.

Other than that, not a whole lot to report. Another boring day at the factory, but at least it was a half day. In this place, that's about as good as it gets.

Unfortunately, there's always another Monday,

Deron Boyd

Log Entry: Day CCCXXXIV

Feeling tired this eve. I guess that's not surprising. In the Camp, one always feels tired. But it's a different kind of tired. Not exhaustion exactly, more of a wearisome tired, like I just don't know what to do with myself anymore.

I just feel stagnated at this point. I love my friends, but even our conversations are starting to get a bit dull. There's never anything new to talk about, of course. No one has ever done anything interesting because all we do is work. I'm even getting a bit sick of our card games.

Maybe I'll take a zombie pill tonight. I haven't since that first night, but I've stocked up plenty, so I can afford to if I want. There's no real good reason for it, but maybe I'll just do it for the sake of changing it up. I know I'll feel refreshed in the morning at least.

We'll see,

Deron Boyd

Log Entry: Day CCCLXV

Well, it's official. Today, I celebrated my campiversary. One whole year it's been, and I can hardly believe it.

Needless to say, it's been a long year. There have been some positives, for sure. I've quit drinking and drugs (mostly), made some new friends, and overcome a lot of turmoil. But there have definitely been a lot of dark times as well. And I wish I had more meaningful reflections, but it's honestly tough to think of any with how long I still have to go.

There's an old saying I think used to be applied to prisons. They say you only do two days: the day you come in and the day you go out. I wish whoever made up that saying was here right now so I could smack them across the head. That is maybe the biggest load of bullshit I've ever heard. You don't do two days. If anything, you do double days. Maybe that's what the saying is actually supposed to be. You do two days in prison for every one day in the real world.

Anyway, I don't know what else to add to this other than to try to give myself some positive words to close. Year one of anything is typically the hardest. Hopefully, that means it's all downhill from here.

Doubtful, but I can dream,

Deron Boyd

Log Entry: Day CDII

Another day, another bother. We all had to stay late today because apparently, they're putting up a new building somewhere in Wexin District and they need a ton of wood for it. It was an extra hour of work, and the most annoying part about it is, it's not like we get any type of compensation for our efforts. No extra beer, no longer break another day. Our only option is to do what we're told or risk being punished, and there's nothing we can do about it.

I feel like I'm writing the same things over and over again in here, but I've got nothing else to talk about. And things are only going to get worse with the impending return of Edwin only a couple months away.

Where's the light,

Deron Boyd

Log Entry: Day CDLVIII

The Devil is back. An already terrible situation just got even worse. I could write paragraphs about it, but I really don't feel like jotting my thoughts right now. God, I hate this place.

Let me out,

Deron Boyd

Log Entry: Day DLV

Randall told us today that he and Andrew got sent home early from the power plant because of some equipment problem, and I nearly told him to go fuck himself. What a great friend I am, honest to God. Something good happens to my friends, and instead of being happy for them, my first reaction is to be jealous.

THE UTOPIA

I wish I could say it was just a momentary lapse, but that wouldn't be true at all. Even now, I still feel envious more than I feel vicariously happy. It really makes me sick. And the worst part about it is that I'm the only one who can't seem to escape the negativity.

After twenty-two years here, Hakeem is still fine. Sakura and Sam have a tough boss too, but they do alright. Randall and Andrew are in a foreign land, and they've adjusted well. Carla is in the exact same boat as me, but she still manages to smile. It's just me who is angry all the time. It's just me who is struggling with all this. There was a point in time when I thought I had finally cleaned my plate of all this angst, but now I feel like that plate is more loaded than when I started. And thinking about it now just makes me even more upset! I just don't know what to do anymore.

Wishing I would just grow the fuck up,

Deron Boyd

Log Entry: Day DCIV

Had an alright one today. Had the dream again, which makes it the third time in the last two weeks alone. Don't really know why it's been appearing more consistently, but a strange pattern I've noticed is that every time I have the dream, the next day seems to be just a little bit better. Nothing crazy happens. It's not like we get the day off or some gourmet meal. I just seem to feel a little more relaxed, a little more positive, better able to take whatever comes in stride. I wish I had the dream every night.

Although I also can't help but feel that perhaps it's all just a setup for something terrible.

Always staying positive,

Deron Boyd

Log Entry: Day DCCXV

Agatha asked me if I wanted to switch to forklift duty, and I could hardly believe it. After nearly two years in this place, I'm finally going to get to do something other than watch wood slide down a conveyor belt all day. I'm scared to say it, but add that to a week where we danced at the bar and played soccer in the park and things are actually looking up.

I hope I haven't just jinxed it,

Deron Boyd

Log Entry: Day DCCCXXVI

Something bad is going to happen. I've never been so sure of it in my life. It's been almost a whole week now, and they still won't tell us why Edwin isn't back. It just doesn't make sense. If he quit or retired, why wouldn't they just tell us that? Keeping us in the dark can only mean trouble.

I almost shouted in joy when they announced he was gone, but now I'm just scared. I have no idea why, but it's one of those times I just trust the feeling. I wish I was wrong. I wish I was just being paranoid. But there's something going on, and I just can't help but feel like I'm going to be in the thick of it. That sounds exorbitantly conceited, but I know I'm not wrong.

Please someone help me,

Deron Boyd

Log Entry: Day DCCCXXVIII

Something bad is happening. I know I've said that over and over the last few days, but this time, I'm talking about the present and not the future. It's all unfolding right before my very eyes.

I saw the area warden on my walk home, and I swear he was getting arrested. I saw two guards talking to him, heard him shout something unintelligible, and then saw him get put into the back of the van, and the group of them drove off.

I know I sound crazy. I know it's entirely possible the guards were just giving the area warden a ride while he sat in the back. I know everything I see in here makes me think the worst is happening, especially recently given the bad feelings I've been having.

But I also trust my intuition on this one. This was not some friendly ride offered by two colleagues. These guards weren't asking; they were demanding. If it hadn't happened in the broad daylight of a Sunday afternoon, I think things could have gotten ugly. I think maybe the area warden might have fought back.

And I think I know why they were bringing him away.

And I think I'm next.

Just why,

Deron Boyd

Log Entry: Day DCCCXXIX

I finally saw it. After years of having the dream, I finally saw what that orange light was over the horizon. It's not the setting sun. It's not the glow of some distant island. It's not something beautiful or majestic at all. It is something utterly terrifying, just like that raven.

This was the closest I had ever gotten to the bird. It looked at me with those naked eyes, staring right through me, staring through me until I was within spitting distance. When it looked back over the water, that's when I saw it: the fire. It was the deadliest conflagration I ever could have imagined, and it wasn't the water that was burning. It wasn't the sky that was lit up in embers. It was a ship engulfed in flames, destined for only one thing: to sink into a hollow grave, never to be seen by the world ever again.

And something tells me I'm about to burn down along with it.

This is the end,

Deron Boyd

***

IT WAS DAY 832 when it happened, and like Deron had come to suspect that it would, the event transpired without any real drama. His only real disappointment was that all his friends were there to witness it. He could have done without that. Seeing the shock on their faces just added some salt to the open wound.

They were at the park playing cards when the guards approached. Deron had known instantly that this was the moment and had stood up before the request was even made. There was no point in dragging this on longer than he had to. He picked up his feet and made his way toward the guard van without muttering a sound.

"What's going on?" Sam asked the guards, who were watching Deron walk.

"Where is he going?" added Andrew, directing his question more toward the group.

Only Carla and Hakeem knew the answer. Not directly in that moment, but they would make the deduction and inform the group before long. It had to be the fight. There was no other explanation.

Before he entered the van—a van that would chauffer him to a holding cell for the second time in his life—he took one last look back toward his friends. Carla was in tears. Sam's face was aghast. Hakeem was praying. Randall, Andrew, and Sakura were looking on with blank stares, all thinking the same thing.

Deron nearly broke down in that moment, realizing that if they wanted to, the State could send him to a place where he would never see any of them again; realizing that if that happened, that would be the end. He could fight no longer. They were the only reason he hadn't given up already.

He turned away, only because seeing how much they cared made him hurt even more, thinking to himself how truly unfair the Camp could be.

He had survived Edwin. He had survived Yuri Yin. And it had all been for naught. It was a sad truth he should have known all along: in this place, if something didn't get you, something else would.

CHAPTER 13

If there was one thing Matthew Tucker had learned since becoming a member of the guards, it was how to keep a good poker face. Sitting in the grandiose lobby of the head parliament building, his expression indicated a relaxed disinterest, like this was just part of his daily routine, and the fact that he was about to meet with the leaders of the Utopia didn't bother him at all.

It was a skill he had developed over time. He hadn't always been like this. As a kid, he'd been brash and reactive. As an adolescent, the same. Even his first years out of school, he'd still tended to show outbursts of emotion. Only after becoming a guard had he started to hone his craft, more as a necessary defence mechanism than a proactive strategy, but up to this point, it had worked. He still had all those emotions, still had many times where he felt like he had no clue what he was doing. But he had gotten very good at pretending.

He looked around the giant foyer with the exquisite paintings and brass statues wondering how on earth he had gotten to this place. Physically, he had taken the train, and mentally, he had a general idea why he had been summoned, but metaphorically, it just didn't make much sense. His whole life, he had done just enough to get by, hadn't cared at all about gaining a solid reputation or being held in good standing, had preferred to just fade into the background when it came to work endeavours. And yet now he was here.

He stood up with Deron Boyd-esque intuition that his time had come, and like his counterpart, he was correct. A guard behind the extensive concierge desk passed along the message and gave him his instructions.

"Tap this card in the elevator and it'll allow you to go to the top floor. Talk to Laurie when you get there. They should be waiting for you in the conference room. Any questions?" Matt shook his head no. "Good. And don't worry about your belongings. Someone here will watch over those no matter how long you're gone. You'll get your weapon and everything else back when you return the card." Matt nodded. "Good luck."

"Thanks," Matt replied, finding the well-wishes weirdly appropriate. He wasn't here to be reprimanded. Quite the opposite, in fact. Yet his feelings behind the mask were eerily similar to the ones Deron Boyd had felt as he stood on trial for the second time waiting for the Computer to hand down his punishment: a burgeoning fear that the future didn't look bright. Whether that was true or not, he would discover soon enough.

Beyond the concierge desk was a short hallway that led to an elevator lobby. There were four in operation, and the first one on the left opened at his request. Inside, he presented the card the guard had given him to the scanner, and up, up, and away he went. Destination: top floor.

His heart rate began to increase as he levelled through the floors. It had been an oddly long time since he'd stepped foot in an elevator outside of those located within an apartment complex. Over two years, in fact. It was when he'd taken a man named Gregory Zimmer for the last ride of his life.

Little had changed between this trip and that. He still drove the same route to and from the Camp five days per week. He still enjoyed his surfing on the weekends and quiet nights at home. He was still single. He'd had a steady girlfriend for over half a year before cutting the cord a couple months ago, deciding he preferred his alone time after the honeymoon phase had passed. He still played chess, although less frequently these days. For the most part, he just concerned himself with work and TV, figuring that combination was about as safe as he could get. He always remembered what happened to the rebels in the back of his mind.

"Tenth floor," the automated voice announced as the doors spread their wings.

THE UTOPIA

Matt stepped out into a corridor that looked similar to the one nine floors below. Beyond it, things changed. The lobby space was much smaller, there were no statues or paintings, and the concierge desk faced the elevator area instead of a main door.

He approached it all the same, with that pale look of indifference on his face, hiding the fear within.

"Hey there," said a woman in a guard uniform. Unsurprisingly, this place was swarming with them. He had counted at least seven in the lobby alone and another dozen more posted at various checkpoints outside.

"Hi," he said, forcing a smile. "My name is Matthew Tucker. I'm here to see Leader Azalea Hawthorne and Leader Mustapha Hakimi at their request."

"Excellent." She smiled back. "They're just finishing up with District Overseer Bhakta, but they should be ready to see you any minute. In the meantime, I'll just check you in and you can take a seat if you like. Can I just have your ID?"

"Absolutely," he said with another fake smile. He handed it to her, thinking that even for the Utopia, this was a bit much. They had ID'd him at the front door, at the lobby concierge desk, and now here. Were they worried he might have transformed into a werewolf on the ride up?

He said nothing, of course, and took a seat at a white leather couch located along the wall to the left of the concierge. From the elevator lobby, the room expanded near the desk to create a more welcoming feel. At least that's what he figured the intention was. For him, it didn't do anything for his nerves.

His gaze fixated on the wall behind the concierge. Unlike the walls downstairs, this one was plain with white paint and no decorations whatsoever. The only thing disrupting the drywall was a set of double doors fabricated from metal. The design was quite contradictory to the charm of the downstairs lobby, but he couldn't argue with the practicality.

His eyes went hollow as he stared off into space, thinking to himself once again how unbelievable it was that he was here. Two days ago, he'd been preparing to go to work same as always, only to receive a call from Azalea Hawthorne's administrative assistant asking if he would consider meeting with the leaders to discuss a new role within the guards, one where he would fill a key position within the organization and receive a special benefit if he accepted the assignment. He had nearly told the woman to go take a long walk off a short pier, sure that this was some type of prank call. God was he thankful he hadn't done that because this was no joke. They needed a position filled, and they really wanted him. Him!

He took the train out the next day and hiked halfway across the country from his home in Wexin to the aptly named State District. He was too late to see the leaders that day, so he spent the night at the station, and then with the help of his GPS and a few buses, he made his way to the head parliament building this morning where he'd been waiting patiently ever since for his chance to speak to the most powerful people in the Utopia. It was not exactly how he'd been planning to spend his Sunday, but it wasn't like he had a choice. If they wanted him here, they were going to get him here one way or another.

He took a few breaths to try to steady his racing heart. He still didn't know exactly what the job was, but it was well understood that it must be something of utmost importance if the leaders of the whole goddamn country wanted to speak to him in person. Anything less than that and they wouldn't waste their time.

Either that or it was a trap, a way to get him here so they could lock him up somewhere and throw away the key. That thought had crossed his mind, of course, but it hadn't lingered long. If they wanted him for something, there were a lot quicker and more effective ways to bring him up on charges. Besides, he could honestly think of nothing he had done wrong. He had made a conscious effort to be a model citizen since the day he'd been released. This really had to be a job offer of some kind. But what kind of job, and why did they want *him*?

He was about to find out.

"Guard Tucker." His eyes blinked hard at the sound of the voice. He gazed toward the guard-secretary. His forehead had started to sweat. "They're ready for you. You may go in now."

"Great," he said. He rose from his seat without hesitation, wiped his head once calmly with his shirt sleeve, and then made his way around the desk and toward the metal doors. Just before he went through, he smiled his warmest smile at the guard-secretary and added one final remark.

"Thank you," he said.

And he really hoped he meant it.

***

AFTER TEN MINUTES OF talking, his first impression of Azalea Hawthorne and Mustapha Hakimi—the current Utopia leaders and grand overseers; the head lawmakers, movers, and shakers—was that they were surprisingly normal.

"Sounds like a lot more fun than sitting here with us," said the skinny man in the black suit. And they all shared a laugh. Matt's was probably the loudest of them all.

"I don't know if I'd go *that* far," he replied somewhat sarcastically. It was a tone he wouldn't have imagined using in a million years before he'd met them, but for some reason, now it felt completely appropriate. More than that, actually. It felt like exactly what they wanted to hear. They all chuckled some more.

Who would've guessed they'd have such a great sense of humour? he thought to himself. Not that he'd expected them to have green skin and long tentacles. He, like the rest of the Utopians, knew exactly what they looked like from their press conferences and public addresses. It had just never dawned on him that they might be this friendly: offer him a glass of water, ask him about his travels. He'd expected a thorough interrogation, but so far, what he'd gotten was smiling faces and humble banter.

In some ways, it made him terribly suspicious, but for the moment, he was unexpectedly comfortable.

"I love to surf too, actually. Of course, our district isn't particularly close to the ocean, so I don't get to go as often as I would like. But any time I can get to the beaches, I love to catch some waves."

"You mean let the waves catch you," the woman in the white dress jested, chuckling. "Let's be honest, Mustapha, you're not exactly Kelly Slater out there."

That got a hearty laugh out of Mustapha, and Matt laughed along too. He had no idea who Kelly Slater was, but he figured it was best to keep up with the positive energy.

"I'm not particularly great myself," he said from across the table. They were sitting at one end of a long conference table, Azalea and Mustapha on one side, him on the other. There was no one else in the room but the three of them. "But it's definitely a good way to relax."

"I agree wholeheartedly," Mustapha replied. He had a bright face that dimpled when he smiled, and it gave him the appearance of someone who was kind, someone you could trust.

Matt would hold off on putting his complete faith in him for now, but he also hadn't yet been given a reason to be skeptical of him either.

"It's a great way to clear your mind. The waves just have this calming aura about them."

"Sure do," Matt concurred. He took a sip of his water, unsure of what else to add.

"Would you like some more?" Azalea asked kindly, pointing to his glass. He hesitated for a moment before declining the offer. She bore a striking resemblance to the girl he had dated for the better part of the last year: dark hair, soft brown eyes, fair skin, and an illuminating smile. He almost wanted to bring it up but thought it unnecessary. They likely already knew that. And everything else about him.

"No, thank you, I'm fine." He smiled. She returned his gaze and then looked to Mustapha. He nodded at her, and that was the moment Matt knew things were about to get serious.

"Well, in that case," Azalea spoke. "We know it's been a long journey to get here, and I'm sure you're eager to get back. So what do you say we get down to business?"

Matt nodded, expecting to start feeling more nervous, but his anxiety wasn't rising, a part of him understanding that the sooner they discussed the nitty-gritty, the sooner he could leave.

"Great. That's great, Matt. So I'll cut to the chase then. For the past few years, we've had some trouble with a certain area warden, a man you're very familiar with: Supervisor Mirko Reynolds."

Matt flinched when he heard the name. Azalea noticed but ignored it and continued.

"Turns out Reynolds has been running a fight club in his area of the Camp the last couple of years. We've known about it for some time, but it's taken a while to gather the necessary evidence and to make sure we had a full grasp on exactly who was involved in the operation. Measures against the offenders are being taken as we speak."

Matt gulped silently. Now his pulse was starting to speed up. He hadn't been told this had anything to do with Reynolds. And this new knowledge was starting to put some serious doubts in his mind.

Maybe this wasn't about a new position after all.

"That's crazy," he said straight-faced. "I had no idea. I—"

"We know, Matt," Mustapha intervened. "I can sense you're nervous, and that is completely understandable. We know we didn't give you much information when we asked you here, but we promise this is not an interrogation. We know you had nothing to do with any of it. Don't worry about that."

"Okay," he said. He thought of denying his nervousness, but there was no point in lying. They would know if he was.

Mustapha continued. "We asked you here, Matt, because now that the area warden has been relieved of his duties, we need someone to fill his position. And we were hoping that someone would be you."

"Me?" Matt nearly shouted; he was so surprised. Suddenly, he was a lot less nervous and a lot more confused.

They seriously want me to be an area warden?

"Yes, Matt," Azalea chimed in. "We've looked through your file and we like what we see. You are devoted to your position, have an exemplary record ever since you've become a member of the guards, are well-liked by your co-workers, and have a very good demeanour, which we have seen here firsthand."

"I appreciate that," Matt replied. "But I'm sure there are other guards who also have great records. I've never been more than a driver. This seems like a huge step up. I'm not sure I'm ready."

"Understandable," Mustapha commented. "You're right; this is definitely a step up in responsibility, but we think you can handle it. We know how seriously you take the work, so much so that you leave yourself with few other commitments. We know you know how to navigate Camp life because you've been there yourself."

Matt looked at them awe-struck. His poker face had abandoned him on the flop, and he hadn't a hope of getting it back by the river. This was so much to take in, and while their reasons were all logical, it still didn't make sense why they would choose him. It still didn't make sense how they even knew who he was.

"I want to show you something. I can tell you're unsure, so I want to be completely transparent with you. I want you to know why we came to this decision because it wasn't by accident."

Mustapha rose from his chair and shifted to his left. In the corner of the room was a filing cabinet, and on top of that was a remote. Mustapha took it, clicked it, and turned on the monitor that was attached to the wall overlooking the table.

What Matt saw when that screen turned on made his eyes pop. It was a list, numbered from one to ten. And number one on that list, in bold black lettering, was the name Matthew Tucker.

"This list, Matt. This list was not compiled by us. This is not a list of the people who *we* believe are best suited for this role because we are not smarter than anyone else in this country. We do not know anything more than the bartender or the bus driver or the administrative worker. We, like everyone else, are just following the guidelines. You know where this list came from, Matt?"

"The Computer."

He said it instantly. For the first time since he'd been here, he didn't need to think. He had intuitively known the answer to the question "why me?" the whole time, it just somehow hadn't clicked. When there's an important decision to make, it isn't a human who is tasked with the obligation. He'd been taught that as a boy and had seen it firsthand every time he entered the courthouse. The big decisions are always left to the Computer.

And the Computer had chosen him.

"That's right, Matt. The Computer chose you. If we're to be perfectly honest with you, less than a week ago, we had no idea who you were or what you did. But we needed a new area warden, and when we asked the Computer who was best suited to fill that position, the answer was you."

Mustapha sat down, and Matt again looked at him with a sense of disbelief. He understood now why he had been summoned here, but what he still didn't get was what could have possibly led the Computer into thinking he was the best option?

"The Computer isn't always right, Matt. We know that is what is taught in school, but nothing is perfect, not even the machine. It chose Supervisor Reynolds, after all, and look how that turned out. But the Computer *is* right much more often than it is wrong, and if it says you're the best candidate, it is our duty, as the current leaders of the Utopia, to take that recommendation very seriously. And now that we have met you, we believe you are the correct choice."

"Of course, you don't have to accept," Azalea added. "If you're happy with your life, no one is going to force you to take this new role. There are clear disadvantages that come with it. It is a lot more responsibility, and you will need to move to the Camp full time. You will have your own setup there, but until you quit or retire, you will have to live on the grounds, and your freedom to leave will be limited. It will be a large adjustment.

"But it also comes with a number of advantages, mainly this: If you accept this position, you need only work for ten years, then you can retire. And once you do, you will have no chance of being picked. It doesn't matter that you will not be sixty years old. That is the perk of greater responsibility: more freedom later on for your troubles."

Matt gazed once more with a surprised face that said what he was thinking. Before he had a chance to chime in, Azalea continued.

"We don't advertise this because we don't want everyone competing to earn the top spots. We want people to naturally climb into their roles so their true nature can be properly analyzed by the Computer. When Mustapha and I were chosen four years ago to become leaders for this seven-year stint, we had no idea our reward for the headaches and pressure would be freedom once we were finished. That is why we were picked. We were put in these roles because they were something we cared about and something that meshed with our personalities, not because we wanted them for the rewards. Do you understand?"

Matt nodded, unsure if he was doing so truthfully or not. This was way too much for his brain to try to comprehend all at once, which was unfortunate because the biggest decision of his life was looming.

"Like I said, no one is going to force you to accept this role. The only thing we ask if you decline is that you never mention to anyone what we have told you about the early retirement advantage. I don't want this to come off as a threat, but legal action may need to be taken if you do. It would threaten to undermine part of the system."

Matt said nothing.

"Otherwise, nothing else changes. You go back to your normal role. You work off your mandatory years and then you can continue, seek something new, or quit and hope you're never chosen. The Computer picked you; you don't have to pick it. But we need to know your answer right away because if you decline, we need to pick someone else to fill this position."

Still nothing from Matt other than a blank stare.

"If it helps at all, you won't be responsible for arresting Reynolds or any of the others. All of that has already been taken care of. You can start there fresh with no inherited problems, other than the ones that are to be expected as part of overseeing such an important operation."

She stopped talking then and gave Matt a look that was not a glare but also not the smile he had grown accustomed to seeing from her either. It was a look someone gives when they're studying intently and are keen to grasp a concept. She wanted to know what his plan was.

He would reveal what that was soon enough, but for the moment, he was desperately trying to sort out his own thoughts. On the one hand, early retirement sounded like an absolute blessing. On the other, he questioned if he would survive to see the end of his term. There were so many unknowns: what exactly this job entailed, how much control of the situation he really had; how long his leash was if he made a few innocent mistakes.

On the surface, the safe choice seemed to be to decline, work this lax job until sixty, and then live his golden years finally free from any State pressure. His job was boring, but it was a hard job to botch. His life wasn't perfect, but it was comfortable and secure. He could continue being a nobody and live his simple life in peace.

But that was on the surface. Below the crust were more vile predicaments he had to reckon with: seeds of doubt growing in his brain. He had something inside of him that saw beneath the surface world and toward the ruin depths, something that questioned the integrity of that "simple life" line of reasoning, something that wondered if he might just suffer an accident or get caught doing something he shouldn't if he didn't take this offer. It was that same something that always seemed to arise in moments like this, the something that told him there really was no choice.

And like usual, it was that something that won out.

"Okay," he said, his voice shaking just a touch, his face calm and content though in spite of the moment. "I accept. I'll take the position."

"Excellent!" Azalea exclaimed, and the genuine excitement in her voice helped Matt relax, helped him think that maybe he really had made the right choice after all and it hadn't just been out of fear. Maybe the Computer was right and this really was a position he was meant to have.

Azalea stood up from the table and presented her hand for Matt to shake. He obliged and then did the same with Mustapha.

"I think you'll make an excellent area warden," Mustapha said. "How do you feel?"

"Good," Matt responded, smiling. And to his own amazement, he actually did. He felt free and light and greatly empowered. This was an exciting new chapter that was about to unfold.

"There're just a few things for you to sign, then you can be on your way," Azalea said, heading over to a nearby counter to collect some papers. She returned in short order and presented him with the forms.

"Okay. So here just says you agree to take the position. There are no real stipulations with it. The rest of these clauses just mean ..."

At some point, Matt checked out and receded into himself, not out of fear for once, but out of genuine excitement.

This is awesome, he thought. *Wow. Me, an area warden. Who ever would have thought? I think I'm going to be glad I did this.*

And in that moment, he really believed it too, believed it all the way out the building and until he got to the station. It was only on the train ride home that the doubt started to return, the doubt that asked him if maybe he had just made the biggest mistake of his life.

CHAPTER 14

Two weeks after he had been arrested and charged for his role in what would come to be portrayed in the media as the Fight Club Fiasco, Deron Boyd sat daydreaming in the local Camp Pub. He was surrounded by the only audience who would ever get a firsthand account of his side of the story, the only ones who could truly sympathize with what he had been through. And he was fighting back tears.

In and out, he took a deep breath as the onlookers commiserated. He had spent the last ten minutes or so rehashing the events leading up to and following his arrest in gory detail, and the magnitude of it all was finally hitting home. He had suffered a lot.

"Two more years? That's bullshit! How can they—" A glaring eye across the table told the rambler to cut it. He caught himself but added softly, "I'm sorry. That just seems so unfair."

Deron said nothing. His body trembled uneasily, battling his emotions. He had heard the words. He had heard the collective sigh that followed despite the raucous crowd noise. But his mind was in another realm, for the moment, unable to return to this world.

Two more years. In his mind's eye, he could actually see his reaction to hearing the news, as if he had caught it all on video and was up in the replay booth reviewing the footage, feeling the life get sucked away from him as he heard the Computer relay his sentence, seeing the screen flash in the Camp's makeshift courtroom that imposed justice against those lawbreakers already locked away. Every time, the picture was painted just a little more vividly. Every time, he understood just a little bit better what it meant.

Two more years. It was like his first 730 days had never even happened.

A hand rubbing on his neck is what brought him back to earth. It was also what caused the first tear to drop, a subtle one that fell directly in his lap. His response was to grab the glass in front of him and take a rather large chug. This was his third stein of the night.

"Sorry, guys. I think the alcohol is getting to me." He forced out a chuckle, which the others refused to accept as authentic.

"You don't have to be sorry, Deron," said the woman beside him, bordering on tears. "Bad things keep happening to you, and you don't deserve any of it. You have the right to be upset. I am."

She started crying for real then, and Deron turned to her and clasped her in a hug. He was again close to breaking up, and he wasn't alone. They all were, even the strongest and most resilient of them all.

"She's right, you know," he said from the seat beside the woman's. Because of their embrace, he was looking Deron directly in the eye, allowing the younger man to see something in the older that he hadn't seen in him before: real anguish in his eyes.

"You don't deserve this, Deron. You truly ... I'm sorry." His eyes blubbered and he began to sob softly to himself. And then, like a chain reaction, it hit them all: Randall, Andrew, Sam, and Sakura. Once they saw Hakeem join Carla in sorrow, it was impossible to hold it in.

Here was a man they respected greatly for his wisdom. Here was a man who they knew hated the Pub but who had put his personal feelings aside to be here for his friend. Here was a man who had suffered for twenty-three years, crying his heart out for the merciless treatment of another. If this man could be broken by Deron's story, how couldn't they?

The seven of them sat at the fragmented table of the shabby Camp bar crying together, unaware of the world or anything but themselves, insensible to the perceptions or stares from those around. Six of them cried for Deron and his losses. Only Deron himself cried for something more.

Like the ocean waters, his blue disposition was covering something

THE UTOPIA

clear. He had cried for his losses plenty, but now he was crying for the one thing they'd let him keep.

He was crying for his friends and how much he loved them.

***

HE WAS BEYOND TIPSY when he went outside to get a breath of fresh air. Three steins will do that to a person, especially one who is used to a ration of one drink per month. The old Deron would have been able to handle this no problem, but the new one was down twenty pounds and a featherweight on the bottle.

"Shit," he said as he stumbled toward the sidewalk. He had no plans of leaving yet. His friends were all still inside, after all. But he wanted to get as far away as possible from the guards bouncing the front door. Public drunkenness wasn't a crime as far as he was aware, but when you were Deron Boyd, you just never knew anymore.

"Oof." He sat down hard against the concrete, his legs crossed just over the curb. There were a few vehicles in sight, as there usually were in the late evenings after the workday had ended. But the road was wide enough that they could comfortably pass without coming within striking range. He watched them go by, smiling contently, and then looked up toward the sky.

"Nice evening out, eh, Deron," he said to himself. "Sure is, Deron. Those stars sure are pretty. Wish they'd come hang out with us."

He laughed to himself at the ridiculousness of his current conversation but then really took a moment to appreciate the sky. It truly was beautiful. Some nights, the pollution was too thick to see the stars, but tonight, they were out in full force, and it made for good feelings.

"Really are pretty," he mumbled quietly. He had mellowed a lot since they'd had their team cry. It had been a good cathartic moment, for all of them, and a much needed one. It was the first time since that evening in the park that they'd all been together.

He continued to stare as he thought back to that instance. How scared had he been that it was the last time he would see any of his friends? It was really beyond words. And for the two days that followed, it was all he could think about—until he got his trial, until he heard the Computer say the words, until he was told the sentence would be added on to the back end of his current one, but that he could continue on living and working where he was. How bittersweet that notion had been. *We will let you keep living in a world that doesn't want you.* As he sat staring up, that was what was on his mind.

That and how damn beautiful the stars were.

"Deron."

Initially, he didn't react upon hearing the call. But after a few more moments of looking toward the heavens, he turned his head around to get a glimpse of who it was. He expected Carla, perhaps Hakeem or Randall, but was surprised to learn it was none of them who had come out to check on him.

It was Sakura instead.

"Sakura, hey." He bumbled his words as she crouched down beside him, partly because of his state of intoxication, but more so because of her. She was the last one he would've expected to take the initiative. She was always so quiet.

"I just wanted to come check on you and make sure you were okay," she whispered softly, almost like she wasn't sure if she really wanted to say it. But as she spoke, she looked at him with real concern in her eyes.

"Well, that's nice of you," he replied. He smiled at her and then looked back up again. "I'm doing alright; just enjoying the stars."

She joined him in that moment in appreciating their beauty. "They are nice, aren't they?" she said, peering up. "I remember on nights like tonight, I used to go out on my balcony and just stare up at the sky, wondering what was out there."

She thought back to those times, alone in her apartment with nothing but time on her side. Some evenings she would spend what felt like hours out there. A few times she even fell asleep under the moonlight, back before all this, when it was easy to see the beauty of the natural world, at least under the right conditions. Her mouth formed a wry smile.

"Only difference was, I was usually fucked up on a lot of drugs." She laughed and so did he.

"Must have made for quite the visions. I'm guessing you probably saw aliens at least once or twice."

THE UTOPIA

She gave a good chuckle at that. Deron turned to her and smiled, but her gaze was still upward.

"No aliens," she said. "No spaceships or comets. I never saw anything spectacular at all really. Just the stars and the bigger picture and infinite possibilities."

When Deron heard that, he felt a weird feeling inside that nearly made him flinch, like a fierce rival had just patted him on the back. It was so unexpected and seemed so out of character. It was her nature to give clean, simple answers, yeses and noes that left little room for interpretation. He hadn't anticipated anything so profound.

And yet ... His smile, which had disappeared for an instant, returned in a flash as he realized it right then. It felt like the most unguarded thing she had ever said to him.

He nodded once to himself and then looked back up at the sky. Only this time, when he did, he felt for the first time that he wasn't looking up alone. He felt the aura of the person beside him, felt connected to something larger, as if cosmic forces were at play.

At that moment, he felt that perhaps he had been wrong in his earlier assessment, that perhaps she was exactly the person who he should have expected to come out and join him.

"And do you still see all that now?" he whispered to her softly. He said it without thinking then turned his gaze back toward her, only this time, she mirrored him.

"No," she said. "No, I don't." And he expected something else profound, some deep words of wisdom. But after a moment of silence that seemed to drag on, what he heard instead was, "Now I'm just seeing double. I knew I shouldn't have had that second beer."

She laughed to herself, and he looked at her amazed. Then he just smiled and laughed along with her.

"Believe me, I know," he chuckled. "Sorry I asked you to drink with me. Everyone just wanted to give me their ration, and I didn't want to drink alone. Not that I would have been able to finish them all anyway. Not this Deron."

She smiled at him brightly. "Oh, don't worry," she said, "I was happy to join. And I'm not actually seeing double; I was just kidding about that.

Definitely feeling it though."

He looked at her and grinned, and then a moment of silence hovered over the scene. Vehicles passed by. People chatted on the street. But for just a moment between the two of them, the world was still as they valued each other's presence.

When Deron spoke next, the words once again came naturally. "You want to go for a walk somewhere? I mean I know—"

"Sure." She cut him off before he had a chance to finish, smiling at him again with a face that showed zero hesitancy at all. "I would love to."

She stood up from her crouch, and after his own moment of indecision, Deron joined her on his feet.

"You think we should tell the others?" he asked, expecting one answer but hearing another.

"They'll be alright," she said. "C'mon, let's walk." And she started down the street before he even had a chance to respond.

What's gotten into her? he thought to himself. *Those beers must be hitting her hard.*

As he watched her stroll down the sidewalk, a part of him did think that was probably just the case, that inebriation was the reason for her current lack of inhibition, that she would sober up soon and make her way home before it got too late, that she would remember this in the morning simply as a funny night out with her friend.

Only this time, his intuition was wrong.

***

WHEN SAKURA AND DERON ended up at the park after twenty minutes of stumbling and bumbling around, it would seem to both of them an odd twist of fate. Neither had planned this destination. Neither would believe at first that the other really wanted to be there. And neither had any inclination exactly how this would end.

Only as the events unfolded would it begin to make sense, would it resonate with them how natural it was, how in times of confusion and dismay, it is normal for people to be drawn to a familiar setting. It is normal for them to seek comfort there, even if that place has a dark shadow overcasting it.

"Sure looks different this late at night," Deron commented, mostly to himself. Sakura was beside him, but at the same time, she was in a different world. She'd been quiet since they'd arrived here.

"Yeah," she said. But her voice sounded adrift, ghostlike almost, like it came out only by conditioning, and her response would have been the same no matter what he had said.

Deron looked at her for the first time with a hint of apprehension. It had been an interesting walk to get here. At some points, they had both been lively and upbeat and the conversation had flowed easily. At others, however, they had both seemed in an almost hypnotic state, lost in their own thoughts, walking only because their brains hadn't told their legs to stop moving.

His concern was that right now, maybe this wasn't the best place to be. It was the park where she had seen him arrested, after all, and they hadn't been back since. While he reckoned that he himself was taking the return here surprisingly well, he wasn't so sure what the emotions were like for her. Perhaps they should just get out of here. It was late now anyway.

"Sakura." He spoke softly, hoping not to startle or frighten her. But the swiftness with which she turned to him made him believe he had failed miserably on that front.

"I'm sorry," she said. And she did look frightened, so much so that it made his heart race—at least that's why he thought it made his heart race. "I'm not sure why we're here, but I doubt this is where you want to be right now. Not after what happened."

It took him a moment to regain his composure, but once he did, he smiled. "No, don't worry about me!" he exclaimed. "I was concerned *you* might be upset. I'm actually quite happy to be here right now, especially with you here. It's peaceful with no one else around."

When Sakura heard him speak, it helped her settle down, but it was really his smile that put her mind at ease, allowed her to see the truth behind the words, to know that he wasn't just trying to act brave or make her feel better.

Later, she would reflect that life is a funny thing. Had they entered a few feet deeper into the park, they wouldn't have been within range of the overhanging streetlights. She would have never seen his face. And if she hadn't seen his face, perhaps she would have requested that they leave, perhaps even asked that they go their separate ways, thinking he wanted no part of this.

Only by seeing his face did she come to know the truth. He really had meant what he had said. He wanted to be here—to be here with her.

She smiled back at him in appreciation and understanding. He'd been concerned for her the same way she had been concerned for him. That realization sparked in her the same confidence she had felt earlier in the night, when for reasons unknown, she had left the safety of the group to ensure the safety another, something she would have only done for two other people she had ever met: Sam and a man named Ronaldo who had once taken her breath away.

"Well, in that case, why don't we go see if our favourite spot is available. For some reason, I think it will be."

Before he even had a chance to respond, Sakura was headed toward the picnic bench they had claimed as their own on many an evening, where they often played cards and laughed amongst friends.

Deron followed her with his eyes before he could with his legs, watching her fade into the darkness beyond the oak tree Randall was prone to taking naps under, past the shrubbery Carla had fallen into on more than one occasion. He smiled brightly as he reminisced about those times. His last experience here had been the bane of his time at the Camp, but in that moment, he got the feeling that perhaps tonight, a new memory might take shape, one where the light overtook the darkness, one that was the result of him finally acting upon what he had felt in his heart for some time.

He chased after her until he caught her for good.

***

FOR A WHILE THEY just sat quietly in the darkness. There was no tension or discomfort; they were simply enjoying the moment, reminiscing on times they had spent together here, surrounded by the ones they loved most, the bright knights in yellow jumpsuits that got them through their days.

In a way, they both almost wished that the others were there. This was a moment that deserved to be shared. These were feelings that deserved to be spread. They all deserved to listen to the peaceful call of the wind as it burrowed through the trees. They all deserved to enjoy the moonlight and the stars above, providing just enough brightness to see the backdrop of the scene. They all deserved to know what the two of them were feeling now. But they had chosen to come alone, and they both knew this moment wouldn't have existed if they hadn't.

"Sakura." It was Deron who started because before anything happened, he had to be sure. There was another in their group he'd had feelings for once, a woman he'd become close with, but only after she had broken his heart. He had rushed into that the same way as this: with alcohol-induced vulnerability. He had to make sure history would not repeat.

That's what he told himself, although somewhere deep down, he believed this was different. But there was only one way to know for sure.

"I really like you."

It was as straightforward as that. No beating around the bush. No excuses or qualifiers. Because in his heart, he knew it was true. He had known it for some time, he'd just been too afraid to tell her out of fear it would ruin the friendship they already had, out of fear she might not like him back, out of fear it would put pressure on a quiet and humble soul who was dealing with enough stresses stemming from this chaotic world in which they lived.

He'd felt this for some time, but he'd never come close to telling her until tonight, when he'd finally believed there was a chance she liked him too.

She turned to him, and the veil of darkness couldn't disguise her smile. She clasped his hand in hers and said the words that made it real.

"I really like you too, Deron."

And the timid part of her wished in that moment that she could just leave it at that, just give her heart to this man she had come to admire and care deeply for, this person who had never made her feel uncomfortable or afraid in a land where all she felt was scared all the time. If she could just leave it at that, she could make this person happy.

But it wasn't so simple. She had loved one before him, one she had cared for on a level she hadn't once thought her heart capable of, one who hadn't left her by choice, one whom she had forced from her memories at one time because the thought that he was gone had caused her too much pain.

She liked Deron a lot, perhaps even loved him. But she did not care for him like that, at least not yet. And he had to understand that.

"But I'm scared. I loved someone before. I lost him very tragically, and I don't know if I can open my heart up and risk that again. I don't know if I can handle it."

She looked at him with bleak eyes. She hadn't teared up. She'd thought she might, but it just hadn't happened, although it didn't make much of a difference. Suddenly, she felt terribly pitiful, like she had already given up before she'd even tried, given up on the thing she had sought after the most for the longest time, and now that she had found it, she'd decided that it wasn't worth the risk. Only when he told her his own story did she know to take the chance.

"I understand." He said it matter-of-factly. There was no added effort made to convince her it was the truth, and somehow, that made her believe him even more. "There was someone I lost once too. She left on the boat, and quite honestly, I've never been the same since. I promise you're not alone."

And then suddenly, he smiled one of the grandest smiles he ever had in his life. After all he had been through mentally, he had finally found someone who could share in his story, someone who knew what he felt, someone who'd convinced *him* that *he* wasn't alone. And when she felt that same energy, there was only one thing left to do.

They kissed under the moonlight. It was a short but passionate kiss, releasing years of pent-up emotion, years of frustration, years of worry and doubt. In that moment, they lifted each other up, the negativity was drained, and all they felt was hope.

After that, they just sat there quietly under the stars, embracing each other and feeling each other's warmth, daydreaming about a future ahead that neither would have ever expected before this very moment, realizing that sometimes, the dreams that come true are the ones you never had.

***

HE SAT IN THE control room, one building over from the guard barracks where he lived in his own penthouse suite. It was almost time to return and get in a good night's rest. It was past curfew, after all, and the split-screens were quiet, thousands of them panning on a rotating basis, showing mostly darkness and red uniforms. Perpetually monitored by ten or twenty guards, and sometimes more during the day, he could leave the overnight task in the hands of just a few. In his first few weeks, he had overseen the night shift on a couple of occasions just to get a feel and hadn't seen a soul who wasn't a member of the guards. That was until tonight.

Tonight, the CCTVs had detected movement near the park. And out from the shadows, two beings had emerged: one woman and one man. They had embraced, kissed each other good night, and then gone on their merry ways. A simple gesture but also one of defiance. They should have been home in their beds with the rest.

Should we intercept them, sir?

That question had been posed by a member of his staff, and so far, he had yet to say jump. He knew in his heart the answer he wanted to give was no, but part of him thought it had to be done, that he had to show his power in the face of such disrespect toward the rules; that as the new leader, he had to prove to his disciples that he had a handle on things; that there would be no corruption like there had been under the previous regime; and, perhaps most importantly, that the ones who were watching *him* could trust he was up to the task.

It was best if it was done, but it was what was in the man's file that was making him hesitate. He had brought it up using facial recognition software, and what he had read in those reports made him reluctant to pull the trigger. This man had suffered. This man had been through a lot in a short period of time. This man should not have even been here in the first place.

And *he* was the one who had brought him to this place.

"No. Not now. Send a command to all units in the area that if they see either of these two, they are not to intercept. I would like to see if they go straight home, and if they do, we will follow their behaviour in the coming weeks. We can always come back to these tapes if discipline is warranted, but let's not make any rash decisions now."

"Yes sir. Right away, sir." The guard picked up his radio. "Attention. Attention all units near the park area. Please be informed that …"

He tuned out before he heard the end, already uncertain if he had made the right call. It was a thought process he had many times a day, like one of his chess games. He had to make sure he was making the right moves with the pieces in play, only when a piece was sacrificed in this game, it was never coming back.

As he watched them walk home, his face was unnerved. But only after they had made it inside their residences did he start to breathe again. Only after he himself had left for the night did he show any emotion.

And only after he himself was tucked away safely in his new home did he begin to feel better.

CHAPTER 15

When Deron woke up the next morning, he felt the best he had in a very long time—too long to remember.

He rose from his bed with a smile on his face, a full thirty minutes before the alarm even sounded, feeling wonderfully energetic, so much so that he left the apartment complex before anyone else stirred and caught the end of the sunrise over the horizon. It was a beautiful morning, which he was sure would transition into a beautiful day. His smile stayed fixed even as he walked to work. The thought that he and Sakura had been out past curfew never crossed his mind.

At work, he drove his forklift like he was racing around a speed track, lapping others in terms of production and fun. Most days, he enjoyed the work for a while and then it got repetitive, but today, every pickup and drop-off was like a new level in his favourite video game. He could play for hours and hours and never once discover boredom.

At lunch, he found Carla and excitedly told her the news—news she was already privy to. She lived in the same building as Sam and Sakura, and most mornings, they caught up before work, but she was more than happy to hear about it for a second time. She had never seen Deron so delighted: not the day they'd first met, not the night they'd been together after he'd vanquished Yuri Yin—never. It made her already cheery disposition that much brighter. Deron deserved to be happy, and she was happy that he was.

When he left work that night, she didn't need to ask where he was going, not that she would have had time to even if she'd wanted to. The man who was usually one of the last out the door was the very first tonight, leaving in a near sprint to get to his destination, not wanting to waste a single second of the evening.

They met at the park, and when he saw her, he ran to her like a kid at the carnival. She laughed, and they embraced. Then they spent the evening skipping rocks at the nearby pond, laughing and kissing and enjoying the evening breeze, all the while their hearts feeling full of love and affection.

When night fell, they departed with one final kiss, promising each other they would be back tomorrow and the next day and the day after that, both excited by the prospect of it all. Sakura left thinking that was the most fun she'd had in years. Deron left mystified by his sudden change in fortune.

He was still at the Camp, still subject to long workdays with very few breaks, the same basic meals, the same lumpy bed, the same sounds and noises keeping him up at night. But suddenly, he didn't care. Suddenly, those things didn't quite bother him so much anymore. Suddenly, he had a reason to overlook those things and focus on the good.

He walked home that night wondering how long it would last.

***

THE ANSWER WAS ABOUT four months, at least in terms of the wholly bliss stage. For four months, it was like they had transferred from the Camp to some variation of heaven. They spent many days just like that first one, working under the same conditions, only with endless energy and enthusiasm, waiting for their chance to meet up together at night.

Some nights, they were alone, but oftentimes, they included their friends in the festivities as well. It felt natural to, and their positive energy infectiously rubbed off on the group. For those four months, it seemed like the spirits of all were lifted, that life in the Camp wasn't only bearable, it was borderline perfect.

That was Deron's perspective anyway. As the steadier personality, Sakura was less prone to the highs and lows of her newfound situation. For her work was still work, the food was still ordinary, and she still slept poorly at night, those keen ears of hers perpetually unsettled.

She was happy though, the happiest she had been since the death of her beloved. She had come to realize that with Deron, it would never be the same as with Ronaldo, but that was just fine. It was better than anything she could have expected, especially in here.

For the ones outside of the relationship, not a whole lot changed. They were happy for Deron and Sakura, but they also had their own lives to live, their own burdens to deal with, and they could only feed off their friends' energy for so long. Like the rest of humanity, they were damned by their own minds.

They were never jealous. Seeing Deron's happiness especially was never a burden in their eyes. All they had ever seen from him was sadness and fatigue. They were happy he was happy, and they wanted that to last.

But they knew before he did that it wouldn't last forever.

The last two months had proven that. Deron's infatuation remained, but over the course of sixty days, his happiness had begun to dwindle for reasons very much outside of his control. Somewhere along the line, the reality of the situation finally clicked in.

He had ignored it for as long as he could, pushed it aside as something he would deal with when the day came nearer. Part of him thought it might never arrive, like how he had been taught in school that the sun would one day absorb the earth, a tidbit he had thought of as a worthless bit of information because he would never see the day. It was so far into the future that he could be reincarnated a million times and still not have to worry. Only recently had he discovered the purpose behind that lesson.

The day always comes: Judgment Day, deadline day, the day of death and rebirth, the day the sun finally absorbs the earth. Whether tomorrow or one billion years into the future, the day always comes. And that's what he was struggling with.

In a few short months, Sakura would be leaving. Her three-year sentence was set to expire, and just like that, she would be gone from his life. Just like that, the relationship they had built would be reduced to rubble. Just like that, his days would return to perpetual dread and drear. When she left, she would take all of his hope and joy with her, and he would be stuck in the Camp for another four years.

He wasn't all selfish. A part of him would be pleased to see her go—the noble part that had fought Yuri for Carla's sake. That part would shed tears of joy when she left, happy that at least one of them would taste sweet freedom once again.

It was just the other ninety percent of him, the human part of him, that would be crushed to see her leave.

They'd had discussions about it, but they had never delved too deeply into the reality of what was coming. It was an uncomfortable topic, and neither was the best at opening up about their feelings, especially the negative ones. One or the other would drop the conversation before it could really get started, telling themselves it was best not to dwell on the inevitable, that it was better to make the best of the time that remained. That they had made it this far, and whatever came next, they would find a way to get through it.

At no point had Deron grown comfortable with the situation. At no point had he given credence to the idea that he wouldn't feel the sting when she was gone. But also at no point had he thought to do anything about it. After all, what was there to do? Ask her to stay with him at the Camp? He was selfish, sure, but he wasn't a psychopath. He wouldn't ask that of his worst enemy (okay, second-worst enemy; he'd probably let Yuri suffer with him), let alone someone he cared deeply for.

No, he was going to have to accept that she was leaving, that the Camp, for him, had been a strange blessing in disguise, but that the day was coming where that would finally change. He'd sinned after all, and while his punishment was harsh, it was nothing he hadn't brought upon himself. He would have to learn to live with that.

He thought about all this as he parked the forklift for the night, cleared his mind as he reached the most satisfying part of the day. A smile grew on his face in anticipation of the card game he and his friends were about to play. It was a time to relish while it lasted and a time he could enjoy even after Sakura left. The rest would still be around, at least for a little while, and that was something he had to remind himself to be thankful for. The ones who had been there for him before he'd even met her, they wouldn't let him break. They would help him to survive, like they had since the beginning.

He had just started to feel good again, and that's when he saw the judge.

DESPITE IT HAVING BEEN almost three years, he recognized him instantly. The shaved-head-and-glasses look was a common one in here, and the face had aged a bit, but there was no question it was him. Robed or not, in or out of court, it made no difference: you don't forget the person who locks you away, his fault or otherwise. In a sea of a thousand, he would have stood out like the Loch Ness Monster.

And right now, it was just the two of them.

"Judge Sanderson," he remarked. It sounded almost like a question, but he wasn't second guessing. He was just totally surprised. How on earth had an officer of the court ended up here?

The judge, himself surprised by the sudden acknowledgement, almost jumped out of his skin. He had been angling toward the changing rooms (they were standing by the glass window just outside the dining hall) but turned suddenly to see who had broached.

"I would appreciate it if you didn't call me that," was the first thing he said. His tone was firm but respectful. "Some in here might not appreciate a judge among the ranks, even if I am just a figurehead, legally speaking."

Deron got the memo. "Sorry," he said. "Didn't mean to startle you or reveal any secrets. I'm just surprised to see you here is all."

This apology seemed to calm the judge somewhat. The look of shock disappeared from his face, and he approached Deron fluidly.

"Well, you're not alone in that," he said. After a moment's hesitation, he stuck out his hand. "Glen." There was another pause. "I'd imagine you know that already if you know me as a judge, but I prefer the formality all the same. And since I can't seem to place you, my intuition tells me that the reason you know me is because I probably sent you to this place."

Deron flinched but held his nerve. "Deron," he said, shaking the man's hand and then quickly drawing his own back. "And yeah, you could say that. Although I don't blame you for it. There wasn't a whole lot you could do." After a pause of his own, he continued. "But I guess you didn't help too much either."

The judge laughed openly at that. Deron smiled awkwardly but didn't laugh along.

"I'm sorry," the judge said. "Please forgive me. I should know better than anyone that a man's freedom is no laughing matter. It's just when you put it in those terms, it really shows how useless my position was." Deron didn't know what to say to that, so he let the judge keep talking. "I mean, I knew the law, sure, but it doesn't take a brain surgeon to know the law in the Utopia. The Computer makes all the decisions. Any man or woman could do the job I did. I really *was* just a figurehead—a figurehead that sentenced people to this deathtrap."

The judge chuckled some more, and Deron wasn't entirely sure he wanted to continue this conversation. He wasn't entirely sure, in fact, why he had started it in the first place, other than out of an odd sense of disbelief. There didn't appear to be much to gain by talking to this man. In here, he was just a prisoner like everyone else.

He was about to leave, about to roll along and try to forget he had even had this exchange. He had an appointment to keep, after all. And with Sakura's time coming to an end, he could hardly afford to stand here and have such a worthless conversation, especially with someone he had no particular attachment toward.

He was about to leave, but then the judge said something that stopped and made him think. And Deron's curiosity got the best of him again.

"But it was an easy job, at least, and maybe it would have been in my best interest to have kept at it for a couple more years. Doubtful I would have ended up here if I had."

"What do you mean?" Deron asked, not quite understanding. *If he quit his job, which is what I assume he means, what would that have to do with him ending up here? How would that have any bearing on ... unless ...* And then he clued in.

"You were chosen!" He exclaimed it louder than he'd wanted to, but he couldn't hold it in. Something about the idea just seemed so unfathomable.

A judge? Getting chosen? And one who had to be somewhere in his fifties and close to retirement anyway. He couldn't put a finger on why, but it felt almost blasphemous. But it was about to get even weirder.

"I'm not sure."

For the first time, he looked at Deron with a real sense of disillusion, without that air of invincibility in his demeanour. He was no longer laughing, but there was no intensity in his face either. He looked genuinely unsure.

"What do you mean—" But before he could get it all out, the judge interrupted. When he did, that intensity returned with so much emphasis that Deron couldn't help but feel afraid.

"Look," he said. He twisted his head back and forth to see if anyone was around. When he realized there was no one there, he continued. "I probably shouldn't tell you this, but if I'm truly the one who sent you here, and I have no reason to assume you're lying, then I will as a courtesy." Deron nodded, unsure of what else to do. "Here's the deal. I truly do not know whether I was chosen or not. If I was, it wasn't by normal means. There was no lottery draw done, at least not in open court, but I still think it's possible I was picked."

How? Deron's brain screamed. But he didn't need to ask the question.

"The reason I think this ..." After a moment of worrying he might be speaking just a touch loudly, he leaned in closer so he could whisper the next bit. "The reason I think this is because I can't for the life of me remember my crime."

And the moment he heard this, Deron felt his muscles freeze and his blood run cold. He could have fainted had his heart not started to pump at a thousand beats per minute. He could have thrown up had his reflexes been functional. He could have done a lot of things, but he just stood there instead.

"It's true. I have no idea. They say I assaulted someone. They even have a video of me doing the deed. But I can't, for the life of me, remember doing it, and I have no idea why. I've never been an angry person, and I've never had an issue with memory lapses either. I don't think I would do that, and even if I did, I'm sure I would remember it!"

Realizing he had started to get worked up, he tried to once again quiet his tone. "That's why a part of me thinks I was chosen. A part of me thinks I was used as some pawn in a chess game and that I never assaulted anyone but they somehow made it look like I did. I know it sounds ridiculous, but I don't know what else to think."

Deron didn't respond. He just stared straight ahead with bulging eyes that looked about ready to pop out of his head, the same stare he'd had since the judge had started his tale of woe, a look of unconditioned fear.

"You okay? You look like you've seen a ghost."

"Yeah, fine," he said. It was clearly a lie, and a judge of the court would see that in a heartbeat, would probably follow up with more questions until he told the truth. But right then, he got a reprieve.

"Deron."

The judge and Deron both looked in the same direction, and their eyes struck Carla. Fresh out of the shower, her hair was still wet, but she otherwise looked every bit the familiar face Deron knew. And needed.

"Well, hello there, young lady." It was the judge that took the initiative, and in that moment, Deron was happy for that too. He had yet to come to grips with anything that had been said. "You waiting for this fine fellow right here?"

"Yes," she said politely, although it took her a moment before she could take her eyes off Deron and look toward the speaker. Her friend looked unwell. "My name is Carla. Pleased to meet you."

She stuck her hand out for the judge to shake, and the man happily obliged. "Glen. Very nice to meet you too."

He then turned to Deron. "Your friend and I here were just catching up. Been a long time since we've had the pleasure of each other's company, right, Deron?" He cracked up at his own joke, and after another moment of emptiness, Deron forced out a chuckle just to seem normal—to them and himself.

"Anyway, I'll leave you two be. I should probably get along now before it gets late. I'm new to this, after all. You two take care of yourselves." He smiled at each and then added, "Nice to see you, Deron. If you have anything else you would like to discuss with me, well, you know where to find me." He laughed to himself again and then headed toward the changing room.

Deron's eyes watched him walk away, but it was more than a few seconds before he truly *saw* him at all. "Likewise," he shouted after him. His face formed a smile, but it was obvious it was forced. Carla spotted it instantly.

"You okay?" she asked. "You look like—"

"Fine," he said. He shook his head to snap back into it, and this time, the smile came about more naturally. "Fine, yeah. Was just really surprised to see that man here is all. He was the judge in my case."

"Actually?"

Her face showed her shock, but Deron continued calmly like what he had said couldn't have been more insignificant. "Yeah. Weird coincidence, right? Just has me a bit thrown off."

"I can imagine," she said. She looked at him with a bit of concern, thinking perhaps there was even more to it than that. She had come to know Deron quite well over the years and could almost always tell when there was something he wasn't saying.

But she would leave it alone for now. "Should we go? I can imagine the others will almost be there by now."

"Yeah. Yeah, right," Deron said. He shook his head again. "I got caught up. That's my bad. I'm just going to take a super quick shower, and then we'll get out of here."

"Okay. Well, I'll wait here for you," she said.

"Great. Thanks," he replied. But he didn't look at her when he said it, and that made her sure that something was amiss. The judge could be part of it. It wouldn't be weird for something like that to throw a person off. But her senses were telling her again there had to be something more.

She watched him walk away, hoping they could discuss it on the walk over to the park or maybe as a big group if it was something truly serious. In a short while, she'd get the chance to ask whatever she wanted.

And her first question would be why he'd chosen not to shower.

***

IT WAS AFTER THE third card game that the conversation started, although it very well could have earlier.

From the moment Deron and Carla arrived, everyone noticed Deron was off in his own world. The questions could have started then. It wouldn't have been weird. When a friend seems down, it's normal to ask him or her what the trouble is and to try to lift their spirits.

But they also all knew their friend and how sensitive he could be when his chemicals were imbalanced. Each was hoping Deron would bring it up himself. They didn't want to prod. Doing so wouldn't have helped if he didn't want to talk. But now it was getting late.

It was past nine o'clock. The sun had set a long time ago, and the only light within reach was the familiar glow of the electric lanterns they traditionally borrowed from the park's activity chest. They couldn't replace the golden orb, but they were enough to clearly define the features of the players sitting around the table they were set up at. All faces were saying the same thing: they wanted answers.

"Should we play one more game?"

Hakeem's question could have been answered by anyone, but it was directed purposely toward Deron, and the others knew not to respond. They had concocted this plan to get Deron talking when he had gone to use the washroom, and they had chosen Hakeem as the speaker of the house. It was a logical decision. Deron was in love with Sakura, and Carla knew him best, but it was Hakeem who had known him first and Hakeem who he felt the greatest respect for. To Hakeem, Deron couldn't lie.

"I'm not sure if I'm up to it, to be honest, but it's up to you guys."

The comment was innocent enough, but it created the perfect segue. Hakeem didn't need any instruction to know to pounce. "Yes, you don't seem especially yourself today, my friend. Is something the matter?"

Deron gulped once, but his heartbeat remained steady. On his way back from the washroom, the table chatter had all but stopped as he approached. He'd suspected they'd noticed his mood and had been discussing it. He'd had an idea this was coming. And quite honestly, a part of him was happy they were going to force him to put it out there because he needed their guidance, perhaps now more than ever.

"It's just ..." He looked around the table, and all eyes were on him. Their focus was intense, and he was somewhat intimidated by it. This was difficult to explain, and there was another thought that was making him a bit uncomfortable as well.

What if I really did do it?

"I met this man from my past today. Who he is isn't all that important, but it's this story he told me that got me thinking about my own life, and I can't seem to shake the thought."

He glanced down at the table. He could feel their eyes still on him, but he didn't know how to proceed. He was just so confused. Was it possible he had been set up? Or was his mind just playing tricks on him because he had never quite been able to accept what he had done? He truly didn't

THE UTOPIA

know, and that's what made it hard. A part of him wished he had never spoken to the judge. And then he heard her voice.

"It's okay, Deron. You can tell us." His eyes glanced to the left, and he caught a glimpse of her seated beside him, a sad smile on her face. She clutched his hand in hers and held it tight with love. "We all just care about you and want you to be okay. We want to look out for you the same way you always look out for us."

He didn't cry then. In fact, the emotion he felt couldn't have been described as powerful at all. A simple smile did the trick, and the look at Sakura reminded him of something she probably hadn't planned on inspiring in him, but it hit him right then. What did he have to lose?

"Thanks, Sakura," he said, feeling some peace in his heart for the first time since he had spoken to the judge.

His friends were there, like they always were, but this time, he didn't sit there thinking he should tell his truth for their sake. This time, he didn't need to justify to himself what he was about to say, ask himself how it might affect them or who he was doing it for. He would tell them for himself so that he could feel better. He would do it selfishly, and there was nothing wrong with that because if what he had to say was true, then he had more than paid his dues.

"The truth that this man made me realize—and I know this might sound crazy, but you all know the story of how I was arrested and how I could never fill in the gaps. Today, I think I realized why."

Unbeknownst to him, the moment the words left his mouth, hearts went into throats. A collective anxiety set in amongst the group as they began to realize that what he was about to talk about wasn't the type of Deron problem they had been expecting—not boredom from work, not soreness in his arms and legs or complaints about the rations, not even an attack on himself for the mistakes he had made. This was something else entirely.

Suddenly, they wished they hadn't coaxed him into discussing this at all. But now it was too late.

"I think I was set up."

When he said it, he closed his eyes, expecting a barrage of questions and loud reactions, perhaps even a rebuttal that what he was saying was impossible. But what he heard was nothing.

When he reopened his eyes, all except Hakeem had their heads down and were staring at the table, like a group of monks praying, only in this circle, silence was compulsory. He was stunned by the reaction, but then he figured he knew why.

"You guys don't believe me, do you? You think I've lost it. Well, I guess I can't blame you. Even in my own head it sounds insane, but you asked me—"

"It's not that, Deron." The interruption came from the only person who could look him in the face in that moment. His eyes wandered toward Hakeem. "It is precisely because we do believe you that your other friends and I are having trouble finding words."

"You ... you do?" Deron's eyes went wide as he looked around the table. "All of you? You believe me, just like that?"

"Of course we do, Deron." It was Hakeem again. He seemed to be the only other one capable of talking at that moment. "It makes perfect sense. A man such as yourself who is by and large a smart and humble and reserved individual—for someone like you to just commit a crime as foolish as breaking into a General Store, and then on top of that, to not remember doing so? Unless you have been lying to us about this—and none of us have ever had reason to think you have been—it would seem much more likely than not that you were, in fact, set up. This is the Utopia, after all."

For just a moment, Deron had no words; he was ill-prepared for this. He had thought of a rebuttal in case they didn't believe him, had considered on the way here that it was possible someone could have slipped him something when he went to use washroom that night out at the bar. It had somehow never occurred to him before because he hadn't remembered seeing anyone, but that very well could have been a result of the drugging. Maybe he had seen someone and just couldn't remember.

He had prepared to make this point. He had prepared for the questions and the shock and perhaps even tears if he could convince them it was true. But never in a million years could he have envisioned this, that they all might have already thought he was innocent before he'd discovered it himself.

"But why?" he said, now starting to realize the reality of the situation. "If you all thought that, why wouldn't you tell me? How could you just let me rot in here all these years and not say anything?"

"Please don't be mad, Deron."

It was Sakura this time, still by his side, still clutching his hand, even though he was now gripping hers with much more ferocity than he had realized. He loosened his grip and looked deeply into her eyes as he let her say her piece.

"We just didn't know what to say. It always seemed conceivable that you were set up, but it's impossible to prove. Of course we wanted to tell you we had our suspicions, but it just seemed like it would only make you feel even worse that you were here. Maybe that was a mistake, but we just didn't want to hurt you, because even if it is true, we knew there was nothing we could do."

There were tears in her eyes now, and that struck Deron at his core. If he had been mad before, he was no longer. Sakura didn't get emotional unless she truly hurt inside.

He was about to tell her it was alright, tell her he understood and that they had done the right thing, that it would have just upset him if they'd all convinced him he was innocent, that it would have made the tortured life he lived that much more unbearable.

He was about to let it be until Hakeem said the words that would change their lives forever.

"There *is* one thing we could do."

And that was the first time that heads raised from their crouches, the first time any of the others showed any signs of life, the first moment since Deron had spoken that they were more confused than afraid.

"I didn't want to mention it because it's an extremely risky plan. It didn't make sense to do it while you were unconvinced of your innocence, but now that you seem sure, there's no reason to hold back. There is one thing we could do."

They all turned to him like he was some great guru, like he was about to bestow upon them some powerful knowledge and open up their minds to something they had never considered.

But somewhere deep down, they all knew what he was about to say, even if they couldn't all entirely believe it. It was an idea they had all pondered at some point or another but never seriously enough to mention it outside of their own minds. It was entirely preposterous, and at the same time, it was the only answer to their problems.

"We could try to escape."

"No way," said Randall.

"That's nuts," echoed Andrew.

Even Sam, who was as rebellious as any of them, couldn't fathom the suggestion. "Hakeem, you know I have a lot of respect for you, but you can't be serious. Not only is it impossible, it's suicide!"

Hakeem didn't answer. For the first time, he was the one who could not return their gazes. He looked down at the table, wondering to himself if he should continue on. The discussion continued amongst the others, but for Hakeem, in that moment, the only chatter was in his brain.

Twenty-four years.

All his mind could think of was the amount of time he had spent at the Camp—almost half a lifetime, and by the end, it would be a lot longer than that. He would die in this place if he couldn't find a way out.

He looked up at Deron. Twenty-four years. For twenty-four years, he'd been waiting for this moment, to find a group of people like him he could convince to take the risk. Alone, he'd never make it, but with them, there was a chance. With them, there was a real possibility they could do this because they had her.

His eyes gazed toward Sakura, understanding that she was the true key to all this because she was to be released, and if they could get her on a van legitimately, they could perhaps find a way to get the rest on board as well. It was a long shot and a plan that would fail a lot more often than it would succeed, but at least there'd be a chance. And after twenty-four years, that was all he wanted. And he thought he just might get it.

Sakura, like Deron, was looking back at Hakeem in that moment with eyes of determination, a look that didn't disparage his comment as completely ludicrous or irrational, a look that inferred that perhaps he was onto something after all, a look that said she might do it.

I'm sorry, my Lord, he thought to himself. He was sorry for a lot of things, and one of those was that he'd lied. He had always intended to mention the possibility of escape when the timing was right. He hadn't thought that day would be today, but the Lord's signs often come without warning, and this was one he could not deny.

Today, Deron had convinced himself he was innocent, and whether he was or not didn't truly matter. He would want to escape, and that was what was important—that and the fact that the girl would do whatever she could to help. He was sorry that he'd lied, but mostly, he was sorry that this girl would have to suffer if they were caught. She didn't deserve that. She didn't deserve that at all.

But he might never get another chance to take them down. And he owed that to the world.

Please accept my repentance, oh merciful Allah. Forgive me for my methods as I carry out this work. Guide me in my trials against the enemies of freedom.

"This suffering must end." He said it aloud, and whether he'd intended it or not, it got the attention of his audience. He looked to each of them one by one. "I know it sounds foolish. Perhaps it even is. I offer it only as a suggestion, and even if it was an option to consider, I would never ask anyone to come along who did not want to. That would never be fair. But as I look around this table, I see a bunch of decent people with genuinely good hearts, a bunch of people who deserve better, a bunch of people who should never have been here in the first place. It isn't right."

He paused to let his words sink in, taking note of each of their reactions. Some looked inspired—those ones, he thought, would probably join the fight. Others looked unconvinced. It wasn't that they didn't believe his words, but they doubted any plan they concocted would have even a glimmer of hope of coming to fruition. They would probably take a pass. But they wouldn't stop the others.

"I have been here for twenty-four years. I hope and pray that none of you should have to endure that type of punishment, but you must understand that even if you get out of here, you will never be truly free. You will need to work for the guards or find some other type of employment, all the while living in fear they might one day send you back. It is no way to live."

"So what do you suggest then?" The comment came from Sam, the first interruption by any of them. "This is the Camp we're talking about!

There are cameras everywhere. It's not like you can just stroll out of here without anyone noticing."

"You're not wrong," he conceded. "But where there's a will, there's a way. I have spent twenty-four years thinking about this problem, and I may just have a plan. It would be dangerous, no doubt, and the odds would be against us, but it's not impossible."

Sam motioned like she was about to rebut him but, in the end, added nothing. She was convinced she was right, but it seemed there was nothing she could say to persuade Hakeem it was impossible. In light of this, Hakeem continued.

"But it would require a sacrifice. From you, Sakura."

"From me?" Her eyes grew at the prospect, and the others perked up as well. If he hadn't had their attention before, he certainly did now.

"Yes. I'm sorry to say. But the only way this is possible is if we take advantage of the fact that you're being released soon. We would need to come with you if we want to have any hope of escaping."

"No fucking way." This time, Sam didn't hold back her comment. She stood up, in fact, to make her position known. "If you want to go on some suicide mission, you be my guest. I won't try to stop you. But there's no way in hell Sakura is giving up her freedom for your loony plan. That you would even have the audacity to suggest such a thing shows a complete lack of respect."

Hakeem didn't argue. "Again, you are right, Sam. I make no bones about the fact it is an incredibly unfair thing to ask." He looked at Sakura. "I want you to know that my intent is not to pressure you into this. To be perfectly straight, you SHOULD NOT go along with my plan. I'm merely stating that if we were to have any chance at all, this is what it would require."

At that moment, Hakeem himself began to stand up. He had laid all the groundwork he could for the night, and there was nothing more to add. He had made his intentions clear, and if he persisted with them any longer, he would only face more resistance. It was best to start fresh another time.

"I think we've all had a long day, and I personally feel in need of some rest. We can discuss this at another time, or we can never discuss this again. I've been here twenty-four years; this is the only life I know anymore anyway." He started to walk away.

"This is crazy," said Andrew. "Absolute madness. Michael Schofield couldn't escape this place." Only Randall got the reference to a show that had been remade five times since the original had aired all those years before. "Should we go with him?" he asked his brother.

"Yeah, let's go. Don't wanna let the old man walk alone. It's late now anyway. Good night, ladies and gent. We'll see you ... when we see you, I guess."

Only Carla mumbled out some form of good night. The rest were still lost in thought until Sam broke the silence.

"Let's go home, girls," she said, starting to walk away herself. "I think I've had enough of these discussions for one night. It's too much."

"Okay," Carla agreed, following behind. Sakura began to stand up as well but hesitated once she was on her feet. Deron stood up and joined her.

"I know what you're thinking," he said. The other girls were still within range but were trying to make it seem like their attention was somewhere else. Deron didn't take notice, nor did he really care. "But you can't do this. You know how much I hate this place and how much I'll miss you when you're gone, but Sam is right. You cannot sacrifice your own freedom. You have nothing to gain and everything to lose."

"I have you to gain." That comment stunned him. He wanted to refute it, but no words were coming to mind. She looked at him with eyes that were fierce, but he couldn't help but notice a gloom in them as well. "I don't know what I'm thinking. This all came about so fast. But what I do know is we don't have to decide tonight. We can talk about it later. Together." She kissed him lightly on the cheek. "I love you, Deron."

Before he could respond, she began to walk away. His mind told him to catch her before she went, but his body wouldn't move. He stood in silence, unable to fully comprehend the enormity of the moment.

I love you, Deron. In all their months of bliss, that was the first time she'd ever said it.

"I love you too." He spun around and called out after her, but she didn't look back. She heard the words though, but to her, they weren't anything new. He'd said them to her at least a dozen times. Every time, her response had been that same kiss on the cheek. Never once had she repeated them back because until this very moment, she hadn't known if they were true. But now it was clear.

You wouldn't be willing to sacrifice your freedom for someone you didn't love.

Deron watched her catch up to the girls and disappear into the night, feeling a weird mix of happiness and sorrow, wondering to himself what in the world he was to do. She had just told him she loved him, and in a few months, she'd be leaving.

And he'd have to risk her life if he wanted to go with her.

CHAPTER 16

Log Entry: Day MXXXV

It's been just over a week since the freedom talk, but sadly, nothing has changed since my last entry on the subject. There is still tension amongst the group, particularly from Sam toward Hakeem. Although the latter hasn't broached the topic with us again, she can tell it's on his mind, and it makes her uncomfortable knowing it's only a matter of time before the discussion resumes.

I can't say I blame her for her feelings. She's concerned for her friend, as she has every right to be. I just hope she understands that Hakeem would never pressure Sakura into helping us escape. I don't think he would have ever even brought it up as a suggestion if it hadn't been for me, if I hadn't said what I'd said about feeling like I was set up. If anything, she should blame me for this, not him. As usual, I'm the one bringing the group trouble.

I just hope she will forgive him soon because I can't stand to see this dissention continue. We've been so tight for so long, so unflappable no matter what's been thrown in our faces. We can't lose that now. We won't survive without each other in the short term or long.

Apart from the group, Sakura and I had our own private conversation

today, and I can report nothing has really changed there either. She still says she's unsure, but I can tell she wants to help me. I continue to tell her I think it's a bad idea, and I honestly do, but …

This is incredibly hard to write, but my rebuffs are losing passion with each passing day, and I think she has taken notice. I want her to see I'm strong. I want to tell her that no matter what she wants to do, it won't matter because I'll refuse to go with her and that will be that. I want to show her that her freedom means more to me than my own.

I want that all to be true, but deep down, I want to get out of here, and it's getting harder and harder to lie to myself about it. If she really wants to help, and I can't convince her otherwise, I don't know if I'll have the fortitude to deny myself this chance, not if Hakeem has a plan that actually might work.

There, I said it. God help my soul.

I wish I was better than this,

Deron Boyd

Log Entry: Day MXL

The raven is back, just when I thought it might have finally decided to leave me alone. It hadn't paid me a visit in nearly six months, but last night, it made its triumphant return, haunting me with its presence like some undead spirit. This time, it wouldn't take its eyes off me, even as I looked over the horizon toward the burning ship.

I think after all these years, I finally see the pattern. I guess looking back, it was obvious from the beginning, but I didn't want to acknowledge it. The raven seems to come as a bearer of bad news, an omen of destruction and devastation. It came to me when I was going through my struggles with Yuri Yin. It came to me when Edwin was about to take over for Agatha. It came to me when I was about to be arrested for the second time. And it's coming to me now, likely to foreshadow that any attempt we make to escape will only end in more heartache. But I have news for this raven.

THE UTOPIA

You will not win. Before, I was afraid of you, but now, I think you're afraid of me. You know I can overcome you like I did Yuri, like I did Edwin, like I did that trial. I outlasted all of them, and I will outlast you. You know that in that vile black heart of yours, and that is why you refuse to come near. I don't know yet whether the escape is going to happen. Talks have been progressing, but there is still some time left before we make that decision. But I promise you one thing: I'll catch you, bird, if it's the last thing I do.

In command of my own ship,

Deron Boyd

Log Entry: Day MLI

Good talks again today. No final decision on whether the escape is a go or not, but at least we have more of a clear indication on where people stand.

Sam is a hard no, as she has been from the beginning. From her perspective, it makes sense. She has less than a year and a half to go on her sentence, and there's no point in risking it. I give her credit though; she's been a lot more supportive the last few weeks about giving everyone autonomy to make their own decisions. She no longer bickers whenever someone brings it up. She makes her stance known and stands up for Sakura, but she hasn't let it affect her friendship with Hakeem or anyone else. I admire her for that. She's a strong person.

Randall and Andrew are also out. They've got a bit less than twenty-eight months left to go on their sentences, so for them as well, the risk isn't worth the reward. Plus, they've openly admitted they're terrified of what will become of them if they're caught, and I can't blame them for feeling that way. The punishment could be anything, even ... I guess I should try not to think about it.

Carla hasn't expressed her thoughts yet one way or the other. I know her though, and she's not going to do it. She got nine years for her crimes and has served just over five of them, so she still has plenty of time left. It would make a bit more sense for her to involve herself in this, but I can tell she doesn't want to go. She's just different in that respect. The rest of us hate it here, but she lives her life like this is a summer camp, not a work camp. I think she honestly feels like she's better off in the Camp than on the outside or, at the very least, that it makes no difference in her world whether she's in here or out there. I can't claim to fully understand it, but I'll accept her choice if that's what it is, even though I'll miss her dearly.

I've decided that I'm going. Hakeem has a number of great ideas, and I think they could work. A lot of them rely on Sakura, of course, and she hasn't yet made her decision (or told us if she has), but even if she decides against helping us, I think Hakeem and I are still going to make an attempt. It will be much harder, but I think the both of us have decided enough is enough. We need the escape to happen, or we at least need to try.

I haven't told Sakura any of this. I've made a promise to myself that I won't tell her I've made up my mind until she makes her own decision. I don't want her to feel pressured into doing this for me. It truly isn't fair what we're asking of her. She has the utmost to lose and by far the least to gain. The least we can do is let her decide on her own if she's willing to risk it all. Honestly, a part of me is really hoping she's not.

And honestly, a part of me is really hoping she is,

Deron Boyd

Log Entry: Day MLIII

Strange encounter with Merlin today. I guess that isn't surprising. The shock would come if I ever had a normal encounter with the man. I can't even picture what that would look like, but I imagine it would feel totally bizarre.

I write about it only because it made me feel nervous. I was discussing our escape plans with Hakeem outside the front of our building when, all of a sudden, we heard something creeping in the bushes around the corner. We thought it was just an animal, so we ignored it at first, but when it didn't go away, we investigated, and sure enough, it was Merlin! He was hiding in the bushes!

I attempted to confront him about it, ask him what he was doing and what he had heard us say. But Hakeem said he would handle it and asked me to leave. In hindsight, that was probably for the best. I was getting too worked up, and if anything, I was making it obvious we'd been scheming something. But I just couldn't control myself.

He makes me anxious, that Merlin. I know I've written that before here at least once or twice, but it isn't because of the way he acts that I feel this anxiety. It's because when I look beyond his antics, I realize how smart he really is. Every time he's played Link or cribbage or any other card game with us, he's always won, and it's not out of dumb luck. I can see his mind working through the cards. It's like he remembers exactly which ones have been played and knows exactly which ones are left in the deck. But he hides his intelligence, and that's part of what makes me nervous. Sometimes I wonder if he really is mentally ill at all. Sometimes I think it's all just part of a larger scheme to get out of work. Or maybe it's so people will leave him alone. Or the worst thought of all, could he even be a spy?

I just don't know, and it really bothers me. I know Hakeem trusts him though, and if Hakeem trusts him, I guess I have to as well. At this point, there's not much else I can do. I just wish he'd at least stop staring at me like he is now.

Creeped out,
Deron Boyd

Log Entry: Day MLX

Another day, another dream. Almost caught the raven last night. Crept up to it real close and was just about to reach out and grab it, and that's when I woke up. Strange how that happened. The raven wasn't moving, and I swear I would have had it, but it's like some force in the dream world wouldn't let me catch it. I guess I should have suspected such. Evil spirits don't die easily. That's one lesson this place has drilled into me like a screw through wood.

Anyway, I'm sure I'll see it again soon. And maybe the next time I do, I'll take care of that bird once and for all. It's only a matter of time.

CHRISTIAN JERRY MARCHIONI

> *Your days are numbered, bird,*
>
> Deron Boyd

Log Entry: Day MLXXVI

It's on.

I can't believe I'm writing this. My hand is literally shaking as I try to put pen to paper. But after everything I've written in here, it would be wrong of me not to document this moment, so here goes nothing.

Sakura finally informed the group of her decision. After a week of back and forth between just myself and her, she finally decided she couldn't take it any longer. She had to tell the rest of them. Understandably, it was weighing on her conscience.

The surprising part was how well everyone seemed to take the news. There was some pushback, of course, mostly from Sam and a little bit from Carla. But by this point, I think they knew it was coming. They're her best friends, after all. I would guess she's been keeping them in the loop at least somewhat, and even if she hasn't been, I'd imagine it didn't take much for them to deduce her intentions. Maybe they've accepted this really is what she wants to do, or maybe they think there's still time for her to wise up and change her mind so there's no point in panicking quite yet. It's not like she signed some binding contract, after all. Until the deed is done, she can back out at any time. They probably understand that, and I hope she does too. I want the escape to happen, but if there's any doubt in her mind, then she needs to back out. Hakeem and I would more than understand.

Anyway, for now it suffices to say that with her in the fold, the plan will really begin to take shape. I also shared my intentions of going with the group, and since Carla voted not to go, that leaves Sakura, Hakeem, and I as the sole conspirators. Once this was settled, we proceeded on with our night like any other. It was eerie really. We all talked and joked like nothing had changed, but inside, I felt it, and I'm sure the others did too.

In the moment she made her announcement, everything became real, like our goal had shifted from a dream to something tangible I could touch, something I could morph with my hands and see with my own eyes, something with a heartbeat that we as a collective had breathed into life, something that we were in charge of.

For maybe the first time since I've been in here, that moment made me feel like I control my own destiny, like I make the rules, like I make the decisions, like I say when we work and what we eat. I say what happens to me at the end of the day.

It felt like the first step in a great movement—a movement to be free. I was never meant to be here. I was never meant for this. I was meant for something more.

And when the world won't let you be what you were meant to be, it's time to change the world.

It's on,

Deron Boyd

Log Entry: Day MLXXXI

Met with just Hakeem and Sakura today so we could start discussing plans. We're just over a month out from Sakura's release, and we need to be prepared. For the escape to succeed, every i must be dotted and every t must be crossed.

Hakeem seems to have an understanding of the procedures involved in releasing campers, and that's a good start. He says the camper is picked up at their housing complex in the morning, and from there, they're transferred out of the Camp. Where they go, he doesn't know, but that's not really of importance. What matters is the pickup point and how we can use it to our advantage.

There are cameras just about everywhere in the Camp, but for some reason, there are blind spots (I have noticed this in our building, and Sakura has confirmed it in hers) in the tiny scan-in areas between the frosted glass doors and the metal doors leading into and out of the complexes. If we can get the attending guard into that location and find a way to subdue him or her, there's a chance we can take the van without any security staff noticing anything suspicious.

We would need a lot of luck. And even in a best-case scenario, they would notice before the day's end what has happened. But it's at least a start. Our bigger question is what we do if the escape does happen. We'll have nowhere safe to go, nowhere to hide. Taking the van is far from a sure thing, but it is the easy part in comparison.

Hakeem says he has a plan for that as well, but he hasn't given us any details as of yet. He says he doesn't want to say anything until he knows for sure that "everything is in order." I don't know what that means or what exactly he's planning, I just know I have to trust him. If anyone can find a way to pull this off, it's him. He prays to the divine every night for answers.

I just hope his God comes through for us on that day,

Deron Boyd

Log Entry: Day MXCV

Just a few weeks to go, and I'm starting to feel a bit nervous. And also paranoid. The new area warden came by my work today. The judge said he used to work at his courthouse, and I honestly think he might have been the guard who drove me here because he looks damn familiar, but that's beside the point. What I'm nervous about is that he might be onto us.

Hakeem and Sakura have said they've both recently seen him at their work as well. Didn't address the campers or even speak much to the guards really, just lurked around and watched the comings and goings. He stayed for about an hour or so and then left. Same thing happened at the sawmill today. He just walked around nonchalantly and never said a word.

The most likely scenario is that he's just making his rounds to learn more about the operations. Perhaps his bosses aren't happy with production, and he wants to see firsthand what can be done about it. The chances he knows what we're up to are slim. We've been very careful to only talk in discrete locations since the Merlin incident. Even if this place is bugged (which, let's be honest, it probably is), it's incredibly unlikely the

THE UTOPIA

microphones would have picked up anything.

No, this has to be about something else. I'm probably right that this is about production and my paranoia is just a classic case of Deron Boyd syndrome. I really should just let it go. I've got enough things to worry about. Real things.

Although I guess maybe it's worth ... Oh, never mind,

Deron Boyd

Log Entry: Day MCIV

Had the dream again for the third night in a row, only this time, it happened. I can't believe I'm writing this, but it finally happened. I caught the bird!

That raven has tricked me for so long, always distracting me with the devastation it has caused, always ensuring I take my eyes off it at the pivotal moment and look toward the ship. But last night, I finally got my revenge. I faked like it had fooled me again, only this time, I reached out and grabbed it even with my gaze elsewhere. I was so quick, it didn't even react. And when I caught it, I snapped its neck and tossed it over the veranda. I looked over the railing just in time to see it land harmlessly in the water, sucked up by the ocean waves.

It sounds heinous, and I felt a cold chill overcome me as I did the deed. Even in the dream world, I couldn't escape that feeling. But it had to be done. That raven has been torturing me ever since I arrived. Enough was enough. Now I just hope its spirit will pass on and it will return to my dreams nevermore.

Quoth,

Deron Boyd

Log Entry: Day MCVIII

Fourth night in a row. Fourth night in a row I've had the dream, and the raven wasn't there. It's unbelievable. I feel amazing. I've been waking up each day with a pep in my step and real honest belief in my heart. It's like I've vanquished my mortal enemy, and now that my adversary is gone, there's nothing that can hold me back.

We're at just over a week to go, and I should be losing my mind at this point. I should be a nervous wreck. But I'm not. I feel absolutely exhilarated. I feel like I could run a marathon or fight Yuri Yin with my hands tied behind my back or, gee, I don't know, maybe escape from this godforsaken place! No more second-guessing. We're getting out of here. We're actually going to do it. I've never been so sure of anything in my life. The curse has been lifted and there's nothing that can stop us now.

One more week,

Deron Boyd

Log Entry: Day MCXII

Four more sleeps to go until we make our escape, and I'm still feeling good. I will admit though that the nerves are starting to grow. I still feel confident that this is all going to work out, but there are also a few unknowns that are making me sweat a bit.

We still don't have our plan set. Hakeem is going on a mission tomorrow to try to find a way to get in touch with some of his old contacts on the outside, and he's taking Merlin with him. I still don't know what he sees in that man, but I'm beyond the point of questioning it. Hakeem works how he works, and if he thinks Merlin can help, who am I to tell him no? It's not like I've contributed much in the way of bright ideas.

There is one thing about their operation tomorrow that is interesting to me though, other than the fact that Merlin is going along for the ride, of course. Hakeem said he and Merlin would do their digging in the morning, and when I asked him how he was going to get away with skipping work, he informed me that he doesn't work on Fridays at all. Apparently, this whole time I've known him, he never has! I asked him how he was able to get a whole day off, and he said it had to do with religious reasons and because of the amount of time he's served, and for a while, I bought that ...

But then I realized Merlin should be working Friday mornings. He's not religious, and I know he has Friday afternoons off because I've seen him walking the streets around the sawmill on Friday afternoons. As little as a month ago I saw him! Plus, he is nowhere near as old as Hakeem, and there is no way he has been here as long. There's no way he would have that same time-served agreement. Something's fishy there. There's something he's not telling me.

I don't doubt Hakeem's loyalty or think he's some undercover spy working for the Camp. I can see the passion on his face whenever he talks about his distaste for the Utopia, and he was the one who suggested the escape. Why would he do that if he really was a spy? What would there be to gain? And why would he befriend me for three years just to trick me now? I could understand if I was some political assassin or if I had been planning some grand scheme to leave the island when I was on the outside. But I did nothing of the sort. I was a nobody out there and am still a nobody in here. It wouldn't make sense to put all that effort into targeting me of all people. I just can't see it.

There's something he isn't telling me, but I don't think it's anything that will cause me harm. It's probably just something personal he hasn't shared with anyone. He is a pretty private person when it comes to his personal life.

I just hope their recon leads to something tangible. It's getting pretty late, and we need to get all our ducks in line. Otherwise, our only chance at freedom might just pass us by.

We can do this,

Deron Boyd

Log Entry: Day MCXV

It's finally here; tomorrow is the day. I can hardly believe that after everything that's happened, it comes down to this: one chance, one moment *where we put everything on the line. A part of me wishes I could see into the future to know how it all turns out, but the rest of me is scared.*

We have a good plan. After some final discussions today, I feel we're about as prepared as we can be and that all the pieces are in place. We'll need a bit of luck. More than that actually: we'll need God on our side. But we have at least put ourselves in a position where there's a chance. I just hope Hakeem has prayed enough for all of us.

I feel bittersweet. On the one hand, I'm ecstatic at the prospect of leaving. It's been the only thing I've wanted since arriving here, the only thought that has constantly been on my mind, my only true ambition.

But on the other hand, I'm also sad—sad because tonight was more than likely the last time I will ever see some of my friends. Even if we do escape, even if everything works out as optimally as it can, I just don't foresee a way where we will ever cross paths again. And in some ways, after all we've been through together, after all the times we've shared and the things we've overcome, in some ways, that's heartbreaking.

I will miss them all. Sam and her fiery demeanour. Randall and Andrew and their constant bickering. Even some of those who were never part of the group but who've fought every bit as hard to survive this place. I'll miss Keith and Jacob and Ashley and Paulette. I'll miss Sandro and Ishan and Selena and Mikhail. I'll even miss Carlos and Shawn and Ray and Merlin. But mostly, I'll miss you ...

His eyes began to water as he looked up from the page and out into the deserted street. It was a quiet night, the heavy traffic of the evening rush long since gone. There wasn't a person in sight, nor was there one coming. It was him and him alone, sitting out in the darkness along the front wall of his apartment complex. Just him and his journal, his pages and pages of memories that would soon be left behind.

He looked back down at the page, eyes still tearing. But he wanted to write more as he sat in the exact spot where, all those years ago, he had cursed the woman's name. He sat there now finding it impossible to put into words how much she meant to him, wishing she would call to him from the shadows.

"I'll miss you." He whispered it to himself in a voice that was meant to soothe his own emotions, but it was never going to work. His tear ducts filled, and the first drops began to fall. They landed on the page, and he didn't try to stop them.

What he did instead was think back—think back through the pages. How many had he filled with stories about her, from the first time they met to the incident at the fun house and their battles with Yuri. He could write a novel about their monumental moments, a drama with twists and turns that would leave the reader wanting more, a story of chaos and adventure and heartbreak and understanding. They were moments that would make the tabloids, moments that would define their relationship from the outside looking in. But when he thought about her now, he didn't think of them at all.

What he thought of was her smile. What he thought of was her laugh. What he thought of was the way she would flick his ear to pester him and that look on her face whenever she'd see him sad. What he thought of was her humour. What he thought of was her smell, somehow always lovely no matter how many hours they had put in at the mill.

What he thought of was the woman he once thought might be the woman of his dreams. What he thought of was only being able to see her when he slept.

More tears fell, and he wiped them with his sleeve. And after he'd taken a deep breath, he felt around his neck, knowing the instrument he'd worn for so long was no longer dangling there. It brought a smile to his face, and he looked up toward the sky.

Kimmy, he thought, *for so long, I thought I would never get over you. But after that night with Sakura, I knew I had done it. I hope you're happy wherever you are.*

But this is not about you, and it's not about Sakura. It's about someone else: a woman who kept me sane through all the insanity, a woman who wouldn't let me quit no matter how badly I wanted to, a woman who kept my heart beating with that infectious smile in the times between you and Sakura. You are my past and Sakura is my future, but she was there for me when I needed her in the present. I hope you don't mind that I gave her your pendant. After all she's done for me, it's the least she deserves.

His smile broadened as he looked back down at the page. Stained by tear marks, some of the ink had run, but that was just fine. He would always remember why. And always remember her. He went back to writing.

But mostly, I'll miss you, Carla. I'll miss you with all my heart every single day.

And I'll love you forever.

Always,

Deron Boyd

CHAPTER 17

That night, Deron didn't dream about Carla. He didn't dream about Kimmy or Sakura or anyone from his past. He didn't dream about his times at the Camp. He didn't dream about the raven or the lighthouse or the ship burning over the horizon. He didn't dream about anything that night because it's hard to dream when you don't catch a wink of sleep.

Normally, a night without slumber would have made him useless the next day. Back in his other life, he had pulled all-nighters for no particular purpose; the drugs just wouldn't let him doze. Taking one too many bumps and the dopamine rush that followed made passing out impossible. Usually, he'd just play video games until he came down, but sometimes he'd have to power through the next day if there was something on the agenda, fighting against the headaches, fighting against the sudden flashes of hot and cold, fighting the feeling of weakness and tightness in his chest that begged him for rest, his body pleading with him to stop acting or even thinking, threatening to do the shutdown itself if he didn't choose to soon. He felt none of that today.

He stood outside of the W-2 apartment complex under the glory of the morning sun, just him and his companions waiting patiently for the guard to show up so they could spring their trap. They were the only ones on the lot, the rest of society having already transferred to their workplaces,

places like factory 4F, where they would soon be wondering why a man named Deron Boyd hadn't shown up for work. As he stood outside the apartments now, he felt anything but tired, anything but weak. He felt the adrenaline coursing through his veins, a rush so intense, it made those times with the cocaine feel like nothing more than a sip of morning coffee. It made him think about how if this kept up, he might need more than the collection of sleep aids he had left in his bag if he ever wanted to sleep again. He felt like he might go crazy if this man or woman didn't show up soon.

"Where are they?" he mumbled, his voice intentionally quiet but involuntarily firm. "It's got to be past nine now. People are going to notice we're not at work if they don't show up soon."

"Settle down, Deron." The voice was Hakeem's. He was standing beside Deron in front of the complex looking down the street. "They'll be here any minute, and don't worry about them noticing you're not there. It's likely they have already, but it doesn't matter. You've never been sick or late, and it's their protocol not to check on anyone with a pristine record until at least after lunch. You know this."

"I know that's what's supposed to happen," he said back, not taking his eyes off the road. "Doesn't mean it will, and every wasted minute is precious."

Hakeem didn't answer back, and Deron didn't pester him with any further comment. He needed to remain calm; Hakeem was right about that. But standing around here out in the open wasn't helping his anxiety and neither was knowing there was nothing he could do about it. Their only option was to wait and stick to the plan.

Deron looked over his shoulder. Sakura was there about ten feet behind, waiting by the door. He was about to call her over and remind her of her part for the umpteenth time just to give his mind something else to focus on, but then he got the word.

"He's coming." Deron immediately snapped his neck around and gazed down the street with Hakeem. "Looks to me like a white guy in his forties. Not an exact match for me, but probably less noticeable than if you do it. What do you think, my friend?"

Hakeem smiled at Deron, and for the first time that morning, Deron managed to crack one of his own. "Won't argue with you there." After a moment's pause, he said, "Thanks, Hakeem."

Hakeem said nothing back audibly, but the words were spoken in his mind. *Thank me if we get out, child, but first thank the Lord because I put our odds at succeeding at less than one percent. Unless it is His will.*

The van pulled up to the curb. The driver exited immediately. As Hakeem had described, he was a white man with short curly brown hair. He was taller than Hakeem but shorter than Deron and not especially well-built. These were useful features for their plan but all irrelevant if he didn't have one more crucial trait: an instinct to trust.

"Excuse me, sir." It was Hakeem who called to him right away. There was no hesitation and even a hint of alarm in his voice. There had to be if this was to work. "We need your help!"

"There a reason you two are here?" he grumbled back. "I'm supposed to be picking up a Sakura Saito, and for some reason, I don't think either of you is her."

"Sakura is our friend," Hakeem added. "We came here to send her off, knowing this would probably be the last time we saw her. But please, sir, you have to listen. Our other friend, he's very sick. I think it's the heat, or perhaps it's something to do with his condition. He needs to see a doctor or at least get to the pharmacy!"

"Woah, woah, woah, okay, slow down." The man waved his arms in a gesture like he was quieting a crowd. "Who? You mean that guy?"

He pointed toward the building where a man was doubled over, holding his stomach, to the left of the doors where Sakura stood. It was a man with pale skin and hair that fell all the way down his back; a man with a round face and goatee, who was as thin as a stick; a man with lost eyes, like they'd spent their whole existence wandering the desert and had just never quite found their way back to civilization; a man named Merlin Leclerc.

Merlin looked up as the guard pointed, convulsed once, and then spat a large glob of phlegm off to one side. The guard recoiled when he saw it.

"That's disgusting, argh. I hate when people spit; it makes me want to puke."

"Please, you've got to help him." It was Deron's turn to talk. "We've been waiting here for someone to come by, but no one has. We don't know what to do."

The guard thought for a quick second, but his response was what they expected. "No can do, gentlemen. I'm sorry. My orders are to take Sakura Saito and that is all. I can call in someone else to help with this situation, but I have no time to take him. I'm already late. Speaking of which ..." He walked past them and approached Sakura. "You Sakura Saito?" he asked.

"Yes sir," she replied. "I have my ID right here. They said you would ask for it."

She handed it to him, and he scanned it with a small device attached to his belt. She felt nervous as she watched him do it. It had nothing to do the scan itself. It was the weapon beside the scanner that made her feel uncomfortable. If their plan worked, it would never leave the holster, but if it didn't ...

Deron and Hakeem approached just as the scan was finishing.

"Alright, you're all good. Congratulations," he said, handing back her ID. "In a few short hours, you'll be done with this place for good." Sakura smiled. The man didn't. "Now if you don't mind, I would like to get a move on. I've got a schedule to keep."

"Okay," she said. "It's just—I really have to use the washroom. I'm sorry. I'll be super quick. I just didn't want you to come by and think I wasn't here and then, I don't know ... Silly me. I should have just gone before." She contorted her face into a look of desperation to drive the point home.

"You're right, you should have," the man said, mildly annoyed. "But as long as you're quick, I'll allow it. You're lucky you're the only one getting out today or I wouldn't be able to afford the time; that almost never happens."

Only one getting out. When Sakura heard that, her face nearly cracked, but she managed to restrain it.

"Thank you so much. I'll be right back." She opened the front door of the building and entered inside.

Hakeem and Deron, meanwhile, had also caught wind of the guard's last comment, and telepathically, their minds seemed to enter the same sphere.

That's very good, they thought. *Very, very good.* But they also held their nerve because they were far from home free.

"Excuse me, sir," Hakeem said.

"You guys again," the guard said, turning back to face them. He knew they'd been lurking but had hoped that perhaps they would just fly away with the breeze. Little did he know, these little birdies had a plan. "Look, I'm sorry. Like I said, I can radio for someone to come pick this man up, but—"

Merlin spewed before the guard could even finish his sentence, and not just a spit of phlegm this time; it looked like parts of his previous night's dinner had come up as well. The guard saw that and nearly threw up himself.

"Oh God, that's gross," he said. He began to walk away but Hakeem and Deron followed.

"Here, have some water," Hakeem offered, taking a bottle out of his supply bag.

"No, no, thank you," the man protested. "That will only make it worse."

He turned away from them again, and the moment he did, Deron and Hakeem made eye contact, and each added a subtle nod. They both understood. This had to happen now, or any hope they had was dead.

"Sir, please, we don't mean to be a bother, but we're begging you here," Hakeem said. "You can clearly see Merlin is sick, and I know you can radio others to come get him, but the truth of the matter is—and I didn't want to say this while I thought he could hear us—but the truth of the matter is, I think part of the reason he's feeling this way is because Sakura is someone he really cares about. I think it pains him to see her go, and part of the reason we want you to take him is so that maybe they can have just a few more moments together."

The guard didn't respond. He was still dealing with his own nausea. But he was listening. Both Hakeem and Deron could tell.

"I know it's probably against protocol, and we don't want you to do anything that could get you in trouble, but all we're asking is that you call your supervisor and maybe ask if you can take Merlin on the way. You said yourself you have a little extra time today, and we know you're going to pass the pharmacy on the way out of the Camp anyway. So please, can you just ask?"

There was a pause in the air, and for a second, Hakeem believed he might need to add one more push, but then the guard turned to them. He looked plenty worse for wear. A glance over at Merlin and he again looked like he might heave, but in that moment, Hakeem saw a look of empathy in his eyes as well. He would do as they asked.

Somewhere, the mighty Allah was smiling down on them.

"Okay, okay, fine. I'll try. You're right; poor guy shouldn't be left out here to suffer. Just ..." He closed his eyes as if he were concentrating hard, but really, he was just trying to calm his stomach. "Maybe I'll take a sip of that water after all."

And when he heard that, Deron's eyes went ballistic.

Hakeem didn't even flinch. "Sure thing," he said. "Here." He handed it to the guard, and the guard sucked back. "Have as much as you would like. It's a hot day out; hydration is important."

The man didn't hold back. He guzzled until the bottle was half empty before handing it back. "Thanks," he said. "I do feel a bit better now."

"You're welcome," Hakeem replied. After a few moments of silence, he pointed over toward Merlin with his eyes.

"Oh, right," the guard said. "Right, right, right. I'll radio to my supervisor, but no promises."

"Understood."

"Alright then."

He reached for his radio, tuned it to the correct channel, and held it to his mouth. "Base. Base, this is Davidson. Do you copy?"

"Copy, Davidson. This is base," the voice replied through the transmitter. "Go ahead."

"I'm requesting permission to take a sick camper to the pharmacy. He's thrown up already, and I'm not sure what's wrong with him. Might just be the heat, but I don't want to take any chances. I don't see anyone else in the area."

There was a pause in the transmission as if the radio itself were thinking. Neither Hakeem nor Deron moved an inch. The plan was in motion, and one way or another, they were going to follow through. They were in too deep now not to. But it would be oh so much easier if, just this one time, the voice on the other side of the instrument could give them good news.

THE UTOPIA

"Copy. Yeah, I checked the monitors, Davidson, and there's no one close by. Some mishap at the power plant apparently, and the closest staff were called in."

Randall and Andrew. Deron's face remained steady, but his mind started to wander to thoughts about his friends. *Thank you, guys. I don't know what you did, but whatever it was, you risked your skin for us. I'll never forget that.*

"The Big Dog isn't around at the moment, but ... God, yeah, alright. I'm giving you the green light, Davidson. I can see the guy on the monitor, and he looks pretty beat up. I'll radio the pharmacy and have someone there look at him. They can transfer him to the infirmary from there if need be."

When Deron heard that, it took almost everything in him not to pump his fist, and everything he had left after that to remind himself that the dangerous part of this was only just beginning.

"Copy that, base. I'll drive the poor sucker. Over and out." The guard looked to Hakeem and Deron. "Well, gentlemen, there you have it. Looks like you got your wish. Must be my lucky day."

He didn't look pleased, and that didn't change even after Hakeem smiled at him broadly. "Well, at least you'll sleep well knowing you did the right thing," he said. He even added a laugh after for good measure, something that was quite out of character. Only he and Deron knew what was so funny.

"Yeah, whatever you say, man. He just better not throw up in my van or I'm going to lose it. I'm not about to spend the rest of my day cleaning puke off a ... off a ... woah."

Davidson moved slightly to his left, but it was more of a stumble than a fluent maneuver, like he had been walking down a flight of stairs and missed the bottom step.

"You alright?" Hakeem asked.

"Yeah, yeah. Fine, I think. Just feeling a little lightheaded all of a sudden."

"Probably just the heat," Deron chimed in. "It's a scorcher today."

"Yeah, maybe. I just better not be catching whatever your friend over there has."

Davidson pointed over at Merlin, who was now sitting with his head between his legs, looking sick as could be. Deron and Hakeem ignored this and instead offered up a suggestion.

"Perhaps you would like to go inside for a moment to get out of the sun."

"No," he said, sounding more aggressive. "What I would like to do is get a move on. Where is that girl? She's taking her sweet time in the bathroom."

Deron and Hakeem looked at each other, unsure of what to do. They both knew what they needed to have happen. What they didn't know was how to make it so. They had pushed this man as much as they could, and another suggestion might cause him to become irate. He was probably wondering by now why they were even still here. He had told them he would take their friend. They had just about run out of ideas, but then Merlin made his move.

"Hey. Hey! Where are you going?"

As Deron and Hakeem turned to see what the problem was, they saw that not only was Merlin now standing, but he had actually creeped up to the front door of the W-2 building. Better than that actually—he had a hold of the handle and was beginning to open the door.

Davidson began to strut toward him with purpose.

"Hold on," Deron said, sounding a bit afraid. "Don't yell at him. He has mental health problems."

Davidson stopped instantly and turned to Deron with a glare. If he was frustrated before, he was now legitimately fuming.

"Oh, now you tell me this! Just what I need."

Merlin was now halfway through the door. "We can get him for—"

"No! The last thing I need is any of your help or any more of your ideas. I'll get him ... I'll get him ..."

All of a sudden, his anger evaporated. His voice got slow and heavy. He sounded the way a person does first thing in the morning, before their blood is flowing and their mind has fully awakened. He sounded like he wanted to crawl back into bed and take a nice long rest.

"Here," Deron said. The guard's energy had abandoned him, and Deron was no longer worried about him putting up a fight. He led him to the door Merlin had entered into.

"Thanks," the man grunted out. His eyes were now half closed. "I don't know what happened. I just feel so tired all of a sudden."

"It's the heat," Deron said, knowing full well it wasn't that. He opened the door for the man and let him walk himself into the narrow scan-in area inside. Deron followed behind him and Hakeem—taking one look behind him to ensure no one was there—after that. Then Hakeem closed the door.

Merlin was leaning against the wall to the left of the metal doors.

"I'm sorry for yelling," the guard said to him. Merlin looked at him blankly, but the guard didn't see a thing. His eyes were now all but closed. Merlin could have given him the finger and he wouldn't have reacted. "I'm sorry. I'm so ... so sleepy ... I'm ..."

The man began to fall, and Deron and Hakeem caught him before he could make a thud.

"Quickly," Hakeem said. "We don't have much time. Those pills should keep him out all day, but I'm sure someone saw all that on the monitors. If we don't leave here quickly, they'll wonder what's going on. Undress him."

Deron didn't need to be told twice. He and Merlin began to rummage through the body like they were battling each other for a coroner's position. It took them a minute or so, but they were able to do the deed.

"Good," said Hakeem. "Now hand me his guard clothes so I can change into them, then put my jumpsuit on him. Quickly now."

They did what was asked, having a bit more trouble with the dressing, but they managed to get it done. When they finished, Hakeem looked like a guard and the guard looked like a camper.

"Where's Sakura?" Merlin asked, saying, for the first time since the guard had arrived, words and not just gargling or gagging. As he spoke, he began to tuck his long hair into his jumpsuit.

"She should be just on the other side of this door," Hakeem said. He knocked twice in rhythm, and then another two knocks followed. It was their secret code saying it was safe to come out. She was with them in a flash.

"No one came by," she said. "But I'm sure at least a few of the girls are here, so we should hurry."

"Alright," Hakeem responded. "Merlin, help me lift him."

The two men reached down to try to lift the body. The deadweight was a handful, but they managed to get him up.

"I did like you asked. I stayed on the couch and kept going through my bag like I was looking for something. God, I hope they bought it."

"You did great." Deron smiled at her. "You did more for us than anyone could have asked. The rest is up to us." Sakura smiled back and they shared a quick kiss.

"Alright, you two lovebirds. No time for that now. We've got to get out of here. Deron, you and Merlin walk him. And everyone keep their heads down. No matter what you do, do not look back! The main cameras are attached to the building. If we move straight ahead, they won't catch our faces. And if they don't catch our faces, we can make it look like I'm the guard, the guard is a passed-out Merlin, and Merlin is me. Everyone ready?"

They each looked at him and nodded. They would never be truly ready, but they were as ready as they'd ever be.

"Let's go."

Hakeem pushed the door open and held it in place. Deron and Merlin maneuvered their way through and dragged the guard toward the van with his arms clasped around their shoulders. The street in front of them was deserted.

"C'mon," Deron mumbled. "Almost there." The heat was excruciating, and sweat was beginning to form on his forehead. He barely noticed it. His focus was the task at hand.

Hakeem and Sakura got to the van first, and Hakeem opened up the back. Sakura went in, and with some help from Hakeem, Deron and Merlin managed to toss Davidson in as well. They then climbed into the back themselves.

"Alright, everyone, let's get the hell out of here."

Merlin gave a thumbs up and untucked his hair. Deron sat and held his head. Sakura posted up against the wall with her neck tilted toward the sky. Hakeem shut the doors and then scrambled toward the driver's seat, tossing things from the belt of his new guard uniform onto the passenger's chair. First went the weapon. Then went the cuffs. He followed

THE UTOPIA

that with the scanner and then, finally, the radio. He expected someone to call, ask what had happened to the man and if they needed help. He had even come up with a script of exactly what he would say. It was all part of the plan. There had to be someone watching.

But the call didn't come, and after Hakeem realized it wasn't going to, he decided it was time to go. Guard Davidson's card was in the pocket of his uniform, and Hakeem used it to start to van. Then he tossed aside the final thing in his arsenal, his bag of supplies, reminding himself of only one thing as he did.

Whatever you do, don't drink the water.

He drove off toward the pharmacy.

***

IN THE BACK OF the van, Deron's heart rate was just starting to return to its normal level. *Thump-thump. Thump-thump.* He had his hand pressed to his chest and could literally feel the pumps circulating through him. Quickly at first, and then slower and slower as the oxygen began to flow, as his nose remembered to breathe, as his mind began to clear.

He sat on the long bench on the driver's side of the van. Sakura was next to him, collecting her own thoughts. Merlin was across, that typical blank stare pouring out of his eyes. The scene reminded Deron of a time just over three years earlier when he and a group of others were taken on a van ride much the same as this, toward an undefined future, where there was just no telling how it would end.

The only difference back then—there was no drug-induced zombie passed out on the floor.

"He'll be fine." The voice belonged to Merlin, who had noticed Deron's gaze toward the guard. "Crushed or not, zombie pills are strong. He'll be out for a while. Probably ten to twelve hours. But when he wakes up, he'll feel just fine. Better than that actually—he'll feel brand new."

Deron nodded. "Yeah, I know," he said softly, now directing his eyes to Merlin. "I used to use them plenty back in my heyday. I'm not so much worried about that. It's just, well, everything else."

At that, Sakura put her left hand into his right and gave it a loving squeeze. She felt tired. She had only been up a few hours and had slept pretty well the night prior, all things considered, but she had used up a lot of adrenaline. The crash was coming. She laid her head against Deron's shoulder and promptly closed her eyes.

When Merlin saw that, he spoke. "You'll be okay. The journey ahead will be a long one, but the trickiest part is over. Once you cross through that gate, there will be people who will help you. You're not alone. Always remember that."

Deron nodded once more. And after he had done so, he rested his head for a moment against Sakura's. Merlin was right. He wasn't alone. He had her, and he had Hakeem.

And he also had him. He lifted his head back up and glanced toward Merlin. Again, the man looked dazed, like someone who had just woken up from an operation, and the nitrous oxide hadn't yet worn off.

His whole time in the Camp, he had only thought of Merlin as some type of burden, someone he couldn't trust because of his condition, someone who was always meddling in his affairs and judging him with his stares. And yet, on the day they needed someone most, it was Merlin who was there.

"Oh, I almost forgot!" Merlin shouted out of nowhere, loud enough to stir Sakura. "Here, you need this."

He reached into his pocket and tossed Deron something he was not prepared to catch. It was a juggling act, but Deron managed to snag it before it fell to the floor.

"A cell phone? Wait, how did you get this?" he said, amazed. At no point had a cell phone been mentioned as part of the plan.

"I've had it for a long time. They gave it to me."

"Why would they—"

"When I got it, it was broken, but because of my condition, they figured there was no harm in giving me a broken phone. They assumed I would just use it to make fake phone calls and it would all be harmless. But I'm pretty handy with these gadgets, and I managed to get it working again. There's a number in there you need to call once you leave the main campground, people I know who will help you."

Deron looked at the now wide-awake Sakura, and she looked back at him equally confused.

THE UTOPIA

Call a number? Call who? I thought Hakeem was the one who knew the people who would help us!

"Wait, Merlin, slow down," Deron pleaded, gesturing at him for calm. "You're confusing me. You say *you* know the people who are going to help us? I thought Hakeem was the one who knew them."

"Oh, he does! Well, sort of. He knows of them through me. Before I came to the Camp, I was part of this ensemble, and Hakeem used to be a member of an earlier faction of The Cause."

"The Cause?"

"Yes, The Cause is what we call it, people who are disenchanted with the way the Utopia runs its operations and want to see things change, specifically, they want the ability to leave the island. Twenty-five is too young to make such a large decision about your future. Most people don't realize what the Utopia does to them until they're older or until they've already been to the Camp. And by then, it's too late. The Cause is about finding ways to get out of here ourselves if the State won't allow it. That's what it's about now, I believe, or at least it was back when I was outside the Camp. I'm not sure what its main goal was when Hakeem was an active member."

Deron glanced over in the direction of Hakeem driving the van, then back toward Merlin. Questions were firing off in his mind at a rate of about a thousand per minute. What on earth was The Cause? He had never heard of them. And if they're so important to their plan, why the hell was he was just learning about them now?

"There's no need to worry, Deron. Everything will be fine. All you need to do is call the number in that phone. Call them and use the word *Valkyrie*. They'll explain the rest. I would tell you more, but there's no time, and besides, I haven't been in contact with them for a number of years."

"What do you mean you haven't been in contact with them?" This question he had to ask. It exploded out of his mouth without any second thought. "I thought you just said you got the phone working. You mean you didn't contact them to check and make sure this could even happen?"

"I couldn't take the chance. If I used the phone, it was possible someone could track it. Unlikely anyone would notice, but it wasn't worth the risk. The phone will work. Like all phones in the Utopia, it has automatic minutes. I'm just not entirely sure the number is still connected. You will only know when you call."

Deron stared at him, astonished. For the moment, he had no words. He could hardly believe that *this* was the plan. When Hakeem had told him about the group of people that would help them, he had made it sound like it was a group of people *he* had known, people *he* could *surely* count on, people he had *already* contacted from inside the Camp via his relationship with a few of the guards, people who knew when and where to wait for their arrival. But this wasn't that. This wasn't that at all. This sounded like a pipe dream. This sounded like a very dangerous game of chance. This sounded almost like …

Something made up.

"Merlin, are you sure these people are real?" Sakura nudged his arm, but he ignored it. It was a brutal question, but he'd decided right then it was something he had to ask. This didn't make any sense, and there were only two possible explanations he could see.

Either Merlin was having a moment of psychosis, mistakenly believing he was the mastermind behind this plan, seeing the work Hakeem had done as his own and fabricating a story to project that, even adding a prop to convince himself it was real—it was either that …

It was either that or Hakeem had lied.

When he looked at Merlin, he expected that same blank stare, the one where he could never quite tell what the man was thinking, the one that seemed to look through him instead of at him, the one that made Deron see him as an enemy. But instead, Merlin just smiled.

"I understand why you'd think that, and you're not wrong to," he said, calmly and in control. "I do have a mental illness. That has never been a lie. I've learned to control it better over the years, but I still have my bad days, as you've surely noticed. On more than one occasion, I've been particularly harsh with you. That's nothing personal, by the way. It's just that Hakeem has helped me so much throughout the years, and the second you showed up, he took a large interest in you. A part of me was jealous of that, the part that has trouble controlling itself. Anyway, this is a long-winded way of saying I didn't make them up. I know they're real, and Hakeem knows it too. Ask him about them. He'll tell you everything you need to know."

Before Deron could respond, the van pulled off to the curb and came to a halt. Hakeem tapped once on the glass, drawing their attention. He pointed off to the side, and Merlin understood the cue.

"I guess this is me." Merlin stood up without hesitation, but rather than leave right away, he stuck his hand across to the other side. Deron looked at it and pondered and then quietly spoke the words.

"I'm sorry," he said. "This whole time, I misjudged you." He stood up, looked at the cell phone, and slid it into his pocket, and then the two of them shook. "Thank you."

Again, Merlin smiled, and then he left the only way Merlin could. "The institution is shady; the celebration is grand. Turns out he doesn't hate me; turns out he is a fan."

He stepped around Davidson and exited through the back. Deron and Sakura watched him close the door again, and just like that, he was gone, out of their lives, his part forever played.

Around the side of the van, Merlin gave a wave to Hakeem as they drove off toward freedom, a sense of inner peace radiating from his body. He would surely miss his friend, but sometimes, sacrifices have to be made for the greater good. He had done all he could and had given them a chance. The rest was up to them.

Will they make it?

"Yes," he said. "Yes, yes, yes." His mind asked the question, but his mouth said the answer, repeating it over and over so he could drill it into his soul. He walked toward the pharmacy without a doubt in his mind.

Because some things aren't true, but you've got to believe them anyway.

***

IT WASN'T LONG AFTER Merlin had departed that Deron decided it was time to get some answers.

Knock-knock. He had waited until he could see out the front windshield that they had reached desolate land. To have revealed himself before would have been dangerous. It was impossible to know if they would pass any checkpoints, and he couldn't afford to be seen by any wandering eye. But now it was time.

Knock-knock. Knock-knock. He repeatedly hit the glass that separated the cabin from the front of the van. He was unsure if the glass could part or not, but that didn't really matter. He knew Hakeem could hear him and that he could hear Hakeem.

"Yes, Deron." Hakeem's voice came over an intercom by his ear. Deron pressed a button and spoke into it.

"I need to talk to you about something. Is there a way to separate this glass?"

Hakeem searched around on the dash. There were buttons of all kinds, but none clearly labelled. He tried one, then two, and the third one did the trick. The glass slid downward like a power window and retracted into the frame.

As this was happening, Deron shifted from the driver's side of the cabin to the passenger's side so he could get a better view of the man he'd be interrogating. In his mind, he had decided that's what this would have to be. He had to know the truth, and he wouldn't get it by dancing around the subject.

And Hakeem knew that too. "This about the cell phone?" he asked straightaway, his eyes peering through the rearview mirror to gauge Deron's reaction.

"Yes. Why didn't you tell us that? What the hell is going on? And what is The Cause?"

Deron was beginning to get a bit worked up. Sakura had joined him at the front of the cabin and was gesturing for calm from across the way, but his attention was diverted. He couldn't believe, that after everything that had happened, Hakeem wouldn't inform him of every detail of the plan, a plan where he'd be risking his life, a plan that required a woman he cared deeply for to sacrifice guaranteed freedom. He couldn't believe this man would betray him like that, this so-called man of God, this so-called friend.

"Deron—"

"No, it's alright, Sakura. He has a right to be upset. I haven't been completely with you, and given the stakes and the trust you've put in me, that is tremendously unfair. I have a lot to explain." Hakeem sighed deeply, his eyes fixated on the road ahead, the emptiness of the surrounding lands a sick metaphor for the emptiness he felt inside. It was true, he had lied, to them and to himself.

"But I must start from the beginning. Do you remember, Deron, our very first conversation? The day we met, it was just you and I and Merlin in the room. Do you remember what I told you?"

Deron thought back but it didn't take much of an effort. It wasn't something easily forgotten.

"Yes, you told me you killed a man because he attacked the woman you considered to be your wife."

Hakeem sighed again as he stared out into the beyond. He was on the verge of tears now, something that only occurred on the rarest of occasions. He didn't want to discuss this. It hurt too much to talk about. But if he ever wanted them to trust him again, he would have to put his sentimental feelings aside.

"Yes, but I never told you *why* he attacked my wife," he said, his voice beginning to shake. "I never told you the whole story. The truth is … Sorry."

His voice was really shaking now, and in the back of the van, Deron's emotions were starting to shift from anger to empathy. He was starting to realize there was a reason Hakeem hadn't told them about the plan, and it had nothing to do with deceit.

Hakeem collected himself and once again began to speak. "The truth is that the man I killed wasn't just any man. He was a high-ranking official for the Utopia, someone I befriended purposely in order to gain access to State secrets."

"State secrets?" Deron repeated, and then it hit him. "Wait, does this have something to do with The Cause?"

"Yes, that's exactly right. I was doing it for this secret entity known only as The Cause, the origins of which date back to the first iteration of the Utopia."

"All the way back then?" Sakura interrupted.

"That's right," Hakeem continued. "But at that time, the group was a lot larger, and it also wasn't secret. The faction was simply a select group of people who didn't agree with the rules that the Utopia was implementing, who thought it unfair that the people of the island would have to leave their homeland if they didn't want to conform to the regime."

"Seems reasonable," Deron added.

"Yes, to you and me maybe. But naturally, the Utopia didn't like this, so they locked the members up, charging them with rebellion against the State, forcing them to do the same laborious tasks we've had to do, only under even worse conditions. The technology back then was not what it is now."

Deron nodded along, now fully invested in the story. In all his time at the Camp, he had never even considered how much worse it would have been in the early days. The campers back then had probably built the very factories they were working in today!

"After that, a new faction of The Cause was created, only this one went underground. Knowing what would happen if they were caught, they became very cautious, only meeting in rare instances and always in a different place, only allowing new members when they were certain those persons could be trusted. About twenty-eight years ago, I became one of those members. And sometime fifteen years later, Merlin did as well. Only I had no way of knowing this at first, of course, as I had already been arrested many years before for killing that official. Is this making any sense?"

"Some," Deron said. He'd been following along as best he could, and he thought he had the gist of it. "You believed that the Utopia was mistreating people and limiting their freedoms, so you joined this underground group who was scheming a way to do something about it."

"Correct."

"And sometime later, after Merlin was arrested and sent to the Camp, you figured out that he was also a member of this organization and that's how you became close," Sakura added. She too was hanging on pins and needles listening in. The idea that there was this secret group out there who had spent the last century conspiring against the Utopia seemed absurdly fantastic.

"Exactly, yes. Except it was actually he who found me. He had heard of me through another member of the organization, and when he name-dropped her during one of our conversations, I knew he had to be a member as well. From then on, we spent many of our days off together, trying to come up with ways to help the organization from within."

"I meant to ask you about that," Deron said, seeing an opening to direct the conversation with more of his questions, "about the Fridays off, why it was that you had them free and also why you never told us."

"It was because I struck a deal," Hakeem replied hastily. "People like to believe the Computer runs everything, but that is simply not true. At the end of the day, humans still make the final call, and I was able to barter one day off a week. In exchange, I promised to admit I was a member of The Cause and accept an indeterminate sentence, even though I knew that would likely mean I would be stuck in the Camp until I died."

"Wow," Deron said softly. Stuck until he died. He couldn't even imagine.

"And so Merlin did the same?" Sakura asked.

"Not exactly! And this is why he was so important to this plan. I originally thought he must have admitted his affiliation to The Cause, but he didn't. He got his deal because of his mental illness and because he was willing to take a few more years in exchange for the day off. They had no clue he was a member, and as far as we can tell, they still don't."

"But *you* knew. And you knew he had contacts you could use. That's where the cell phone came in," Sakura added. She thought she had a pretty good grasp on the situation now.

"Very good. That's exactly right. Merlin's contacts were much more recent than mine, and I thought if we could somehow get a phone, we could reach out to one of them and get ourselves some help."

"Good plan," Sakura complimented. She was about to say more before Deron interrupted.

"But why didn't you just tell us that?" he exclaimed. He, like Sakura, now thought he understood Hakeem's plan, but what he didn't understand was why. Why did he feel the need to keep all that a secret from them?

"Because I was afraid that if you knew about the cell phone, you wouldn't trust Merlin. And I was afraid that if you knew I hadn't told you the whole truth about my wife, you wouldn't trust me." His voice was starting to crack again. There was nothing difficult about explaining the plan to them—that he had known he would have to do one way or another. It was this part that was hard. "Ironic, isn't it? Lying to someone in order to gain their trust."

Deron said nothing. He could hear the emotion in Hakeem's voice and knew whatever was coming next would be incredibly difficult for him to say. He would contest him after if he had to, but for now, he had to listen.

"I just didn't want to admit to you that the reason everything happened was because of me. No one from The Cause put me up to it. I made the decision on my own, made the decision to try to investigate this powerful man, thinking I could play him for a fool; meanwhile, he was the one playing me, he was the one doing the investigating and learning my weak points and realizing that the way to hurt me most was to go after my wife—to attack her. And he didn't just do that."

His frantic pace slowed, his voice got quiet, and he said the thing they knew was coming but were desperately hoping not to hear. "The part of the story I left out was that he didn't just attack her, but he hurt her brutally."

When Deron and Sakura heard that, their hearts began to pound harder in their chests. Both felt heavy in their bodies and sick in their guts. Neither could say anything.

"I'm not proud of what I did to him. It puts me in a class just as low as him. But I saw no other choice. If I didn't kill him, they could have arrested me anyway for my association with The Cause, and he could have gone after her all over again. But that doesn't change the fact that if it hadn't been for my own foolishness none of that would have happened. It doesn't change the fact that—"

"Hakeem." It was Deron who finally interrupted. He climbed over to the driver's side of the van and reached through the opening to put a hand on his shoulder. "It's not your fault. I'm sorry. I'm so very sorry."

Tears were streaming down Hakeem's face as the van slowed to a crawl. Eventually, it stopped for good so Hakeem could weep to himself. Deron stood behind him with his hand on Hakeem's shoulder, and Sakura joined with love and tears of her own. It was finally clear to them both why he hadn't told his story.

"I'm sorry," Hakeem said after he had finally settled down.

"It's okay, Hakeem. You have nothing to apologize for," Sakura offered. Deron nodded in agreement.

"But I do," he said. "Because I lied to you both. I have you out here risking everything on false pretenses. I don't even know if the number in

THE UTOPIA

that phone is going to work. Maybe everything else I can justify, but that I cannot. I don't know what I was thinking."

Deron and Sakura looked to each other. What they should have felt in the moment was fear, perhaps even anger that their lives were being risked without their fully informed consent. But what they felt instead was pity.

"We would be here anyway," Deron said. And when he did, he felt his body surge with an energy he hadn't felt in some time. It was a moment of realization and truth that made all of his other thoughts seem meaningless.

Who had he been kidding? Once the suggestion had been made, this was always going to happen. God himself could have told him it was impossible and still, he would have tried.

"That's right," Sakura agreed. "And either way, we're here now, so there's only one thing left to do."

She glanced over at Deron, who didn't need the look to understand. He slipped his hand into his pocket, grasped hold of the cell phone, and held it out for Hakeem.

"It should be you," he said. "This is your plan. Plus I've never much enjoyed talking on the phone. I'm much more of a texter."

Hakeem gave a muffled chuckle, the first sign of life from him since his heartfelt confession. He stared at the phone and then turned in his seat to look back at his friends. "Thank you."

"Of course," said Sakura.

"You can thank us by calling," Deron added, pointing with his eyes to the phone his outstretched arm was still holding. "We shouldn't waste any more time."

"You're right." Hakeem nodded. He snatched the phone from Deron's grasp, unlocked it with the code Merlin had instructed him to memorize, then found his way to the contacts list. There was only one number.

"Valkyrie?" Deron asked.

"Valkyrie," Hakeem concurred. "Let's just hope whoever is on the other end chooses to let us live." He pressed the screen and began the call.

Ring-ring. Ring-ring. Ring-ring.

"Hello?"

Their eyes went wide. Hakeem spoke calmly. "Valkyrie," he said.

There was a pause on the other end. For each moment there was no response, their collective anxiety grew exponentially. Then, after about ten seconds, ten minutes, or ten hours (who could tell?), the voice responded.

"Who gave you this number?"

"Merlin. Merlin Leclerc."

There was another pause, causing the triangle of conspirators to hold their collective breath as they wondered if this call would lead to their salvation or demise.

"How many are you, and what are your names?"

"Three. Sakura Saito, Deron Boyd, and Hakeem Syed."

Another pause and some clicking in the background as though the person was on a computer somewhere.

"Where are you right now?"

"Still on the Camp side of the Wall. Probably forty-five minutes from the gates, the ones closest to Unglow District."

More typing in the background, and then after a few moments, the voice on the other side said, "Okay. Androloch Conservation Area. West parking lot. Be there at five forty-five this afternoon. There will be a van there waiting for you with a yellow backpack in the front seat. The van will be unlocked, and the backpack will have instructions inside detailing how to proceed. Understood?"

"Yes."

"Good. Now delete this number and destroy this phone before someone can trace it. This will be our last interaction. Good luck."

"Thank you!" Hakeem said, but the person on the line had already dropped the call.

The three friends looked at each other, straight-faced at first, but a smile soon began to form on each one's face.

"Let's go!" shouted Deron, giving a fist pump. Sakura laughed and clapped her hands. Hakeem was the calmest, but even he was beaming. The sadness he had felt discussing his wife's assault was a distant memory.

"That had to have been legit, right?" Deron asked. "There's no way that was some State agent on the call, is there?"

"I highly doubt it," Hakeem agreed. "I'm not sure they would be able to intercept a call that quickly. And I don't believe they would ask us to destroy the phone if they had. Speaking of which ..."

He tapped through the phone and quickly deleted the number. Then he shut it off and opened the driver's side door.

"I'm going to smash this thing and then bury the pieces. After that, we'll continue on. Any objections?"

"None from me," Deron beamed. "Wooo!"

Sakura laughed as Hakeem left to go take care of business. "Settle down," she said. "We're not out of here yet, and you don't want to wake Davidson." She knew they needed to be careful, but in her heart, she was just as excited. She gave Deron a hug.

"You're right; I'm sorry," he said, sounding not particularly sorry at all. "It's just, this is going about as well as we could have hoped, and, well ..." He paused for just a moment. "I'm just really happy I'm here right now. With you."

"You're sweet," she said. "I'm really happy too." She might have said more if Hakeem hadn't returned right then.

"Alright. Let's roll," he said. "I'm going to close the window again if you don't mind, just in case we pass someone or for when we get close to the gate. I want everything to look proper."

"Sounds good," Sakura agreed, breaking off from Deron. "I think I'm going to take a quick nap anyway if no one minds."

"Do your thing," Deron said. But he didn't let her get away before a quick kiss. She smiled at him after and then lay down along the cabin's driver's side bench and closed her eyes.

Up front, Hakeem hit the button to return the window into place, but as he was doing so, Deron caught a glimpse of his face through the rearview mirror. He was smiling ear to ear. Deron didn't think he had ever seen the man so happy in their entire time together.

As the window closed for good, Deron took a seat on the bench opposite Sakura. With her entering the dream world and Hakeem now out of reach, he took a moment to just appreciate all they had endured to get to this point: the fights, the risks, the sacrifices. All of them were needed to make this moment possible, and while they weren't out yet, the fact that they were even this close was a testament to them, to who they were, to how far they'd come, to how they'd refused to quit in the face of any and all adversity. It felt like something he had to write about in his journal. And as they rolled along on the road to their new lives, the words seemed to come without any exerted thought.

Log Entry: *Day MCXVI*

This last log marks the final frontier.
What I've written in here is a man's quest to see clear
beyond a surface world encapsulated by fear
and his attempt to understand what it is he holds dear.
None of it matters.
Pages of uncircumscribed thoughts,
stages of ever-changing locks,
built by sages, bots, emotionally raging, lost,
and all along, I was taught only one thing:
none of it matters.
Here or there, it's all the same.
Happiness's existence is a hollow vein.
The goal is pleasure, but life is pain,
so accept, attain, and don't mind constraints
because none of it matters.
Took me my whole life to hear those words,
appreciate the message I was meant to learn,
In a herd of sheep, absurd reasoning is birthed
to disguise the hurt that
none of it matters.
I was one, but now I see those words for what they truly are,
allowing them to light my mind up like the brightest star.
Near or far, cages, guards,
Satan's dark enslaving heart:
none of it matters.
Everything important is within me now.
I've travelled through the portal: they can't hold me down.
Lost or found; sink, swim, or drown,
don't ask about, who, what, when, where, why, or how
because none of it matters.

And yet, it couldn't mean more.

-Deron Boyd

***

WHEN DERON FINISHED HIS poem, he felt happiness eluding him. The elation he had felt earlier was gone, and what he was feeling now would have been more aptly described as perplexity.

He had written pretty much in a trance, not really even thinking about the words he was putting down, like he was some kind of prophet and the word of God was flowing through his pen. He reread what he wrote and thought it quite profound but felt something just didn't feel right with it.

"Oh, wow."

He glanced up from his page just in time to see Sakura stretching herself awake. He closed up his journal and slipped it underneath his supply bag just as she was sitting up. He would further analyze it later.

"That was a nice nap. How long was I asleep for?" she asked, blinking a few times to adjust her eyes.

"Not long. Half hour maybe. Good thing you woke up though: you were snoring so loudly, you almost woke Davidson."

"Oh, shut it," she said. "Was not. And if anything, I'm the one who would hear something. You know how good my ears are."

He gave a smile at that but couldn't force out a laugh. Something still just didn't feel right.

You're probably nervous about getting through the gates. We should be close now. You'll feel better once you're out of the Camp for good.

And that line of reasoning made sense, but ... he just wasn't so sure that was it.

"I'm going to ask Hakeem how far we are," he said, mostly so he didn't have to say anything else.

"Good idea."

He scurried up to the front of the cabin, hopped over Davidson's outstretched body—poor Davidson; he really didn't deserve this, but there was no other way—and pressed the intercom button.

"Hey, Hakeem, just checking in. Wanted to know how far we are from the gates."

The response was almost instant. "Not too far now. I can see the bridges. Your timing is impeccable because I was just about to call for you myself. You should begin preparing yourselves."

"Alright, sounds good. Plan A or B?"

"Plan A for now. I haven't seen or heard about any trouble. It's been quiet on the radio, and I haven't seen any guard vans on the road at all—only transport and moving trucks."

"That's good," Deron said. It seemed odd to him that there wasn't much chatter on the radio, but perhaps Hakeem meant he hadn't heard anything noteworthy. Either way, it was better than an emergency bulletin telling all units to be on the lookout for the campers who had escaped. "Anyone behind us?"

"Just a moving truck. Same one has been behind us for a while. Not worried about it though. Figure it just caught up to us when we pulled over."

"Makes sense." He felt the need to add something more, but he wasn't sure what. Eventually, he settled on, "Alright, we'll get plan A rolling. Keep us updated."

"Affirmative."

Deron turned back to Sakura. "You get all that?"

"Yep," she confirmed. "Plan A, which is basically the status quo mixed with a hope and a prayer that when they make these exit runs, they don't check the back of the van."

"That's one way of putting it," he replied. But in essence, that was it. They were in a van without any specialized equipment and no real clue what the exit procedures entailed. All they could really hope for was that the process was the same as the one used upon entry: open the side window, have Sakura smile for the camera, and then proceed on their merry way. If that was the case, they'd be okay.

As long as the guards didn't have any questions for the new driver.

Deron returned to his original spot and began to ponder quietly to himself, wondering what, if anything, he could do to help improve their odds. That celebration from earlier now seemed woefully premature. He began to flex his fingers in and out in frustration.

THE UTOPIA

From across the cabin, Sakura noticed this, as she usually did whenever Deron was upset. And like the other times he'd been upset, she wanted to speak up. She just couldn't find the words.

He's doing it again, she thought, *worrying about the things he has no control over, seeing ghosts that aren't really there.*

She wanted to speak, but in that moment, she began to feel a lot more like crying instead. Twice in one hour would have been a lot for her, but if there ever was a day, this was it. And if there ever was a person worth crying over, this was him.

She watched him put his head in his hands and begin to rub his face, oblivious to the outside world and the effect his gestures had on anyone else, lost in his own mind.

She could empathize with that, and not just because she loved him and wanted him to break the cycle, but because in a lot of ways, she was like that too: a lot on her mind, and it wasn't often positive. It was one of the reasons she had never been much of a talker.

But I've gotten better with it, she told herself. And over her three years at the Camp, she really had. She'd learned what she could do to make the best of her situation, taken solace in her friendships during the toughest times.

It wasn't perfect. Many days, she wished for something better than what she had. But for the most part, she could accept whatever came her way. For Deron, it always seemed like he was looking for something he was never going to find.

She looked at him and thought of their moments of bliss, how even during those times, she could sense a certain inevitability, that one day she would be leaving, and when that happened, the positive strides Deron took would be reversed times ten. It was why she had chosen to try to help him escape.

But not just for him, she reminded herself. *For Hakeem and for me too.*

She was doing this for herself because she had no idea what was next, no idea what her life would become once she re-entered civilization, how she would fare if they made her become a member of the guards, made her become an enforcer of a way of life she hadn't chosen for herself.

She also had no idea what life would be like if their plan worked out, if they escaped the Utopia and found themselves somewhere else, in a country with different rules, a country with a different way of thinking. She had no clue whether this would be a net positive or a loss, but she'd made the decision to try because going back to her old life wasn't the answer. There was nothing transcendent for her here.

Either way, she'd have struggles. Either way, she'd still face the never-ending challenge of the battle against her brain. Either way, she'd have regrets. But at least this way, she had hope of something different. At least this way, she could do something positive for her friends. At least she had chosen this path for herself.

And that made it all the more heartbreaking the moment she realized they were never going to make it.

***

"HEY, GUYS." THE VOICE was Hakeem's over the intercom. It wasn't a panicked voice, but it was enough to startle both Deron and Sakura back into the real world. "I think something's wrong."

Sakura and Deron took a frightened look at each other, then Deron scrambled with reckless abandon to the intercom, nearly stepping on Davidson in the process. "Wrong how? What do you mean?" he barked.

The answer he received was succinct. "That moving truck followed us onto the bridge."

Deron's initial reaction was to think, *So what?* But then he remembered. Each of the four bridges has its own designated purpose: one in for camper transport, one out for camper transport, one in for goods, one out for goods. Why would a truck be on a "camper bridge," as they called them, unless …

Unless its purpose wasn't to transfer goods at all.

"You think it's the guards in disguise?" he asked into the intercom. The response he got was not what he wanted to hear.

"Impossible to say for sure. But if I had to guess, I would say yes."

Sakura, who had rushed up to the front of the cabin as this conversation was ongoing, now pressed the button and added her own two cents. "But you can't say that for sure. You just said so yourself, right?" she asked, playing devil's advocate. "It's possible the driver just made a mistake. You said they've been behind us the whole time; perhaps they just got distracted and absentmindedly followed us. I'm sure it wouldn't be the first time something like that has happened."

She looked to Deron for support, but Deron said nothing. In his mind, what she was saying sounded like a completely reasonable explanation, perhaps even the most likely one on any given day. But it wasn't what was happening. He knew it, and so did Hakeem.

"It's a fair point, Sakura, but I don't know if we can take that chance."

"What do you mean?" she shouted back into the intercom. "What other choice is there?"

Again, she looked to Deron, and again, he said nothing. It was like he was paralyzed.

She turned her attention toward the glass screen instead. Through it, she could see out the front windshield just enough to know they were within a few kilometres of the security booth. Whatever the choice was, they would have to make it soon.

Hakeem saw it too. There was a booth overlooking the single laneway they were on. To the left and right of it were others, but those were irrelevant to the current predicament.

Each bridge was a single road that ended at its own booth. There was no way to transfer to any other lane, and with the moving truck behind them, there was no way to reverse course either. The only way to proceed on was to advance with permission past the arm barrier, the ten-foot-long piece of aluminum that separated prisoners from their freedom.

Within a minute or two, they would arrive at it, and when they did, it would all be over. The longer they glided along the path, the surer Hakeem became. Through his side mirrors, he was privy to information the others were not. In the moving truck behind them were three men who weren't wearing guard uniforms, and they didn't have weapons at the ready. But the giveaway was the radio the one man was holding, a man Hakeem was finally realizing looked a lot like a person of prominence from the Camp.

He looked at his own radio lying on the seat next to him and thought of flipping through the channels to see if he could overhear the conversation ongoing. He thought better of it when he realized there was truly no point. He likely wouldn't find it fast enough, and even if he did, it would make no difference at all. He had already decided what needed to be done.

"I'm going to drive through the arm barrier," he said over the intercom. "I'm sorry; I know that was never the plan, but we've come too far to give up now. It's our only chance."

For the second time that day, his eyes began to water as he felt sorrow overcome him and a sadness in his heart. He would never forgive himself for what he had put these kids through, but he couldn't bail on the mission now. After all the Utopia had done to him, he was not about to go down without a fight. He had prayed to Allah, the greatest of planners, and the Lord's guidance had gotten them this far. The rest was up to him. He pushed his foot down on the gas.

In the back, Sakura and Deron nearly stumbled at the sudden speed increase but managed—barely—to hold their ground. For Sakura, this was especially important. Hakeem was losing his mind, and she needed to convince him that what he had planned was not the way to go.

"Hakeem, you can't!" she screamed, truly afraid now. "Even if you get through the barrier, what do you expect will happen? That they'll just let it go? Someone will call for backup, and they'll be on us in minutes!"

She looked toward the back doors, wishing they had windows so she could see what Hakeem saw. Would it have changed her opinion? Unlikely. But at least then she could have tried to come up with a plan of her own.

As it stood, she was stuck with trying to talk Hakeem off the ledge.

"Our only hope is that maybe you're wrong and they're not after us! We have to stick to the original plan; it's our only chance!"

She didn't honestly believe her pleading would work, but she had to try. As she peered through the glass again, she could see the security booth fast approaching. If they didn't slow down soon, it would be too late. They would crash through the arm barrier, and that would be the end. If the guards weren't on to them before, they certainly would be then.

She pounded on the glass, but Hakeem was unresponsive. He had made up his mind, and there was nothing she could do or say to change it. There was only one other thing left to try now.

She would have to convince someone else to convince him.

"Deron," she turned around and cried out. And for the first time, his

THE UTOPIA

paralysis seemed to break. He didn't speak then, but his eyes fixated on her instantly. "Deron, please, you have to tell him not to do this. I know how badly you want to get out of here, and you have to know how badly I want us to get out of here too. The thought of going back is sickening, especially after all we've been through." Her voice was starting to shake but she did her best to hold her nerve. "But this won't work. You have to know that. This is not the way. If we break through that gate, they'll send the cavalry after us. We'll never make it."

She was very close to tears again, and seeing her eyes water was beginning to make Deron's tear up as well. This was not at all what he wanted.

"Maybe Hakeem is right. Maybe the truck behind us is full of guards, and maybe they arrest us. But at least if we give up, maybe there's a chance they show us some compassion. Maybe they send us back to the Camp, and I know that's not what you want, and trust me, it's not what I want either, not after I had the opportunity to leave in the palm of my hand. But maybe they'll at least let us go back to how things were. Maybe they'll let us stay together. Us and Hakeem and Sam and Carla and the twins. Would that really be so bad?"

Now the tears were falling, and she didn't try to control them. *Would that really be so bad?*

"No. No it wouldn't." His mouth just spat it out before he even had a chance to think. With tears still in his eyes, he walked over to the intercom.

"Hakeem," he spoke. "Hakeem, please …"

He began to hesitate.

You'll never make it, his mind said. *You'll never make it if you go back.*

His stare was toward the intercom, but in that moment, his eyes didn't see a thing. His conscience was looking inward.

You know they won't put you together. You know your punishment will be for the rest of your life. That's if they even let you live.

"Hakeem."

Don't fool yourself, Deron. You had to know something like this was probably going to happen. You had to know your odds of making it were slim. You were willing to do whatever it took to get out. Don't give up on that now.

"I'm asking you to please …"

You'll regret this, Deron. If you stop, you're done for. If you drive through, at least there's a chance. Think of all they've done to you. They locked you away after framing you for something you didn't even do. They gave you two more years for standing up for yourself. You deserve better than this. Don't let the Utopia do this to you. If you're going to go down, go down fighting. Show them who you are! Make them remember you! Do it for yourself! Do it for Carla! Do it for Hakeem! Do it for Sam and Randall and Andrew!

Do it for Sakura.

"Please don't do this. Sakura is right; we'll never make it. Our only chance is with the plan."

He sat down on the cabin floor. His eyes teared up, but he didn't sob. His body lay limp, an empty shell, his soul lost somewhere in the dark corners of his mind.

Sakura came to him and sat, grasped his hand in hers, and laid her head down on his shoulder the same way she had done earlier in the day, the same way she often did when they were alone together, the same way that seemed to always make him feel good no matter what the circumstances, the same way it did now.

They sat there together as the van chugged along.

***

IN ANOTHER LIFE, DERON'S speech would have affected Hakeem deeply, would have made him realize the impossibility of what he was about to attempt, would have made him understand that sometimes giving up is a necessary act. It doesn't make you weak. It doesn't invalidate everything you stood for. It is just the only choice that will allow you to survive.

But this wasn't another life. This was Hakeem in the here and now. And this Hakeem—this Hakeem was not ready to give up. This Hakeem was determined to fight off his oppressors no matter what it took.

This Hakeem would die for The Cause. This Hakeem would find a way to see his wife again if it was the last thing he ever did.

So when he heard Deron's words, this Hakeem didn't even flinch. If anything, he became even more determined. They were breaking through that barrier gate, and nothing was going to stop them.

If only he had realized before it was too late that they had activated the spike strips.

THE UTOPIA

Crash! When they busted through the arm barrier, it sent shockwaves through the vehicle, but their momentum carried them through. The problem was that their momentum wasn't going to last very long.

Pop! Almost simultaneous to the crash came the sound of popping tires, the holes courtesy of expertly designed spike strips built right into the ground, an attack Hakeem should have anticipated had he been thinking more clearly.

"Argh!" He shouted something unintelligible as he slowly pushed the breaks. He had no other choice. If they tried to continue on at that pace, they would simply crash and burn.

He looked in the side-view mirrors. The moving truck had stopped at the security booth, but Hakeem was sure that would only be momentary. As soon as the spike strips were deactivated, the truck and its inhabitants would come for them all.

In the back, Sakura and Deron were just now scrambling to their feet. Their peaceful moment of serenity had quickly died upon hearing the crash, and now they were just confused. They hadn't seen what had happened and didn't know why they had stopped.

But that confusion was about to turn into fear very quickly.

"Hakeem. Hakeem, what are you doing?" Deron shouted, forgetting for the moment that his friend couldn't hear him unless he spoke to him through the intercom. He banged on the glass instead.

Hakeem heard this but didn't react. Instead, he was staring down at the seat beside him, the seat that held all of Davidson's belongings: his handcuffs, his ID card, and his radio and scanner. But most notable was the thing no longer in the chair—the weapon Hakeem had taken hold of in his hands.

"I'm sorry, Lord. This is not the way I wanted things to end. But it is our only chance of escape now. Whatever result stems from my actions, I will humbly accept, for you are the best of judges."

He said the words to himself. He spoke them quietly and then silently said a prayer. He knew what he was about to do was wrong, but it was his only chance.

He pressed the intercom. "I'm sorry, friends, that it has come to this, but this is the only way. I've come too far to quit now. And the Utopia will surely put me to death if we are caught. I promise I will get you out of here or die trying."

"Hakeem! Hakeem, no!" This time, Deron had remembered to press the intercom button. "Put down the weapon!"

But it was already too late. The man's mind was made up and nothing was going to change it. He stepped out of the vehicle and fired three rounds toward the approaching moving truck.

Bang! Bang! Bang!

The sound of the gun blast echoed through the air. The truck turned sideways, and the guards inside ducked below the dash.

"Give me the vehicle and no one gets hurt!" Hakeem shouted. He was less than fifty feet from the truck now, capable of putting down any guard who popped his head up with a well-aimed shot—capable in theory anyway. He had no plans to kill anyone.

"I just want to live in peace! The Utopia is a cesspool of corruption! It is the antithesis of freedom! I have strived my whole life to bring it down, but I will settle for the chance to leave! Will you grant me this wish? Will you …"

He paused. One of the guards was getting out of the truck, the one he recognized.

"Hakeem," the guard said. His heart was beating a mile a minute, but he did his best to remain calm. He came out with his hands up to show he was unarmed. "Your name is Hakeem, right? Hakeem, nobody wants to hurt you." He was entirely outside the truck now, facing Hakeem head on, his hands still raised in innocence.

"And I don't want to hurt anyone either," Hakeem replied. "All I want is to be gone from this place. After what it has done to me, that doesn't feel like too much to ask."

The other guards were starting to get out of the truck as well, both through the same passenger's side door their leader had exited from. They slipped in behind him cautiously and then spread out, one on each side.

"Now, Hakeem, you know I can't do that. You and your friends tried to escape the Camp, and I understand you had your reasons for it, but I can't just let you leave. You know that. I have no choice here."

Hakeem held the gun steady. The other two guards had their guns on him now, but to him, it made no difference. He had one goal in mind, and he would accomplish it no matter what.

"That's where you're wrong my friend. There is always a choice in this life. Always. And I have made mine, so now, it's time for you to make yours."

"I can't just let you go," the guard said. He was almost pleading with Hakeem. "You have to understand that. I can't. I can bring you back, and I can maybe find a way for you and your friends to stay together, but you can't get what you want. It's impossible."

The man looked at Hakeem with a real heartfelt sense of compassion in his eyes, like he felt true empathy for Hakeem and his friends, like he wanted to do right by them. Those eyes said his heart was in the right place. But his mouth said nothing more; he wasn't going to give the order.

Hakeem recognized that and knew what it meant. That allowed him to smile for the first time since they had made their freedom call—and for the last time in his life.

"I understand," Hakeem said. "But it was worth a try."

His face turned to a scowl, and quick as lightning, he shifted his gun toward the guard on his far left. He didn't pull the trigger.

***

IN HINDSIGHT, MATT WAS pretty sure—no, almost positive—the man's finger hadn't even been on the trigger at all.

But he knew what he was doing, and the frightened guard on the left fired his weapon without a second thought. It struck Hakeem in the chest, the bullet penetrating his heart, killing him almost instantly.

Matt turned to the shooter, who said, "I'm sorry, Supervisor Tucker. It was so fast. I thought he was going to shoot. I thought—"

"It's okay, Billy," Matt said. The outcome was not what he had hoped for, but there was nothing he could do. He had known when he'd first gotten word of the escape that this was a possibility. "It's not your fault. Just, please, let's cover him with something from the back of the truck. I don't want the others seeing him like this."

"Yes. I ... Okay." The kid was lost, but he would do what he was told.

The hallmarks of being a guard, Matt thought.

He took the other guard and approached the stolen van. In the past, an event like this would have caused him hesitation, would have paralyzed him with fear as his mind raced in a thousand different directions trying to decide what to do. But today, his mind was on autopilot, as it often was these days, just counting down the days until he could be done with this shit for good.

When he opened the back doors, Sakura and Deron were sitting on the driver's side bench facing the far wall. It was obvious they'd been crying, and equally obvious they knew exactly what had occurred. They put up no resistance when he ordered them out, only a request that they could ride together in the truck. He saw no harm in it. It was probably the last time they would ever see each other.

Matt nearly broke when he thought about that, and to cover up his emotions, he ordered the other guard to secure them in the back of the moving truck. The guard did as asked and led them toward the truck. They saw a covered body as they walked and knew it was Hakeem. It would have ripped apart their souls had they not already been in tatters.

Matt didn't dare watch them walk. Instead, he searched through the back of the van and got on his radio.

"HQ, this is Supervisor Tucker. I'm going to need an EMT, possibly two, at the Wall, Unglow District entrance. We have two bodies here: one deceased and one who looks like he might be passed out on zombie pills, but I would like to have someone check on him."

"Ten-four, Supervisor Tucker. A team is being deployed."

"Ten-four."

He put away his radio and thought to himself. *I guess I should leave Chang here. It would be cruel to leave Lander after what he just did. Poor guy.*

He looked out the back of the van and saw his understudy looking blankly into the beyond. It would be a while before he recovered from this.

But at least this isn't a Zimmer situation. Have to look at it that way, I guess.

He was about to step out when he noticed something on the floor that he hadn't previously picked up on. Purposefully or not, it was almost hidden below the passenger's side bench. He bent down and picked it up. It was a Camp book, one of the ones they gave away with the first-day instructions.

He opened it to a random page and began to read.

"Anything else, Supervisor Tucker?" It was Chang at the back doors. "I handcuffed the two, what with them trying to escape and all, but they're comfortable back there."

"Good," Matt said, his head still buried in the book. He read a few more lines. Realizing his heart was starting to race, he closed it up. "Thank you, Chang. That is all. I'm just going to need you to stay here and wait for the EMTs. I don't want to leave Lander here."

"For sure," Chang agreed. "I'll wait with the booth guards, I guess, and you can pick me up on your way back?"

"I think that's a good plan."

Matt got out of the van, stuck his hand out for Chang to shake, then headed over to the truck. "You take passenger, Billy. I'll drive," he called out to his comrade.

"Okay. Thank you, Supervisor Tucker. I'm just—"

"Don't mention it, Billy."

They got into the truck after Matt had ensured the back door was secured. He started the vehicle with his ID and began to drive toward the cities. Sakura and Deron, in the back of his truck, were ironically going in the direction they wanted to go but were never destined to reach their destination of choice. Matt knew they were there, knew what they'd done, but otherwise didn't know much about them at all aside from the brief notes he had taken from their files.

He'd learn plenty more soon enough.

CHAPTER 18

Today is the end.

As he sat strapped to the operating table, his torso at a slight incline, his mind fired the thought off without his consent. As he glanced at the wall that was as blank as his stare, he found no energy to fight it off. He was alone in this empty room of death, lying next to the machine that would soon help take his life. Any reason he had for optimism had already passed on.

The last three days had been a whirlwind, a tornado of chaos and punishment and despair. The events seemed to all mash together, and there were really only bits and pieces he could remember with any clarity.

He and Sakura had arrived at a holding jail sometime in the early eve on the day of the escape. After being allowed a few moments together, they were split apart for good. There was no grand farewell, no moment of resistance, no begging or pleading for their release. They had simply accepted the inevitable and gone their separate ways.

The following day was just a blur of loneliness and contempt as the meaning of the next day's trial sunk in. He would either be sent back to the Camp, likely for a good portion of what remained of his life, or he'd be sentenced to death, not an unlikely scenario given the severity of his crimes.

Perhaps, if they had given themselves up prior to crashing through the arm barrier during the escape, it would have been the former, but it had turned out to be the latter, the well-enshrined three strikes rule coming into effect. He had still held out a bit of hope that maybe since his first sentence had been so unjustified, they might let him live, but sadly, this was the Utopia, a place where the sun shines so bright that it blinds you to the truth, a place where the water is so clean because it sweeps its dirt below, a place where everything is free except freedom itself.

After that, he'd just sat and stewed, waiting for this moment, thinking about the world, thinking about his friends, thinking about everything that had led him to this point. If he'd had a book and a pen, he would have written it all down. But there was nothing left to write and nothing left to do.

Today was the end.

The door to the hallway creeped open, and he hardly moved a muscle. There was really no point. He wasn't getting out, and he'd have no attachment toward whoever was entering. It wasn't Sakura walking through that door. It wasn't Carla or Sam or Andrew or Randall. It wasn't Marla or Diego or Charlie. It wasn't Kimmy, and it certainly wasn't Hakeem. It wouldn't be anyone who mattered at all in his life.

Until suddenly, it was. And two for the price of one.

"Deron Boyd."

It wasn't the call of his name that brought him back to life but the recognition of who had said it: a woman with dark hair, soft brown eyes, and fair skin; a woman in a white dress, the same one he had seen her wearing on more than one occasion when she was speaking on the TV screen. Her name was Azalea Hawthorne, but he knew her by a different title: co-leader of the Utopia.

And she was with the other one, the man in the black suit, who went by the name of Mustapha Hakimi. He'd let his curly hair grow out, and he'd added a short beard along with it, but there was no doubt it was him. He closed the door silently and then approached with Azalea.

"You know who we are, I assume?" Azalea asked, giving Deron no time to come to grips with the situation he was in. She was now standing by the foot of the operating table with Mustapha at her side.

"Yes," Deron said. Without really thinking, he added, "Why are you here?"

THE UTOPIA

He stared at them but without a glare or scowl. His eyes were still hollow—the look of a man who didn't care much about the answer but felt a need to fill the air.

"We want to understand why you tried to escape," Mustapha replied, getting straight to the point. There was no reason to attempt any small talk. It would only make things worse for all of them.

"Why we tried to escape?" Deron repeated the words as if he didn't understand the question.

"Yes," Mustapha said. "Believe it or not, statistically speaking, attempts to escape from the Camp are very rare. Each year, there are only a handful, and most of these cases involve campers who have long-term sentences, sentences that will take up the majority of their remaining years. And even in those cases, the camper will often have a disease of the mind which makes him or her more prone to rash choices. But you are different, and we want to understand why."

Why? He looked down from them toward his feet. *You want to understand why someone would want to escape a place where you're worked to the bone for no incentive or reward?*

He thought about the words he could say, the arguments he could give. God knows there were plenty, but he wasn't sure what good it would do. If they didn't understand already, it was quite likely they never would.

As if reading his mind, Mustapha said, "We have some inclination, of course. The hours are long and hard. The accommodations wouldn't necessarily be described as the most pristine. And yet even with those factors, it's very rare we get a case like yours, someone who knows they can get out with more than half a lifetime in front of them but risks it all anyway. It is most unusual. And your friend is even more fascinating. She *was* getting out, but she chose …"

Sakura.

Mustapha's voice faded out as Deron thought about her.

You risked it all for us and look how it ended up.

His eyes stayed hollow as he looked inward, within himself. It was a thought he'd had a lot over the last few days. He felt guilt over what had happened, self-reproach for the damage he had caused, because if it hadn't been for him, Sakura would be living life as a free woman. But he had taken that from her, taken that from her without a hope or a prayer of their plan ever succeeding. Somewhere deep down, he had known that, and yet, he'd still been selfish enough to try.

You never should have met me. You'd have been better off if you hadn't. None of this would have happened if it hadn't been for me. Or if it hadn't been for them.

He looked up, and when he did, he felt a fire inside that he hadn't felt in days, a passion reignited by the presence of the two people now before him.

What happened to Sakura was his fault. For three days, he had known he would take that to his grave. But it wasn't his alone. No, it was also theirs. He had known it then and he knew it now. If he hadn't been framed, none of this would have happened.

Suddenly, he felt like giving an explanation might be worthwhile after all, if not for him, for the future ones like him.

But not before they answered something for him first.

"What did you do to her?" he said, forcefully enough to stop Mustapha's monologue.

It was Azalea who answered. "Her trial has not concluded, but the likely outcome is she will be sentenced to another stint in the Camp. Her crime, while serious, is only her second offence, and technically her previous sentence had elapsed prior to this incident and that plays in her favour as well. It is therefore her choice what she wishes to do. She can choose to go back, or she can choose ... the other route."

Deron didn't need for her to spell out what "the other route" meant. He knew it all too well, of course. It was the path he was facing himself.

He shook his head solemnly. "Why can't you just let her go," he said. His voice was low, but there was clear emotion in it as well. "It was Hakeem and I who convinced her to do what she did. It wasn't her fault. She doesn't deserve this."

"Her position is not an enviable one; we can agree on that," Azalea said. Her face remained emotionless, and her tone stayed steady. "But decisions like these are not up to us. They're up to the Computer."

Deron could only shake his head. He knew that answer was coming, but it was just so difficult to accept. "But they don't have to be," he pleaded.

"It's just a machine. You're the co-leaders of the Utopia. You can override it. You can let her go if you choose!"

He looked back and forth between them. Strapped to the table, his muscles could barely move, but with the energy he'd exerted shuffling, he'd started to work up a sweat. Had the lights above been old fluorescents, he might have been bathing in it.

They saw this but were unnerved.

"We cannot, Deron," Azalea said. "These decisions must be the Computer's. It is the only way to eliminate any and all emotion. It is the only way to crunch all the variables in a truly objective way. It is the only way to be fair."

"Fair!" This time he shouted. "I was sent to the Camp for doing absolutely nothing! That's the only reason any of this happened in the first place—because the Computer judged me guilty even though I did literally nothing wrong! How can you say that's fair?"

He was panting by the time he finished his outburst, but the co-leaders didn't flinch. "Deron, we would be happy to explain that to you if you'll allow us. But we need you to calm down," Mustapha said.

Easy for you to say, you arrogant prick. Try being in my position. That's what he wanted to say, but the words never left his mind. Upset or not, he was coherent enough to know they would do him no good.

He scrunched his eyes together, and when he reopened them, he released some tension. "I'm all ears," he said quietly.

"Okay then." This time, it was Mustapha's turn to make the point. "Okay then. I will explain."

Mustapha looked toward Azalea, who gave him a quick nod of approval. He then put his gaze back toward Deron, and after a few more moments spent trying to conjure up the right words, he began speaking.

"You're right, Deron. What was done to you wasn't fair." He paused, thinking again. "You're right that you were set up. There's a special State team that does this from time to time. They make it look like a crime was committed when, in fact, there was none—or at least not one done voluntarily. And that was the case with you."

Deron's heart began to palpitate faster and faster as he heard the words. Somewhere deep down, he had known all along this was the case, well before talking to the judge and discussing it with his friends. He had always known there was something that didn't fit, that the crime he was accused of was something he wouldn't do. He knew that somehow, someway, he was set up—drugged and convinced to do it or perhaps a fake video. Something had happened that he could not explain, and there had to be a reason. It had never made sense why he hadn't just waited, and now the truth was finally being confirmed.

It made him feel like throwing up.

"But," Mustapha continued. "This is not because the State had any vendetta toward you. Perhaps you think that, and if you do, I understand why you would, but that is just not the case. You were simply chosen by the Computer."

Bullshit! Again, his mind screamed but his mouth didn't move. He had a feeling an explanation was coming without the need for prodding.

"Now, I know what you're probably thinking. If the Computer chose me, then why didn't I have a normal hearing like others who are chosen? Why create this elaborate hoax when you could have just followed the law? The answer to those questions is a State secret, but given your position, I will tell you if you want to hear."

Deron tried to swallow but felt his mouth had run dry. His heart was beating rapidly. This was not what he had been expecting to hear. But now that he was hearing it, he needed to hear it to the end. He nodded.

"Okay then. The truth is this. The Computer has a certain algorithm it follows to create the best version of the Utopia. Incorporated into this algorithm is a ratio for the workforce based on the population: a certain number of people need to be guards, a certain number of people need to be doctors, and a certain number of people need to be campers. Is this making sense so far?"

Deron just nodded. This time, his mind had no words; he was simply following along.

"Now, as I'm sure you have become aware, the campers are the lifeblood of the Utopia. They do the grunt work necessary to keep everything else functional: farm the food, collect the raw materials, transform those materials into usable products. Most of the truly crucial jobs in society are in their hands. And because of this, a steady source of labour is

THE UTOPIA

needed. This is the reason for the chosen law.

"Believe it or not, every year, the percentage of the population required to be campers decreases. This is because of constantly improving technologies created by those technicians who are free to spend their time developing these advancements thanks to the work of the campers. Without their labour, these technicians would have to worry about food and shelter, but because of the campers, they can focus all their energy on creating new products that in turn make camper labour less and less necessary. It all works together."

For the first time, Deron noticed a smile on Mustapha's face, a joyous one, not put there to make him feel at ease or as a front to convince him. The man was truly enjoying explaining this to him.

"Now, you're probably wondering what any of this has to do with your situation. The answer is this. As I said, every year, the percentage of the population required to be campers decreases, but there are more real crimes committed in some years than in others. Crime is low in all years because everyone's needs are met. But once in a while, the rate will be exceedingly low, and in a year like that, more people than usual will need to be chosen. Usually, this is not a problem. People understand the rules and accept the possibility that if they don't volunteer, they could be picked. But a few years ago, the year you were chosen, not only was there an extremely low crime rate, but it was also a year where an abnormally large number of campers were scheduled to be released."

Finally, Mustapha's smile faded, and as it did, Deron could sense a different energy coming from him. He had seemingly enjoyed discussing how the system worked; but it appeared like he would not enjoy this next part.

"The year you were chosen was the year the most people were chosen in the history of the Utopia. This was a problem. We didn't want people living in overbearing fear of being chosen and to therefore risk the possibility of society descending into chaos. Because of that, we used the same strategy leaders of the Utopia have used since the dawn of its existence, the same strategy we continue to use when it is necessary. We have our task force manufacture crimes for people, people the Computer would have chosen anyway. And you were one of those people."

Mustapha sighed and, for the first time since he'd started speaking, looked away from Deron. Azalea continued for him.

"It's not a perfect system, Deron. I don't want you to get the impression that we think it is. But we believe that it's the most equitable for everyone. The Computer treats everyone the same and plays no favourites. If you volunteer, you can't be picked. If you don't, you can. Everyone receives the same education. Everyone grows up under the same conditions. Everyone gets food, water, shelter, and the chance to have a life. There will just always be people needed to do the grunt work. There's nothing we can do about it."

Deron said nothing. He stared beyond them blankly toward the wall. His heart rate had begun to slow; it was his mind that was racing now.

"As Mustapha said, one day, the technology will be so advanced that we won't need as many people, or if we do need as many people, we won't need them for as many hours. But for now, this is what we've got. Progress requires pain. Our goal is for there to be less of it each year."

Deron continued to stare toward the wall. His mind was adrift. Thoughts of all sorts were entering and leaving his mind. But there was one that he couldn't shake.

"I didn't choose this life though," he mumbled so quietly they almost didn't hear. "The Computer chose all this for me ... That can't be right ... You say this is a fair system, but it's not. It can't be."

"It's not the system, Deron." It was Mustapha speaking again. "As Azalea said, we don't think this is perfect, but we believe it's the best we can do. The biggest problem is people. People always want more. People always want better. Nothing will ever be good enough for them. They can never just be content with what they have."

"You might not like it, Deron," Azalea added. "There will always be people like you who don't. But what you need to understand is that the alternative you think so highly of—it isn't better. You're thinking of more choice, but you're not thinking of the poverty, not thinking of the war, not thinking of the hunger and homelessness and struggle. We're not perfect, but we're not that. And deep down, you know it. Otherwise, you would have chosen to leave the Utopia when you had the chance."

Deron's eyes began to tear. His muscles began to shudder. "It's not right," he repeated. "It can't be right."

Azalea and Mustapha made their way toward him, one on each side. Mustapha produced a tablet out of his blazer.

"I'm going to ask you to take this now, Deron. It's a zombie pill, as I'm sure you know."

He stuck his fingers in front of Deron's mouth. Deron could have chomped down on them, perhaps even bitten one off if he had clamped with enough force. But what would be the point?

He swallowed the pill.

"That's good. Thank you, Deron. It will only be a few minutes now. I want to thank you for giving us your time. I think we understand now why you did what you did. I'm sorry it has to be this way, but you made your choice, and the Computer has made its."

Deron didn't say a word. He just stared forward at the wall, a blank canvas of white, a perfect metaphor for the current state of his mind. There was nothing inside: no fear; no anger, hatred, or resentment; no longing or sadness. Nothing at all. He had given up the fight.

He began to doze off.

"Okay, Deron, I'm going to put the mask on now. I promise you won't feel a thing," Mustapha added.

Deron whimpered out a nod, his body shutting down into a mode of rest, feeling good and high the way he used to during the peak of his drug addiction, feeling it for the last time.

His eyes shut tight. Azalea might have said something to him at the last moment, but he would never know for sure. In the real world, he would never hear another thing; never say another word; never again touch, love, or taste; fight, cry, or argue; write, drink, or dance. Never again would he wake up with a hangover wishing he was dead. He would no longer have to wish.

This was the end.

***

HE STOOD WITHIN A lighthouse gallery overlooking the ocean. At first, he felt afraid. It was dark, and there was this ominous orange light spread beyond the horizon. But the breeze was calm and steady. He heard the waves harmlessly crashing into the rocks below. Once he gave in to his surroundings, he felt an inner peace, like it was somewhere he was meant to be.

And it helped that he wasn't alone.

To his left was a raven, a beautiful bird, sleek and strong. He felt a warmth coming from it, drawing him in. As he approached, it didn't stir. It stayed rested on the guardrail looking into the beyond.

"Hello there," he said. The raven gave no answer, but when he pet its head, it didn't flee, as if it knew he meant no harm, as if it trusted him as a friend.

The raven continued to stare out toward the water, and eventually, he did the same. And when he saw it, he nearly teared up. He couldn't believe his eyes.

There was a ship within his sightline. It was approaching fast, lit up in a display of orange. It was the most beautiful thing he'd ever seen.

"Should we go down?" he asked the raven.

His friend gave him a nod. And within the blink of an eye, they were down by the rocks awaiting the ship's arrival. The closer it got, the clearer he could see.

The passengers on board were holding candles. They were dancing and singing songs. It looked like the most fun. When they got close enough, they smiled at him and waved.

"Come aboard!" one yelled, a beautiful woman with short wavy black hair.

He waved back and smiled too. The ship released a gangway for him to climb. He took a few steps toward it and then stopped.

"If I go, you can't come with me, can you?"

He stuck his arm out for his friend to crawl on. The raven worked its way down to his wrist and looked at him face to face. It shook its head no.

A puzzled look formed on his face as he looked back out toward the ship. If he didn't go soon, he would miss it. He jogged toward it, stopping just in front of the gangway.

"Come on," a man said as he waved. He was older than the woman and had brown skin and bushy hair.

Deron nodded his head but didn't move an inch. Instead, he looked at the bird.

THE UTOPIA

"I don't want to leave you. I don't know what to do. I don't—"

Yes, you do.

He heard a voice in his head say it, a voice that startled him because the voice was not his own. But when he heard it, he didn't question it. He looked at the raven and gave an understanding nod.

The raven did the same, then it spread its wings and rose into the sky. It only descended once he had climbed onto the ship where he was approached by his fellow passengers.

Marla gave him a hug. "It's been too long," she said, then passed him on to Diego.

"Nice to see you, man. Really nice."

And Charlie followed. "Told you we'd meet again. I told you. Missed you, pal."

Then he hugged Randall and Andrew and Sam and Hakeem and Carla. And finally, Sakura.

"I'm sorry," he said. "I'm sorry. I—"

"Don't," she said. "Please, Deron, it's not your fault. I made my choice like you did yours. It's time to let it go."

He pulled back from her and saw a smile on her face. Behind her, the others had the same grin. And when he saw that, he couldn't help but smile again himself.

His friends. They were with him to the very end.

He turned around and waved as the island started to fade, waved to the lighthouse, waved to the rocks, waved to the raven he would never see again, waved with all the love and joy left within his body.

He waved until it was all gone, until his heart beat for the last time.

CHAPTER 19

As the evening drew to a close, she gave her hands a good shake. They were sore from the day's work, as they often were. Her technique had improved greatly over the last few years, but her hands—they felt pain. They had never quite adjusted the way the rest of her body had.

She looked up from them only when she heard a voice. "Hey, Sakura, we're going down to the bar. You want to come with us?"

Just beyond her machine was the smiling face of Rhonda, a woman who used to be one of the biggest objectors to her quality of work, a woman she had developed a bond with since those early days to the point where the woman had missed her the week she was absent.

Sakura smiled back politely. "Not today, I don't think. I promised some others I would meet up with them. Another time though."

Rhonda patted her on the shoulder. "Well, alrighty, Ms. Popular, if you've got other plans, I won't object. If I don't see you in the changing room, I'll see you tomorrow then."

"See you, Rhonda. Next time though, I promise." And she meant it too.

Rhonda gave her a thumbs-up and walked away. Sakura smiled after her, feeling grateful. She was pleased she had earned her respect. She was happy the woman valued her company. But mostly, she was thankful Rhonda had believed her story.

She had told everyone who had asked that her week away was simply an administrative error. She had been wrongly transferred to another part of the Camp, and they had brought her back as soon as the mistake was corrected. Any rumour that her sentence had lapsed and she had returned only because she had committed another crime was patently false. Any of her closest friends could attest to that.

Speaking of which… Her smile brightened as one of them approached, a blonde-haired woman with daring hazel eyes and a feistiness to match.

"What are you still sitting there for, girl? There's no overtime bonus."

Sakura laughed. "I know," she said. *I'm just soaking in being back.*

She thought of saying it but decided against it in the end. She could humour herself with her own misfortune, but Sam would have none of it. The fact that Sam hadn't condemned Hakeem or Deron yet was purely out of respect for lives lost.

"You're right, let's go."

Sam grabbed her hand, and together they began to walk toward the changing room, laughing and joking like nothing had changed. All the while, Sakura knew it wouldn't always be like this.

At some point, I'll cry again, she thought to herself, *knowing that Deron is gone and I'll never see him again, thinking about Hakeem's story and how much he suffered, understanding that for what I did, I'll be stuck here long after the others are gone.*

They arrived at the door and slipped in, their first steps toward a night of fun and games. Maybe they'd even play cards.

I'll miss you, Deron. And Hakeem. But after that, I'll feel happy—happy that I got to know you, happy that I did all I could for you and for myself, happy that I get to stay close to my friends, the ones I need now more than ever, the ones that make this life worth living. I know they'll miss you too. But…

Her smile stayed attached.

But if it's all connected, you'll stay a part of us forever.

CHAPTER 20

*Lost or found; sink, swim, or drown,
don't ask about, who, what, when, where, why, or how
because none of it matters.*

And yet, it couldn't mean more.

-Deron Boyd

    Matt's eyes began to tear up as he read the last line. Beside his bed was a nightstand, and placed upon it was a tissue box that was dwindling toward empty. He had used a lot over the last few days.
    "God," he mumbled to himself, sniffling his nose as he wiped his eyes. "Just had to read it, didn't you? Just couldn't help yourself."
    He'd known it was wrong the second he'd opened the cover. These were a man's private thoughts, a man who, in the time since Matt had found the book, had been sent to the gallows. He should have left it alone, but he just couldn't help himself.
    And now he was going to pay for it.
    He blew his nose, got up from his bed, and started to pace around the room he had lived in for the last nine and half months, his private sanctuary in the palace of hell, his oasis in the desert, the place where he was supposed to feel safe, the place where he was supposed to be able to block out all the bad

he saw on a daily basis. But there was no salvation here or anywhere else.

No matter where he went or what he did, he just couldn't escape it.

"You had no choice," he mumbled to himself. His voice sounded agitated, like he was demanding his mind accept the proposition whether it wanted to or not. "It was you or them. If you had let them get away, you would have paid for it. You would have ended up just like Reynolds. You did the right thing."

It was true; he had made the right choice for himself. But in the grand scheme of life, he wasn't so sure, and that's what he was finding the most difficult to accept.

"You had to do it," he repeated. "You had to. You were doing your job. You didn't force them to run. That was their choice. They had to know what the consequences would be."

Back and forth. Back and forth he paced. Back and forth on a never-ending loop.

"And besides, it wasn't you who handed out the punishment. No, that was the Computer. If it was up to you, you would have done something different, but it's not up to you. None of it is up to you."

He went back and forth, back and forth, sometimes feeling out of breath, sometimes feeling strong.

"You did what you had to do, and you'd do it again because it's the only way."

He sometimes headed in one direction, sometimes, the other. His head was spinning. Eventually, he stopped.

He sat down on his bed. "I did what I had to do," he whispered to himself. "I'm sorry."

He lay down and stared at the ceiling. In his heart, he felt pity—pity for himself, pity for the campers, pity for the guards, pity for those on each side of the Wall, pity for those on each side of the world. He turned his head and glanced toward the book lying motionless on his mattress, wishing, just for a moment, he could trade places with its author.

He grabbed a pen and the book and added one final entry.

Pity the living, for only the dead are free.

-Matthew Tucker

EPILOGUE

She walked out of the tunnel and headed up the stairs, nearly slipping on one soaked in an orange soda. The handrail caught her fall as her purse banged the concrete wall. The gentleman behind her asked if she was okay, and she smiled and said that she was. She let him pass then continued her climb toward the natural light of the outdoors. Behind her, she could hear the echo of a moving train rumbling on toward its next destination.

She would be back to catch a different one tomorrow morning, but right now, she was headed home, her working day concluded. It was a typical nine-to-five, except they'd had a cake at lunch in celebration of Barbara's birthday. That was pretty nice—a longer break and a sweet treat to go with it. Although she'd been disappointed that half the cake had ended up in the garbage.

She emerged from the subway exit and headed east. Her apartment was a few blocks away. There was actually a closer stop, but she preferred to walk from here. All day, she sat in her little cubicle staring at her screen. It was nice to enjoy the outdoors and get a little blood flowing.

As she made her way to the intersection, she reached into her purse. Her wallet was inside, and within that was some change. She grabbed a couple coins in anticipation, and sure enough, when she turned the corner, there he was.

"Thank you, darling. Much obliged," he said as she dropped them in the hat he'd placed on the ground in front of him.

She smiled and said, "You're welcome." She then proceeded on her way, kicking herself that she hadn't thought to bring him a piece of cake.

Next time, she thought as she continued down the street. *I'll bring him something next time.* Her heart wished there wouldn't be a next time, but her mind knew that he'd be there.

A block and a half later, she had made it to her building. Her key fob let her in. She climbed the stairs to the third floor and entered apartment 32.

"I'm home," she yelled, not expecting a response. She took off her heels, noticing the orange soda had stained the bottom of her right one.

Dang it, she thought. She would have to clean that up before tomorrow. Her boss would not be happy if she didn't look presentable. But she would worry about that later. For now, her priority was a feline friend. She found her in the living area.

"There you are, Muffins," she said with a smile. "You miss your mom?"

The cat gave a soft meow, and she scratched her behind the ears.

"Knew it," she said. After a few more moments of scratching, she went to fetch her food and poured it in her bowl.

The cat ate hastily. She watched her do so with a smile, thinking to herself. *That's done. Now what?*

The answer was in the kitchen.

She flicked the light on and made her way over to the fridge. On the door, she'd taped a list of things to do. It was a bit old-school, but she found it beneficial. Even after living here for almost seven years, there were still little things she would sometimes overlook.

Pay the rent: check. Bills: check. Oh right, the dryer sheets.

She had meant to research a new brand, one that hopefully offered more wrinkle resistance. But she'd forgotten just how many options there could be. She needed to choose one before she ran out of her current supply. She would do that right now.

She walked back into her living area and found her laptop on the table just beyond the couch. Muffins joined her as she waited for it to boot.

"Really need to get a new one, Muffins, when I can afford it," she said to the cat. "Over there, I had the same laptop my whole life. Things just

THE UTOPIA

don't last the same way here. I'll never understand it."

After several minutes, she was finally good to go. "About time. Okay, let's see here." She began her search.

She read up on various companies, formed opinions based on the various critiques she read from people around the world, and decided on a best option.

After that, she made herself dinner and watched some TV, learning about efforts to further the civil rights movement, foreign trade policy, and the newest fully immersive video game technology. It was all very interesting, as things often were in this great big world she had set out to see. There were some things she liked, some things she didn't, some things she strongly agreed with, and some things she disagreed with. And when she went to bed that night, she thought the same thing as always: she had set out to see the great big world and she didn't regret it.

But sometimes, she really missed the Utopia.

Printed in Canada